John H

To-Day

Essays and Miscellanies; Vol. 2: Night Thoughts

SALZWASSER
VERLAG

John Hollingshead

To-Day

Essays and Miscellanies; Vol. 2: Night Thoughts

Reprint of the original, first published in 1865.

1st Edition 2022 | ISBN: 978-3-75259-078-4

Verlag (Publisher): Salzwasser Verlag GmbH, Zeilweg 44, 60439 Frankfurt, Deutschland
Vertretungsberechtigt (Authorized to represent): E. Roepke, Zeilweg 44, 60439 Frankfurt, Deutschland
Druck (Print): Books on Demand GmbH, In de Tarpen 42, 22848 Norderstedt, Deutschland

TO-DAY

ESSAYS AND MISCELLANIES

BY

JOHN HOLLINGSHEAD

VOL. II.—NIGHT THOUGHTS.

LONDON

MDCCCLXV.

CONTENTS.

TO-DAY.

MAKING A GENIUS.

It has generally been assumed that the quality which we call Genius is one of the rarest things under the sun. Most people have agreed to consider it as something which may be born, but not made, and which cannot be ordered by the yard, the pound, or the bushel. Every man, however, likes to believe that he possesses a grain of this precious treasure, and few men like to be told bluntly that they have no hope of this distinction. The mothers of large families, with a faith which does honour to their hearts, if not to their heads, are never tired of tracing the sparkling light of this jewel in the most leaden-eyed of their children. Fathers of families are not free from the same amiable weakness; and, sometimes, relations and friends affect to be just as trusting and discerning.

Taking the popular idea of Genius, which is the broadest we can get, and not troubling ourselves with the close definitions of keen hair-splitters, we shall find that its chief requisites may be readily taught in the schools as an ordinary part of a classical and commercial education.

The usual forcing and cramming system, found at most schools, by which the dullest dog is made to take a polish which looks very well for the time, but which can never be honestly warranted to wear, is not, by any means, the system for producing Geniuses. Its fault is, that it lays out too much work for the pupil, and does not give sufficient play to idleness and extravagance. A weak respect for industry underlies all its machinery, as it was never meant to manufacture anything but showy hard-working men.

The plan upon which Geniuses, according to the popular model, can be made in any quantity to suit the demand, is so simple, that it may almost be conveyed in a few paragraphs. The marvel is, that educational reformers, inventors, or speculators, have not hit upon something of the kind before.

The chief thing necessary to do in training a commonplace youth, so that he may become a popular Genius, is to deprive him of all the homely virtues he may possess. He must be taught to despise punctuality, to see the folly of keeping his word, and to regard steady reliability as only worthy of mill-horses. He must also be filled with a belief in the dash and spirit of the opposite qualities, and must be taught the propriety of doing nothing like plodding average men.

The drilling which the Genius will undergo at this new school will only give him a few rules for his guidance in after-life, and much must be left to his native impudence. If he wishes for that worldly distinction which is the daily bread of Geniuses, he will not fail to act up to his early teaching. It is impossible to tell him all that he should do, and all that he should not do; but if he really wants to be looked upon as a wonder, he must contrive to live somewhat in the following fashion:—

At the beginning of his career he must write an epic poem with a sounding name, and get it printed. The task is not difficult; but if he objects to so much inventive labour, he had better steal, and adapt some old poem, or batch of poems, or get a journeyman writer to provide him with the necessary quantity of metre. It is not indispensable that the epic should be complete; it may be the first six "books" out of a promised twenty, or a huge block of blank verse, which may be called "A Fragment."

Some years ago, in magazine writing, these "fragments," or literary broken victuals, were very fashionable; and they have now been so long banished from literature, that their re-appearance would be looked upon as a revival. The poem, whether it be complete or not, must deal with some lofty subject; if lofty enough to be out of sight, so much the better. It must allude very freely to the Infinite and the Vast, and must be written in dignified rumbling language.

With a poem like this, well published, to work upon, the popular Genius will be fairly started in business. He will require an assistant, or confederate, in the shape of a friend who believes thoroughly, or is supposed to believe thoroughly, in his master's ability. The assistant will be much better than the confederate for this work, and a man may easily be found who will grow into a strong faith in the powers of the Genius. Hundreds of such men, with weak judgments and strong feelings, are always wandering about the world seeking for some mental idol to worship, and it will be very strange if a watchful Genius is not able to secure one of these blind admirers.

The assistant—or admirer—will be drawn towards the Genius, in the first instance, by a feeling of toadyism. He will be proud of being noticed by a great epic poet.

He will tell his friends of this intimacy with a distinguished man, and will thus act as a walking advertisement for the popular Genius. To increase his own importance, he will fall into the old trap, and magnify his patron whenever he speaks of him.

"Surprising man," he will probably say, alluding to the popular Genius; "never eats vegetables."

"Indeed!" says an interested listener.

"Likes them very much, but says they destroy the imagination—particularly cabbage. Surprising man: never seems to work—and yet he *must* work; always seems to be lounging about with a Turkish pipe."

"Indeed!" again says the interested listener, rather drowsily; "perhaps he always *is* lounging about with a Turkish pipe."

"Not he—not he," returns the believing friend or advertising assistant. "He thinks a long time before he writes—not like your hasty, superficial authors—and when he *does* give us something, it's worth having."

So much for the believing friend, advertising assistant, confederate, or whatever we may choose to call him, who is always talking about the popular Genius in this strain. If his enthusiasm flags, or his judgment is faulty, he can always be properly set going again with a little judicious training.

The popular Genius, for his part, must begin his career with a decided antipathy to facts and figures. He must profess an utter inability to understand accounts—the relations of debtor and creditor, and the value of money. By borrowing and overdrawing, he may always take care of himself, and leave to others the trouble of keeping ledgers. His cue is to exhibit a great ignorance of the world, a great horror of all forms of business, and a great dislike of anything like reins and curb-chains. As he is the courser, the race-horse, the fiery Pegasus, who will be immediately benefited by this love of freedom, there is every inducement for him to affect this character.

The part is not difficult—it runs much more smoothly than many more honest and painstaking characters—and it will give his believing friend an opportunity for discoursing upon his large-mindedness.

The popular Genius having acquired a good sound reputation for carelessness and imprudence, must be careful that he says or does nothing likely to injure this reputation. For example, we will suppose that he has to go through the ceremony of receiving a cheque from a publisher or a patron. An ordinary man would give a receipt, pay the money into his bankers'—if he had a banker—or take it home quietly, and make good use of it. This course may do for average, commonplace men, but it would be fatal to the popular Genius. Unless that eccentric but highly-gifted being excites misgivings in the mind of his publisher or his patron, as to the use he is likely to make of the money, he may rest assured that his reputation is damaged. The first step he must take with the cheque, whether it is crossed or uncrossed, must be to get it changed. As he is not allowed to keep a banker (keeping a banker is another mark of prudence which would be fatal to the reputation of a popular Genius) he must go to the lowest tavern or public-house he knows, and so contrive, that when the cheque is returned to the drawer, it may be defiled with the stains of rum-and-water, tobacco and beer. He may take home as much money as he likes out of this cheque, or he may lodge it safely in some savings' bank, but he must come out at night with seven shillings and sixpence, a short clay-pipe, a tattered coat, and a battered hat, and must be found lying in some street gutter, in a helpless condition. When taken to the station-house, as a matter of course he must send round to his publisher, or his patron, to act as bail, and the melancholy state in which he was found will thus be made known in the proper quarter. The inference will be, that, like a true popular Genius, he changed the cheque at a public-house, drank one-fourth of it, was robbed of another fourth, lost the remainder, and was found with spoilt clothes, and a few shillings, worse off than ever. No explanations will be required of him—his reputation will stand in the place of them—and he will, most probably, get another cheque, this time turned into cash by a respectable clerk, who will deliver the money to him carefully at his own lodgings.

The popular Genius must not cling too much to this trick, good and productive as it is, but must vary it so as to give variety for the money. He will, of course, take credit for anything, from anybody who will give it, and seek credit from most people who are likely to trust him; and will so contrive that his affairs may come to a financial dead-lock about once in three years. He must then hear of a number of debts for the first time; of others which he thoroughly believes have been paid; and must talk loudly of bills that he has given to renew other bills without the originals having been returned to him. While he has thoroughly feathered his nest, he must seem to be in a hopeless tangle, unable to get out without the assistance of friends, and unable to go on with his great hidden work. His admirers will pity his position, while his creditors will probably arrest him and seize his goods, and, in the confusion, his great hidden poem will, of course, be lost. After being well fed in prison by his faithful admirers, he will at last go through the Court, with the sympathy of the Commissioner, who rather likes popular Geniuses.

When he steps into the world again a free man, furnished, to all appearance, with nothing but the legal amount of "excepted" articles, he need do nothing but sit quiet. His admirers, stimulated by his believing friend, will rally round him. A committee will be formed to aid the "poor dreamer," as he is patronizingly called, and every so-called practical man will be delighted to show his superiority to the popular Genius, by feeding and clothing him. One practical man will kindly tell him how to manage his affairs, while giving him a ten-pound note; another practical man will explain the law of bills of exchange, while presenting him with a piano, and a case of books; and a third practical man will tell him to be more cautious and prudent in future, while giving him a Turkey carpet and an oaken writing-table. Each patron will chuckle while doing these things, to find himself such a clear-headed, common-sense worker; and the popular Genius will sit with dignity to receive all these offerings, being really far more practical than most of his admirers.

This is the electro-plated Genius demanded by a large public—a Genius all show and no work, whose greatest effects are produced by standing still—and surely there can be little difficulty in supplying such an article. If industry is a vice in literature—as some critics, who do little, and who measure every man's powers of labour by their own, would have us suppose—we can easily grow the pleasant virtue of idleness. If a low moral tone of life, a disposition to stand still and be fed, and a self-indulgent spirit, are true signs of Genius, we may easily increase the number of our idols. While the new gods are being raised, however, the great old gods must be displaced, for none of them bear any resemblance to the popular Genius. Chaucer, with his book-keeping talent, and business prompitude; Shakspere with his industry, thrift, and rapid production (he wrote more than two great plays a-year, besides his minor works), and Milton with his clerkly precision and reliability, must all be taken from their lofty thrones. According to the new lights, they are nothing but steady, painstaking, plodding men; the very opposite of popular Geniuses.

RELIGIOUS BOOK TITLES.

I KNOW I am about to tread on delicate ground, and that I shall find myself in the position of a performer who is dancing a hornpipe amongst a number of eggs. I cannot help it. If I am sent to perdition by saints and preachers, I must still have my say. I have often been lectured upon sins and vices that I never possessed, and I now feel that I have a call to lecture the lecturers.

Without any malice, any prejudice, any particular tincture of any particular infidelity, I do not honestly think that the conductors of cheap, would-be-popular literature are going exactly in the right way. They mean well, no doubt—as well as many notorious sinners have meant—but I need scarcely allude to the proverb which represents "another place" as being paved with such intentions. My accusation against the conductors of cheap, would-be-popular religious literature, and also against certain authors of religious books, is short and simple. I think that in endeavouring to run on level terms with the light and "comic" publications of the age, they have become flippant—almost dangerously flippant—without being more amusing. They have acknowledged the character of their pills by laying on a meretricious and shallow gilding—they have danced to the pipings of scoffers and unbelievers, they have eaten out of the same flesh-pots, they have dwelt in the same Ichabod palaces, they have wallowed in the same mire of false and mistaken wit, and only to succeed in alarming or disgusting their friends, without attracting any converts from the ranks of their enemies.

There is a certain epic dignity about all religious subjects and biblical records which it is not wise to disturb. The line is so thin, and so easily broken, which divides the ridiculous from the sublime, that it will not bear the touch of the lightest trespassor, much less the clumsy kicking of undiscerning men. A single letter will derange the ideas of nineteen centuries. The name of Solomon has the calm, cold, statuesque dignity of an Egyptian sphynx; the name of Solomons is suggestive of fried fish, auction-mart "riggers," second-hand garments, and the slums of Aldgate. The "Israel in Egypt" is a great work of a great master, in which the Red Sea gapes and roars even within the walls of a conventional concert-room; but call it Israels in Egypt, before a note is sounded, and it will suggest no picture but the Pyramids half covered with placards of an advertising tailor. The conductors of would-be-popular moral and religious literature—honest and persevering as they may be—have not been sufficiently careful, or sufficiently endowed with a pure sense of the ludicrous, to avoid this rock, and for this reason they have lost ground, to my thinking, instead of gaining it. A large circulation of tracts, handbills, periodicals, and books, is good as a trading speculation, or as an engine for spreading certain ideas; but not good if the ideas it spreads are the very opposite to those which the writers and publishers are supposed to be teaching. I look upon the titles of all such publications as of the utmost importance. It is the only thing placed before the public in preliminary advertisements; it forms a phase which is always in the mouth of buyer and seller, and which is often the only vestige of a work which lingers in the mind of an average reader. No amount of bad writing can wholly destroy the effect of a good title; and no amount of good writing can atone for, or destroy the influence of a bad one. This holds good, I imagine, to a great degree in books; to a greater degree in periodicals and the titles of articles; to a far greater degree in slender tracts; and to the greatest degree of all in literary handbills. In proportion as the matter becomes meagre in quantity, so does the influence—the grappling force of the title increase, until in some cases—no mean majority, perhaps—it is the undisturbed master of the situation.

If there is any truth in this reasoning, what must we say to a variety of moral and religious titles of books, pamphlets, and handbills, which are being disseminated at the present moment under the most distinguished and spotless authority, and if not, what must we say to them with equal justice upon purely artistic grounds?

I will first take the "Illustrated Handbills (compiled by the Editor of the 'British Workman')," which, according to the advertisement, "embrace Religion, Sabbath Observance, the Sacred Scriptures, Temperance, Peace, Kindness to Animals, Truthfulness, Swearing, War, Smoking, etc." So far, so good,—in fact, very good; but how about some of the titles? "Oh, this Hard Lump," "The Cabman's Dying Cry," "How to manage an Ass," "My Father's at the Helm," and "The Bullet in the Bible," are five titles selected out of fifty, and what must any unprejudiced reader think of their taste, judgment, and adaptability to the lower orders? What class of people can they be, who, according to supposition, are only to be reached by such false and dangerous familiarity? Is the awful chariot of Jehovah likely to be more respected after being dragged through the mud like a catsmeat barrow at the heels of a powerful but mistaken Association? Is the Gospel likely to be more largely drunk and relished when brought down to the level of 3*d.* a pot in our own mugs? The first of these titles ("Oh! this Hard Lump") can only suggest indigestion; "The Cabman's Dying Cry" tempts one to ask if it was "four shillings a mile." "How to manage an Ass" sounds exceedingly disrespectful to converts. "The Bullet in the Bible" might be the name of a conjuring trick, performed by some distinguished wizard, while "My Father's at the Helm" is a very fair specimen of that playfully familiar style of dealing with the most sacred subjects, which only religious Societies and licensed preachers can adopt without fear of reproof, of warning, or of excommunication.

Passing from these "Illustrated Handbills"—whose objectionable titles can easily be altered—to another stratum of moral and religious publications, I find a variety of books, tracts, and articles, all, apparently, christened at the same font. As my object is not to attack individual writers or individual publishers, I avoid as much as possible the mentioning of names, but I am obliged to quote the *bonâ fide* titles of existing or announced works in order to strengthen my argument. As two other examples of that familiarity with sacred subjects, which is calculated, according to my views, to breed contempt, I will take such a title as "Christ Knocking at the Door of the Soul." Will any one say that the taste which framed this title would shrink from adapting the negro song of "Who's that Knocking at the Door?" to the work of sectarian proselytism? What appreciable difference is there between such a religious title as "The Night, the Dawn, and the Day," and those theatrical tableaux which are usually supposed to form an attraction in the playbill of a Victoria melodrama?

If I were to take two other strictly religious titles, viz., "Pearls from the Ocean," and "Echoes of Eternity," what man who reads this letter would be able to give me the lie if I said that the first was a well-known popular quadrille, and the second a highly-effective waltz by Jullien? If I went still further, and after taking two other titles of similar works, "The Early and the Latter Rain," and "Good Seed for the Lord's Field," thought proper to add "by Mr. Thorley, author of the 'Food for Cattle,'" what sign would there be on the surface, or in the last title, to show that I had practised a deception? Another such title, called "Bread from Heaven," might be improved in the same direction by adding "Down again to Ninepence" (or whatever is the price of Bibles); while "A Book you will like" might be provided with a couple of worthy companions, having the same shopkeeping twang, in the shape of "Is there any other article?" and "Can we send it home for you?"

I pass over such books as "The Lamplighter," which has come and gone, and such an alarming title as "The Great Tribulation coming on the Earth," which latter, I suppose, could only allude to the fact that a new book was in the press, author Dr. Cumming. Though I pass over these things without comment, I cannot abstain from noticing a book that was recently announced, called "Nuggets from the Oldest Diggings; or, Researches in the Mosaic Creation." This title is, doubtless, considered likely to popularize that most unpopular of all compounds, a mixture of theology and geology. As no particular "mission" is claimed for it, except the one great mission to be sold, I will leave it as it stands, merely hoping that the world may not be destined to lose, in the warfare of religious discussion, so evident and promising a "comic writer" as the author of such a title.

In these days of Spurgeonesque preaching we ought not to be surprised at anything, and it is wrong, perhaps, to expect our popular, or would-be-popular, religious literature to do more than reflect the religious manners and whims of the time. The same theological literary taste is now at work which produced Richard Baxter's "Heavy Shove," "A Salve for Sore Eyes," "Pins and Needles for the Ungodly," and a hundred other similar titles; and the true interests of religion, to say nothing of public decency, are likely to benefit as much by the one as they, doubtless, did by the other. This rage for "taking" title-making in religious works may not end with its present efforts; and as a man of the world, of the earth, earthy, I venture to make a few suggestions for further progress. I think the following titles would circulate widely, and do a deal of good, if they did not, like their predecessors, cause a leak in one part of the spiritual ship while they were pumping out the black water in another. These are:—"Box and Cox Converted and Baptized," "How the Wandering Minstrel (Jem Baggs) was gathered into the Fold," "Did you ever send your Wife to Camberwell New Chapel," "Harlequin, Day of Judgment; or, I'm a-looking at you," "The Reformed Skittle-sharp," and "The Repentant Pot-boy." When once you begin to dabble in flippant and comic titles, *it* is worse than useless to stand still. The seasoning must be made stronger with every succeeding dose, or the palate will begin at once to loathe its mixture.

I cannot be accused of any attempt to undermine religion in offering these additional titles, as I should be much more gratified by their utter rejection, and the total destruction of all those which have gone before them. I think it is far better that the pure stream of religion should be left in dimness and mystery, high up in the distant, everlasting hills, than that it should be turned on with vulgar familiarity in every man's house, like New River water, or Imperial gas, or should be hawked about the streets as our fine, old, original, gospel fluid, only a penny a glass, with the usual trading reduction upon taking a quantity.

FASHIONABLE PUBLISHERS.

LITERATURE and the stage are both peculiar professions; peculiar in being largely followed for something beyond mere pecuniary profit,—peculiar in being attended by crowds of "amateurs." A watchmaker never sends one of his mechanical productions to a distributor of watches with a hope that the "article" may be found suitable to the shelves or pocket of the receiver, and a statement that payment is not required. A cheesemonger never opens a warehouse for the purpose of appearing before the public as a chief counterman, and never feels rewarded by seeing his name upon a handbill. Filthy lucre,—circulating medium,—gross, palpable profit, are all such workmen and tradesmen fight for; and it is only authors and actors who ever take the form of "amateurs," and work for nothing more substantial than barren applause.

Labour like this extracts its sustenance from vanity, and never annoys its employers with combinations and strikes. It is only too happy to be beckoned off the ranks, and to be driven anywhere at its own expense. There is only one drawback to this disinterested industry, and that is its practically valueless character. It breaks down at the very point where support is most needed, and it never inspires its public with a genuine belief in its excellence.

Though hundreds of great poems have been written without a thought about pecuniary profit, and though, in the very nature of things, a thousand more must yet be so written, still the best and most popular literature of a country is that which is fairly bought and sold. Ths most unthinking reader shuns the offerings of "amateur" generosity with a kind of instinct, and editors of periodicals are governed by the same feeling. Long years expended in fruitless examination of manuscripts, digging patiently for the hidden treasure that is never found, has taught them to look coldly upon that mass of "voluntary contributions" which no barrier of official contempt can keep out. In one leading weekly journal of general literature, published in London, under the editorship of a distinguished novelist, the weekly average of manuscripts, on all subjects and of all sizes, sent in from unknown, unsolicited writers, has been about sixty. This flood of unprinted literature, floating towards and swept away from this particular journal, has been ebbing and flowing for ten years, during which time at least thirty thousand articles, tales, sketches, poems, and plays have been offered for insertion, and not thirty have been found worthy of a place. A few even of this small number had to be entirely re-written, as their style and construction were not equal to their subject-matter.

This is only a leaf of literary statistics taken from one journal, and a dozen more, selected from different sources, might possibly furnish us with very similar results. Together they would show us how vast is that literary suburb outside the recognized literary world, the inhabitants of which are always pressing into the centre, and seeking to bring themselves into public notice. Some few of them, by virtue of their perseverance and natural aptitude, succeed in attaining the coveted position, others drop by the way; and others resolve to purchase the bubble reputation with solid gold. At this point an agent, a crafty middleman, steps in, and offers to guide the panting, unrecognized genius to his proper pedestal. This agent seeks no reward, according to his own showing, for this timely service, except the barest trade per-centage. His duty is to extricate literature from the blotted mazes of manuscript; his title is the fashionable publisher.

If the fashionable publisher's own account of himself—contained in his trade circulars, or printed advice to inexperienced writers—were a faithful portrait, he would seem to conduct his business on sentimental principles. He is especially tender towards the young author, who knows nothing of the pitfalls of publishing, and careful to impress him with a thorough faith in his guide. He advises inexperienced writers not to meddle with the edged tools of printing, paper, and advertising, but to leave them to be handled by the faithful fashionable publisher, who has made them the study of his life. Wisdom is folly where ignorance is bliss, and all businesses *will* have their little harmless mysteries, however we may try to penetrate them. The whole trade of fashionable publishing is so reduced by excessive competition to the lowest per-centage of profit, that it is cruel to prevent it earning a stray shilling where it has a chance.

The first duty of the fashionable publisher is to speak kindly and encouragingly to the young author. That sensitive and highly-gifted being has, doubtless, been much bruised and irritated in his encounters with blind and deaf editors before he flies to the fashionable publisher, and he wants comfort, not further annoyance. This the guide, instructor, and friend, would be bound to administer as a man, did not policy dictate humanity in the way of business.

When a thoroughly amiable feeling is established on both sides, and the fashionable publisher says he never saw a more promising work, while the inexperienced writer thinks he never met a more agreeable yet competent critic, the usual common-places of such interviews may be safely exchanged. It may be remarked, without apology, by the fashionable publisher, that business is business, and that printers and paper-makers *will* be paid. Whatever may be the importance of a work to an expectant public, there are certain preliminary charges attending its mechanical production which *must* be provided for. As fashionable publishing, properly so called, is strictly confined to printing for authors and possessors of manuscripts, these charges are always drawn in advance from the young and inexperienced writer.

When the fashionable publisher has obtained his cash deposit from the young author, he sets his machinery in motion, but not before. This cash deposit varies according to circumstances, but, for the sake of argument, we will call it a hundred pounds. When anything like a three-volume novel, of the true fashionable publishing breed, is going to the printers, the cash deposit is never less than fifty pounds, while very often it reaches a hundred. The simple rule that guides the fashionable publisher is that he shall always retain a balance in hand, and make a profit in any turn of affairs. The author, it is almost needless to say, is seldom gratified by receiving back any portion of his advance.

The printing of the great work is carried on in the country, say at Winchester, or Guildford, because country prices are at least a third lower than London prices. The fashionable publisher has discovered this in the course of a long business experience, and he is entitled, so he thinks, to keep his knowledge to himself. The "proof sheets," if not corrected by an engaged "reader" (in many cases the publisher himself), are sent to the author only through the publisher, and when the balance-sheet of receipts and expenditure is prepared, the London price of printing figures in its proper place.

The paper for the work is selected from the lowest samples, for the young and inexperienced writer can hardly expect to be printed on ivory at starting. A leading, established, and popular author may luxuriate on a material worth thirty shillings a ream, but the untried amateur must be content with something far more humble. Though issued at Mayfair, for Mayfair readers, at the Mayfair inflated fancy library price of one pound eleven shillings and sixpence for each three volumes, he must not shudder if he detects in the thin muddy medium that conveys his cherished ideas the twelve shillings a ream paper so popular with Whitechapel ballad-mongers.

The binding of the volumes will be in perfect keeping with the rest of the manufacture, being done by poor, unskilful workmen, at two-thirds of the fair market price. The "edition," or number printed, will vary according to the amount of cash deposit, but upon the basis of a hundred pounds, an issue of 250 copies, or 750 volumes, will be suggested and ordered.

The principle upon which a hundred of these copies are disposed of is simple and unfailing. There are, perhaps, a hundred libraries in town and country that only exist upon a contract to supply their customers with *all* the *new books* as soon as they come out. The work by our young and inexperienced writer is essentially new if not original, and it therefore follows that each library must take at least one copy as soon as it is advertised. By a trade arrangement, the fancy price of one pound eleven shillings and sixpence is held to mean fifteen shillings, or less than one-half; but, for all this, a certain amount of cash receipts from an *edition of anything* can be securely counted upon. The hundred copies, or three hundred volumes, sold are all that are bound, and the unmoveable "remainder," which no bookseller can be induced to purchase, even at half-a-crown a volume, is left in broad flat sheets for the author to look at. When a period has elapsed sufficient to prove that the interests of the young author are not being sacrificed by any undue haste on the part of the fashionable publisher, an account current is rendered, showing the supposed expenses of the edition. This bill, delivered by the fashionable publisher to the young and inexperienced writer, will run somewhat as follows:—

Edition of a new novel, in three volumes, running to 250 copies.

AUTHOR'S ACCOUNT.

	£	s.	d.
Composition and printing . . .	56	5	0
Corrections	9	15	0
Paper (twenty-four reams) . . .	28	16	0
Binding 100 copies (300 volumes) at 1*s*. . .	15	0	0
Advertisements	29	9	0
Publisher's commission, 10 per cent. on sales of £75	7	10	0
	£146	15	0

The real cost of the edition, if traced through the fashionable publisher's private books, may be stated in this form:—

Edition of a new novel, in three volumes, running to 250 copies.

PUBLISHER'S ACCOUNT.

	£	s.	d.
Composition and printing . . .	37	10	0
Corrections (*nil*)	0	0	0
Paper (twenty-four reams) . . .	14	8	0
Binding 100 copies (300 volumes, at 42*s*. per 100)	6	6	0
Advertisements (less discount and insertions in trade circulars)	15	0	0
	£73	4	0

The balance-sheet, rendered to the author, will run thus:—

Inexperienced writer in account with fashionable publisher.

Dr.	£	s.	d.
Expences of edition, as per statement rendered .	146	15	0
Cash balance, handed over to author, with 150 copies of novel (*unbound*)—450 vols. .	28	5	0
	£175	0	0

Cr.	£	s.	d.
Cash advanced	100	0	0
Sales, 100 copies of novel, 300 vols., at 15*s*. per copy, published at £1 11*s*. 6*d*. . .	75	0	0
	£175	0	0

By these figures it will be seen that the fashionable publisher, after obtaining the cash advance of a hundred pounds from the young and inexperienced writer, never expends more than seventy-three pounds four shillings on the edition, and so retains a balance of twenty-six pounds sixteen shillings in hand. When the seventy-five pounds receipts from sales to "the libraries" begin to come in, this balance is considerably increased, and at the final settlement of accounts, the guide, instructor, and friend has secured for himself a nett profit of seventy-three pounds and eleven shillings. The young and inexperienced writer in this case receives back twenty-eight pounds and five shillings out of his hundred pounds advanced, and finds that he has written his work and paid nearly seventy pounds sterling to circulate a hundred copies. He has had the satisfaction of seeing himself in print,—of reading one highly flattering notice of his work inserted by his own publisher in a pliable "organ;" of presenting a few copies of his book to a few friends; and of earning a place in the British Museum catalogue. He *discovers*, in a few months, that "the *trade*" have but one price for his remaining 150 unbound copies, the low, degrading sum of threepence a volume! He parts with the whole mass reluctantly for about five pounds, and sees them finally bound up, three vols. in one, and "jobbed off" into obscurity at one shilling and sixpence a copy.

ADVERTISING LITERATURE.

THERE is a class of literature struggling hard to secure a place in the world of letters, the fate of which has hitherto been to die almost as soon as born. It has taken the form of poetry, and the form of prose. It has affected humour, and history, and narrative; and it has called in the pencil of the illustrator to its aid; but in spite of this it has found no resting-place, either upon drawing-room tables or on library shelves. It has always worn two faces under one hat, and with such shallow hypocrisy, that the dullest reader refused to be deceived. Its Shaksperes and its Miltons have tuned their harps to sing the praise of cheap clothing or of quack medicines, and have perished miserably in the attempt.

This class of literature, we need hardly say, is Advertising Literature. It has always fretted under the weakness which caused it to die so young, and without being beloved by the gods. It has contaminated its fingers with trade bribes, and yet has not had nerve enough to face the inevitable punishment. It has been carried to the waste-paper buyers, as unwillingly as a child is taken to the dentist's; and it has endeavoured to arrest the destructive hand of the rude boors who were blind to its literary merits, by the external charms of a costly and elaborate binding.

There was a time, not a quarter of a century back,

when grammar and spelling were considered very unimportant in tradesmen's handbooks or handbills, and purity or elegance of type was a thing undreamed of. Now we may see every variety of ornamental printing, if we only examine the cards that are thrust into our hands or into our letter-boxes. We are told where to buy our soap and candles in the old red and black Anglo-Catholic type; while fancy ironmongers have rushed wildly into Gothic and cursive print; and railway bills have gone back to the numerals of the fifteenth century. Blank spaces are engaged and paid for in the advertising columns of accommodating journals; Greek names are given to waterproof goloshes and six-shilling shirts; and these names are printed upside down between the blank spaces, in order to attain more force in striking the eye of the reader. The day when Black-Letter type will be applied to advertisements of hats or umbrellas is evidently not far distant.

Perhaps the rudest form of advertising literature is that which endeavours to fasten the puffing of a particular hat, or a particular pair of boots, upon some great contemporaneous political event. This form was popular in London during the early days of cheap clothing; but it has now given way, in obedience to a more advanced and artistic taste. The provinces still cling to it, as being the best and latest style they know, like our metropolitan dressmakers, who are content to copy the garments which Paris has worn the year before.

In Scotland, we find an energetic address to the people, containing, amongst heaps of similar matter, the following rousing phrases, set forth with all the art of large and varied type :—" The Disastrous War between France and Austria! Fifty thousand human beings destroyed to no purpose! Thousands upon thousands of disfigured, bloated corpses choking the magnificent serpentine rivers, and fattening the fertile plains of Lombardy. Despots, tyrants, are you men or beasts? Humbug peace; it cannot last, pity if it should! Treachery to the cause of Italian independence! the professed objects of the war overlooked." This is all very stirring political writing—sufficiently stirring to stand no chance of admission into France; but why is it illustrated with the picture of an ordinary beaver hat? Further on you may read half a long column about the late Italian War, the French alliance, and "Italy, garden of the earth! lovely, romantic Italy! left by a deceptive peace in a worse, because more precarious position, than when the war commenced;" but still the shadow of that hateful, commonplace, every-day black hat hangs over all this English composition and dims its fire. When you get to the end of the article, you find that you have been listening to the not-altogether-disinterested outpourings of an advertising hatter, who informs you that his stock is very large at present, that he has splendid satin hats, light and durable, from six shillings and sixpence, and a delicious production at eighteen shillings. What would not such an enterprising tradesman with literary tastes have given if Burns had sung in this strain?—

Scots wha ha' wi' Wallace bled—
Scots wham Bruce has often led—
If you want a graceful head
Go to Ross, the hatter.

This is the simplest and least artistic form of advertising literature. The main object—to state the name, the address, the leading article, and the average price—is concealed, it is true, until the reader arrives at the end of the essay or poem, but then it comes upon him with the shock of a most fearful anti-climax. He is not let into the gaping mart of the enterprising trader, in a gentle, persuasive way; he is addressed by earnest politicians, or sung to by beguiling poets, who suddenly throw off their masks, and stand confessed as noisy touters demanding his custom or his life. His nerves are jarred; his taste is offended; and a feeling of antagonism grows up within him. He will not only not buy, but what is worse, he will neither read nor listen with anything like attention in future. His faith has been severely shaken; and the clumsiness of the puffing trader has created a cynical sceptic.

Sometimes this literature indulges in certain eccentricities, by attempting to address the inhabitants of a foreign country in their own tongue, without proper guidance, or by soaring into the lofty regions of tragic poetry. As a fair sample of the latter kind, we may take a tragedy in four acts, called "Alexander the Great," which is "dedicated to the stage" by the author, Mr. Paulin H. Pearce, who describes himself as a "sea-actor." In all publications like this, there is a large share of literary pretension, and while the instinct of the tradesman (or professor) leads him to advertise his everyday trading occupation, he yet preserves the sensitiveness of the author. We would not willingly say a word to wound the feelings of the highly expert swimmer who has written this tragedy of "Alexander the Great," but as it comes into the category of "advertising literature," we merely describe it as it stands, as tenderly as though we loved it.

The author very judiciously begins with swimming, and his preface runs thus:—"A *few* rules I submit with confidence to your notice on SWIMMING, for I have taught above five thousand persons the art, and performed the parts of Julius Cæsar, Hercules, and Alexander the Great in the open sea; and swam to the Brake Buoy and back, at Ramsgate, before thousands of spectators, likewise from Dover to Calais, Margate, Broadstairs, and other places; cooked and ate dinners, caught fish, fired blunderbusses, bows and arrows, flew several kites at one time, sailed on the water, dressed and undressed," etc., etc. Mr. Pearce then tells us how to swim well—how to float on our backs—how to swim on our backs—how to turn back when we are swimming—how to turn from our stomachs on to our backs, and the reverse—how to stand in the water—and how to dive. Then comes the tragedy, written in blank verse, with occasional burst of rhyme, from which we give a short quotation:—

ACT 1, SCENE 2ND.—THE SUN AND MEADOWS.

Enter Diogenes with his tub rolling.

DIOGENES. The massy sun sheds golden beams of day,
Illumes the waving sea and gushing spray,
The eastern sky unfolds harmonious sounds
Through all the spheres vibrate to ocean's bounds,
Creation, order touch the golden strings
And planets roll upon their aerial wings,
Soft yellow clouds with waving lustre shine,
Shaded with solar halos bright divine.
Hail! glorious sun, clear shining light of day,
Thy vital beams revive the dormant clay,
And vivify the air with beaming light,
All nature glories in thy massy might;
I pay thee homage for thy glowing heat,
Few are my wants, fresh herbs my daily meat:
What are ambitious conquerors to me,
Whom all the gaping crowds now run to see?
There's Alexander, swelling in his pride,
To make the world an ass, that he may stride
The stubborn brute, for this his father sighed;

Some future time he'll ride the hornéd moon.
Ha! ha! he thinks new cares are quite a boor
And I will bask within the bright sunshine,
Nor let this hero turn this brain of mine. (*Basks.*)

When Mr. Pearce has waded through his tragedy in some such style as this, he gives us his address, where he is always to be found, and then concludes by telling us how to swim on our sides; how to swim feet first; and how to swim like lions and serpents. How to swim and recite his tragedy at the same time to crowds of listening and admiring spectators, he does not inform us.

As a sample of the foreign advertiser endeavouring to address himself to a strange people, we may take the treatise of a Dutch quack doctor, printed in what he fondly supposes to be English by John Enschede, of the City of Haarlem, in Holland. We have all heard of the enterprise and advertising daring of our leading English dealers in quack medicines; and we have all been told that there is no language in the world which does not set forth their specific remedies. Perhaps our Dutch quack doctor may not be the only bold advertiser whose language may have been laughed at by the alien and the stranger.

"This medicine (he says) works miraclas with every one, that makes use of it, and the Grace of the Omnipotedt God is experiencedt in it to admiration........When you take this Remedy, it unites it fell to the stomaeh, and is the fame as a flying mercury, not letting the vapours rife without being mixed with them. It likewife prevente at moist hum hurs from running through the veins or nerves. ....If you take fifteen drops of this Remedy after supper, going to bed, it wil expel all gravel or stone without the loast inconvenience; and what we admire most, is hat it dissolves suhtoe time it cals, same inwardly hy the etat........A fick man Abraham van Nut having been under cure of the most eminent phyficians for opwards of three years, was at laft car ried to Amsterdam to undergo an operation appogref wo weak that the could not bearone. Abut freely making of our Remedy haw entriruft lyrostored to his perfect health........It cures all Anxie ty Megrims, Giddines, and Headakes, big smetling it, or by putting it in the eras of the fick person a little bal of cot ton loaked in the same Medicamentum........You may anoint Ulcers, Malingant sores, all cankres be assured of its perfecticure. ....The greatestt Pain of Colick that cambe, immediately ceases with ihitty Drops ot he fame Remedy........This is the content of our Medicamentum Gratia Probatum, or the Remedey approved by Grate; but I find no remedey for those thae follow bed Couneil, or advice; nor for those thae do not libe medicine; munch lefs for those that seems too delicate in taking it........This Medicamentum is made and sold in tho City of Haarlem, in thi Provincie of Holland, at the house of Nicolas de Koning Tilly' who is the author of the fame, since the year 764, and so was his Grandfather Claas Tilly before him, that was the Chief Inventor of it, since the year·1898."

The favourite form which advertising literature has long taken and kept, is that of the Almanac. A certain distinguished example, which was started, we believe, for the purpose of making known a few patent medicines, has now attained a circulation, although professedly published at a shilling, reputed to reach nearly half-a-million every year. The chief object for which such publications are issued is apparent on nearly every page; and you are advised in what months you ought to give your children a particular dose of a certain physic or your cattle a particular allowance of a certain food.

The highest order of advertising literature, and the one in which may be seen the earliest attempts to secure a permanent position on the library-table or the library-shelf, is the trade history. We have one of the Umbrella, another of Boots and Shoes, another of the Cocoa-Nut palm, and another of Wool and Woollens. To this we may add a republished series of letters upon the use of Fire-arms.

The first of these is issued by a well-known umbrella manufacturer, but it contains nothing that might not have been collected and put together by any one unacquainted with that particular trade. It is meant to be readable; it strives to be amusing; and it is illustrated by a distinguished comic artist. We have fancy pictures of Jonas Hanway, and Egyptian frescoes, a few patches of Greek and Latin quotation, a few doubtful stories, and a postscript, which means business, at the end.

In the second of these trade histories—the one of boots and shoes—we have even more learning in the Egyptian fresco style: a good deal about Greek, Roman, and Saxon shoes; an illustrated account of foot costume in England; and a discourse upon the anatomy and treatment of the foot. All this is made to revolve very skilfully round a certain patent leather, which the author has invented, and manufactures into shoes for tender feet. The account of the cocoa-nut palm is framed in the same way, and for a similar trading purpose; and the letters upon care with fire-arms, while they contain much useful information, are intended as an index pointing to a certain shop at the West-End. Although they are addressed "to all true lovers of the trigger and friends of humanity," it is difficult to believe that their spirit is purely disinterested. A clumsy sportsman, who shoots *himself* on his own doorstep, is a gun customer destroyed, and the literature which attempts to preserve him may be the same as that of the Scotch hatter, in which the "Fifty thousand human beings destroyed to no purpose" are loudly lamented, because, being dead, they can no longer want hats.

We next meet with a specimen of what we may call the Gay Archæological Advertisement:—

"While strolling down Addle Street, yesterday, ruminating on the mutability of mundane matter, and wondering where Athelstan's palace stood of yore, I chanced to turn down Philip Lane, and 'a change came o'er the spirit of my dream,' for I saw a very old friend putting on a new face, in that the ancient hostelry of 'Ye King's Arms,' better known, perhaps, as the 'Old Yorkshire,' was being re-juvenized. What a pity, thought I, that poor humanity cannot undergo the process! and in fancy I again peopled the arena with those political gladiators, who, in my hot youth, were wont to engage in deadly (political) combat here. Again I beheld the sarcastic Smith, ubiquitous Wilson, the jester Peat, and Harrison the robust, and those other master spirits, whose speeches were 'wont to set the table in a roar,' no, I don't mean that, but the coruscations of whose brilliant fancy have shed undying radiance upon its hospitable roof. A falling brick quickly dispelled the illusion, and I exclaimed, in the prophetic language of that great orator of our time (I need hardly say that I allude to Unsworth), 'Where are we now?' and Echo, who answers for everything and everybody, replied, 'Where?' An intelligent specimen of muscular Christianity informed me that the present spirited proprietor, whose high moral character and courteous demeanour has endeared him to all with whom he has come in contact, has, with that spirit of enterprise which is the great characteristic of the present day, determined to renovate and restore the entire establishment to its pristine glory, so that not only that ever-increasing circle of town friends should have their comfort increased, while their legs were stretched beneath his mahogany, but that he would be able to open wide his portals and his arms for his country friends; and as he offers us extraordinary dinners at less than ordinary prices, let us hope that he will reap no niggard harvest for his investment, and as we have the authority of the Bard of Avon for stating that there is a tide in the affairs of each of us, which, if taken at the flood, leads on to fortune, we trust that his flood is near at hand, and we believe he knows how to take advantage of it, so that with the hatchet of war buried in the back garden, and the calumet of peace, filled with the choicest bird's-eye, in his mouth, and surrounded by his friends, we trust that there are very many years of unalloyed happiness in store for him."

The triumph, however, in this kind of literature was reserved for an advertising firm of cheap tailors to enjoy. "The Wool and Woollen Manufactures of Great Britain," written, we presume, by Samuel Brothers, as their name appears upon the title-page, and published by Piper, Stephenson, and Co., is a trade history, as far removed from those before mentioned, as a "Lay of Ancient Rome" is removed from a Catnach ballad. A large octavo book, of nearly two hundred pages, with broad margins, printed in the highest style, upon the finest gilt-edged, glazed paper, and published at 10*s*. 6*d*., in an ornamental cover, is an example of advertising literature of which the age may be proud. That it is armed to fight for that coveted place on the drawing-room table, or the library-shelf, is evident from the style in which it is published; and that it is never meant to attain a large and fleeting circulation, is also as evident from its price. People who give half-a-guinea for a book, or who are presented with a volume whose price is half-a-guinea, will take good care to secure it from the waste-basket, even if they are not interested in, or capable of judging of, its contents. This is the truth which Messrs. Samuel Brothers have discovered, and by acting upon it, in a bold and enterprising spirit, they will secure a certain amount of breeches-pocket respect for their volume (the first of a promised historical and descriptive series), and be handed down in indissoluble connection with "Wool and Woollens" long after the ephemeral cheap or gratis trade histories which surround them are forgotten.

A REALLY PRACTICAL POET.

There is a popular notion that a poet is a bright-eyed, long-haired, wild, and unpractical creature, who passes much of his time in "communion with nature," never answers letters, and never keeps an appointment. These two last defects,—defects from a business point of view,—are held to be undoubted signs of genius. Without them, a man may be a very good statist, a tolerable historian, a pungent leader-writer, and an able reviewer, but he can never hope to rise to those lofty heights where minstrels are ever striking their golden lyres. The examples that tell against this theory are conveniently forgotten. Chaucer, the excellent clerk and accountant; Shakespeare, the successful manager of a playhouse; Milton, the reliable political secretary; and Pope, the best man of business in the eighteenth century, are never alluded to. The proofs that ordinary prudence, trading skill, and average punctuality are never united to the poetical faculty are always sought for and found amongst the secondary class of geniuses. Even here the search is not always successful, and we have a poet of this quality now before us who is one of the most practical writers of the day.

Most of our readers may have never heard of a great poem called the "Londoniad," which has appeared in seven parts during the last seven years. It is one of those productions which few persons will read, precisely because so many other persons are anxious to see it read. It is a poem, according to its author, that comes out "under the auspices of the Queen, the Prince Consort, the Emperor Napoleon III., Leopold, King of the Belgians; Otho, King of Greece; Sir Joseph Paxton, Sir Charles L. Eastlake,"—in large letters,—"his Grace the Archbishop of Canterbury, friend of the author; his eminence, Cardinal Wiseman, writer on art; the Governor-General of Canada, the Governor-General of India, the Lord-Lieutenant of Ireland, upwards of two hundred and fifty members representing literature, science, and art, in both houses of the British Parliament; and one thousand gentlemen, illustrious as inventors, manufacturers, and authors throughout the world." This highly-patronized poem is published in a "home, colonial, royal, and parliamentary edition," and its author is Mr. James Torrington Spencer Lidstone, of Torquay, Devon, late of Toronto, Upper Canada, and author, by his own showing, of the "Conquest of Canada," "Ancient America," and a "Pictorial Description of the British Provinces in North America."*

There is always a pleasure in discovering new poetical genius, and in being the first to bring it before the world. When Charles Lamb and his friends introduced John Clare,

* "The seventh 'Londoniad' (complete in itself), giving a full description of the principal establishments, together with the most honourable and substantial business men in the capital of England. Also containing the great prize poems on Prince Albert, and Leopold, King of the Belgians, and pieces on some of the most celebrated personages in the kingdom, and in the provinces of British North America, forming altogether episodes in a grand national poem on the arts." Published by the author, at his town residence, 12, Lower Calthorpe Street, London, W.C. 1860.

the Northamptonshire peasant, to London society, they were more delighted with what they had done than with all the works they had ever written. Their kindness took the shape of late hours and heavy drinking, and the peasant poet, in due course, became an inmate of a mad-house. His patrons, however, were hardly to blame, for they never contemplated such a melancholy result. Their "intentions were honourable," and so are ours. In introducing Mr. Lidstone to the general public, we are actuated by nothing but a friendly love for literature. Notwithstanding the solid titles of those books which he places after his name, we have a strong suspicion that he is not very widely known. Without going into his presumed merits as an historian and a writer of travels, we merely introduce him as that rarity amongst authors, a really practical poet.

In turning over the pages of the "Londoniad," we are struck by the originality of the subjects chosen by the "Muse." There is no nonsense about the moon; no running after skylarks and nightingales, in the style of Shelley and Keats; and no "pottering over" water-lilies and purling brooks. The minstrel sweeps the strings to no love-sick strain, but twangs them in shops and counting-houses to the tune of trade. His poem might have begun:—

> "Arm-chairs and the man, I sing,
> Who makes them cheaply,
> And who stuffs them best."

The London shopkeepers have waited long and patiently for their epic poet, and they have got him at last. He was sure to come, in the fulness of time, like railways, telegraphs, and other signs of "progress." To parody another well-known passage:—

"The poet's eye in a fine frenzy rolling
Glances from lords to hatters,
Thence to pumps, to clocks, to lamps,
And those that make them
(Always to those that make them),
Nothing is passed."

The real design of Mr. Lidstone's poem may, perhaps, be gathered from the following lines, which are given by the poet in the form of a dialogue:—

Col. Sykes. "Do you not think it derogatory
To your own fame and the Muse's glory,
And that your genius, Mr. Lidstone, errs
In taking for heroes manufacturers?"

Bard. "It is the pride and honour of my days,
That I to men of science poured my lays;
I list to what each coming age imparts,
When the world calls me poet of the Arts!
Those giant minds that gave the Arts their birth
Are all but walking gods upon the earth.
Besides, they always paid for what they got,
Which you, Lieutenant-Colonel Sykes, did not."

If the great practical poet wishes us to read the last passage in a prosaic sense, it may serve as an explanatory guide to this wonderful epic. It may explain the hidden meaning of what the poet calls the "Great Scagliola Poem," the "School Furniture Poem," the "Great Cement Poem," the "Farinaceous Poem," the "State Poem," the "Great Pump Poem," the "Light Carriage Poem," and the "Vegetable Leather Poem," which are all component parts of the great work. Never, perhaps, had any inspired minstrel so much "method in his madness." After a long apostrophe to Apsley Pellatt and Company (which the distinguished glass-maker and parliamentary candidate is doubtless very proud of), the poet winds up with the following significant note:—"Osler and many others have presented their cards, but it would be a great piece of impolicy either to introduce a Brummagem house through the 'Londoniad,' or any inferior firm, while I can honour myself, and do more justice to my friends, by taking as hero one acknowledged to be the head manufacturer in Great Britain."

To speak of a poem, and not give a taste of its quality, is an unpardonable crime in a reviewer, so we quote the bard upon marble chimney-pieces:—

"I've heard of marbles, and my heart doth warm
Towards monuments that many nations charm,
Th' Carrara gives t' our age a just renown;
Was in the distant Julian era known.
The Parian, though yellow now with time,
Has borne bright trophies from each classic clime.
Blest Paros! ever midst Cyclades flow,
O Muse-enchanted Archipelago!
By th' magic wand of Art, for Demosthus
Leaped statues from th' quarries o' Pentelicus;
And Mount Hymettus, famed of old for bees,
And Luini upon the Tuscan Seas."

We will not spoil this lofty strain by any allusion to the "firm" in whose interest it appears to be written, nor by giving, by way of anti-climax, the prosaic trade advertisement attached to the lines.

If we read the poet rightly, in his poem upon fire-proof safes he seems to be aware of his "mission":—

"Had nature not here stamped the literary man,
Gladly I'd represent thy house, John Vann,
Then should thy saving art myself inspire,
Although I might not strike the awful lyre."

We might quote the great practical bard upon compressed vegetables and their vendors, upon coach and harness-makers, gas-fitters, carpet-manufacturers, bell-hangers, and a dozen other trades. We might quote him upon Alderman Copeland, or rather, as he puts it, "W. T. Copeland (late Copeland and Spode)," whom he calls the "Mighty Potter," with capital letters. We might quote some stanzas he has written to his mother, which may have been put into the book to flavour it with a little sentiment, but we are checked by our limited space. One prose passage, however, referring to past, present, and future poems, we are compelled to quote:—"The present 'Londoniad' will be found to contain a greater number of patentees than any yet published." The poet, we presume, has not included his mother. "Every poem in the 'Londoniad' is copyrighted, and is the sole property of the author; but any gentleman taking one thousand copies and upwards can use the poem written for himself, provided that it does not fall into the hands of publishers." There is little danger of that. "Should I live to be an old man, I intend to sit down and make with these pieces one grand national poem on the arts. At present, although each is complete in itself, all are like the links of a chain that are not yet joined." We like them better as they are. "The first five 'Londoniads' are now scarce. . . . ." We may add fortunately scarce. " . . . . The seventh is the first of the 'Londoniads' through which I have *heartily entered into business* with many gentlemen therein mentioned."

On looking over the list of names of "gentlemen therein mentioned," we are glad to find that poetry, in these supposed hard times, can boast of so many rich and influential patrons. We hope that old and respectable houses like Broadwood and Sons, and Maudslay, Sons, and Field, are able to trace a clear trade profit in being the favourites of the "Muse." A poem like the "Londoniad" may be profitable to the practical bard, but is it equally profitable to the "heroes" of its pages? Thousands of copies may be thrown down areas, or crammed into private letter-boxes, but readers, as we have said before, are a very obstinate class, and generally reject the "literature" that is forced upon them gratis.

ANOTHER PRACTICAL POET.*

EACH literary man of any distinguished mark or position has raised at least one monster, who seizes his style, his principles, his peculiar modes of thought, and carries them headlong downwards into the great gulf of absurdity. This Frankenstein—this attendant spirit—is faithful, but unruly. It multiplies every action, whim, or fancy that it copies by three or four; it leaps higher, dives lower, speaks louder, and goes farther than its master; and often succeeds in so far dazzling a certain circle of admirers that they often prefer the coarse copy to the pure original. Mr. Thomas Carlyle must be often haunted by some such phantom, who speaks to him in crabbed sentences more affected than his own, and exhibits even more fretful impatience of shams and windbags. Mr. Charles Dickens has often suffered from demons of this kind, who have visited him in huge genial masks, in huge pathetic masks, and in huge humorous masks; and Mr. Thackeray has been unable to shut out electro-plated familiars, who have shown him his own image, distorted and magnified.

Most authors of this rank have had their trials, and now comes the turn of Mr. Ralph Waldo Emerson. A nature worshipper so devout; a mystic so often incom-

* "Leaves of Grass." Boston (U.S.): Thayer and Eldridge. 1860-61.

prehensible; a prose poet who uses language, as some people think it ought to be used, to conceal thoughts, or perhaps the want of thoughts, could hardly hope to escape imitators, where imitation was so easy. He may have expected the visitation to fall rather heavily when it came in the fulness of time; but he could never have been prepared for such a muscular caricature as Walt Whitman. The sternest enemy of the American philosopher and of the great fog-bank school to which he, in some measure, belongs, cannot fail to pity him under such an affliction.

Walt Whitman, or, as we should prefer to call him, Emerson's monster, or wild poet of the woods, is a thoroughly untamed, muscular, unconventional writer. What Emerson talks about doing, or seems to wish to do, Walt Whitman to all appearance does. Emerson only asks for health and a day to make the pomp of emperors ridiculous; Walt Whitman has got health of the rudest kind, with many days, and he glorifies the whole weighable, pinchable, material universe. No form or manifestation of matter is mean or contemptible to him. Like the great practical poet alluded to in our last paper, he would chant a great guano lyric, though with a far louder voice, and in a very different tune. If he fell in a gutter, he would rise up shaking his muddy locks, and dash onwards like the "strong-breasted bull" which meets with his admiration. He describes himself in a coarse, sing-song, rugged stanza as—

"Free, fresh, savage,
Fluent, luxuriant, self-content, fond of persons and places,
Fond of fish-shaped Paumanok, where I was born,
Fond of the sea."

He might have added in plain prose, and no one would

have discovered the difference—"fond of rump steaks and oyster sauce, legs of mutton, pots of beer, cart-horses, wrestling, and lifting weights." He chants in this strain page after page:—

"No dainty dolce affettuoso I;
Bearded, sunburnt, grey-necked, forbidding, I have arrived
To be wrestled with as I pass, for the solid prizes of the universe." . . . .

The dustman, the "navvy," the slaughterer of oxen, have at length found their poet. He sings the song of all creation. His invitations have no limit:—

"This is the meal pleasantly set—this is the meat and drink for natural hunger.

"It is for the wicked just the same as the righteous. I make appointments with all; I will not have a single person slighted or left away. The * * * * * *, sponger, thief, are hereby invited. The heavy-lipped slave is invited—the * * * * * is invited.

"There shall be no difference between them and the rest."

The entertainment is the same, whether for man or for beast. If anything, perhaps, Walt Whitman has a partiality for the beast:—

"I behold the picturesque giant and love him—
And I do not stop there,
I go with the team also."

* * * * *

"Oxen that rattle the yoke or halt in the shade!
What is that you express in your eyes?
It seems to me more than all the print I have read in my life."

* * * * *

"The wild gander leads his flock through the cool night,
Ya-honk! he says, and sounds it down to me like an invitation;
The pert may suppose it meaningless, but I listen close,
I find its purpose and place up there toward the wintry sky.

The sharp-hoofed moose of the north, the cat on the house-sill, the
chickadee, the prairie-dog,
The litter of the grunting sow as they tug at her teats,
The brood of the turkey-hen. . . . .
I see in them and myself the same old law."

Every word of this might have been written by Emerson muscularized;—by Emerson at the age of thirty-two, trained by a New York "rowdy" into a state of firm, animal, pugilistic vigour. To come a little nearer home, every line might have been written by one of Barclay and Perkins's draymen, by a Rotherhithe coal-whipper, by a Billingsgate fish-hauler, a canal bargeman, a sewer-cleanser, a meat-porter of Newgate market, or an average pot-boy who had learned to read and spell. What Dr. Johnson said of the famous Percy ballads, may be said of poems like these "leaves of grass;"—they can be spun by any one at the rate of six yards an hour. This is a chant of the lands:—

"O the lands!
Lands scorning invaders! Interlinked, food-yielding lands!
Land of coal and iron! Land of gold! Lands of cotton, sugar, rice!
Odorous and sunny land! Floridian land!
Land of the spinal river, the Mississippi! Land of the Alleghanies!
Ohio's land!
Land of wheat, beef, pork! Land of wool and hemp!
Land of the potato, the apple, and the grape!"

This goes on for many pages more, and there is really no reason why it should ever stop at all. Cyclopædias, commercial dictionaries, directories, and such books are plentiful enough, and in the slang of our wild poet of the woods they contain thousands, millions of such poems. Everything is a poem in the Walt Whitman sense, as everything, by a similar wrenching of language, might have been called a fish-kettle, a pitchfork, or a blacking-bottle. There used to be a favourite class of comic songs which proved all men to be gardeners, scrubbing-brushes, or lucifer-matches, according as the whim started. These dreary pieces of laboured humour are not as popular now as they were twenty years ago; but Walt Whitman, if he gains such a hearing here as he has in America, ought certainly to bring them once more into fashion.

There is a certain philosophy in all this muscular poetry—the philosophy of making money by creating a sensation. The world is always on the look out for anything wild, strange, and eccentric. If Walt Whitman had had the power or the inclination to put his common-places into intelligible forms and language, the "leaves of grass" would never have made hay while the sun shone. The tricks of authorship are not yet half catalogued, or half exhausted. We must have treatises upon logic written by street tumblers, or rather we must have authors of such works keen enough to take to street tumbling to stimulate the sale of their books. We must have an epic poem written by the keeper of a Shoreditch baked-potato-can, or rather we must have the writer of an epic poem go out with a potato-can to make his poetry popular. The science of advertising is in its infancy, and America, so it seems, can give the mother country a "few wrinkles" on this subject. When Walt Whitman, as the story goes, drove an omnibus along Broadway to oblige the regular driver, who was laid up with a fever, we have no doubt that his charity proved a remarkably good investment. We have no means of overhauling his publishing accounts, to see what effect the public excitement had upon his "editions," but we have no doubt that many people never bought his book until after they found him driving an omnibus.

As it is not fair to blame the son alone while the father is living, we should like to have Mr. Emerson's calm opinion of his literary offspring. The rumour runs that the philosopher is rather proud of his wild poet of the woods, and reads the "leaves of grass" with infinite pleasure. If this is so, he must be deceived by the poet's "yearnings after the infinite," which are about as intelligible as a dog's baying at the moon. The inventory of nature is the only thing solid in a book, one-half of which is quite as coarse as Rabelais, and just as obscure. The passages that look profound are not worthy of sustained thought and investigation, because they are deliberately made nonsense-riddles that never had an "answer."

SLOP-SHOP LITERATURE.

THE title at the head of this paper, without much stretching, could be made to include a very broad area of literature. It would take in those very learned, neatly-printed, and profusely-illustrated trade histories, which are only published for the purpose of advertising a particular business. Waxend on the Human Foot, Daniel Lambert on Corns, and Sleeveboard on the Roman Toga, are not authors wishing to make their fellow-creatures more learned, and to secure for themselves the immortality of the British Museum Library, but shoemakers anxious to sell a particular boot, and tailors interested in the sale of paletots and sixteen-shilling trousers. We have most of us seen a treatise upon umbrellas, a history of boots and shoes, another of the cocoa-nut palm, and a discourse upon teeth, which point with unerring constancy to the shops of their masters. We have only just noticed a very costly, gilt-edged history of wool and woollens, written, so the title-page asserts, by Messrs. Samuel Brothers. Moses and Son have long kept a poet of no mean ability in their establishment; but the clothiers of Ludgate Hill, so it seems, are more ambitious. The task of writing the history of their trade was one that could not be entrusted to hireling hands, so the inventors of the "Sydenham trousers" became themselves the Hume and Smollett of their raw material. About eighteen months ago a similar volume was issued under the somewhat inflated title of "Commercial Enterprise and Social Progress; or, Gleanings in London, Sheffield, Glasgow, and Dublin." The "gleanings" appeared to consist chiefly of advertisements of second-rate firms, and the descriptions were all written with a palpable advertising object.

This, however, is not the kind of slop-shop literature to which I wish to direct attention; as I am not fond of exposing adulterations in every other trade but my own. The slop-shop literature of which I speak is that which is written as literature, published as literature, and bought and read as literature. The people who write it and put it together are called "authors" and "literary men," and the people who sell it are called "publishers." The English language is very elastic, and those who use it often stretch it to the utmost.

The first place amongst real slop-shop literature ought to be given to the modern British drama. It claims a position in the world of letters to which it has not been entitled for years. The clever tradesmen who have discovered how much easier it is to take the product of a Frenchman's wit and ingenuity, and turn it into English, than to invent a coherent plot, and fill it up with natural characters, may be complimented for their shrewdness, but for nothing else. Six easy lessons in the French language, and a good French and English dictionary, are all the modern dramatic author requires to start him fairly in business. The managers look upon him with favour, and open their doors to him, because he brings them nothing possessing any dangerous originality. The cost of producing a piece is ten times the "author's" fee for translating it; and therefore the conductors of London theatres are can-tions in selecting their ventures. A drama that has been successful in Paris has been tried and not found wanting, and the theatrical speculator welcomes its appearance in an English dress because he can produce it with less risk than would attend the production of an original piece.

All this is very clever trading on the part of both manager and "author," but nothing more. Even when the translator aspires to become an "adapter,"—a softener down of French manners for the English market, a man who has sufficient talent to turn the Italian Boulevard, Paris, into Regent Street, London, and the gardens of the Tuileries into St. James's Park,—he is still nothing more than a slop-shop author. He may take his wages as a crafty middleman, he may flatter himself, in his secret heart, that Shakespeare borrowed his plots and characters in the same unscrupulous way, but he must be kept down to his proper level in the world of literature. If he turns virtuous after a long and profitable career, and writes books with not over clean hands, like the "Eighth Commandment" by Mr. Charles Reade, it shall not absolve him from his original sin. His motto must still be the trading principle that has always governed him:—"Gentlemen's own materials made up."

A slop-shop drama produces a slop-shop order of criticism, for no journal cares to devote much space or capital to the analysis of mere "amusements." What was formerly treated as an art by actors, upheld as an art by managers, and jealously preserved as an art by literary critics, like William Hazlitt, is now chiefly watched over by reporters and "general writers." The literature of the stage is "noticed," not criticised; and in the leading literary organs the record of its productions is stuffed away in a lumber-corner for paragraphs. No able editor cares a straw about it, but devotes his attention to telegrams and universal politics. An attempt was made, about two years ago, in the daily press, by Mr. John Oxenford, to alter the system of scribbling long criticisms upon plays in a hurried hour after the performance, by presenting a weekly digest instead. This would have given time for reflection and careful writing on the part of the critic, but the "Times" declined to adhere to the suggestion, and it fell to the ground. It was the only sympton of a "revival" in real dramatic criticism, that we have seen for some years past; but it was not strong enough to overthrow the established slop-shop plan.

If dramatic criticism shows symptoms of degeneracy and even of approaching extinction, the censorship of general literature is in no healthier condition. A hundred books on all subjects,—science, art, and politics; works of imagination and collections of facts, will flow in weekly to an important literary journal; and flow out to three, six, or at the most to a dozen "reviewers," as they are called. No one ordinary man can understand thoroughly more than one subject, and yet he is called upon to pass judgment upon twenty. Lord Brougham, great and exceptionable as he undoubtedly is, has an encyclopædical reputation only among encyclopædical men; and when a writer who has devoted himself to one branch of human knowledge tests him upon that branch, an exposure of his lordship's superficial acquirements naturally follows. If Lord Brougham, and wonders of his class, are not infallible at all times upon all subjects, how shall the nameless critic's opinions upon everything be regarded? Sound common sense, a logical head, and a stock of well-defined principles, may uphold a writer upon "all things and many others" to a certain extent, but they can never preserve him from exposing his weakness to the initiated when he writes upon subjects he knows little about. If he is not content to manufacture agreeable articles out of books he is incapable of analyzing, he is sure to do an injustice to the authors, and to injure the property of the publishers. He will fall into the dogmatic cant of ignorant criticism, which any literary slop-worker can easily assume; and instead of presenting the readers of his journal with the condensed contents of the volumes before him, he will point out errors that have no existence, and make suggestions that can never be followed. Those uninquiring minds that are entirely governed by the "opinions of the press," will at once see how superior the reviewer is to the author, and will duly pity the ignorance of the latter, as directed.

Not one of the so-called "critical journals" is so managed that each book is invariably sent to the right man and to no other. When an important volume is announced, a volume that will excite much discussion and interest, and become a landmark of that particular publishing "season," a critic is sought for whose researches have been carried on in the same workings as the author. It would be dangerous to place such a book in any other hands than those of a special reviewer, and, for once, an article appears whose verdict, favourable or unfavourable, is uttered with a voice of real authority. This is the exception, however, and not the rule; and nine-tenths of the books which appear every year are cut open, tasted, and marked with black or white brands (the whitey-brown or medium brand is almost unknown in such "noticing") by a small knot of slop-shop reviewers.

Another obtrusive branch of slop-shop literature is the newspaper "leader." It has been manufactured for years on a certain mechanical and unvarying plan. It must nearly always be of a certain length, no matter what may be its subject matter; and its writers must generally be men with very dormant, elastic, or negative opinions. A writer who is not cast in this mould is soon disposed of as an impracticable man, a grit that is always getting into the very sensitive machinery of a daily organ. Some honourable exceptions there are, both amongst editors and contributors, to this melancholy rule, men who respect each other, and neither write, nor cause to be written, that which is not meant; but they are very few. The Swiss—the free lances—with the ready pen and unquestioning mind, are those who provide most of the daily thinking material for those who only think they think. Such writers are shielded from observation, and speak only through the brazen head. Their morality is on a par with that of the outcasts of the street, but no "midnight meeting" is ever held to reform them.

Apart from the principles which animate most leader-writers, it is curious to examine the construction of their articles. The fixed length or framework which they have to fill up imposes on them a style of composition which is somewhat monotonous. The middle of their articles contains all they really have to say, the introduction and peroration being mostly devoted to ornament. The kernel of a leader can generally be extracted from a few lines near the centre, and nothing will ever be lost by passing over the first two or three paragraphs. The learning which the cheap press often displays is very encouraging to those who wish well to such organs. If you want Greek, Latin, French, Johnsonian words, and scraps of pedantry from all quarters of the globe, you can have it in any quantity for the small charge of a penny. Although most of these leaders, social and political, which the common people try to read and digest, undoubtedly belong to slop-shop literature, to do them justice, they resemble in their effects a grand display of fireworks.

Another most common manifestation of slop-shop literature is "graphic writing." Until the trick was discovered, it was considered very wonderful; but now its secret is known, it is practised by all. The commonest account of a fire is now embellished with parodies of those descriptive touches which have made the literary fortune of "our own correspondent" in different parts of the world. The atmospheric aspects of fire are enlarged upon; the flames are said to lick the adjoining houses; a picture is made of the firemen in the ring; the sparks are played with in what is called "a happy vein of fancy;" the grey distant spire of some church is picked out, and described under the new colours thrown upon its surface; and, altogether, the old style of "penny-a-lining" is put to the blush. The representative of the new school throws about his similes with a lavish hand, and rather thinks himself an unappreciated genius. Like a boy who has been sitting for years on the banks of the stream of literature watching the swimmers, he falls in, and is surprised to learn how easy it is to float like his fellows.

The companion of "graphic writing" in slop-shop literature is "forcible writing," and this is now so general that it has descended to Catnach and his compeers. The beauties of English composition are no longer confined to our great literary works; they adorn the meanest catchpenny publication that issues from the press. The occupation of "Jem Ward," the well-known "one-eyed patterer," and all the distinguished bards of Seven Dials, must assuredly be gone, when sketches like the following are issued by a Whitechapel printer and publisher:—

"THE MYSTERIOUS MURDER OF AN OLD MISER LADY AT STEPNEY.

"All readers of romance are familiar with the ideal of a miser. It is an aged, attenuated, yellow anatomy, who lives like a grub in a cheerless house, and ultimately dies, either crouching on a heap of gold, or leering into a chest full of mortgage deeds, or is murdered by burglars. The late Mr. James took hold of the idea, and produced Mr. Scarves, who dwelt in solitude with his golden-haired daughter, until fear compelled him to employ a servitor with a knotted stick to watch and guard the dismal but opulent habitation. All the misers upon record have exhibited the same characteristics. Their secretiveness is equal to their penury; they love to see and touch their hoarded wealth; they disdain all pride except that emptiest pride of riches, as if in the whole of Vanity Fair there were a booth more loathsome, more wicked, more hateful than that of the miser. They wear the meanest apparel; they eat the most sordid food; they patch a broken pane of glass with brown paper; they are hard in their bargains, and relentless in the despotism of their extortion; and, generally, as though under some dread retributive law, their ends are ignominious and miserable. 'Thou fool! this night thy life shall be required of thee!' That doom is recorded against the misers one and all. They live in expectation of a day which never comes, and they die unhallowed deaths. The most degraded and desperate of men dog their footsteps; robbery is for ever on their thresholds; they are envied by the very miscreants to whom blood is not sacred, and innumerable have been the instances in which they have perished under an assassin's hand amid the glut of their unfructifying lucre. These remarks apply especially to the fearful event at Stepney. Mrs. Emsley, the dust-contractor's widow, was the shabbiest Dives of East London. Her fortune was splendid. She was proprietor, it is believed, of not less than from eight hundred to a thousand houses, chiefly let to the poor, from whom she exacted her rents with rapacious punctuality. She was old and litigious; she lived solitary, without even a servant. A poor charwoman cleansed her abode every Saturday. Her collecting day Monday, when she sallied forth with a strong-pocketed apron like that of a toll-collector, to receive her due, which, next morning, was deposited in the bank. There it lay, unblessed and worthless, accumulating from one week to another, but of no human value except in the imagination of the insatiable widow. For how did she enjoy her possessions? By leaving her kindred miserably poor; by eating scraps of fly-blown meat haggled for after regular business hours at the butchers' shops; by sustaining her existence upon garbage and water, while she lurked, like a spider in its web, or a wolf in its den, perpetually famished, and waiting for the regular Monday prowl. Then the flies were caught, and the sheep devoured, and the Old Woman of Stepney went back to her haunt, to gloat over heaps of notes and coin, and to indulge in the malignant misery of self-starvation.

"Suddenly her solitude is broken upon. Murder enters her house, and she is struck down amid her mortgage deeds, agreements, securities, and all the dusty addenda of wealth. There she lies, dead, her skull crushed in, her blood staining the floor, her treasure despoiled, and from Monday to Friday, we may presume, her body remains undiscovered. Why should the neighbours wonder? was she not habitually isolated and taciturn? They might have fancied that she was, as usual, gnawing her bone in an attic, in greedy expectation of the next Monday, which was to augment her balance at the bank. No friendly hand touched her knocker. No child or sister cared for her existence. But at length a tenant sent for two brass taps which, with the customary instinct of miserdom, she had delayed providing for the water-butts in one of her own houses. Then was it discovered that her corpse lay stark in an upper room, in the midst of documents relating to her property. In all likelihood some one well acquainted with her character and means had called, had followed her up stairs, had stunned her as she entered her apartment, and had completed his work of murder as she lay senseless in the doorway."

If Mr. Dickens can boast of many imitators, Mr. Thackeray numbers almost as many, and the imitations are openly carried into the lowest works of the hour. A novel is now being issued in penny weekly numbers which is thus boldly advertised on its own cover. It is called "The Woman with the Yellow Hair."

"This most powerful fiction, from the pen of the First Comic

AUTHOR and most picturesque essayist of the day, is wonderfully quaint and eccentric in its humour, philosophical in its satire, and deeply affecting in its pathos. The writer so nearly resembles DICKENS and THACKERAY, in his sketches of LONDON LIFE, that his anonymous articles in the principal journals of the day have frequently been attributed to those authors.

"The present work, by the fearlessness of its language, and its utter defiance of all those powerful conventionalities which have cramped and fettered modern novelists, making their books but fit for the entertainment of prim BOARDING-SCHOOL MISSES, threatens to revolutionize the world of novel writing, and shows that there still remains in our time some of the strength and vigour which of yore characterized the GIANTS OF LITERATURE.

"The object of the author in this story is to unmask VICE and HYPOCRISY in every rank of society; to depict life as it really is, and expose in all their ghastly deformity the fearful cankers gnawing at the heart of civilization, which a FALSE PRUDERY would gloss over and ignore."

The following is a taste of its Thackerayian quality:—

"CHAPTER THE FOURTH.—'THOSE CREATURES!'

"'To the Haymarket!' The Haymarket, where midnight is noon-day—where roses are carmine—where there is much drinking but little thirst—where the same faces pass and repass each other every night, and all night long, with the same threadbare badinage, the same senseless joke, the same dreary, weary smirk on the thin cracked lips.

"It has gone twelve—put up your shutters, respectable tradesmen! Get you home, honest people! Stop your ears, Pity! Turn away your head, Mercy! Clench your hand, Charity! We are among the outcasts—'the ulcers and incubuses of society'—the rouged and ragged, flaunting, tawdry—pretty faced and tastefully dressed;—in short, among '*those creatures!*' and we are come to find your husband, madam, your brother, or your son, whichever it is that you have been sitting up for so patiently these many hours. Be of good cheer, dear lady, he is in right merry company, and in no hurry to get

home to you. Be not hard upon him when he comes in; you know he has a sufficiency of your society any day, and he is now amongst such jolly fellows, and such pretty women. Ay! They will be pretty, you know, some of them, with their audaciously bold faces, much prettier than you are. Besides, you know, boys will be boys, and the good world smiles not unkindly upon their innocent gambolling."

This kind of slop-shop literature can be produced in any quantity, and, bad as it is, it appears to sell. Our railway bookstalls are largely supplied with such material, not in the periodical form, but bound up as gaudy books. It is a comfort to know that bookselling at railway stations is almost extinct, for it has done little more than support the slop-shop literature of its own creation. The gamboge covers of such literature have generally been in harmony with the contents of the volumes they brought so unpleasingly before the eye. The days of "Bubble and Squeak," by Ernest Maltravers, and "Mr. Collywobbles' Confessions of a Bagman," by the author of "Mixed Pickles," with a host of similar volumes with similar titles are happily numbered. Such books belong pre-eminently to slop-shop literature, are issued by slop-shop publishers, and were bought by slop-shop readers. Their crackling covers fell to pieces in the hand in the course of a six hours' journey, and no library shelf was ever enriched by the addition of such ragged mockeries. A few old bookstalls upon the line—an egg-chest crammed full of twopenny English classics—an odd volume of the "Spectator"—of Cibber—of anybody of the last century, would have furnished far more nourishing travelling refreshment to the British public than all such indigestible collections of literary pastry.

POCKET-MONEY AUTHORS.

During the last ten years—a period remarkable for the advance of periodical literature—more has been done by false friends to destroy the class-feeling of literary men than any open enemies could well have accomplished. In proportion as the area of journalism increases, as authors (we use the old term) become tolerably well fed, well clothed, and decently independent, so does the binding power of the profession, its spirit of working fellowship, seem to die away, and we become little more than a noisy, self-asserting rabble. The increase of writing men, the widening of the old parochial limits which hedged in the author, may have something to do with this, but a hypocritical, pocket-money, cock-a-whoopy tone, which is too general just now in many newspapers and magazines, has far more to do with it. We are all struggling to set ourselves above our neighbours; all busy pooh-poohing the labourers in the same vineyard. Never, at any time, so it seems, were so many superior persons writing for the press, or making books on various subjects for a little pocket-money. The "amateur" author—the duke in disguise—who never used to make his mark, and whose special magazines, started to publish his harmless productions, were always notorious failures—now seems to be the only person who has got the public fairly by the ear, if we are to judge by the tone of a flood of articles. Hundreds of writers now write as if they were ashamed of their business; as if they wished the world to suppose that they wrote only for their own amusement. Some pride themselves on mere accidents of birth and fortune; others range themselves in some particular literary sub-class, and treat all other literary sub-classes as contemptible inferiors. Imitators of these supercilious ones spring up in rank luxuriance, and our ears are dinned with cries almost as vulgar as "no connection with any other establishment."

No people are so full of vulgarity as your superior persons, and we are, therefore, not surprised to find them indulging in slang. They never lose an opportunity of abusing those humble newspaper reporters whom they have christened penny-a-liners in a paroxysm of contempt. The title is about as genteel as most other nick-names, such as "greasy" for a butcher, "doughy" for a baker, or any other piece of street wit applied to trades. It was invented to throw discredit upon a hardworking, useful class, whose labours the public pays for and demands. If there is anything so very contemptible in "penny-a-lining," in the act of collecting information and placing it before the readers of newspapers, those who encourage it ought to come in for their share of the blame—the master ought to be despised as well as the servant. A report of a fire, of a murder, of a railway accident, of a birth of four children at once, or even of a remarkable gooseberry, may or may not be a very polished literary production, but it conveys information which many people think useful and necessary. Penny-a-lining is as much a part of our fully-developed journalism as leader-writing, special reporting, or even editing. Worked at industriously and conscientiously it is no more deserving of the contempt it so largely receives than any other occupation of the same standing and value.

The habit of underrating our fellow-labourers, like all unamiable, unjust habits, is more easily acquired than got rid of. A man may soon school himself or be schooled into a belief that he fills a far higher position in his profession than nine-tenths of his companions and equals. The possession of a little more money, the membership of a particular club, the faculty for hitting the taste of a particular magazine, the opinion of one or two toadies or weak-minded friends, a favourable review of his productions in a journal of some authority, or a dozen other such influences, may have the effect of turning a writer's brain, and leading him to think, write, and act like an insufferable egotist. Not content with his own absorbing sense of elevation, not trying earnestly to soar above his competitors in a fair open struggle, he stands still with folded arms, and tries to rise in appearance by assuming that all who work near him are beneath him. This is hardly the way in which great men of any profession have been made, for, supposing it to be successful, it would only create one giant at the expense of a hundred dwarfs.

The abuse and derision once kept for chance reporters,—the penny-a-liners, as they are called—is now shared by special reporters, London correspondents, and leader-writers. If the attempt now often made in various journals to show that some literary work is mechanical, some offensive, and very little of it wonderful, is intended for very ignorant readers it may not be thrown away; but surely educated, intelligent people are not in need of such information? They are not accustomed to regard authors with open-mouthed astonishment, to look upon a book, or a newspaper, or a magazine, as a mysterious production; nor to read leading articles, and to be governed by their teachings. Professional writers who go out of their way to analyze and expose their own craft—to take their readers behind the scenes of a newspaper or a magazine office, are much more likely to be thinking of their craft than the public, and to be filled with an overweening sense of its social importance.

There is really no occasion to overrate nor underrate the literary profession. Like every other trade it only wants to be left alone. Some of its members may be geniuses, some may be fools, and many may be good working-men. Let them all pull together in the team as long as they can, each one taking his well-earned feed of corn. Let each one think highly of himself and lowly of his brother-in-harness, if he will feel so disposed, but let him chew his one-sided opinion in silence. It is hardly fair to the public to take up their scanty time with personal squabbles, explanations, or self-glorifications, when so many great subjects are waiting for a patient discussion.

NEWSPAPER PROFITS.

The simple fact that two popular weekly newspapers, claiming a large circulation, have been respectively reduced in price from twopence to one penny, since the repeal of the paper-duty, seems to have created something like a trade union amongst the newsvendors. Under the old Protectionist plea of a wish for the public good, and with the old Protectionist claim to know better what the public want than they do themselves, these distributors of journals have held indignation meetings. At these meetings they have of course considered their own position, but their chief anxiety has been about the public. No class-interest ever wanted to benefit itself; it always struggled to benefit the public. The newsvendors are just as patriotic as any other trade, clique, or union. They wish to put down the newspaper-hawking boys for the public good, and to raise the price of newspapers for the same worthy object. While they complain of the labour they have to go through in distributing the penny journals, thereby bearing witness to the enormous circulation and popularity of those journals, they coolly tell the crowd of buyers that they don't want a penny newspaper. Coddling is the public friend, not Short; and Coddling recommends nothing but twopenny newspapers. He looks upon a penny newspaper as a great mistake—a financial impossibility—a speculation drifting headlong on to the rocks of bankruptcy. He has read the penny "Daily Telegraph" and the "Morning Star" for several years, and has generally found them well-informed and well-conducted, but this has not convinced him that penny newspapers are commercially practicable. He clings to a belief that daily journals are produced for some sentimental or mysterious political reasons, far above a sordid desire for trading profits. He thinks that the Government pays the expenses of one "organ" out of the Secret Service money, and that the Opposition supports the other by a liberal subscription. Nothing will convince him that a penny newspaper is a paying speculation, whether it appears six times a week, with original matter, or only once a week, with three-fourth of its contents borrowed.

It is not a pleasing sight to see three thousand respectable tradesmen making themselves ridiculous. If there is no cause why a driver of fat oxen should himself be fat, there is surely some cause why a distributor of advanced news and literature should be fairly intelligent. A very little inquiry would convince the newsvendors that a penny popular weekly journal is a very profitable speculation. The best of all arguments is the logic of figures, and we therefore take the liberty of presenting a few balance-sheets to our readers, which will show *them*, at any rate, what they ought to get for a penny in the shape of a popular journal.

In newspapers everything depends upon the weight—not of the writing, but of the paper. The weight of the penny "Morning Star" is $1\frac{7}{8}$ ounces when printed, and the weight of "Lloyd's Paper," when printed, and when it was sold at twopence, was $1\frac{15}{16}$ths ounces. Both these journals were then printed on mixed straw-paper, made by the same manufacturer, and, considering the expenses which a daily newspaper must always incur, but which a weekly newspaper need never incur, our readers may easily judge which was the cheapest journal.

When the paper-duty came off, Mr. Lloyd reduced his price one-half, and he was quite wise to do so. At two-pence he would have been beaten out of the field in less than a year, and even now he will have to struggle to maintain his ground. The failure of the Messrs. Kelly, the proprietors of the "Penny Newsman," is no proof of the unsoundness of penny weekly journals. Their failure arose from many other causes, and their cheap newspaper was fast growing into a lucrative property. Let us, however, look at some figures showing the cost and profits of a penny weekly journal the same size and *weight* as "Lloyd's Newspaper" is now:—

Balance Sheet, No. 1. This is an estimate where composition, printing, and machining are done with the proprietor's plant: the best method of working off a journal with a large circulation.

Basis of 100,000 Copies per Week.

Dr.

Paper, 11,000 lbs. at current prices		£206	5	0
Composition	Labour	20	0	0
	Interest on Plant, etc.	9	0	0
Machining	Labour, etc.	25	0	0
	Coals, etc.	3	0	0
	Interest on Plant, etc.	16	0	0
	Ink	8	0	0
Literary and Editorial Work*		20	0	0
Publishing, Rent, etc.		8	0	0
Posters and Advertising		20	0	0
		£335	5	0

* This matter is nearly all "lifted" or borrowed

Cr.

100,000 copies at 1*d.*	£415	0	0			
31 per cent. off	130	0	0			
				285	0	0
Advertisements, say 5 columns at £10*				50	0	0
Note.—Shows no profit.				£335	0	0

Balance Sheet, No. 2. Estimate under the same conditions.

Basis of 200,000 Copies per Week.

Dr.

Paper, 22,000 lbs. at current prices	£412	10	0
Composition, etc. (see Balance Sheet, No. 1)	29	0	0
Machining: Labour, etc.	25	0	0
Machining: Coals, etc.	3	0	0
Machining: Interest on Plant, etc.	16	0	0
Machining: Ink	16	0	0
Literary and Editorial Work	20	0	0
Publishing, Rent, etc.	8	0	0
Posters and Advertising	20	0	0
	£549	10	0
Profit *per Week*	100	10	0
	£650	0	0

Cr.

200,000 copies at 1*d.*	£830	0	0			
31 per cent. off	260	0	0			
				570	0	0
Advertisements, say 8 columns at £10				80	0	0
				£650	0	0

Note.—Profit £100 *per Week.*

Balance Sheet, No. 3. Estimate under the same conditions.

Basis of 300,000 Copies per Week.

Dr.

Paper, 33,000 lbs. at current prices	£618	15	0
Composition, etc. (see No. 1)	29	0	0
Machining, etc. (see No. 1)	44	0	0

* This estimate of Advertisements is based upon facts.

Ink	£24	0	0
Literary and Editorial Work	20	0	0
Publishing, Rent, etc.	8	0	0
Posters and Advertising	20	0	0
	£763	15	0
Profit *per Week*	191	5	0
	£955	0	0

Cr.

300,000 copies at 1*d.*	£1245	0	0			
31 per cent. off	390	0	0	855	0	0
Advertisements, say 10 columns at £10				100	0	0
				£955	0	0

Note.—Profit nearly £200 *per Week.*

DETAILS OF MACHINE LABOUR, ETC.

1 Engineer	per Week	£2	0	0
1 Stoker (allowing for night work)	"	2	0	0
Machinery—1 Superintendent	"	4	0	0
" 8 Feeders (2 to relieve)	"	10	0	0
Counter, Wetter } Wetting Room	"	5	0	0
Sundries, Oil, Rags, etc.	"	2	0	0
Coals, etc.	"	3	0	0
Interest on Plant, 10 per cent. on £8000, charge per Week		16	0	0
		£44	0	0
Ink (this item increases £8 with each 100,000 copies)		8	0	0
		£52	0	0

DETAILS OF COMPOSITION, LABOUR, ETC.

Labour		£20	0	0
Interest on Plant, about 40 per cent. on Type, cost £1000, and about 10 per cent. on Fittings, cost £500	Weekly charge	9	0	0
		£29	0	0

CAPITAL ACCOUNT.

	£	s.	d.
1 Hoe's Machine, to print 13,000 to 16,000 an hour .	£3500	0	0
1 ditto (reserve)	3500	0	0
1 Engine	200	0	0
1 ditto (reserve)	200	0	0
Boilers	300	0	0
Fittings, etc. (charged in accounts at 10 per cent. *per annum*, interest on capital, and wear and tear) .	300	0	0
	£8000	0	0
7000 lbs. of mixed type (charged in accounts at 40 per cent. *per annum* for wear and tear, etc. Old type sells for metal at 3*d*. per lb.) about	1000	0	0
Fittings (charged in accounts at 10 per cent. *per annum*)	500	0	0
	£9500	0	0

These figures are not invented by a mere literary dreamer, but are gathered from practical working men in the trade. The literary dreamer has only marshalled them with the best skill at his command. Making every allowance for errors or mis-statements, they show that the proprietors of popular penny newspapers have not met the demand too soon, and ought not to end their days in the workhouse.

THE PUBLISHERS' BOGIE.

Mr. Mudie ought to feel proud of his commercial position, for, in spite of the exertions of many competitors, he is still the publishers' bogie. The formidable opposition of the great newspaper distributors, the energetic rivalry of a joint-stock company, and the threatening combination of certain West-end librarians, have not rendered him of less importance to book producers. The ignorant cry about his "monopoly" has certainly not been heard since it has been shown how easy it is to start in the same business; but an involuntary tribute is constantly being paid to his trading pre-eminence by complaining of his mode of buying books. No other librarian has yet reached the high honour of being loudly grumbled at by discontented publishers; and as no sensible tradesman ever traded on the rules laid down as good by these grumblers, we must assume that all other librarians are still very unimportant book-buyers. We are sorry to have to think that this is the case, because real and successful competition is wholesome for the public. Mr. Mudie, by the admission of his enemies, has evidently not lost much ground at present, and he is still as much a "monopolist" as he ever was; that is, he still retains his large capital, reputation, and connections. He is still as much a monopolist as Messrs. Simpkin, Marshall, and Co., or those other few leading book-buyers in the "Row," who buy such disgracefully large parcels of every published book which they feel they can place upon the market. Mr. Mudie is still Mr. Mudie —the so-called "Autocrat of New Oxford Street"—the supposed arbiter of current literature; and he is still published at by a large class of book-manufacturers.

A man who enjoys the profits and influence of a position like this must be content to suffer a good deal of badgering. He can hardly please everybody at all times, unless he trades upon a loose, sentimental system. The book-trade and its money-making features do not differ in any way from the sausage-trade, and an easy buyer will make as bad a seller in the one case as he would in the other. Mr. Mudie must expect to be taught his business every day in the week by people whose interest it is to push off a particular article. He must expect to hear, probably in a single hour, that his customers adore travels, that they detest travels; that they are sick of fiction, that they are ravenous for fiction; that they seek a healthier literary diet in works of theology and science, that they detest any book which conveys the slightest useful information; that they are languishing for poetry, that they have had enough of verse; and a dozen more such contradictory assertions. Knowing better what his customers want, through the simple inquiries over his counter, than the cleverest of his book-suppliers, through their interested theories, he may possibly decline to purchase a work of permanent value. With nothing but his trading instincts and experience to guide him, as a sound tradesman he may very properly turn his back upon a new Bacon, or look coldly upon a budding Macaulay, waiting patiently for his customers, the public, to give the first sign of appreciation. It is not his duty to make people more virtuous than they really are, to improve their tastes or to educate them in any way, but simply to act as an active agent for his numerous clients, to supply them with exactly what they want with as little delay as possible, and not to try to force any book, whether bad or good, into circulation, by buying it blindly and pushing it energetically.

This, we take it, is Mr. Mudie, the brisk, prosperous, trading librarian—the only man who has ever managed the large and successful business in New Oxford Street. The other Mr. Mudie—that sentimental or usurious shadow who is always supposed to be either acting the patron of literature, or the grinder-down of publishers—we take to be a pure creature of the imagination. We have our doubts about the existence of the patron of literature, because Mr. Mudie is reported to be wealthy, and has certainly never been in the "Gazette;" and as to the huckster—that bogie which only very hard dealers are ever frightened at—these are not the days in which to pelt a man for buying in the cheapest market. Moreover, while books are notoriously published at fancy prices, and a movement has only just set in to do away with figures that always involve large discounts, it is too much to expect a simple bookseller not to higgle. We have all within us that healthy desire to get as much as possible for what we sell, and to give as little as possible for what we buy, which shows that the head is clear, and that the heart is in the right place; and why should Mr. Mudie be abused for being in such a sound condition? Mr. Mudie has, doubtless, made mistakes; he has unwisely claimed to be the founder of a "select" library; he has given reasons in letters for offering less for a book than the subscribed price; but many of us have also attempted more than we have been able to perform, or have put words upon paper that have proved slightly injudicious. We think it very injudicious and undignified when publishers—young or old—cannot always reject Mr. Mudie's offers, or wait for the public demand for their books, without writing articles in journals under their command which they must eventually feel ashamed of. If Mr. Mudie claims to be nothing but the keeper of a vast mixed circulating library; if he states in simple figures what he will give for a book, without any attempt to justify his low estimate of its value, no one can say a word that will even seem to touch his character as a trader. If he underestimates the value of the book, he will have to raise his price, as thousands of other traders have to do every hour of the day; and if he tries, from mistaken economy, to shut books out of his library that are really in demand, he will soon find the error he has committed by his withered subscription list. That he has not plunged into this folly at present is proved by his well-earned success, and the undoubted competition which he has now to meet is not likely to make him less watchful in future.

The sentimental duties of bookselling, which are very unreasonably expected from Mr. Mudie alone, might with equal justice be looked for from publishers. The patronage of high literature, in defiance of sound trading principles, is a thing involving a little honour and much loss; and it is only fair that those who share the credit of publishing sterling but unprofitable books should also contribute to the expenses. If a publisher has sown sentiment, he can hardly expect to reap guineas; and he certainly ought not to ask Mr. Mudie to pay for an unsaleable crop which that gentleman had no hand in raising. As sentimental dealings, however, have now been given up between author and publisher,—as periodical literature has made writers more independent, and extended markets have given publishers the means of being more liberal,—let us hope that none of the old Grub Street failings, cast off by literary men, will linger amongst library-keepers and book-makers. Literature has now been reduced to something like a respectable, reliable trade; it has thrown off its titled patrons, and it wants no support or encouragement but what it can give full value for. Those authors who think otherwise had better exchange their pens for some other working tools; those publishers who think otherwise had better turn their capital into other channels.

OUR ROYAL LITERARY PENSIONS.

Lord Palmerston seems to be working hard with us to bring the royal literary bounty into contempt. We lately spoke in no very respectful terms of that civil list pension fund of £1200 per annum, which is annually doled out to "men of learning and genius." We consider such flunkey halfpence thrown to literary beggars as degrading to the whole body of authors and journalists. The receivers of these kitchen sweepings—these crumbs from the royal table—are not to be condemned. In many cases they merit our warmest pity and help. It is the body—the craft—the guild, that is disgraced, when even its humblest member is left to depend upon such cold, ignorant charity. The great grandmothers of a royal pimp, or the bastard scum of imported kings who could hardly read and write, are treated with far more liberality and respect. If literary men had any class-union amongst them, any class-spirit and independence, they would speak and act in this matter in a way that could not be mistaken. Their apathy in the face of these annual insults is the wonder of half the societies of literature in the world. They are smitten on one cheek, and they turn the other. Each leader of the tribe retires within his tent, and comforts himself with the belief that *he* has not been relieved. Never were men of discernment more deceived than in this. No fortress is stronger than its weakest point. The mountains may be mountains, but they are only part of the plain. The fund-holding, shirt-frilled book-maker, who dubs himself a Member of the Royal Society of Literature, or who is a thick-and-thin supporter of the Literary Fund, can never get rid of his connection with the ragged tobacco-smoking Bohemian. That unsavoury phantom comes up before him at his *conversázioni* and dinner-tables, and says to him, "Am I not a man and a brother?" It is the old story of the rich prosperous man with "poor relations." The shabby visitor is known to belong to "master;" and "master" is considered "unnatural" when he turns him over to the workhouse.

The Royal Literary Pension Fund, as we call it, for the sake of clearness, has not often fallen like a refreshing dew upon the withered plants of literature. It has comforted schoolmistresses, paralytic cooks, stern warriors, and discoverers; as well as authors of all-work and rural poets. Literature is not disgraced to the extent of the whole twelve hundred pounds every year, as various kinds of pensioners are allowed to join in the scramble. Perhaps, on the average, one-half of that amount is yearly bestowed upon broken-down writers and their representatives, and literature bears this corporate stain for the sake of a mere milk-score. It would be difficult to show, upon logical grounds, why the trade of book-writing should be more entitled to this slice out of the national taxes, than boot-making, sausage-making, or the manufacture of beer-bottles. As a craft or profession it is surely as well able to take care of itself as any other branch of industry. Almost every interest except the writing interest employed in the manufacture of a book, is able to maintain its independence without royal or spasmodic charity. The bookbinder, the book-printer, the papermaker, and even the inkmaker, has got his provident organization for periods of distress, and is as strong as a thorough class-union can make him. The literary man, on the other hand, is as weak as a thorough class *dis*-union can make him. Like all weak bodies, he gets offensively patronised; the committees of his societies are mostly formed of patrons, instead of fellow-workers and friends; the stewards of his public dinners generally bear the same complexion; and the charitable pension-givers of course take their tone from what they see and hear in "polite society."

It has seldom been easy to guess upon what principle the royal literary bounty has been bestowed, until Lord Palmerston took the direction of the springs of benevolence. That highly jaunty and well-advertised comic statesman has evidently regarded the whole affair as a financial "lark." He has tied up his small packets of sovereigns in the usual dog's-meat bundles, and after satisfying the appetites of the nearest claimants, has looked about for the most ridiculous representative of literature he could find. His lordship's sympathy with letters is notoriously confined to that practical, everyday branch which can render him good political service in the shape of newspaper leaders. For this reason, perhaps, we ought to make allowance for his singular taste in poetry; but we certainly expected something better from an old squib-writer in the days of Hookham Frere, than a pension granted to a rhyming Joseph Ady in the wilds of Westmoreland. His lordship's selection of such a "rural poet" as Mr. J. Close, of Kirby Stephen, for a pension of £50 a year,* can only be accounted for on the theory that

* Mr. Close's pension has been withdrawn, but this does not affect the argument. The Royal Literary Pensions are still bestowed with equal taste and judgment.

the giver wished to bring literature and the royal bounty into contempt. By tying-up several well-known and respected literary names with the self-styled "Poet-Laureate to the King of Grand Bonny" in the same bundle of gifts, he has snubbed what is generally considered a highly sensitive profession. If those who are individually or collectively interested in maintaining the dignity of themselves and their order only now act with becoming vigour and spirit, the present year ought to see the last of these degrading pensions.

We are spared the task of going into the merits of Mr. Close's "poetry," because our contemporary, the "Critic," has exhausted that very uninteresting subject. By a timely analysis of the pensioner's published fly-leaves and poems, our contemporary has shown the poet-laureate to the grand King of Bonny to be an ignorant charlatan; and has caused Mr. Stirling, M.P., to take the necessary steps for bringing the whole matter before Parliament. When the hour comes, we hope the literary members of the House will be found at their posts, and that the whole question of literary pensions will be thoroughly investigated. We are not advocating the claims of country against town, or town against country, in this matter; we only wish to see the whole profession or calling of literature relieved from this annual royal patronage and class disgrace. If the crown and its advisers think proper to bestow a part of the Civil List funds every year upon any warbling idiot recommended by two or more political adherents, that will then be a question for financial reformers, not for authors. At present, Mr. J. Close, of Kirby Stephen, trades, so to speak, under a royal license as a literary man, and this is what we think the profession ought not to tolerate. Battered, divided, angular, apathetic, as it is, we hope it will kick at this. It kicks at most things brought forward to do it good; let it kick at things which do it evident harm. Without reproducing those proofs of Mr. Close's designing imbecility which the "Critic" has produced to some purpose, we may say, in support of our strictures, that the "poet's" paid advocates speak of him as a drivelling idiot. Like the satirists of the last century, the bard of Kirby Stephen seems to have cultivated the lampoon, and to have withheld his poetical lash at times for a satisfactory consideration. Some of the local gentry seem to have declined to purchase the good word of the bard; upon which the muse of satire began to sweep the strings. An action for libel against Mr. Close sprang out of these poetical attacks, in which the "poet" was cast in damages to the extent of three hundred pounds. The counsel employed by the defendant on this occasion could make no better excuse for his client's errors than by bringing forward the reputation for imbecility which the "poet" enjoyed in his village.

The most dangerous fact in connection with this royal literary pensioner is his possession of a printing-press. He can rush at any moment into print, without editorial check or guidance, and where the type is so handy, it is not possible that he ever "declines" himself "with thanks." The praises that he has already showered upon the dear, kind premier are only limited by his ink and paper; and the curses that he prints at his enemies are only kept in bounds by the same materials. In dwelling upon his case at this length, we are not anxious to snatch from him his miserable pension, but to show literature how it is degraded in the person of this patronized rural "poet." The grant, as long as it lasts, will be a monument to foreigners, to point out how the state recognises the man of letters in the England of to-day.

THE SHOP-SIDE OF LITERATURE.

The longer we live in the world, and the more we look about us, the more proofs we find that life is full of compensations. If we are inclined to envy greatness when we see it gathering its hard-earned laurels, we ought to think of the thorns concealed under the green leaves. Literary notoriety is a fine thing—a good marketable commodity, if properly traded with—but it has its bitters. It often leads to indigestion and to sleepless nights, if not always to laborious days. It attracts the critical hornets from all sides, and its unhappy possessor, if ordinarily sensitive, is generally stung to death. Even the last sleep brings no repose to the distinguished martyr. His body may be at rest, but his works are alive—and kicking. Long after his poor bones have melted into the damp earth, he is either condescendingly patronized by cold-blooded admirers, or questioned as to his right to immortality. He suffers from indiscreet friends as much as from discreet enemies, and may be edited at any moment by fools and dunces. When the spell of his copyright is dissolved, his works become the property of the crowd, and are often seized with eagerness by slop-shop publishers. He may be printed upon sugar-paper or yellow tinder, and illustrated in a style known as "penny plain and twopence coloured." His text may be corrupted; his best thoughts stolen without acknowledgment, and his plots worked up into sensational dramas by catchpenny playwrights. He may be torn to pieces by burlesque-writing vultures, while ungrateful crowds look on and smile at his contortions.

These are only a few of the torments which fat, comfortable obscurity escapes, and many more might be added to swell the melancholy list. As time advances, and the ingenuity of man increases, a variety of new tortures will probably be invented. This may seem a gloomy anticipation, but, unfortunately, it is founded upon facts. Our age is one in which the showman is abroad, seeking whom he may devour, and nothing that will turn a penny is allowed to escape him. When the book is used up as a source of profit—when the writer no longer attracts as a wax-figure or a plaster-model—then the old printer-stained manuscript is hunted up and exhibited in the manner of Barnum to a carefully-prepared public. Those who wander into the British Museum Library to gaze upon illuminated Eastern manuscripts, each one the work of an individual life; to learn history from documents like the Duke of Monmouth's diary; or to wonder at the clerkly clearness of Ben Jonson's writing, and the Waverley manuscripts—the latter produced largely in the din of a Scotch law court, with scarcely an erasure or an interlineary word—can hardly imagine the life and adventures of many other literary curiosities which have not been gathered into the national fold. Now and then an advertisement tells us something of the fate of these scattered jewels, in much the same way as certain country papers kept the friends of Bampfylde Moore Carew informed about his gipsy excesses. Taste may be shocked; feelings may be hurt; the dead author, through his manuscript, may be trotted out like a performing pony, or the late Miss Julia Pastrana, but the showman has got his property, and intends to make the most of it. The latest sign of this Barnum spirit, on the shop-side of literature, was shown in the following advertisement, which appeared in the "Times'" supplement of July 18th, 1861:—

"Gray's Elegy.—The original autograph manuscript of Gray's Elegy, to be seen for a very brief period (two or three weeks only), prior to its departure for ever to Trans-Atlantic shores. Mr. Robert Charles Wrightson has the honour of submitting this precious manuscript to the élite of the world. It is a rarity unique, absolute, and exclusive, being neither more nor less than the original draft of 'the immortal Elegy,' written on a single sheet of post-quarto letter paper, somewhat embrowned and time-tinged truly, yet preserving almost unblemished every letter, line, and verse of the exquisitely clear and beautiful handwriting of the inspired Poet. It cost, at public sale, £131, and was competed for by the chief learned and literary societies, the British Museum, the Oxford and Cambridge Universities, the leading London publishers, Stevens, the great autograph collector of America, the learned savans, and chief dilettanti of Europe, and was ultimately carried off triumphantly by its comparatively unknown and obscure possessor. See accounts of the excitement the sale occasioned in the 'Illustrated London News' (April 12, 1854), the 'Times,' 'Athenæum,' and current newspapers, hebdomadal and daily. Lord Byron says of this poem, 'its fame became instant and eternal.' General Wolfe received a copy on the eve of the battle of Quebec, and was so struck with its beauties that he exclaimed he would sooner be the author of this poem than the victor in the projected attack in which he so gloriously lost his life. Dr. Johnson (stern and uncompromising critic) pronounced it without flaw or blemish. 'This inestimable treasure,' exclaimed a distinguished living poet, as he gazed upon the time-stained sheet. 'Every line a jewel, and every verse a cluster of brilliants,' uttered an orator and wit; 'and, following the example of my consort at her jeweller's, I often borrow some on going out for the evening.' 'Glorious!' exclaimed a learned Theban, 'I wouldn't have missed the sight of it for twenty guineas.' In short, 'the Elegy' has been long acknowledged the most elegant and original poem which the English language has produced. Poets, philosophers, wits, warriors, orators, statesmen, and the universal voice unite in rendering it homage, acknowledging it to be, in the language of Shakspere, an 'entire and perfect chrysolite.' And in a few short weeks this inestimable treasure will leave the land which gave it birth for ever, and be far away over the blue waters of the Atlantic to return no more. Immediate applications for inspection (at your own establishments only) are necessary, naming day and hour. Individual appointments, fee, one guinea, to cover cab-hire, incidentals, and advertising expenses. Household parties at a much diminished charge. Address, without delay. Mr. R. C. Wrightson, 24, Jermyn Street, St. James's."

Some few people may be weak enough to consider this as fame, and to think that Thomas Gray is honoured by such "Brummagem" notice. There is no accounting for tastes, but it seems to us that the "precious manuscript," by being made the subject of such an advertisement, is degraded to the level of Harper Twelvetrees's beetle-exterminator, or the latest quack remedy for gravel and lumbago. It seems hard, after a century of popular appreciation, to be introduced to the world by an obscure showman, with all kinds of ridiculous testimonials as to character. If the "inspired poet" could be asked his opinion of this Barnum patronage, there can be little doubt as to the nature of his answer. He would be inclined to regret that he had ever written a line, and to envy all the "mute inglorious Miltons" of the universe. If Dr. Johnson—"stern and uncompromising critic"—could see himself chained to Mr. Wrightson's advertising van, not even the quality of his companions would calm his anger. When we are told that "the chief learned and literary societies, the British Museum, and the Oxford and Cambridge Universities" competed for this "inestimable treasure" without saving it from the clutch of its "comparatively unknown and obscure possessor," we are annoyed that they did not protect an English classic from defilement at any cost. Surely one of those auction-room combinations, so familiar to all brokers, might have been effected in this case, and the manuscript snatched from the enterprising showman. Money is not generally considered to be scarce amongst the institutions mentioned, and in this instance a little extravagance would have been judicious and commendable. The advertisement which we have quoted may have been put out by Mr. Wrightson as a feeler for a public bidding, notwithstanding the pathetic assertion that the "treasure" was about to "take its departure for ever to Trans-Atlantic shores." No response appears to have been made by the British Museum authorities to this indirect appeal, and the manuscript has doubtless "left the land which gave it birth," and is "far away over the blue waters of the Atlantic." The best of friends must often part, when the sole *nexus* between man and man is not forthcoming. We cherish a belief, however, that we shall see the interesting literary emigrant again, although we do not suppose that the suggested family inspections of it were a paying speculation. It has, doubtless, been passed on from one showman to another, and will come back to this country as surely as a racket-ball returns from the wall. Its departure must have been a sad effort of sailing against the stream—a single literary export from England to America, in the face of many imported tight-rope dancers, tramway projectors, African explorers, scheming dramatists, spiritualists, and tragic actors. It will, doubtless, return in a few months, a little stained with tobacco juice and brandy smash, perhaps with the real author of the great African book, the nurse of Washington, and the woolly horse.

LITERARY MANURE.

"After the Lord Mayor's Show always comes a dung-cart."

Popular Saying.

ONE great incentive to literary production is the hope of immortality. Every man who once gets his name across the title-page of a book, considers that he has secured a chance of being read by future ages. He fondly believes that posterity will have to refer to his volumes to find many things not contained in the works of contemporary writers. Periodical literature may be brilliant and fleeting; journalism, however meritorious, may and does die, almost as soon as born; art is perishable; music requires sympathetic listeners and skilled performers; but literature in the form of published books is a monument whose foundations are not easily shaken. Nothing but an irruption of Goths, an earthquake, or a national fire, can destroy the great library collected by Act of Parliament, and, therefore, Mr. Pigmy knows that, as far as the British Museum is concerned, he will last as long as Lord Macaulay, or the philosopher of Chelsea.

The knowledge, however, that a printed volume always secures a place in the great Bloomsbury temple, is not enough to account for half the existing literary activity. The hope of immortality, or even lengthened popularity, reaches far beyond that one vast catalogue and those national bookshelves. It pictures the petted volume—the child of many sleepless nights—amusing the family circle, bearing the stroller company in a country walk, or lulling the impatient traveller into a forgetfulness of time. It pictures it as the friend of old age, the favourite of manhood, and the chosen monitor of youth. It pictures it circulating from house to house in quiet villages, years after its happy author is laid in the dust, or worn into honourable raggedness as the most popular of books at the Mechanics' Institutes. It pictures it reprinted in many forms by enterprising publishers, now in a library shape, bound in fragrant morocco, now in the Roxburghe style for fastidious collectors, now in the illustrated folio style for drawing-room tables, and now in the convenient pocket form—the true reward of a classic. It pictures generations of leading artists striving who shall be foremost in the work of illustrating the cherished volume, and hundreds of eager commentators quarrelling over the meaning of its faintest allusions.

This is the rosy vision—the waking dream—the flattering tale, based upon nothing, too often told by the hope of immortality. What is the reality—the dark unrelenting reality—the doom of ninety-nine hundredths of our current literature? It is painful to have to draw the curtain—to play the part of a death's-head at the feast; but some one must undertake this disagreeable task, and who so well qualified as the critics?

We are not about to allude to the trunkmaker. After a jocular existence of more than a century it is as well, perhaps, that this bogie should be treated as dead. He was doubtless a literary ogre with a voracious appetite, but his principal food was newspapers and clean broad sheets, rather than printed volumes. He fattened upon unbound books in sheets, but seldom touched those stagnant unsaleable works which were protected by the armour of cloth and leather. The trunkmaker, as a good nursery rod, once had power to frighten bad authors and voluminous publishers; but punishments, like mustard, lose their sting, if they are used too much on one palate.

Next to the trunkmaker comes the traditional butterman; and by butterman we may be held to mean any tradesman who uses paper in his business. This devourer of bad literature still exists in full health and strength, with powers of consumption increased rather than diminished. Anything once brought within his destroying grasp may be looked upon as lost, although we have heard a few wonderful stories of literary rescues. The butterman is no respecter of quality or style, and often even shocks the feelings of his customers by his literary indifference. We once knew an old lady who took offence at this boorish method of dealing with literature, and wrote the following note to the offending butterman:—

"Mrs. Blank presents her compliments to Mr. Greasy, and begs that in future he will not send her the butter enveloped in portions of the Holy Scriptures."

Devouring trunkmakers and hungry cheesemongers are bad enough, but the new doom of literature is something far more fearful to contemplate. It is alluded to in a recent article upon Mudie's library, which appeared in "Once a Week," where the writer, after describing the great underground charnel-house for worn-out volumes, gives us the substance of the following dialogue:—

Writer.—Wouldn't these books do for the butterman?
Mudie's Shopman.—Too dirty for that.

Writer.—Nor for old trunks?

Mudie's Shopman.—Much too greasy for that.

Writer.—What are they good for, then?

Mudie's Shopman (*with no emotion*).—For manure.

It would be difficult to imagine any fate more degrading for literature than this, for few people can look upon manure in a proper philosophical spirit. It is all very well to be told that every good citizen should help to fertilize his native land, and that the public benefactor is one who causes two blades of grass to grow where only one grew before. Authors will tell us this with an air of authority, but it would be curious to trace their change of tone when they discovered that their own volumes were to be the fertilizing agents. What effect different kinds of literature may have upon different soils we are not learned enough in such matters to say, but a friend at our elbow says that old books, taken generally, form the best of manures. We are sorry to hear it, for there would have been some little satisfaction in knowing that nothing was got by such apparent Vandalism. We only hope that a certain decency is observed, even in fertilizing the soil, and that Mr. Manwaring's publications are carefully separated from Mr. Murray's. We hope that no orthodox churchman has been fed upon turnips manured with the "Essays and Reviews," and that no sound Tory has eaten strawberries forced into premature life by Lord Macaulay's History.

If any proper division is made in laying down this literary manure, Tennyson might be devoted to flower-forcing, Dr. Livingstone to exotics, and Mr. Timbs to all plants that are to be raised from cuttings. It would be useless, we presume, to try to lighten heavy soils with volumes like those issued by the Parker Society, or to make light soils more solid by mixing them with popular magazine literature. Some care must be exercised when this literary manure is applied, and a little more trouble would make such high farming perfect.

The prospect of being carted away on to the bleak cold land, when we expected to be reposing in snug libraries, is not very cheering to the literary producer. It is like a dim allegory of life and death acted before us to teach us that we are only mortal. It ought to make even the most prosperous author meek and humble, reminding him of that sad saying, so full of old Burton's philosophy, which was born in the streets:—"After the Lord Mayor's Show always comes a dung-cart."

LITERARY FILTER-BEDS.

THERE is a compact body of tinkering philanthropists in this country whose fingers are itching to be in every man's pie. Their intentions are often so good and so plentiful, that Pandemonium never need be in want of pavement. Their theology is "low," their desire to proselytize is powerful, and they hunt down poor sinners with feeble tracts, and tickets for tabernacle broth. They affect to be on the most playful terms with the Holy Trinity, and address the Deity—in book-titles—with the most blasphemous familiarity.

Among other things of a hopeless, meddling nature, these righteous overmuch people have invented a Literary Filter. There is not much of novelty in its main idea; for the Romish Church has worked it for many years in the much-abused *Index*. The Evangelical party, so it seems, are not above doing as Rome does, when it answers their purpose, and the Earl of Shaftesbury, to carry out his pernicious views, is willing to take a hint from the Scarlet Traviata. A number of ornamental committee-men have been got together under the presidency of this distinguished missionary, and it is charitable to suppose that the majority of them are unaware of the impudent nonsense put forward in their name. The strings are pulled by the two or three officers who work the organization, and it is announced that the Great Filter is engaged in sifting all modern literature into two classes. One of these is called pure, and that gives the title of the "Pure Literature Society" to this knot of busy-bodies; and the other is called impure, by implication. When the whole of our vast current literature has been strained through this purifying sieve, it comes out—in the Society's catalogue of approved books—a shrunken pool of milky goodness, and would-be pious pap, without any sign of bone and muscle. Its purity, however, is less the result of virtue than of extreme weakness, for it has hardly strength to move on without the assistance of a patronizing society.

The operations of this Literary Filter—this inquisitorial association of angelic Paul Prys—may be classed under three heads. First, there is an agency for the collection and distribution of "good periodicals," that is, periodicals pronounced to be good by tasters with a confirmed palate, who start to arrive at a forgone conclusion. Secondly, there are the selection and criticism of publications; and thirdly, the granting of libraries to certain favoured institutions at half price.

The importance of the first branch of the Society's labours—the agency for the collection and distribution of good periodicals—according to its advocates, is hardly so well understood as it deserves to be.

"Whilst almost every kind of objectionable cheap serial" (they say,) "was to be had at every little shop in town or country, there was considerable difficulty in obtaining periodicals of a better stamp. The booksellers did not care to supply a shilling monthly parcel, which would perhaps contain a dozen different serials, involving considerable trouble in their collection, and producing very little profit. Under these circumstances, the committee determined to establish a central office in London, at which the various good publications of different prices might be collected, and then distributed by post or otherwise throughout the country. The value of such an agency is now increasingly acknowledged, and upwards of 120,000 periodicals are sent out annually, divided amongst some six hundred and fifty monthly parcels."

This statement contains a falsehood, and apologizes for the "central office"—the carrying out of the secretarial design. The booksellers who refused to supply "a shilling monthly parcel," or even a single penny periodical, are purely imaginary characters, invented to strengthen the hands of the Association.

Three or four booksellers may have shown a desire to pick their custom, but hundreds more can be found who will even deliver a penny journal every week within a reasonable distance of their shops. The great distributors of this class of literature are the barbers, snuff-shop keepers, and sweetmeat-sellers in the suburbs, and these are not mentioned by the Society. An office is started, on philanthropic trading principles, and what is it able to do? With all the advantage of its overgrown committee, and that freemasonry which is supposed to animate the religious world, the society can only point to a sale of one hundred and twenty thousand "good" periodicals in the course of the year! Why this is not one-fiftieth part of the circulation of the "Leisure Hour," a journal recommended by the Society, which is able to walk without a leader. The "London Journal" has a reputation for four times this circulation, or two hundred times more than the Society can obtain for its adopted children; and the swarms of other "bad" periodicals, if put together with their annual figures, would rather check the crowing of the Filter managers.

The list of periodicals recommended by the Society is remarkably meagre, and leads to a belief that all current literature must be desperately wicked. These are the "Leisure Hour," before mentioned, the "British Workman," "Old Jonathan," and the "Youth's Magazine," with some eighteen or twenty minor periodicals of a "distinctly religious character," for adults and children. The leading peculiarity of these "distinctly religious" journals is that their contents are largely stolen from contemporary and other writers. The reader may be benefited; the Society or the publisher may grow fat, while the robbed author may starve. To sue for payment when a copyright book is bundled piecemeal into these heavenly journals, is to be worldly and flesh-potty, and to impose obstacles in the way of sectarian education.

Of the four journals first named, the "British Workman" is a shining example of vicious goodness. When it advocates temperance, it is useful enough; but while it professes to worship the tea-pot, it has sold its soul to the demon of getting on. Week after week it is filled with accounts of "celebrated tinkers," "celebrated dustmen," "celebrated pot-boys," and "celebrated sweeps." It never touches a representative working-man, unless he is one of those rare beings who have raised themselves from a coal-shed to the wool-sack. The lives of these exceptional heroes are set forth with all the false glitter which surrounds "self-made men." Their biographies are taken from popular sources without inquiry, and every anecdote that ignorant wonder or idle invention has plastered on to the original foundation is recorded as a gospel truth. The beginnings of such men are always lowered, and their endings raised, so that the distance of the rise, or self-making, is in appearance increased. The clerk becomes a shop-boy, the cook a scullion, the well-to-do man a millionaire, and the patentee a demi-god. False heroes are mixed with the true, and drunkards and railway-jobbers, like the late Robert Stephenson, are held up as models to be copied.

The lessons taught by such writing and such illustrations of character are greasy and pernicious. They make too much of the fat paunch and the full purse. They cause thousands to be discontented with an humble position in life which can never be altered. They incite thousands to start in an exciting race, in which one man *may* win, but in which millions *must* fail. They breed a race of restless inventors with no invention, who starve themselves and their children, and neglect their allotted work to register useless patents, in the vain search for wealth. They talk to their listeners only of the score or two who succeed, and not of the common-place crowds who must stand where they are placed. Such reading may be thought "good" by those who create it, and may be sold under the stamp and authority of a "Pure Literature Society," but it is doubtful whether any more unhealthy stimulus could be found for working men, or the unformed minds of young children.

"The critical work" (we are told) "of examining books for admission to the Society's catalogue has been carried on during the past year with increased assiduity. The value of this catalogue is now very generally felt, and applications are received from all parts of the country from persons anxious to avail themselves of its aid in forming a library."

Who these persons are we are not told; but evangelical as they undoubtedly must be, they are as willing to be led blindfold by a central committee as any adherents of the Roman Church—the scarlet abomination—were ever supposed to be. The Society professes only to admit books after a careful perusal, and in this part of their report it is that their cool impudence shows itself. "There have been 507 volumes," they say, "brought under the notice of readers for approval in the past year. Of these, 25 have been read by three persons, 289 by two, and 116 by one reader; the latter class being generally that of books which were plainly unsuitable to our purpose. The remaining 77 are still in hand." This is the inner mechanism of the Literary Filter. Six tasters seem to do all the work of the Society, and they undertake, without a misgiving, to give a decided opinion upon all published books. This beats the easy confidence of the critical journals. The six tasters, perhaps, get quickly through their work, by looking at the author's name on the title-page. There is "Palissy the Potter," for example, written by Mr. Henry Morley, and published by Messrs. Chapman and Hall. The author is a man of sound reputation, and the publishers are without reproach; but neither of them is "good" enough for the "Pure Literature Society." "Palissy the Potter" certainly appears in the celestial list, but it is a reduced edition, stolen from Mr. Morley's work, and published without a twinge by the "Religious Tract Society."

The catalogue of books passed through the Literary Filter shows a little broader spirit than the list of periodicals, though this is not saying much in its favour. Everywhere you may find traces of sectarian feeling, and a determination to arrive at a foregone conclusion. The periodicals recommended by the Society seem to be partly edited by the Society, to judge from the following passage in the report we have been quoting:—

"The journals recommended" (it says) "are, from time to time, examined, and suggestions are occasionally offered which are invariably received in the same friendly spirit that dictated them. A kindly intercourse is thus maintained between the Society and the editors of the periodicals."

This is a pleasant way of putting it, and the Emperor of

the French might copy this part of the report, to describe his friendly intercourse with the Parisian journals.

The whole plan of the Society is one for inquisitorial meddling in everybody's business—especially the business of the poor—and for keeping everybody, especially the poor, in leading-strings. A taste for what is called sensational literature is not confined to the supporters of penny journals. The fact is, that while low literature, as it is called, has vastly improved within the last half-century, high literature has stood still, if it has not lowered its standard. Some of us are old enough to remember the time—not more than twenty years ago—when "Lloyd's Penny Sunday Times," a ghastly feast, formed the sole literary food for the lower orders. Now we may have to register a "Reynold's Miscellany," a "Blue Dwarf," a "Mormon's Daughter," a "Charley Wag," and a few other like publications, which are kept alive by licentious description; but these are nothing compared to the mass of successful cheap publications, whose stories may be highly spiced, but whose "padding" is unexceptionable. This is the literature which can afford to laugh at the Filter Beds. It pours down, like a mighty river, purifying itself in its course, while puddling societies squat upon its banks, and strain a spoonful of its contents with some such an air as Mrs. Partington showed when she tried to sweep back the Atlantic.

A SLASHING REVIEW.*

WHAT is "Bradawl's Guide?" What place does it take in English literature? The dullest observer must see that it is not witty; that it is lighted up with no flashes of humour; that it is remarkable for no peculiar vein of poetry. It is not enlivened by any intense narrative, or any subtle delineations of character. It is not a work that is eagerly demanded at every circulating library; that is read aloud to listening families and delighted audiences; that is devoured in solitude by persons of an imaginative temperament. It is nothing if not statistical. Its greatest admirers never claim for it any other character than that of a "compendium of information relating to railways." It teaches a certain amount of geography in the driest and least attractive way, and its pages are only a little more interesting than those of a day-book or a ledger. It is often accused of being complicated and bewildering, but it has always been looked upon as containing the truth, if its readers have only the patience to dig for it.

In dealing with works of this kind, it has long been too much the custom to take their reputation for granted. It has generally been assumed that a dull and unreadable book has compensating qualities in its usefulness and reliability.

* "Bradawl's Railway and Steam Navigation Guide for Great Britain and Ireland." London: W. J. Adams. 1861.

A profusion of figures, a mass of undigested details lying on the surface, have seldom failed to deceive an indolent public. Your brilliant author is looked upon as clever, but wanting in "ballast," while your leaden writer has the character forced upon him of being "learned and laborious." It is thus that hundreds of books like "Bradawl's Guide" are suffered to pass unexamined from year to year with their ignorance unexposed, their authority unshaken. When a critic is at last found with discernment, industry, and courage sufficient to undertake the task, he is seldom thanked for dispelling a time-honoured and agreeable delusion.

Of all the books that have contrived to combine an appearance of minute precision with a reality of slipshod carelessness, we know of none that can equal "Bradawl." We turn to its index of towns in Great Britain and Ireland, and choose a word at random, which happens to be "Alexandria."

Now Alexandria, as every charity-boy is aware, is a city of Egypt, fourteen miles west of the Rosetta, or western mouth of the Nile, in lat. 31 deg. 12 min. N.; long. 29 deg. 53 min. E.; and 112 miles N.W. Cairo.

Having got over our wonder at finding the name of an ancient Egyptian city in a "Railway Guide for Great Britain and Ireland," we open the reliable "Bradawl," as directed, at page 169, to seek for an explanation of the mystery. There we find it coolly stated that Alexandria is in Dumbartonshire, exactly nineteen miles from Glasgow, measuring from the Queen Street railway station (observe the "Queen Street"), and that it can be reached in an hour, at a fourth-class cost of tenpence! Take other towns the very echo of whose names would tell any person, with a most moderate geographical knowledge, that they *must* be in Egypt, in Palestine, or the East—take Aber, Balmaha, Bacup, Bassaleg, Corstorphine, Joppa, Jarrow, Patna, Scarva, and Tanderagee; and then take "Bradawl's Guide" —"for Great Britain and Ireland," bear in mind—to see if it has the ignorant audacity to mention them. There they are, sure enough, as if the editor worked with an idea that Hindostan, or any other distant country, might crop up in England, Ireland, and Scotland, like that part of the parish of Clerkenwell which is found at Muswell Hill, or that portion of the county of Cambridgeshire which is said to be at the foot of Holborn. Aber, we are told by the dry, but infallible "Bradawl," is fifty-four miles from Chester, on the Holyhead line; Balmaha, is said to be on the road to Loch Lomond, Scotland; Bacup is put in East Lancashire, about two-and-twenty miles from Manchester; Bassaleg is placed in Monmouthshire, and called a railway junction; and Corstorphine is stated to be about three miles out of Edinburgh!

This is not all. Joppa—dear, delightful oriental Joppa (sometimes called Yaffa or Jaffa, Jopha or Japho), is placed in North Britain, on the Musselburgh line; Jarrow is planted on the North-Eastern, in connection with Hartlepool, Durham, and Sunderland; Patna, the city of rice, of sugar, and of Hindoo temples, is stated to be in Scotland, about nine miles from Ayr; while Scarva and Tanderagee are both said to be in Ireland, on the railway that runs from Belfast to Dublin!

The more we examine this extraordinary work, the more reason we have to be startled with fresh geographical curiosities. We always thought, if upon no higher authority than a cultivated ear, that Ulleskelf, Gort, Oola, Carluke, Insch, Golcar, Yarm, Drigg, Instow, Wark, and Dromkeen were names of Russian towns, the inhabitants of which were under the government of the czar. "Bradawl's Guide for Great Britain and Ireland" attempts the task of undeceiving us. Ulleskelf, we are told, is not far from Harrogate or York; Gort is said to be in Ireland, in the neighbourhood of Limerick, while Oola and Dromkeen are on the same line; Carluke is placed on the Motherwell junction of the Glasgow and Carlisle railway; Insch is planted in the north of Scotland, about half-way between Aberdeen and Keith; Golcar is stated to be three miles out of Huddersfield, in Yorkshire; Yarm is placed in the same county, about four miles from Stockton-on-Tees; Drigg is said to be on the road from Ulverston, in the lake country, to Whitehaven; Instow is put in North Devonshire, between Bideford and Barnstaple; and Wark is placed near Cornhill, between Berwick and Kelso!

There are marvellous statements enough here to suit any moderate appetite for the wonderful, if we closed the "Guide" at this point, and our investigation also. Our curiosity, however, impels us to sketch out another geographical route, and to see what places the daring "Bradawl" has transplanted into the United Kingdom from the south of Europe. We will take the following towns—Eastrea, Bynea, Donabate, Moy, Aspatria, Manea, Pallas, Eassie, Fintona, and Etruria, which no intelligent reader will deny to be purely Italian. "Bradawl" gathers them all into the Britannic fold—annexes them, insatiable conqueror that he is, and incorporates them with his own country. Bynea, he tells us, is close to Llanelly, in South Wales; Eastrea he calmly places within seven miles of the swampy cathedral city of Peterborough; Donabate he decides to be near Dublin; Moy he can place nowhere but in Ireland, on the Dungannon junction; Aspatria, he tells us, is between Carlisle and Maryport; Manea not far from

Ely, in the Eastern Counties; Pallas in Ireland, on the Limerick line, between the Russian towns of Oola and Dromkeen before alluded to; Eassie he declares to be in Scotland, some five-and-twenty miles from Perth; Fintona, he informs us, is in Ireland, between Enniskillen and Londonderry; and Etruria, which we all connect with the glories of ancient Italy and Etruscan vases, he tells us is a small pottery station in the midst of smoky Staffordshire!

If Italy is thus robbed in this unblushing manner Spain is no better treated by the unscrupulous "Bradawl.' The towns of Torre, Clonsilla, Bures, Pontardulais, Potto, Alrewas, Poyntypass, Moira, Alves, and Pontrillas, are all appropriated for the United Kingdom by this remarkable "guide," although the sound of each and all of them is so unmistakably Spanish. Torre he places in Devonshire, on the Torquay railway branch (we are glad to see that he plants it in the south); Clonsilla he asserts to be a few miles out of Dublin; Bures he puts near Sudbury, in the grazing county of Suffolk; Pontardulais, he tells us, is about seven miles from Llanelly, in South Wales; Potto, if we believe him, will be found in Yorkshire, not far from the Russian town of Yarm; Alrewas he decides to be between Derby and Birmingham; Poyntypass he places on the Dublin and Belfast junction, close to the eastern towns of Scarva and Tanderagee; Moira he declares to be not far from Burton-upon-Trent; Alves he states to be about one-and-thirty miles from Inverness, in Scotland, and only fifty miles from the Russian town of Insch; and Pontrillas he places about half-way between Hereford and Abergavenny!

We have not done with our friend "Bradawl" yet, and we will take him as our "guide" in what we should consider a little tour through France. We will put together the Gallic-sounding towns of St. Germains, Linacre, Oyne,

St. Devereux, Haselour, Goitre, St. Cyres, Doune, Foynes, Beauparc, and Plessy, and ask him where he imagines them to be. He claims them, as usual, in his own dry, but original way, for the already swollen wallet of the United Kingdom. St. Germains, he tells us, is about ten miles from Plymouth; Linacre he states to be about four miles out of Liverpool; Oyne he places in Scotland, on the road to Inverness, and about three miles on the south side of the Russian town of Insch; St. Devereux he puts near Hereford, and close to the Spanish town of Pontrillas; Haselour he places in Staffordshire, not far from Tamworth; Goitre he used to place some five miles from Abergavenny, but he appears to have had some little doubt about this in his last edition, and to have altered the name to "Llanvair;" St. Cyres, he tells us, is about five miles out of Exeter; Doune he plants in central Scotland, on the road from Stirling to Loch Katrine; Foynes he decides to be in Ireland, somewhere near Limerick; and Beauparc, he tells us, we may reach from Dublin in an hour and a half, if we start from the *Amiens* Street station! Our friend "Bradawl" must surely mean the Amiens station, leaving out the "street;" and why does he insist upon dragging us past the Italian town of Donabate? Not content with this, he has the assurance to inform us that Plessy is not more than eleven miles north of Newcastle-upon-Tyne!

As our friend "Bradawl" is so daring in his appropriation of French towns, we will try him with a little group that sound as if they belong to Hungary and Poland. Pelaw, Wem, Ince, Chirk, Piel, Balfron, Magerhafelt, Cam, Starbeck, and Usk, are names of towns that few intelligent persons would expect to find in a railway "guide" for Great Britain and Ireland.. When Koskiusco arrives in this country with a little capital, and starts, perhaps, as an industrious tradesman in the fancy biscuit-line, he is soon made aware that there is something the matter with his name, that it sticks in the throats of his customers, and bewilders the postman. He takes counsel of British subjects, who are learned in the ways of trade, and in due time he is seized by a "partner" who is happy in having the common title of "Brown," and is ultimately found conducting a thriving business under the style of "Brown and Company."

"Bradawl" knows this as well as we do; and yet he annexes these ten Polish and Hungarian looking settlements, and fixes their roots in British soil, without altering their original titles! Pelaw, he tells us, is now a thriving railway junction, about six miles from Newcastle-upon-Tyne; Wem he believes to be doing well, about ten miles out of Shrewsbury; Ince, he says, is doing a small business between Southport and Liverpool; Chirk he has planted firmly within one-and-twenty miles of Chester, on the road to Wolverhampton; Piel he has placed in the lake district, not very far from Ulverston; Balfron he considers safe in Scotland, some twenty miles out of Stirling; Magerhafelt he has planted in Northern Ireland, about two-and-forty miles from Belfast; Cam he has placed on the Dursley branch, about four-and-twenty miles from Bristol; Starbeck he has put in Yorkshire, as the station for water-bibbing Harrogate; and Usk, he tells us, is on the Monmouth line, about fourteen miles from Newport!

While searching further in the index of this wonderful railway "guide" for Great Britain and Ireland, we pick out a group of ten towns that are nothing if not Danish. We take Elsenham, Bargoed, Esk-bank, Troon, Elslack, Bodorgen, Yaxham, Goathland, Florden, and Tong, and ask any reader, with any ear for languages, if these are not towns in some part of Denmark? If a man that is born in Elsenham or Goathland is not a northern "foreigner," in every sense of the word, what is he? The dashing "Bradawl" rushes forward to answer the question, and says, "an Englishman." Elsenham, he tells us, is a quiet village, near Bishop's Stortford, in Hertfordshire, and Goathland is a small settlement not far from Whitby, in Yorkshire; Bargoed he places in South Wales, about nineteen miles from Cardiff; Esk-bank, he informs us, is about eight miles out of Edinburgh, towards Hawick; Troon he states to be in Scotland, about seven miles from Ayr; Elslack he puts upon the Yorkshire and Lancashire line, a short distance out of Skipton; Bodorgen he places half-way between Bangor and Holyhead; Yaxham, he tells us, is in Norfolk, about twenty miles from Norwich; Florden he declares to be only eight miles from this last city; and Tong, he tells us, is in Yorkshire, between Bradford and Wakefield!

Before we finally close the pages of this extraordinary book, we wish to know the exact position in the United Kingdom of some eight towns that we always thought were in different parts of Germany. Friockheim, Mulben, Dolwen, Boher, Kippen, Innerleithen, Helensburgh, and Droylsden, are names that certainly smack of the Rhine; but really, since reading this marvellous "guide," we have almost come to believe that there is no other country in the world besides Great Britain and Ireland. We have heard that our shores afford a refuge to travellers from all countries, but we never heard that these travellers brought their countries with them. It appears, however, from "Bradawl's Guide," that this double importation must have been very common, and we thus find ourselves in possession of lumps of Spain, of Russia, France, Italy,

Denmark, Hungary, Poland, and the East generally. A slice of what seems to be Germany remains to be added in the shape of the eight towns just mentioned, and the indefatigable, voracious "Bradawl" is not slow to add it. Friockheim, he tells us, is in Scotland, within five miles of Keith; Dolwen he puts in Wales, on the Oswestry and Llanidloes line; Boher he states to be in Ireland, six miles from the Italian town of Pallas, and three miles from the Russian town of Dromkeen; Kippen he plants in Scotland, about nine miles from Stirling; Helensburgh he places between Glasgow and Balloch; Innerleithen he also puts in Scotland, but does not commit himself by saying exactly where; and Droylsden, he informs us, is on the Lancashire and Yorkshire line, a few miles out of Manchester!

If "Bradawl" is to be believed, and is to be taken as a reliable "guide," our kingdom is in a very equivocal position. We are using towns that evidently do not belong to us; and which may be claimed, at any moment, by their rightful owners. We may have included people in our recent census whom we have no right to claim as British subjects. We may have driven many people mad by allowing them to book themselves, by certain railways, for certain English villages, and causing them to be aroused in the dead of the night by hearing the name of some wild and unfamiliar place, which has led them to believe themselves in Greenland or the Himalayas. We may have started many "travelled" impostors in polite society who are looked up to as having made a tour round half the world, when they have only been to a few places with foreign names in different parts of England. These and many more similar things may easily occur, if "Bradawl's Guide for Great Britain and Ireland" is to be pronounced reliable. If, however, we pronounce judgment on the other side—a course we are unwillingly compelled to adopt—we shall have shown that a dull and unreadable book is not necessarily an authority upon facts; and that a vast array of names, dates, and figures may exist in conjunction with a vast amount of deplorable ignorance.

Extract from a Letter from the Editor of the "Critical Journal," declining the foregoing contribution:—

"Your article would be very powerful, but for two things: you have mis-spelled the name of the publication you are attacking, and your conclusions are not based upon sound premises. The publication alluded to is "Bradshaw's Guide," and NOT "Bradawl's Guide," and we are surprised that, with your very sensitive ear, you should have fallen into this mistake. Your sensitiveness of ear has helped you to discover many curious foreign names attached to towns in the United Kingdom, but the logical error you fall into is in assuming that the existence of these names implies the existence of corresponding towns in the different countries to which they seem to belong, and the non-existence of these towns throughout England, Ireland, and Scotland. In the few cases in which duplicate towns exist—one abroad and the other at home—you appear to have rashly concluded that only the foreign town can be treated as a reality. Strange as it may seem, the faithful 'Bradshaw' (not 'Bradawl') is correct in his account of these remarkably named places, and if we accepted your contribution you would be hoisted on your own petard."

OUR POSTAL REFORMERS.

THE sudden retirement of Sir Rowland Hill from the practical management of the Post Office has filled most people with regret, and a desire to see a great public benefactor honourably rewarded. We are not niggardly to our heroes of the fire, famine, and slaughter type, and it is bad policy to put Jenner's statue in a lumber-room and to snub our greatest postmaster. The great department which was re-organized by Sir Rowland Hill, has grown more during the four-and-twenty years of his management than during the previous two centuries of its existence. Part of this growth is due to the establishment of railways; part of it to the increase of population —a set-off against the acknowledged evils of living in crowds—but more of it to that clear sight which saw the necessity of a new system, and that determined patience which first set it in motion, and then made it perfect in most of its details.

The British Post Office, as at present constituted, is a Government monopoly, conducted for the benefit of the public. It is the only important trading department of the State which yields a large annual profit applied to the expenses of Government. With few exceptions, it

* I am indebted for most of my facts to the nine Annual Reports of the Post Office, and other official documents.—J. H.

has an exclusive authority to convey letters within the United Kingdom. It is also required to convey newspapers, and it undertakes the conveyance and the remittance and guardianship of small sums of money; but it is only as regards letters that the office possesses any privilege, the other branches of its business being open to any persons who may choose to undertake them. In the United Kingdom the Lords of the Treasury have power, within limits prescribed by law, to fix the rates of postage; and the Postmaster-General has authority to determine the frequency and speed with which the mails shall be conveyed and letters delivered.

The British Post Office is a very old plant of slow and gradual growth, and it owes very little to royal and noble patrons. While profligate kings and greedy ministers have saddled it with enormous pensions, and useless or obstructive officers, it has been chiefly made as productive as it is by three working-men—an upholsterer, an actor, and a schoolmaster.

The postal service in this country began with special messengers, sent by public and private personages, and with common carriers, who travelled with pack-horses, in that thorny time when the wars of the Roses were in full activity. As these carriers went through their journeys without changing horses, their pace was very slow, and the blame was chiefly laid upon the badness of the roads. Their charges, however, were not high, for the Bristol corporation only paid a penny for the carriage of a letter to London; but it must be borne in mind that a penny then represented a far higher value than it does now. Government posts, that is, relays of horses and men, were not established until nearly two centuries later, though "post-horses" had long been kept by innkeepers and private individuals for hire. James the First set on foot a post-office for the benefit of English merchants having trade abroad, but it was not until the reign of Charles the First that a post-office for inland letters was established. This postal arrangement covered a few main-roads and by-roads—chiefly the lines from London to Edinburgh, London to Chester and Holyhead, and London to Exeter and Plymouth, Oxford and Bristol, and Colchester and Norwich. The rates of postage were, of course, somewhat high, as the object of the Crown in establishing this letter-post was as much the formation of a profitable monopoly as the accommodation of the public. Twopence was charged for the carriage of a single letter for any distance under eighty miles, fourpence up to a hundred and forty miles, sixpence for any longer distance in England, and eightpence to any place in Scotland. The post between London and Edinburgh was commanded to run thither and come back in six days—it now does the double journey in a day and night—and on one occasion the London office sent only a single letter. The prohibition which followed of the carrying of letters by persons other than those employed by the king's postmaster caused great dissatisfaction, and the subject was brought before a committee of the House of Commons. The utility of the institution, however, was too great to admit of its abandonment, and nothing was done except to put down a rival post-office started by the corporation of the City of London in 1649, when the amount of the revenue derived from the posts was £5000. From that time the trade of letter-carrying has been in the hands of Government.

In 1680, a Penny Post for the conveyance of letters and small parcels about London and its suburbs, was set up by Robert Murray, an upholsterer, who assigned his interest in it to William Dockwra. This was the first great postal reform, and it is thus spoken of by a contemporary writer:—

"The Penny Post Office is a late office at London only, whereby for one penny any letter or parcel, not exceeding one pound weight or ten pounds value, is most speedily and safely conveyed, to the great benefit of the City of London, and all the parts adjacent only within twelve miles round." This was a London foot-post, like the present, with seven sorting-houses, between four and five hundred receiving-houses, and with four deliveries a day. Dockwra, in the face of much opposition, conducted his undertaking with such success for some years, that it excited the jealousy of Government. It was at last seized, on the ground that it was an infringement of the rights of the Crown, and it was not until some time after that a pension of two hundred a year was granted to him by way of compensation. This was the commencement of the London District Post, of which Dockwra was subsequently appointed comptroller, and which, up to 1854, existed as a separate department of the General Post Office. He was the first to stamp letters with the hour at which they left his office for delivery, and the first probably to see that combustibles and perishable materials were not conveyed in the form of letters and parcels. He was accused of forbidding the taking in of bandboxes, and of delaying physic sent by doctors, and so hazarding the lives of patients. In 1698, he was removed from his office on a charge of mismanagement, which may or may not have been a conspiracy against him; and, in 1708, an attempt was made by Mr. Povey to establish a halfpenny post in opposition to the official penny post; but this enterprise, like Dockwra's, was speedily suppressed by a lawsuit.

In 1710, during the reign of Queen Anne, the Post Offices of England, Ireland, and Scotland were brought by Act of Parliament under one management; and, in 1720, a great improvement was effected by Ralph Allen, who re-organized the "cross-posts" under a contract, brought many neglected districts within the postal service, and realized more than half a million sterling by his ingenuity. He spent his money mainly in works of charity, and sat to Fielding for the portrait of Squire Allworthy in "Tom Jones." On his death, in 1764, the "cross-posts" were put under a manager, with a salary of three hundred pounds a year; and the annual profits from this source at this time were about twenty thousand pounds, notwithstanding the loss to the revenue arising from illegal letter-carrying The muddy, lazy post-boys, striding their lean hack-steeds, and struggling through side lanes that were half ditch, half forest, would act as private messengers, and do a little postal business on their own account, in spite of many whippings, many imprisonments, and more warnings. The service was much interfered with by too generous gentry, "who did give much money to the riders, whereby they were very subject to get in liquor, which stopes the males;" and by old broken-down or apprentice highwaymen, who were not fit for more dangerous work. Robbing the mail in those days was looked upon as mere child's play, requiring neither courage nor experience, a something about equal to stealing linen off a hedge, or fish out of a pond. It was not only on country main-roads and in country bye-lanes that this crime was committed with comparative impunity, but in the thoroughfares of the City. At more than one of the narrow outlets from London it was customary to draw a string across from wall to wall, over which the ambling post-boy would stumble, losing his bags in the fall, and having to return to the head office to report the robbery. The annual expense attending these robberies—to say nothing of the loss of property—was, of course, very great, and in 1783 it was at least four thousand pounds.

The great reform, that speedily altered this unsatisfactory state of things, and gave security as well as increased speed to the national correspondence, was one designed and carried out by John Palmer, the lessee and manager of the Bath Theatre, in 1784, which may be shortly described as a system of trunk-lines and feeders. He connected letter-carrying with the mail-coach service, to the great improvement of both; and post-boys on horseback, hobbling along at the rate of three or four miles an hour, and inviting or conniving at robberies of the mail-bags, were abolished on all the coach lines. This plan was vehemently opposed by the officers of the Post Office, but Mr. Pitt saw its merits, and it was adopted by Parliament. Mr. Palmer was appointed Comptroller-General of the Post Office to carry out his scheme, at a salary of fifteen hundred pounds a year, and a commission on all receipts above a certain amount. The speed of the mails was at once increased to six miles an hour, and subsequently to nine or ten miles. The correspondence and revenue increased, and as they continued to advance steadily for many years afterwards, Mr. Palmer was discharged abruptly in 1792. Three thousand pounds a year—a large sum, but one much below the emoluments to which he was entitled under his agreement—were paid to him; but he was not so easily satisfied, and, after a struggle of twenty-one years, he got a Parliamentary grant of fifty thousand pounds. His chief opponents were men who were abusing the privilege of "franking"—the official and Parliamentary right of sending letters free by post—and who granted covers to their friends, or even sold them through agents, which gave a right of passage to everything, from a note to a mattrass. This franking system began with the post-office charter in 1660, and was only got rid of in 1840 on the establishment of the penny postage.

The year of Mr. Palmer's discharge, 1792, was distinguished by the opening of the first Money Order Office. This office was originally managed by a few of the Post Office clerks for their own profit, but in 1838 it became a recognized branch of the establishment.

About the year 1818, Mr. Macadam's improved road-making began to be of great service to the Post Office, by enabling the mails to be much accelerated; and the opening of the line between Liverpool and Manchester in 1830, inaugurated the great system of railway letter-carrying. Since then, the railways and the Post Office, two noble twins, have grown up together, the progress and statistics of the one being as remarkable as the progress and statistics of the other. Following close upon this important change, in the early part of 1837, came the last and greatest reform of the postal service. In that year Mr. Rowland Hill broached his great plan of inland penny postage, and met with some support, but with far more opposition and ridicule. He published a pamphlet, showing nearly every step in his laborious calculation, which proved that a uniform penny rate was at once both just and practicable; and he did more than this, he forced the House of Commons to consider his scheme. After a full investigation by a Royal Commission and a select committee—in the latter of which the late Mr. Wallace, M.P. for Greenock, was honourably prominent—the great penny plan was grudgingly adopted by the Legislature in the session of 1839, and carried into effect, under the superintendence of Mr. Rowland Hill, with many breaks and hindrances, in the beginning of 1840. No further proof can be needed that the plan had been carefully worked out by Mr. Hill in all its details, than the fact that it was the production of an obscure man, and yet was so soon accepted and acted upon.

The accession of Mr. Hill—now Sir Rowland Hill, K.C.B—marked the death of what we may call the wax and wafer age, and the birth of the gum and envelope age. As mails increased in speed and number, the formal habit of letter-writing gave place to something far more rapid and unceremonious. One by one, mechanical improvements were encouraged to appear—adhesive labels, with their ingenious perforated divisional lines; envelopes, first ungummed and then gummed; the travelling post-office on railways—a carriage fitted up for clerks, where the operations of sorting and stamping are performed while the train is in motion; the exchanging apparatus, by which mail-bags are discharged from or gathered into the travelling post-office while going at full speed; and, finally, the pneumatic tube, at present laid down from St. Martin's-le-Grand to Euston Square, by which the packages of letters and newspapers are blown from the chief office to the railway terminus.

The results of postal reform have exceeded Sir Rowland Hill's most sanguine expectations. When his pamphlet was published, the lowest general post rate was fourpence; and the old rate required to carry a letter from London to Reading or Chatham, is now more than sufficient for its conveyance to any part of Canada, India, or Australia. During the twenty years from 1815 to 1835 (inclusive) there was no increase whatever in the post office revenue, whether gross or net. What a contrast this forms with the rate of increase under the new system, which has been in operation for about an equal period. In the first year of penny postage, the letters more than doubled; every year has shown a considerable advance on the preceding year, and the first year's number is nearly quadrupled.

The revenue, of course, showed a large falling off at first—about a million in the gross and still more in the net revenue. Since then, however, both in its gross and net forms it has rapidly advanced, and it now even exceeds its former amount. A comparison of the year 1863 with 1838—the last complete year under the old system—shows that the number of chargeable letters has risen from seventy-six millions to six hundred and forty-two millions; and the revenue has risen, the gross from £2,346,000 to about £3,870,000, and the net from £1,660,000 to about £1,790,000. In this comparison of revenue, the mode of calculation in use before the adoption of penny postage has, of course, been retained, and the cost of the packets on the one hand, with the produce of impressed newspaper stamps on the other, have been excluded. The number of newspapers delivered in the year is now more than seventy-three millions, and the number of book-packets is more than fourteen millions. The number of returned letters—letters returned to the writers owing to failure in the attempts to deliver them—is more than two millions each year; and the undelivered newspapers and packets are about four hundred thousand. The dead letters, an accumulated mass, reach six hundred thousand. In the London district alone, the number of letters is now nearly double that which, before the adoption of penny postage, was delivered in the whole of the United Kingdom, London included.

The number of officers and servants of the department, including those in the colonies and agents in foreign countries, now reaches more than twenty-five thousand, divided into: one Postmaster-General—a ministerial and sometimes a purely ornamental officer; five secretaries, including the principal secretary—the post lately occupied by Sir Rowland Hill; twenty heads of departments, fourteen surveyors, eleven thousand and three hundred postmasters, sixteen hundred clerks, one hundred and seventy mail-guards and porters, twelve thousand letter-carriers and messengers, seven marine mail-officers, twenty-two postmasters, clerks, etc., in the Colonies, and seventy-three foreign agents. The average annual salary received by these officers amounts to about eighty pounds, while the five thousand officers of the Customs get one hundred and forty pounds, and the five thousand officers of the Inland Revenue one hundred and sixty pounds. The number of post offices now exceed eleven thousand, of which more than eight hundred are head offices; the road or pillar letter-boxes number nearly three thousand five hundred—making nearly fifteen thousand receptacles for letters in the United Kingdom, or more than ten thousand above those existing before the establishment of penny postage. The distance over which mails are now conveyed every day is nearly one hundred and sixty thousand miles.

While the revenue of the Post Office has thus more than recovered its former amount, the indirect benefit to the general revenue of the country, arising from the greatly increased facilities afforded to commercial transactions, must be very large. This indirect benefit is partly manifested in the development of the money order system, under which, since the year 1839, the first year of its official existence, it has risen from a little over three hundred thousand pounds to sixteen millions and a half, or fifty-two fold. The unclaimed money orders are always carried to a fund to assist the officers of the department in insuring their lives. The organization thus so greatly improved and extended for postal purposes stands available for other objects, and, passing over minor matters, has already been applied with great and remarkable advantage to the new system of Savings' Banks.

The organic improvements in the postal service, which have been the work of Sir Rowland Hill during his twenty-four years' tenure of office, are worth enumerating. First came the large reduction in the rates of postage of all correspondence, whether inland, foreign, or colonial. Letters are now conveyed even from the Channel to the Shetland Islands at one-fourth of the charge previously levied on letters passing between post towns only a few miles apart. Then followed the adoption of charge by weight, which, by abolishing the charge for mere inclosures, largely extended the reduction of rates; the stamp arrangements, which have led to the almost universal pre-payment of correspondence; the simplification of the mechanism and accounts of the department generally, by these and other means; the establishment of the book post—including in its operation all printed and much written matter—at very low rates, and its modified extension to our Colonies, and to many foreign countries; increased security in the transmission of valuable letters afforded, and temptation to the letter-carriers and others greatly diminished, by reducing the registration fee from one shilling to fourpence, by making registration of letters containing coin, as far as possible, compulsory, and by other means; a reduction to about one-third in the cost, including postage, of money orders, combined with a great extension and improvement of the system; more frequent and rapid communication between the metropolis and the larger provincial towns, and also between one provincial town and another; a vast extension of the rural distribution—many thousands of places, and probably some millions of inhabitants having, for the first time, been included within the postal system. To these improvements have been added a great extension of free deliveries. Before the adoption of penny postage, many considerable towns, and portions of nearly all the larger towns, had either no delivery at all, or deliveries on condition of an extra charge. Now, ninety-four per cent. of all the letters carried are delivered free at their addresses.

A more prompt despatch of letters when posted, and a more prompt delivery on arrival; an improvement in the condition of the officers, by a reduction of Sunday work, with other important advantages; and greatly increased facilities for the transmission of foreign and colonial correspondence, by improved treaties with foreign countries, by a better arrangement of the packet service, by sorting on board, and other means, but chiefly by the mere force of example, complete a noble list of reforms.

The importance of the last reform, and the influence it has had on the whole civilized world, can hardly be overrated. There is scarcely a lonely island where any Robinson Crusoe could find shelter, which is now cut off from all postal communication. The weary digger in his hut, the worn soldier keeping guard in Indian ravines, the "surplus" sempstresses who have sought a kinder land, and the mothers, brothers, and sisters left at home, have all cause to bless those postal reforms with which the name of Sir Rowland Hill will always be associated.

When a letter is now dropped into a pillar-box, or left in the little side-office of a grocer's or a druggist's, though it may have to go from pillar to bag, from bag to chief-office, from chief-office to van or pneumatic tube, from van or tube to railway, from railway to ship, from ship to railway again; once more from railway to ship, from ship to camel, and from camel to ship, there is very little doubt felt about its safe delivery.

The men who have charge of that letter—poor and unimportant as it may be, except to those who wrote it and those who are to receive it, are known never to desert their trust, but to guard it even at the risk of their lives. The punctuality of the mail-packets—ninety-six in number—often furnishes a remarkable proof of the conscientious character of the service. Four mails were despatched from various points, one from Sydney, New South Wales, distant nearly thirteen thousand miles, on the 22nd September, 1862, another from Calcutta, distant eight thousand miles, on the 10th of October, another from Shanghai, distant upwards of eleven thousand miles, on the 19th of September, and another from Hong Kong, distant upwards of ten thousand miles, on the 27th of September. These mails were all due in London on the 13th of November at midnight, and they arrived one hour and ten minutes before that time. The mails for the West Indies and Central America, despatched from Southampton on the 17th of September, were delivered at the Island of St. Thomas, distant more than four thousand miles, at the precise moment at which they were due. On the same voyage the mails for Jamaica and Demerara, conveyed in each case by a separate branch packet, were delivered within a few minutes of the time at which they were due, while the mails for parts of Central America and for the Pacific were delivered at Colon, on the eastern coast of the Isthmus of Panama, distant five thousand four hundred miles, thirty minutes after time, the packet having been detained at sea that precise period by H.M.S. Orlando. The mails for Chili, after having been conveyed with others across the Isthmus of Panama, were delivered at Valparaiso, distant nearly nine thousand miles from Southampton, two hours before the time appointed.

The duty left by Sir Rowland Hill for his successor to perform is rather an onerous one. Admirably as the Post Office is now worked, there is ample room for further improvement, and the public will naturally expect more from new officers than from old ones. It must throw less labour on the public for the sake of economy, and the creation of a showy annual surplus. Life is short; we have all many things to learn, and have very little time to study postal districts. The most the Post Office can demand from the public is tolerably clear handwriting, a correct numbering of houses, and the re-naming of forty-nine out of fifty King-streets or Queen-streets. These are concessions which no good citizen would deny it. On the other hand, the public demand a large increase in the number of pillar letter-boxes—structures which cost little, either to build, maintain, or clean, and which ought to be as plentiful as lamp-posts. The abolition of the rule forbidding the posting of manuscripts and newspapers in these boxes, and of that other rule which demands fourpence for a letter a fraction above the twopenny weight—a rule that seems to be antagonistic to the spirit of penny-postage,—would be a further improvement. The same may be said of any change which would save the public from a large amount of thinking.

While the Post Office shows a large profit, as it does, we are entitled to ask for these and other reforms, as this profit is as much a tax as the duty on railways and hackney carriages. The one is a tax upon the free circulation of thought and information; the other is a tax upon the free circulation of individuals. Until every penny of the Post Office profits—properly so called—is spent upon the improvement of the postal service, these profits exist as a tax upon letter-writers, or a tax upon those who write many letters for the benefit of those who write few. The answer that no one feels the pressure of this tax, because the money is drawn in such infinitesimal quantities, is often used in apologies for many other bad taxes. The principle of partial taxation is radically unsound, whether it deals with pence, shillings, or pounds; and a tax upon the free circulation of thought must also be radically bad, even if it pressed with equal force upon every class of the community.

ROADS.

It was once laid down by a very eminent writer, that "man is the least transportable species of luggage." He cannot be tied up in a parcel, taken down to a booking-office, and sent wherever a carrier may choose to take him. Unless he is a Queen's messenger, a commercial traveller, a rural postman, or some such wandering officer, he picks his road, and if there is no road to pick, he stays at home. With every disposition to travel and see the world, he will only move from his fireside or his garden on certain conditions. In one age he demands a pack-horse, going at the rate of two miles an hour; in another he asks for a "flying-coach;" and in another he ventures his limbs in a four-horse mail. Travelling is an art, like ground and lofty tumbling, which can only be learnt by degrees. It is a question of confidence. From the handspring you go to the flip-flap, and from the flip-flap to the summersault. The traveller who once had his doubts about stage-coaches, leaps from them on to the luggage train, and from the luggage-train to the wild express. Like the traditional beggar on horseback, he is often a noisy upstart. He will hardly allow the poor iron-horse five minutes to take in water, and grumbles at the slow speed of fifty miles an hour.

As we look back a few years into the past, we are surprised to find how the world seems to have shrunk up. We walk distances, three or four times a day now, which our grandfathers used to regard as a long coach journey. We never rise early to catch a Paddington coach in these days, or are troubled about the hours at which the Bank stages start from Chelsea. We have come to regard Brighton as a place lying at our doors, and Margate as a sea-side village flourishing round the corner. Birmingham, Bristol, Dover, Southampton, and Norwich, all seem to have drawn nearer to town, and to have sunk into the character of London suburbs.

The genii who have brought about these changes in the relations of places are the hard-working road-makers. They have bridged over time and space, have trebled the life of man, when measured by what it can do, and have turned withered villages into thriving cities. They have given us channels as good as money, weights and measures, or any other contrivance for facilitating commerce. They have doubled the size of the poor man's loaf, and of the poor man's fire, and have clothed thousands who, but for them, would have gone naked. Every piece of sound, open, free road is a good Samaritan, that will not let the weary traveller perish by the wayside.

We have all heard a good deal about Roman roads, and some of us have felt the benefit arising from these ancient legacies; but many generations came, and went before the great thoroughfare-makers were copied by our countrymen. The art of road-making in England is not much more than a century old, and this gives us many centuries of rough "bridle-paths" in the dark ages. If any devout believer in the good old times would wish to taste the pleasure of travelling like his forefathers, let him look about for what is called an "undedicated road" in the neighbourhood of London. He will find plenty in those outskirts where brick-fields and market-gardens are ceasing to make bricks and grow cabbages, and are turning their attention to the cultivation of detached villas. An undedicated road means a passage still retained by the owner of the land, and not handed over to the parish authorities as a public thoroughfare. It is undedicated to the local board of works, and defies the monthly reports of the district surveyor, but it is dedicated to all kinds of slush and rubbish. It is generally known as the "back-road" amongst neighbouring schools and families, and is the terror of all right-minded persons who have the care of young children. It is the place were Tommy loses one of his boots in the sucking clay, and hops home for nearly a mile in a fit of nervous excitement. It is the place where Dicky gets a black eye or a cracked head, because he will play at see-saw across an old bar-gate put at the end of the road to mark its private character. It is the place where Sarah Jane breaks the perambulator while pushing it over the uncovered hole of a new coal-cellar; where Master Edward spoils two suits of clothes in three weeks, to the great joy of the local tailor; and where costermongers play undisturbed chuck-farthing on a Sunday morning. The road is a row of soft muddy ridges, formed of brickdust and wet clay, looking like a potato-field; and here and there is a pool of thick fluid the colour of jalap. Some of the children, wishing to make a way into the depths of this wilderness, have planted brickbats in the slush, at easy distances from each other, like the stepping-stones of brooks, and on these they hop in defiance of the mud-billows on either side. Sometimes a foolish traveller, allured by the promise of a short cut, is tempted to try these stepping-stones in the undedicated road, but he generally sticks fast in the centre of the swamp, afraid to go on and hardly knowing how to turn back. Occasionally, during one or two of the dry winter and summer months, the undedicated road may be explored with safety, but for four-fifths of the year it is an impassable bog announced "to be let on building leases."

On some such roads as these, in the good old times, the English traveller made his weary pilgrimage. He trusted to nature, and soon became aware that nature only provides the raw material of roadways. The "merry greenwood," about which so many fancy romances have been written, must have been often as moist and untidy as a scavenger's yard, while outside the magic limits of the brave old oaks, the pathways must have been moats in the rainy season.

The first act of parliament in which a regular provision is made for the formation and repair of roads in England, is the statute known as the twenty-eighth of Philip and Mary (about 1555). The preamble to this statute describes the roads as "tedious and noisome to travel on," and dangerous to passengers and carriages. Under its powers two surveyors of highways were to be chosen annually in every parish, and the inhabitants of all parishes were obliged, according to their respective ability, to provide labourers, carriages, tools, etc., for four days each year, to work upon the roads under the direction of the surveyors. Rude as this system was, it was considered very perfect even up to the reign of Charles the Second, when, owing to the increase of carriages, particularly about London, it became necessary to adopt a more effective plan, and the toll system, therefore, made its first appearance. This system, however, was not placed upon anything like a solid footing, any more than the roads were, until about

1767, when it was extended to the great roads in all parts of the country, while the contributions of labour, under the old act, were confined to the cross or country roads.

London was no better than the country in these days, although "good and true scavengers" were chosen annually in many of the parishes, and it may date all its improvements under foot to the Westminster Paving Act of 1762. The streets, at this time, were often ditches, obstructed with stalls, sheds, sign-posts, and various other projections. Each inhabitant paved the space in front of his own door, according to his fancy, or his means, and the result generally was to give the passengers a footway of egg-shaped stones, such as we may now find in the outskirts of Birmingham, Leicester, or Nottingham. Those only who have walked a few miles on these half-buried globes in not overthick boots, can realize the agony suffered by our unfortunate forefathers. Kerb-stones were unknown in London a century ago, and the carriage-way was undivided from the footway, except in a few of the principal streets, where chained posts or wooden railings were fixed at the side, as they are still fixed in some of the old suburbs. A constant struggle was made by the passengers to get the wall, as it was called, and so avoid a little of the slush thrown up from the gutter in the centre. The etiquette of the wall was even laid down in books, and fixed in that saying which gives that side to the weakest. "In the last age," said Dr. Johnson, "when my mother lived in London, there were two sets of people, those who gave the wall, and those who took it—the peaceable and the quarrelsome. Now, it is fixed that every man keeps to the right, or, if one is taking the wall, another yields it, and it is never a dispute." Since that time the rule has been changed, at least for drivers, as we may learn pleasantly from the following epigram :—

> "The rule of the road is a paradox quite,
> In driving your carriage along;
> If you go to the left, you are sure to go right,
> If you go to the right you go wrong."

The plan for extending turnpike-roads from London to distant parts of the country met with the most violent protective opposition. A certain Blandford waggoner, handed down in the pages of anecdote, gave expression to the popular opinion. "Roads," he said, "on'y be good for wun thing—for waggon-drivin'. I on'y wunt vour-foot width in a leane, an' arl the rest may goo to the devil. The gentry ought to steay at whoam, rot 'em, an' not run gossippin' oop and deown the coontry."

This intelligent native knew exactly what he was talking about, and was not out of tune with his age. The counties in the neighbourhood of London petitioned parliament against the extension of turnpike-roads, on the ground that the remoter counties would be able, from the comparative cheapness of labour in them, to sell their produce in London at a much lower rate than they could do. They complained that their rents would be reduced, and cultivation ruined by the new system. The new system however, like many other reforms, was carried out in spite of this narrow-minded opposition, and the croakers woke up, in a few years afterwards, to find themselves richer than ever.

The improvement of roads, when once begun, proceeded rapidly enough, because good roads helped, more than anything, to increase our capital and population. It is a mistake to suppose that our forefathers were more benighted than we are, or that we have no men, like the Blandford waggoner, thriving amongst us. Mankind, we may feel pretty sure, always liked good roads, good lights, good police, and all the adjuncts of our well-advertised civilization; but they could only get these things by the force of numbers. Roads, lights, and constables have to be paid for by something like a poll-tax, and the fewer the polls, the heavier the burden for each individual.

Even now we could double our police without feeling too secure in our "castles," but we are held back from indulging in this luxury by considering the rates. We often grumble that a policeman can never be found when he is wanted, by which we mean that these officers are not as numerous as lamp-posts, but we forget that the remedy is in our own hands, and that we can have any number of constables if we choose to pay for them.

It is almost impossible to take up any book which deals with the last century, without coming upon whole chapters describing the miseries of travelling. People who had any state appearance to keep up were the most unlucky of all, for walking on the side-path was better than riding on the rough flinty roads, and riding on horseback was bettor than travelling in a carriage. Dukes, lords, ambassadors, and persons of dignity, were in a position like that in which the Irishman found himself when the bottom of his sedan-chair came out, which made him think that he might as well walk, if it were not for the look of the thing. Goods of all kinds in Scotland were conveyed on horseback for speed and cheapness; even oatmeal, coals, turf, straw, and hay, being carried in this way for short distances. A set of people known by the name of cadgers, who have given a word to our slang dictionaries, plied regularly between different places, selling salt, fish, poultry, eggs, and earthenware. These things were carried on pack-horses, in sacks or baskets suspended on each side of the animal. In carrying goods between distant places it was necessary to employ a cart, as all that a horse could carry on his back was not sufficient to pay for a long journey. These carriers, if we include delays, often went at the rate of a quarter of a mile an hour! Mr. J. R. McCulloch records it as a fact that the common carrier from Selkirk to Edinburgh, *thirty-eight* miles distant, required a *fortnight* for his journey between the two places, going and returning! The road, it must be said, was originally one of the most dangerous in the whole country, for a large part of it lay in the bottom of a district called Gala-water, from the name of the chief stream, the channel of the water being, when not flooded, the track chosen as the most level, and the easiest to travel in.

Between the largest cities, says the same authority, the means of travelling were very little better. In 1678, an agreement was made to run a coach between Edinburgh and Glasgow, a distance of forty-four miles, which was to be drawn by *six* horses, and to perform the journey from Glasgow to Edinburgh and back in *six* days. Even a century later it took a day and a half for the stage-coach to travel from Edinburgh to Glasgow.

As late as 1763, there was but one stage-coach from Edinburgh to London, which set out once a month, taking from twelve to fourteen days to perform the journey. In 1830, six or seven coaches set out each day from both ends on the same road, and the time for executing the journey was reduced to about forty-eight hours. Now, it is almost needless to say, that by the Post-office limited mail express train, we may travel the same distance on a comfortable couch in ten hours and a half.

At this time the "franking" of letters was a valuable privilege conceded to members of parliament, and others in authority, and largely used for the accommodation of their friends. The Post-office managers complain very loudly of the strange articles at present sent through the post, but in those days their complaints were much louder. The "franking," which began with letters, gradually extended to small parcels, from small parcels it got to cover large ones, and at last the mail-carriers were very much shocked at seeing a huge feather-bed registered as a free letter. Inquiry, indignation, an improved system of mail-carrying, the extension of population and correspondence, and reduced charges for postage, at last put an end to the franking privilege.

While almost anybody could rob the post through this abused "free-list," the poor mails were just as ill-treated on the road. The most feeble thief of the day could rob a postboy, and rob him by a most feeble contrivance. The French mail was often stopped on its road to Dover by a piece of string stretched across the entrance of Kent-street, Borough. This caught the horse's legs, caused him to stumble, and throw the postboy off, who returned to the chief office, and coolly reported the loss of his mail-bags. Rural postmen were always ready to be robbed by any stranger who appeared on the road, and it was long before stage coachmen, fed, as they were, with lying stories about the daring of fancy highwaymen, had courage not to stand and deliver at the first impudent summons. The feather-beds, so liberally franked at the expense of the country, were very often carried off into criminal bondage, and few tax-payers can help rejoicing at this punishment of their enemies.

Mr. Samuel Smiles, in his recent "Lives of the Engineers," has collected from various sources a number of amusing details about English roads and road-travelling in the last century. In 1690, Lord Chancellor Cowper politely described Sussex as a "sink of about fourteen miles broad." People in some parts used to travel by swimming; and it was almost as difficult for old people to get to church in Sussex during winter as it was in the Lincoln Fens, where they rowed there in boats. Fuller once saw an old lady being drawn to church in her own coach by the aid of six oxen. The Sussex roads were so bad as to pass into a by-word. A contemporary says that in travelling through a slough of extraordinary miryness, it used to be called "the Sussex bit of the road;" and he satirically adds, that the reason why the Sussex girls were so long-limbed was because of the tenacity of the mud in that county; the practice of pulling the foot out of it by the strength of the ankle tending to stretch the muscle and lengthen the bone.

The roads in the neighbourhood of London were as bad as those in Sussex. Chertsey was a two days' journey from town; and Lord Hervey, writing from Kensington in 1736, says:—"The road from this place to London is so infamously bad, that we live here in the same solitude as we would do if cast upon a rock in the middle of the ocean; and all the Londoners tell us that there is between them and us an impassable gulf of mud." Royal carriages stuck fast in the mud for hours together, defying all efforts to remove them.

It was only a few of the main roads out of London that were in any way practicable for coaches. On the occasion of any state visits, labourers went before the royal train to mend the ways. Judges were thrown into bog-holes while going on circuit, and kept the juries waiting while they were being dug out. Sometimes they fell into sloughs, and had to be hauled out by plough-horses.

It was said, in 1752, that a Londoner would no more think of travelling into the west of England for pleasure, than of going to Nubia. "Of all the cursed roads," says Arthur Young in 1769, "that ever disgraced this kingdom in the very ages of barbarism, none ever equalled that from Billericay to Tilbury. It is for near twelve miles so narrow that a mouse cannot pass by any carriage. I saw a fellow creep under his waggon to assist me to lift, if possible, my chaise over a hedge. To add to all the infamous circumstances which occur to plague a traveller, I must not forget the eternally meeting with chalk waggons, themselves frequently stuck fast, till a collection of them are in the same situation, and twenty or thirty horses may be tacked to each to draw them out, one by one." In Essex, generally, he found the roads full of ruts "of an incredible depth;" he found the turnpike road between Bury and Sudbury, in Suffolk, as bad "as any unmended lane in Wales;" full of ponds of liquid dirt, and horse-laming flints. Between Titsworth and Oxford he found the turnpike-road, as it was called, abounding in loose stones, as large as a man's head, and full of holes, and deep ruts; from Gloucester to Newnham, a distance of twelve miles, he found another "cursed road," "infamously stony, with ruts all the way;" and from Newnham to Chepstow he describes the road as a series of hills, like "the roofs of houses joined."

Going to the north, a short time afterwards, this unfortunate but observant traveller found the roads no better in that quarter. Between Richmond and Darlington they were "like to dislocate his bones;" and when he has to speak of the roads in Lancashire, he foams with rage. He cautions us to avoid them as we would the Evil One, for he measured ruts in them four feet deep, that were full of floating mud.

The roads in the Midland Counties, and in Kent, were no better. When Mr. Rennie, the engineer, was engaged in surveying the Weald with a view to the cutting of a canal through it in 1802, he found the country almost destitute of practicable roads.

In Northamptonshire, the only way of getting along some of the main roads in rainy weather was by swimming. Even now it is no uncommon thing, as I can testify by personal observation, to find miles of the railway from Blisworth to Peterborough under water during the wet season. All over the country inland lighthouses—land beacons—were humanely stationed to keep benighted travellers out of quagmires, ponds, and bogs. In Staffordshire, before the great network of canals was made, the roads were so bad, and so much like roads in every other part of the kingdom, that the carriage of earthenware in panniers was one shilling per ton per mile, or eight shillings for a journey of ten miles. This, too, was in the days of the great artist-manufacturer, Wedgwood.

Modes of travelling changed with the gradual improvement of the roads. The foot passengers occasionally took to horse, while ladies rode on pillions, or in horse-litters. Pack-horses gave way to carriers' carts and waggons, and the latter heavy rumbling vehicles, which did more to wear out good roads than any monsters ever framed by coach-builders, were largely supplanted by stage-coaches about 1650. The waggons crawled along, perhaps, at the rate of ten miles in twelve hours, but the stage-coaches, with much jolting, were able to reach four miles an hour. The waggons were solid, slow, and safe, while the coaches were high and unsafe, and their drivers were drunken bullies. No change in the mode of travelling was carried out without a noisy agitation against it. Class interests were as clamorous then as they are now, and as desirous that their particular business should be regarded as beyond improvement.

The condition of the road to York in the last century is never considered in the popular account of Dick Turpin's half-legendary ride. He is represented mounted on a fiery blood mare, leaping over carts and toll-bars, and flying along a hard, smooth ground granite road, like a jockey at Epsom. This is the fancy picture, and it is almost a pity to disturb it. The York road in most places was like those which made Arthur Young so savage; and bold Turpin's pace *may* have been a broken amble of four miles an hour.

In 1754 the first "flying coach" was established by a knot of Manchester men to run between that town and London. Their notion of "flying" was to do the journey in four days and a half, and yet this moderate speed was looked upon with distrust. Lord Campbell tells us that he was warned not to travel by Palmer's improved mail-coaches, the first vehicles that ventured upon eight miles an hour, towards the close of the last century. He was told of certain passengers who had come through by these coaches from Edinburgh to London, and had died of apoplexy from the rapidity of the motion. This eight miles an hour was afterwards increased to ten or twelve, with the improvement in the leading lines of road; and at the latter point the rate of fast travelling stopped, until the best road of all was made—the railroad.

The railway reports, issued from time to time by the

Board of Trade, give us a full statistical account of our railroads. The miles opened in 1860 for regular traffic in the United Kingdom were nearly ten thousand five hundred. The travellers during the same year, also in the United Kingdom, were one hundred and sixty-three millions and a half, besides nearly fifty thousand holders of season tickets, who probably made many journeys. Altogether, there must have been nearly six journeys in the year for each member of our population. The trains of all kinds travelled more than one hundred and two millions of miles, or more than four thousand times round the world. Three hundred and fifty-seven thousand and more dogs, and over a quarter of a million of horses, made railway journeys during the same period. The goods traffic represented the carriage of over twelve millions of cattle, sheep, and pigs, and nearly ninety millions of tons of minerals and general merchandise. The receipts of our railways, from all kinds of traffic, were nearly twenty-eight millions sterling (equal to the interest on our national debt), a little less than one-half of which came from passengers and the mails, and the rest, or largest half, from goods. The expenditure of the companies was about forty-seven per cent. of the gross receipts, leaving fourteen millions and a half sterling as the net receipts. The compensation paid for accidents and losses amounted to a little over one hundred and eighty-one thousand pounds. The rolling stock comprised five thousand eight hundred locomotives, over fifteen thousand passenger carriages, and nearly one hundred and eighty-one thousand waggons for goods. Comparing 1860 with 1859, the passengers (or journeys) were increased nearly fourteen millions, the minerals nearly nine millions of tons, the receipts more than two millions sterling, and the miles travelled nearly nine millions. The trains run in the course of the year were upwards of ten thousand a day. The increase every year now is steadily progressive.

The inland roads of Great Britain, however, can never lose their importance as great feeding arteries of towns, even under any possible extension of railways. They have been chiefly made what they are by the greatest engineers, and some of the works of Rennie and Telford of this kind need not hide their heads by the side of the famous Alpine Simplon. Leaving the railway behind us, at any point, we may find much to be proud of amongst our monuments of road-making on the hills and in the valleys of our country. What we have got, however, should not blind us to what we have not got, and while six bridges, practically closed by a toll, are spanning the river Thames between Chelsea and Southwark, we ought not to consider our road-making thoroughly finished.

Before we close these remarks, we must say a few words about London tramways.

The public and parochial discussions about the merits and demerits of tramways have somewhat died away of late, consequent upon a decrease of energy on the part of certain projectors.

Street tramways have undoubtedly had much prejudice to contend against, to say nothing about local interests, public fears, and a little national jealousy. The practical difficulties in the way of working them have been overrated and misstated, and their history has been completely overlooked. They come to us now ostensibly from America, but only in the character of a re-importation. Like steam-navigation, which Fulton borrowed from this country, and extended on the vast lakes and rivers of the United States, street tramways were tried in and about London before they became a "great fact" in America. Lord Palmerston seemed to be unaware of this, if we are to judge by his speech delivered in Parliament when this subject was recently debated. He alluded to the tramways, or, rather, Roman pavements of Milan, forgetting that he had a fair specimen far nearer home, in the humble neighbourhood of Whitechapel.

One of the earliest modern London tramways, laid down in stone, still exists in the Commercial Road, forming the communication between the East and West India Docks, and the great commercial warehouses in the Eastern parts of London. In consequence of the great wear and tear to which this road was subjected, the trustees decided, in 1827, to lay down a stone tramway, after the manner of the Roman pavements before alluded to, which travelled gentlemen like Lord Palmerston have seen in Florence, Sienna, Milan, and other Italian cities, although they may not have seen it at Whitechapel. The tramway consists of a carriage-way, with two courses of large stone blocks for the wheels to run on, with a space between them for the horses, laid with ordinary gravel.

Besides the great gain which such a roadway offered in point of durability, it promised advantages in increasing the ease of draught to the horses employed upon it, and cheapening proportionally the carriage of goods between the docks and the city. This caused the plan to be very favourably received by the directors of the dock companies, and obtained for it, as far as needful, their cordial co-operation.

The preference which was then given to stone over iron, was chiefly dictated by the consideration that in rainy or frosty weather iron rails are more slippery than stone rails, and more likely to cause injurious accidents. Iron rails had not been tested by railroads in 1827, as they have been since, so the road was inlaid with stone, and the stone, renewed from time to time, still remains. Among the remains of Pompeii there is a stoneway of this description, the blocks of which are worn half through in ruts, thus showing the antiquity of these contrivances, and the comparative softness of the material used.

The original stone employed in the Commercial Road tramway was all granite, the greater part being obtained from Aberdeen, a considerable portion from Herne Island, some from Mount Sorrel, Leicestershire, and some from Guernsey and Jersey. The stones were all cut in one form and size—not tapering towards the bottom, according to the old absurd practice, but perfectly square, and dressed so as to fit closely to each other. The interposition of any substances between them which might cause a disturbance of position, whether from top or bottom, is thus prevented. To guard against any subsidence from the general level, the stones are laid on a firm bottom of cement and gravel. This was the bottoming found at Pompeii, which, after the lapse of many centuries, was almost perfectly level, while the superincumbent stones were half worn through.

On a common road it is considered good work if a horse can draw one ton at the rate of four miles an hour; but in the Commercial Road, six and seven, and sometimes nine tons, are drawn at this rate by ordinary horses employed in the heavy London traffic. The transport of heavy goods in this road is greater than in any other quarter of the metropolis.

The common objections to tramways in crowded

thoroughfares are to a great extent disposed of by the example of London Bridge, the most crowded and way-worn thoroughfare in the world. The eleven thousand vehicles of all weights and shapes which daily pass over this bridge, can only be kept in order by an elaborate tramway system. As rails are not laid down along the road, except stoneways along the gutters on each side, the city police have to take their laborious stand, from morn to dewy eve, and divide the traffic into four streams. This is nothing but a street tramway of the rudest kind; a tramway where no mechanical science is allowed to aid in the work, but where all the labour falls upon human indexes bearing the stamp of official authority, clouded by the mud of London traffic, who stand at intervals in the centre of the road. This is the late Mr. Daniel Whittle Harvey's, the late City Chief Police Commissioner's live tramway, which, one day, when the crowds of vehicles increase so as to be altogether unmanageable, will probably give place to something more in accordance with the railway spirit of the age.

CITY TRAFFIC.

The City traffic has always been a subject of interest to citizens, and those who use the City; as the first have to pay for its partial regulation, and the second are daily annoyed by its bulk and complications. Though, in company with a large and influential majority of the Common Council, we may not approve of the Traffic Regulation Bill, we are quite ready to admit the pressing nature of the difficulty. Martial law is not a thing to look forward to with rapture, nor to cure the evil—if evil it be; and we believe that the cost of delays and blocks acting upon the sensitive frame of commerce will eventually do more to regulate the circulation of vehicles within the City than any unpopular law.

The labour which the City traffic now throws upon the City police is undoubtedly very harassing and costly. We shall probably be within the mark if we say that the police management of London Bridge absorbs twenty constables, who represent an annual charge of a thousand pounds a year. Half the work of the six hundred well-selected and well-officered constables who form the City police consists of a daily struggle with the traffic, and may be put down as not being paid for with less than fifteen thousand pounds a year.

The City traffic, of course, has grown with the population, and without referring to official records, it would be as easy to calculate the number of carts and people flowing in and out of the City during twenty-four hours as it would be to reckon how many coats a certain mass of people is likely to wear, or how many loaves an army is likely to consume in a day. As records exist, however, which give us precise figures concerning the City traffic at different periods during the last fifty years, it may not be uninteresting to present a few of these facts at the present time.

Blackfriars Bridge seems to have been regarded with interest in 1808, and men were placed there to guage the daily traffic for six weeks in the summer and winter of that year. They reported that 48,000 persons passed over the bridge every twenty-four hours, but that, on a fine Sunday morning in August, this number was increased to upwards of 70,000 persons. Holiday-making must have been very popular then in "St. George's Fields."

In 1811 a calculation was made on the Blackfriars and London bridges on the same day, to ascertain the average number of passengers and vehicles that daily passed along these roads. The result is given in the following table :—

	Blackfriars Bridge.	Old London Bridge.
Foot passengers	61,069	89,640
Horses	822	764
Waggons	533	769
Carts and Drays	1,502	2,924
Coaches	900	1,240
Gigs and taxed carts	500	485
Total of vehicles	3,435	5,418

The metropolitan population at this time was about one million.

Another account was taken of the daily average number

of carts, waggons, coaches, chaises, etc., which passed over London Bridge on the 16th and 17th of May, 1828, and 13th and 14th of June 1828, between 6 o'clock a.m. and 8 o'clock p.m. This account also gives the routes from which the bridge was approached :—

	Carts.	Coaches.
From Upper Thames Street over London Bridge	400	13
From Lower Thames Street ditto.................	2376	28
From the City ditto	829	773
From the Borough ditto	2700	767
	6305	1,581
	1581	
Total of vehicles...........	7886	

The number of persons who came with loads over the bridge in one day was 862, and the metropolitan population at this time was about 1,400,000.

The waggons and carts alone which now pass daily over this bridge, at a time when our London population is about 2,800,000, must be at least 12,000, while the journeys to and fro swell this number to 24,000.

Cheapside is more blocked up than London Bridge, because of the side streams of traffic, and the stoppages at shops and warehouses. Thirteen thousand vehicles flow through it every afternoon, from east to west and west to east, between four and five o'clock. This only shows the state of one channel for traffic, and there are many other streets—amongst which we may reckon Ludgate Hill—in the same condition. How the city is now fed with traffic may be gathered from the following table, which shows the number of persons and vehicles that lately entered the City on an average day, and the streets through which they entered :—

STREETS through which they entered the City.	No. of Vehicles.	No. of Passengers in Vehicles.	No of Foot Passengers.	Total No. of Passengers.
Aldersgate Street	2,052	4,952	21,060	26,012
Aldgate	4,978	12,548	42,574	55,122
Artillery Street	148	232	4,110	4,342
Bishopgate Street	8,461	19,388	34,160	53,548
Blackfriars Bridge	4,108	7,293	31,642	38,935
Blackfriars Pier	......	......	2,140	2,140
Blackwall Railway	......	......	7,032	7,032
Blomfield Street	719	1,260	10,052	11,312
Brook Street	254	413	4,530	4,943
Catherine-wheel Alley	......	......	1,876	1,876
Chancery Lane	1,279	7,593	13,057	20,650
Church Street	257	375	2,530	2,905
Custom-house Stairs	......	......	109	109
Devereux Court	......	......	4,466	4,466
Dyers' Hall Pier	......	......	1,439	1,439
Finsbury Place	8,451	11,060	27,024	38,084
Golden Lane	247	352	8,140	8,492
Half Moon Street	114	159	2,886	3,045
Harrow Alley	81	107	6,220	6,327
Hatton Garden	423	815	8,332	9,147
Haydon Square	262	456	2,333	2,789
Holborn Bars	9,060	36,094	41,610	77,704
Leather Lane	162	237	5,830	6,067
Little Moorfields	150	228	5,230	5,458
London Bridge	10,429	30,799	54,128	84,927
London Bridge Wharf	......	......	1,110	1,110
Milton Street	215	357	4,580	4,937
Minories	2,456	3,571	18,208	21,779
Moor Lane	140	175	6,041	6,216
Paul's Wharf	......	......	1,271	1,271
Primrose Street	6	6	1,630	1,636
Ropemaker Street	128	172	2,436	2,608
Rosemary Lane	384	571	3,034	3,605
Shades Pier	......	......	2,500	2,500
Skinner Street	61	86	2,006	2,092
Smithfield Bars	2,439	4,012	24,830	28,842
Somerset Street	584	932	7,210	8,142
Southwark Bridge	497	1,465	875	2,340
Stoney Lane	126	141	7,672	7,813
Sun Street	1,119	1,799	11,970	13,769
Swan Pier	......	......	3,835	3,835
Swan Street	509	713	4,154	4,867
Temple Bar	2,159	13,724	36,950	50,674
Tower Stairs	......	......	197	197
Union Street	1,254	1,861	11,356	13,217
Victoria Street	1,748	3,114	12,650	15,764
Whitecross Street	2,305	4,026	24,890	28,916
Widegate Street	......	......	8,620	8,620
Forty-eight streets—Total	57,765	171,086	535,535	706,621

At the time when this account was taken, part of the pavement was up in Fleet Street, which had the effect of bringing less vehicles into the City through Temple Bar, and more than usual through Holborn Bars. Out of this total of passengers (706,621), forty-nine-thousand, or less than one-fourteenth, entered during the night—that is, between the hours of 11 p.m, and 7 a.m. These numbers are irrespective of the resident population of the City, which is one hundred and thirteen thousand. Half of these people daily help to swell the City crowd, to find work for the City police, and to drive some of the City officials into preparing impracticable Acts of Parliament.

THE UNDERGROUND RAILWAY.

TIME and money have at length done their appointed work, and the Underground Railway is now opened for traffic. It is no longer a mysterious cavern peeped into by children, gaped into by full-grown idlers, gossiped about in tap-rooms and parlours with more or less incredulity, and watched over lovingly by graphic and statistical reporters. It is no longer a withering nuisance to blighted shopkeepers, and a source of perpetual alarm and vexation to quiet housekeepers. Its course has been often marked by local earthquakes, and its capital has been called in to heal those gaping wounds of property. It has threatened utter destruction to workhouses and mansions; and it has itself been threatened with utter destruction by an unruly sewer. It has been nearly ten years before the public upon paper, and three years round them and under them on clay and gravel. As much nonsense has been talked by friends about its "mission," and as many doubts have been expressed by enemies about its powers, as if it had been the first railway ever planned and constructed. The fine old ignorant love of wonders, and the fine old conservative hatred of novelties, have both found abundant food in the Underground Railway.

The origin of the enterprise, if clearly traced, will show what the new railway was really designed to be and to do.

To a certain extent it is the last desperate throw of a board of directors who manage the finest and the least profitable main line in the kingdom. The Great Western Railway, originally planned by a man who was a dangerous compound of the showman and the engineer, has been sinking commercially, year by year, though it is still one of the most striking sights of the country. Its expenditure has been a broad gauge expenditure. Its rails and carriages, if we except the second class, are all on a grand scale, and it has the proud distinction of standing almost alone amongst its fellows. Its gauge is not the gauge of other lines, and, therefore, when it visits its neighbours, the costly preparation of an extra rail has to be made for its reception. An ordinary commercial engineer would have built it in harmony with the general railway system; but the late Mr. Brunel was far above all such vulgar considerations. His father constructed the Thames Tunnel—and he constructed the "Great Eastern." It was a family failing not to care for shareholders, and to show a lordly contempt for dividends. The Great Western Railway is only suffering the usual penalties of a Brunel enterprise, and its chance of fruitfulness has probably not been increased by its many extensions. Most of these extensions, however, were forced upon it by railway competition, and we are not inclined to blame it for struggling with its opponents. When it can fairly earn three or four per cent. annual net profit, we shall think it has done its duty. The public ought not to pay more for the use of railway capital, and the shareholders ought not to expect more. Railway investments being quite as secure as the national funds, ought not to produce higher gains than the natural rate of profit.

The managers of the Great Western, in their competition with two or three other main lines, thought it wise to draw nearer to the heart of London. Instead of waiting for goods and passengers to flow to Paddington, they determined to push out and meet their customers on the road. They were helped in this scheme by powerful and interested allies. The Corporation of the City of London, in its zeal for exterminating rookeries, had become the possessors of a vast unprofitable desert. New Victoria Street, Clerkenwell, which was hailed as a great city reformation nearly ten years ago, was suddenly checked in its progress. Like all incomplete things it gradually fell into decay, and was found out to be rather overrated as a metropolitan improvement. It had destroyed many disreputable lodgings without destroying the lodgers; it had caused a low neighbourhood to be more crowded by creating a rise in rents; it had provided a muddy playground for troops of poor little ragamuffins, and had opened up rather depressing views of Field Lane and Frying-pan Alley. Its black slimy arches were sometimes used as a tomb for murdered infants, and always as a school for teaching pitch and toss, and the rudiments of "the noble art of self-defence." Some of these things might have been tolerated if the thoroughfare had encouraged building speculators, but neither warehouses, shops, nor model dwellings rose on either side of its footway. Under these circumstances the Metropolitan Railway was welcomed as a deliverer; and doubtless in the hope of encouraging the erection of a great goods station, and reaping plentiful harvests of created ground-rents, the Corporation went into partnership with the promoters of the Great Western extension. Out of the million and a quarter sterling sunk in the Underground Railway, the city, we believe, finds two hundred thousand pounds, the rest being supplied by the shareholders of the

Great Western and the Great Northern Railways, assisted by the general public.

The fact that the city has taken a large interest in this railway seems to have led a great number of writers to predict the immediate relief of the city traffic. The Common Council is certainly goaded into unusual activity at the present moment by the difficulty caused by the crowds of passengers and vehicles in the city thoroughfares; but there is no more real connection between the city railway investment, and the desire lately shown by the Common Council to take the whole business of the city into custody, than there was between the Goodwin Sands and old Tenterden steeple. One is a commercial sprat thrown out to catch a salmon; the other is a wild aspiration of embarrassed Authority, which will struggle to gain its ends by a new police bill.

The ability of the Underground Railway to relieve the city traffic has been ridiculously overrated. The line starts from the Great Western at Paddington, and reaches King's Cross in a direct line, under the New Road—a thoroughfare always able to accommodate at least ten times the vehicles ever seen upon its surface. From King's Cross it goes close to the foot of Holborn Hill, along the bed of the Fleet valley, and casts out all its goods and passengers to struggle up Snow Hill, and increase the agony of the traffic in the narrow gorge of Newgate Street. What it may do in the future we will not discuss. We are only examining it as it now exists; and can see in it a feeder, but no reliever of the traffic. Its influence may be very slightly felt at Holborn Bars—a point next in importance to London Bridge as a feeder of the city traffic: but Cheapside will not have cause to thank it for one truck the less, or for the absence of one jostled and impatient passenger.

There are at least a dozen more crowded thoroughfares in the city, where it can never have any effect either in reducing or increasing the traffic, and it ought not to be puffed into popularity for purely imaginary powers.

Of its prospects as a commercial speculation we are fortunately not called upon to speak, as we cannot bring ourselves to look upon it as a free and independent undertaking. We are told that the cost of its construction, which amounts to something like £350,000 a mile, is very moderate compared with the cost of viaducts through cities. We are very glad to hear it. As a dozen similar projects are before Parliament for the east, west, south, and north of London, we presume that shareholders can be found who are satisfied with these investments. Our estimate of just railway profits is not a very high one, and probably the gains of the Underground Railway will reach that modest estimate. In any case, however, the undertaking, after having been a nuisance for two or three years, may now be fairly praised as a great public convenience. No regard need be paid to the trifling difficulties which have sprung up during the first few days of working. The rumoured choke-damp, the fainting porter, the rawness of the arrangements, the engines with defective smoke-consuming apparatus, and half a dozen other drawbacks, will be remedied as quickly as they are recorded. No railway was ever opened for business in a perfect condition; and when we hear that the Underground Railway was inspected for nearly three months by the officers of the Board of Trade, we are surprised that so few faults can be found in its working. The travelling on the line, on the second day of its opening, was rapid and comfortable. The carriages are broad, and well-lighted with gas; the first-class carriages contain five seats on each side. The lowest fare is threepence for travelling from one end of the line to the other, and the highest is sixpence. Starting from Farringdon Street, King's Cross is reached in three minutes; Gower Street, the next station, is reached in about the same time; and so on to the Portland Road, the Edgware Road, and the terminus at Bishop's Road. The stations, though lighted with a sickly reflection from porcelain tiles, seem well-built, and supplied with every accommodation. The time consumed in the journeys is about one-half of the time taken by omnibuses: and although the fares of these latter vehicles have been very generally reduced, the railway still has the advantage in point of cheapness. Without praising it for engineering points, which are beyond our area of discussion, or joining the cry which hails it as the one traffic reformer of the age, we may congratulate its proprietors on its safe completion, and the public on the possession of another railway.*

* Since this was written, the Corporation of the City of London have sold their shares in the line.

FOOD FOR FISHES.

IF Doctor Johnson were alive at the present moment, and were required to give a definition of a submarine telegraphic cable, we are afraid that some very bitter epigrammatic sentence would be put upon record. The man who described a fishing-rod as a stick with a worm at one end and a fool at the other, could hardly be scientifically precise, or decently amiable, when speaking of such failures as the Atlantic and Red Sea cables. The contemplation of so much capital sunk or destroyed, of so much advancement checked, would scarcely be calculated to decrease a certain biliousness of thought, or to soften a certain irritability of language. The temptation to look upon a submarine cable as a rope with many hundred destructive worms at one end, and many blind, trusting capitalists at the other, would certainly be too great. It is well, perhaps, for the battered cause of submarine telegraphy, that Doctor Johnson has not to "define" its aims in a single sentence.

The most unprejudiced observer or inquirer, however, who has no desire to appear smart at the expense of truth, will feel a uncontrollable desire to lose his temper when dealing with submarine telegraphs. He will see a most difficult application of a mysterious science, made more difficult, if not impossible, by contracting leeches and "intermediate" interests. He will find that slop-work is the rule and not the exception; and that every advantage is taken of natural checks and hindrances. The antagonism of the elements is used as a shield to cover the most clumsy and ignorant processes; and the true causes of failure are artfully concealed under the inevitable hocus-pocus of such undertakings. Because a cable, containing a gigantic capital in wire and coating, has to be laid in the bed of the sea, it seems to be assumed that it must necessarily be a wreck. The whole process of laying submarine telegraphic cables is apparently regarded as a ceremony required to satisfy the minds of a few amiable scientific enthusiasts; and, therefore, the least spent upon it, the soonest mended. The plan is so arranged that what is entrusted to the fishes shall bear but a small proportion to what is devoured by the land-sharks in the shape of "preliminary" and "incidental" expenses. Of the eighty thousand pounds sterling paid up by the shareholders for the Dover and Ostend line, only thirty-three thousand pounds, or about two-fifths, have been devoted to the cable; and this is waste compared with the stricter economy shown in the line from Dover to Calais. There, only one-fifth of the capital has been cast overboard; for, out of seventy-five thousand pounds sterling paid up, only fifteen thousand pounds have been sunk in the Channel cable. When we find this evident distrust of the treacherous element operating so largely on the minds of telegraphic projectors and managers, we can hardly feel surprised that out of nine thousand miles of submarine telegraph laid down, not more than three thousand miles can be said to } in working order, the remaining six thousand miles being perfectly useless.

One of the principal scientific causes of failure is to be found in the fact that telegraphic cables have never been thoroughly tested under water before they have been deposited in the ocean. The first considerable failure of a submarine cable was that of the Atlantic Telegraph Company. Before this property was thrown into the sea, it was often strongly urged by the Institution of Civil Engineers, that the cable should be tested during its manufacture, and that it should not be laid until it had been tested under water as nearly as possible under the conditions to which it would be subjected in the ocean. In violation of all these precautions the cable was laid, with the conviction of its not being in a perfect state; a capital of three hundred thousand pounds sterling was sunk; and the cause of electric telegraphy was seriously jeopardized.

That some mischance should happen to the Atlantic cable was not surprising, when the limited experience then obtained in submarine telegraphy in deep water is taken into account. This, however, is the chief scientific defence that can be set up on the side of the directors and managers. The moral causes of the failure are more apparent and less defensible. The details were arranged before anything was practically known about deep sea cables. Great mistakes were made in organizing the undertaking—the radical fault being the precipitate manner in which the contracts were let—precluding any preliminary experiments.

The gross failure of the Atlantic Telegraph—or, as some prefer to say, in elastic language, the lesson taught us by this magnificent experiment—has been cast into the shade by the failure of the Red Sea Telegraph. This second "magnificent experiment" is a phantom in the sea; but a very solid reality upon the earth. It has gone down with eight hundred thousand pounds sterling, as costly food for fishes; but it has left its mark in the national account-books. The country is saddled with thirty-six thousand pounds per annum for half a century (a guaranteed dividend of four and a half per cent. per annum, upon the before-mentioned capital), representing an amount of nearly two millions sterling, even if we say nothing about compound interest. The contract for this half-hidden monument of official folly was so recklessly made, that no one—not even the usual "man of straw"—is fixed with any responsibility. The details of the scheme set forth that the cable was to be divided into six sections—three in the Red Sea—Suez to Kossier, 254 knots; Kossier to Suakin, 475 knots; and Suakin to Aden, 630 knots; or, in all, 1359 knots of direct distance; and three in the Indian Ocean—Aden to the Kooria-Mooria Islands, 716 knots; Kooria-Mooria to Muscat, 486 knots; and Muscat to Kurrachee, 481 knots; or, in all, 1683 knots: making the total length of the two lines, 3042 knots. Messages had been transmitted between Suez and Aden for about nine months, and separate sections of this line had been worked for eighteen months. The line from Aden to Kurrachee had also been worked, by means of translation, at very good speed; but the whole distance from Suez to Kurrachee was never worked throughout. If, however, for Suez we read Stock Exchange, and for Kurrachee, we substitute Downing Street, we shall obtain very different results. The whole distance between these two latter important points was worked with most marvellous success. The laying down, or "paying out" (a most significant phrase in the present instance), was without a flaw; the messages sent were duly received, and duly recorded, docketed, and pigeon-holed, after the fashion of red-tape. The clerkly work was absolutely faultless, as the letter-books, diaries, and Treasury minutes will show; but beyond this the business presents a fog-bank—a dreary waste. The barren ceremony of manufacturing and submerging the cable might have been shuffled through, even more unsatisfactorily than it was, for any active superintendence that the government gave to the undertaking. They guaranteed the dividend; or, in other words, they gave away the public money, and there they seem to have fancied that their duty began and ended. Government made a subsequent attempt to wriggle out of its own agreement, and was only called to a sense of its duty by the higher moral sense of the country.

The real secret history of this Red Sea failure will most probably never be written, because it is not likely that any individual or journal unfortified by exceptional profits on a telegraphic contract, will brave the costly and uncertain law of libel. One Blue-book has added a little to our knowledge of these submarine transactions, and another promises to inform us further; but as the chief actor in the Red Sea farce, Mr. Lionel Gisborne, is dead, an important tap of evidence is necessarily frozen up. In the mean time, we use the narrative contained in Mr. Charles Manby's very able summary of a long and important discussion at the Institution of Civil Engineers on this subject.

In the year 1855, application was made to Messrs. Glass and Elliott by the late Mr. Lionel Gisborne—better known, perhaps, as the government engineer who surveyed the Isthmus of Panama, and forgot to mention the mountains — who represented himself as acting under the authority of her Majesty's government, for information to enable him to prepare estimates for a telegraphic line to the East. On his assurance (we are quoting Messrs. Glass and Elliott's words) that the firm to whom he applied should be placed in a position to tender for the execution of the work, when he had completed certain arrangements with the Turkish government, the necessary information was given him, accompanied by specimens of submarine cables. Upon this, Mr. Gisborne proceeded to Constantinople, and obtained the necessary firman from the Sultan to lay down the Red Sea line. Shortly after his return to England, these concessions were placed at the disposal of a body of gentlemen, who formed themselves into a company—the Red Sea Telegraph Company—for the purpose of laying down the lines. In the month of August, 1857, the directors of the company called upon Messrs. Glass and Elliott for information, and to ask that firm to tender for the execution of the whole, or one half of the line. The required information was furnished, and a prospectus, founded on Messrs. Glass and Elliott's estimates, was issued to the public. As certain statements, however, appeared in the public journals, to the effect that it was impossible to lay a cable in the Red Sea, from its great depth, and other causes, an insufficient amount of capital was subscribed, and the project flagged.

In this state of things, Messrs. Glass and Elliott suggested an application to government to cause a survey to be made, with a view of testing the truth of these statements. This course was adopted, and the "Cyclops" was ordered on the expedition, and instructions forwarded, on the firm's suggestion, to the Admiralty, through the hydrographer, were sent out to the officers in command of the ship. The result of the survey having been considered satisfactory, a fresh attempt was made by the directors to carry out the line. The undertaking had not proceeded further, before it was found that the agreement between Mr. Gisborne and the directors of the Red Sea Telegraph Company had lapsed by a few days; and on being called upon to renew it, he consented, but insisted that in addition to the fifteen thousand pounds agreed to be paid to him as consideration for the "concessions," he should be appointed engineer to the company, and that the whole of the work should be given to Messrs. Newall and Co., without tender, on the ground that that firm had become interested with him in the concessions. The company were thus saddled with an engineer and a contractor as part of the "concession;" practically, the form of the cable was decided upon, and little remained for the board to do but to pay. With these private and confidential arrangements, it is not surprising that unprotected iron wire, scarcely larger than bell-wire, was used for the covering of the cable, although there was abundance of experience to prove that, after being only a few months in the sea, it would become so rusted, that when repairs were necessary, it would be impossible to lift it to the surface. It is not surprising that such a close contract was taken for a lump sum, thereby offering a premium upon the chances of saving some part of the slack or surplus cable; and so causing the fractures attributable to the tightness with which the cable was laid.

Ruinous as this private and confidential contract arrangement was, the directors of the company felt that no other course was left open to them than to make the best of it; and they therefore held together, and supported their engineer and contractor. The rival contractors—Messrs. Glass and Elliott—on seeing the estimates of Messrs. Newall and Co., approved, of course, by Mr. Gisborne, to carry out the work for a sum of six hundred and fifty thousand pounds, or thereabouts, offered to carry out similar work for ONE HUNDRED THOUSAND POUNDS LESS. Their offer was not accepted, their claims upon the undertaking were ignored, and the Treasury were led to believe by the Directors, that the work was laid out in the surest manner to lead to success. The warning addressed by Messrs. Glass and Elliott to the Lords Commissioners of the Treasury, dated June 26th, 1858, was only answered by a Treasury minute of the usual stamp, dated August 4th, 1858. As it shows the nominal character of the supervision exercised by the Government over the undertaking, we present the document entire:—

"Inform Messrs. Glass, Elliott, and Company, that my lords have made an arrangement with the Red Sea Telegraph Company, by which, on certain conditions, a guarantee on the part of her Majesty's government is granted to that company.

"It is one of the conditions in the arrangement, that the line of telegraph shall be laid down on the responsibility of the company; my lords do not propose to interfere in the selection of the parties who are to execute the work, further than to see that its proper execution is sufficiently secured. My lords have no doubt that the company will adopt the proper means of procuring contracts for the execution of the work on the best terms, and can only refer Messrs. Glass, Elliott, and Co. to the directors of the company."

The directors were immovable, and they comforted themselves and the Treasury with the belief that the "early and satisfactory completion of the enterprise would be most effectually promoted by the selection of the contractors who combined the highest reputation," etc., etc. What they meant by "selection of contractors," is not quite clear, when it was notorious that only one contractor was forced upon them; but as their policy was to get the government guarantee at all hazards, we can hardly feel surprised at the tone of their communications with the authorities. In their contempt for the saving of one hundred thousand pounds, the directors of the company seem to have caught the infectious liberality of our imperial expenditure. The maxim that the ship should never be spoilt (although it invariably is spoilt) for a hundred thousand pounds' worth of tar, which is so familiar to "my lords," as they delight to style themselves, is not often the guiding principle of cautious mercantile bodies, who work with a fear of the Court of Bankruptcy before their eyes. But, to do the Treasury justice, one of "my lords"—Lord Stanley—seems to have grown uneasy about this hole and corner contract, some two months after the official minute, just quoted, was recorded. To his credit, he complained, through the usual secretary, in the usual form, that the system of competition was not resorted to.

A contract, huddled up as this was, pointed to failure from the beginning, and turned the concession of the Turkish government into a barren permission to throw certain vast sums of public money into certain Oriental seas. It provided that the laying of the cable should be left entirely in the hands of the contractors, and so absolved the engineers of the company from all responsibility. Failures in the line declared themselves almost immediately, and a vessel was engaged for one hundred and eighty-two days in abortive attempts to repair one hundred and eighty-four miles of cable.

The scientific, mechanical, and natural enemies of telegraphic enterprise, do not seem to be half as formidable as its moral enemies. Gutta-percha—the present popular material for what is called the insulating medium, or covering necessary to protect the wire from air and water—may be difficult to manufacture entirely free from small cavities; currents may be troublesome in washing these specks of bad workmanship into gaping holes; sharp rocks, hungry fishes; too much tightness in laying the cable producing fractures; or too much slackness producing "kinks," or tangles; rigid instead of elastic machinery for paying out the cable; storms, which come on just at the critical moment of the paying-out process, forcibly dividing the paying-out ships from their long tail of cable; a want of careful submarine surveys; variations in temperature, not known or provided for, which melt the insulating medium; the action of sea-water upon the outer iron covering of cables; ships' anchors; movements of the sea; antagonistic vegetation gathering round the cable; gas currents; want of sufficient thickness in the cable; and a dozen other defects and opposing forces may silently and rapidly convert a great undertaking into a hopeless wreck. These are powerful opponents that have to be met with skill and judgment, but, before they are conquered, other enemies have to be guarded against. The insulation of the conducting wire may be brought to absolute perfection, but this will avail little unless the insulation of contractors and jobbing concessionists is also attended to. Of all destroying agencies against which an electric telegraph may have to contend, there is not one that will be found so destructive as a commission agency. Gold is a great misconductor in these cases, a sort of metallic covering that is sure to be spread over a multitude of flaws. A per-centage upon economy of scientific and mechanical outlay, in a cable intended for shallow governments rather than for shallow waters, is apt to produce a belief that gingerbread may serve as an excellent insulating medium. Government assistance, in the shape of a financial guarantee, can hardly be dispensed with in such speculative and international undertakings; although the lullaby patronage of the official mind is dearly bought, even at thirty-six thousand pounds per annum. The only safe course which presents itself to practical men in connexion with submarine telegraphs, is simply to deal with contractors known to be responsible and trustworthy, to pay them a sum not exceeding the actual cost of the cable, and to allow a certain liberal per-centage for its use during the time that it actually remains in working order. Under such conditions, there appears to be no reason to despair of the success of submarine telegraphy.

THE BRITISH SOLDIER.

I PASSED, one morning, along one of those narrow back streets in the neighbourhood of Westminster, where many public-houses hang out their projecting signs, and flavour the air with a scent of sawdust, beer, and gin; a street where heavy, dingy, tobacco-coloured tap-rooms are seen through half-open windows, filled with a noisy crowd, in which the scarlet coat of the full-blown soldier mingles with the ragged clay-stained jacket of the brown-faced country labourer or vagabond, who has just taken, or is about to take, the Queen's shilling. I passed along such a street at an hour which, though not particularly early, was yet too early to allow the business of the day, in that market-place for the purchase and sale of boys and men, to be commenced; and I saw a model tailor's pattern, over-dressed, be-ribboned recruiting-sergeant hanging up a picture at a prominent house-corner, as if he was baiting a trap to catch a number of sparrows or rats. It was the old, old story. A thousand, or perhaps ten thousand, "fine young men" were wanted immediately for active service in the choicest of regiments, in the most delicious of climates. They always have been so wanted, and probably always will be. There was pay to be had, imperishable glory to be earned, the gratitude of an admiring country to be secured, honours and rewards without number, within the reach of all. Why hesitate? why pause to reflect? Look at that picture of the elegant dragoon in the tight-fitting costume, who stands with as much ease, as much elegance, as much perfection of toilet and sense of enjoyment in the front of a gunpowder-clouded battle-field, which is rudely depicted in the background, as if he was merely showing himself, for the credit of the service, in one or other of the fashionable parks.

And so the recruiting-sergeant, having hung up this triumph of imaginative art, retired to his watch-box in an opposite beer-shop, to await the effect of his tempting appeal, or proceeded to other similar stations, where he knew that it was profitable to set up other similar baits. The sight of this recruiting-sergeant, with his gold-headed cane and fluttering ribbons, filled me with no feeling of indignation against him, the instrument of a bad system; it only led me to study more closely the actual social and sanitary condition of the soldier, and to see if something can be done, in the shape of giving publicity to his case, that will be the first step in bringing about an improvement where there is so much to be improved.

The British soldier, upon whom the safety and prosperity of the country so much depend, and whom we are always praising in speeches and print, begins his career of twenty-one years' service, in most cases, as the victim of a recruiting sergeant's artful wheedling. He finds himself in a position little better than that of a privileged prisoner; his hopeful dreams in the enlisting pothouse are all dissipated with a few weeks' hard drill, and he is sometimes transferred, against his will, to an inferior regiment, being too poor and ignorant to seek a remedy at law. His social importance, as a labourer at thirteenpence a day, is not very great, but he is entitled to be dealt honestly with for all that.

The first punishment he suffers is in the article of dress. The uniform that looked so tempting in the highly-coloured picture, and even still looks tempting in its substance, to the ignorant or superficial observer, is made up of instruments of torture, from the hat to the boots. His shako, or field hat, is sometimes a thick, black, shining leather pannikin, in shape like an inverted melting crucible; sometimes a rough drum of hair (as in the case of the artillery service), like a lady's hand-muff, or the well-known grenadier's hat, which resembles a large upright bag. Either of these hats will outweigh half a dozen ordinary civilian hats, and will more than equal the weight which ought to represent his whole summer clothing, with the exception of his boots.

Next comes the stock, an iron-like leather collar, which, in one form or other, has now been in use for nearly two hundred years. It was introduced by the military Croats, and took their name at first, until corrupted into cravat, and afterwards altered to stock—the title it now bears. It almost gave plausibility to the jocular explanation of its use, as presenting a ready means, by tightening the buckle at the back, as much as the men could bear without suffocation, of making those soldiers look ruddy and healthy, who were suffering from overwork, or an insufficiency of food. These instruments of torture have, in their time, been made of horsehair, and have been further stiffened with slips of wood; but the leather army stock of the present hour, although slightly improved, still preserves enough of its ancestral peculiarities to make it the aversion of all the junior officers and men.

The trousers are tight where they ought to be loose, and loose where they ought to be tight; the coats are buttoned up over the chest, without any reference to the weather; and the material is of the same substance in the tropical heat of July as in the pinching cold of February. The boots are made of such hard, unyielding material—not because it is the most durable—that their wearers are crippled after a few miles' march; and the regulation knapsack, a square box, is strapped on the men in such a way as to compress the chief muscles used in moving the arms, to strangle certain blood-vessels and nerves, and render the arms almost useless, as well as to impede the breathing, and help to induce consumption.

The next punishment which the British soldier suffers is in the article of food. There is little to be said against the quantity and quality of what is supplied, but a good deal to be said against sometimes condemning a man to live upon boiled beef for one-and-twenty years. One half of the soldier's meals are thrown or given away, and he flies to his canteen when in camp, or his public-house when in barracks, for a substitute for refreshment, in the shape of tobacco and beer. If he "roughs it under canvas," he is no worse off for variety of food, and no better, as the faithful regulation diet, like the regulation uniform, will follow him everywhere, from Edinburgh Castle to the Dover heights.

There is not only this sickening and unhealthy monotony of food, which the British soldier has to fight against, but there is another cause at work to account for the fearful mortality in the army—the want of properly constructed barrack accommodation. While the painful fact is before us, that the deaths in the bulk of the army are double those in the civil population, and that sickness is almost as active in thinning the ranks of men of all ages, as the destruction of war, we are led to look about for an explanation, and we find it in the indifferent ventilation, crowded state, and defective sewerage of the British soldier's home. Night duty, intemperance, vice, regulation cooking, and want of exercise and suitable employment, have all their share in pulling the soldier down; but the disgraceful existing state of some of the barracks most certainly heads the list. There is neither comfort, decency, nor a wholesome supply of air in these buildings, which are costly to the nation, and destructive to the service. They have been mostly erected in the centre of populous districts, to the equal detriment of the soldier and the civilian. Nearly nine millions of money have been expended in thirty-four years, and there is little more to show for it than a few huts, a number of buildings worse than useless, and a leading line in the Registrar General's melancholy account of human class decay.

The huts at Aldershot (the model military settlement, according to the Horse Guards) are no improvement upon this state of things, any more than the lofty range of barracks already built and still building at this place. The former are low, crowded wooden structures, too slender to keep out the heat as well as the cold; the latter are showy to the eye, but placed in the worst valley situation in the whole camp. The general position of this great home of the British soldier is considered excellent from a medical point of view; but it has nothing to show in the shape of drainage, except a few iron gratings that peep up here and there, in the gutters at the side of the gravelly slopes. Twenty thousand men are now stationed here, in a small space, making it less healthy every day they remain. It is worse now than it was two years ago; and in another two years' time, under the present system of neglect and abuse, it will begin to cry out loudly for sanitary reform.

The want of useful employment, amongst other evils, is the chief dry-rot of the whole British army. It haunts the common soldier in his lonely sentry-box, in his tavern carousings, in his stifling barracks, in his crowded, den-like guard-room, under his canvas tent on the sand or grass, in the dust and excitement of a grand field-day, in the dulness and monotony of an ordinary parade. He sees nothing before him but a blank day of unproductiveness—the shouldering of a musket, the cleaning of a horse, the guarding of something as invisible as air, the taking off of one oppressive hat, and the putting on of another. He goes to bed at ten; he rises at five, and all for what? He keeps the hours of industry, and nothing more. To multiply numbers in one place only adds to his misery. In each comrade's face and movements he only sees the reflection of himself—a man who is pining for want of something useful to do. He knows that one hundred thousand creatures like himself are driving gun-carriages up hills, to drive them down again; are lounging about barrack-yards or places of public resort; are standing like living statues, or tailor's shop blocks, at the doors of water-colour galleries, the British Museum, the Mint on Tower Hill, at the Bank of England, the Tower and its wharves, and certain theatres at the west end of London. He feels that in this sentry-duty, especially, he is only used as an empty show, while the one policeman, who stands by him, and half a dozen like him, is the guardian of order really meant for work. He knows that the man who picks a pocket, disfigures a picture, creates a disturbance in a public building, or steals a note from a banking-house, or a book from a library, is neither deterred from these crimes by the scarlet spectre at the gate, nor marched off to prison by the same spectre, at the point of the military sword. Men hurry by him, towards evening, stained with the marks of toil, going from that which has grown under their hands, to return to it again on the morrow with fresh hope and with fresh strength, while he can only gaze after them like one who is motionless in a land of activity—like one who is dry and unfruitful in a land of wealth.

The British officer, relatively to his position, is not better circumstanced than the men. There is a large and increasing number of the officers who have resources of their own to fall back upon, and who find leisure, not only for professional study, but for honourable devotion to many works of usefulness and philanthropy. But there are also many whose time hangs heavily on their hands. At the camps, such are the most miserable, least self-reliant creatures under the sun. Whatever Aldershot may be to the common soldier, with all the recognized field amusements, which the authorities hear of, and which are little used, and all the unrecognized amusements of the suddenly-created town, which the authorities never hear of, but which are extensively used—whatever this Aldershot may be to the British soldier in his lowest form, it is nothing but a penal settlement to many an officer. A costly club-house amongst the huts, where the luxuries of Pall Mall are sought for, and partly obtained, between zinc walls and under a zinc roof; a fashionable London barber, represented by a hut full of toilet unnecessaries, where heads are washed in the oriental fashion, and handkerchiefs are scented, and fragrant vapours are wafted from half-open doors across the wilderness of yellow stones and dust; a library that is little used, and a number of musical bands that are little listened to—form all that the British officer, in his present condition, can call his recreative resources at the camp. He rises, on ordinary occasions, very late in the morning; he appears, on ordinary occasions, for an hour on parade; and from that time, until the hour for the mess-dinner, he is left the entire master of himself. Billiards (at the club) do not contain within themselves the secret of perpetual freshness, and having one's hair cut and washed is an expensive amusement that wearies upon repetition. The art of reading, in the sense of enjoying a book, is not acquired by all men under the spur of necessity, and there is nothing left for it but to yawn, and lounge, and sleep. Gambling is a thing that helps to pass away the weary time; and the mess-dinner is prolonged, with its wine party afterwards, as the one amusement to look forward to at the end of each dreary day. Over all this hangs the cloud of extravagance and dissipation, the sense of wasted powers and a purposeless life, and the knowledge, in many instances, that debt and difficulty are accumulating at the back of those artificial and gratified wants which the regimental income, without private property, is wholly inadequate to supply.

This is not the life for any large body of healthy men to lead, whether officers or privates, who find nearly eight hours of each working day left unemployed upon their hands. As you cannot increase their monotonous military labour without producing a dangerous degree of disgust, you must find some occupation for them that will produce a tangible profitable result, and that can be carried on otherwise than under the perpetual distressing sense of military restraint. It is the duty of those to do this who hold the moral and physical welfare of the soldier in their hands. What form the labour shall take, whether agricultural or mechanical, whether labour for sale or labour for consumption (as the production of most of those things which are now purchased under such a wasteful system, from "contractors for stores"), is a question of details with which the advocates of the principle have little to do.* With regard to the profits derivable from this work, it has been well suggested that they should be paid in to the credit of the soldier at the regimental savings bank, and be returned to him, with interest, at the end of his service.

Whatever is done should be done at once, and done thoroughly and well. The British soldier will then find himself really respected, for the first time, and will begin to respect himself. The ringing of the smith's anvil, or the bricklayer's trowel, will no longer be a reproach in his ear; the sight of the bending ploughman, or the powdered mason, will no longer be a reproach to his eye. The glare and trickery of the recruiting-sergeant, which are considered necessary to entrap him at his outset, will disappear: and instead of the too common idleness and dissipation of his middle course, and the disgrace and misery which too often embitter his end, he will from the first assume that position in the social scale to which his useful services entitle him.†

* These views are advocated in principle, and also, to some extent, in detail, by all sound military authorities. We may quote the pamphlet before mentioned; the Hon. Colonel Lindsay; Colonel Jebb; Colonel Tulloch; Sir Richard Airey, Quartermaster-General of Her Majesty's Forces; Colonel North; the Right Hon. Sidney Herbert; besides many other gentlemen of equal importance.

† Since this was written, some movement has been made to improve the soldier's condition; and I may quote the following remarks from the "Daily News" of July 8, 1864:—

"We hope that what is doing now at Aldershot may be taken as a proof that better counsels are prevailing at the Horse Guards. Aldershot has produced an Industrial Exhibition. Under the guidance and encouragement of officers who show that they are worthy to command, the soldiers at that camp have furnished the products of their skill and industry, which are now displayed in the Aldershot Club-house, forming a most interesting collection. Every regiment in camp—horse, foot, artillery, and engineers—has sent something for exhibition; and not only the men, but their wives and children, and the wives of the officers, have contributed articles. Besides armourers' and smiths' work, harness, accoutrements, and military engineering instruments, there are specimens of carving, carpentering, cabinet work, photography, leather and cloth work, which show the men to be equal to the demands either of military or civil life. The remarkable feature of the exhibition is the evidence it offers of the correctness of the opinion of those officers who reported three years ago in favour of encouraging the soldier to pursue some industrial occupation in his leisure time. We may take it for certain that the men who have furnished the stalls at this exhibition are not the worst, but the best, men in their several corps; and we have in this display of their work an indication of the way in which a good soldier is led by choice, when left to his own good sense, to spend his spare time. It may be said that the testimony of the men themselves is now added to that of the officers, who supported in favour of General Crauford's recommendation. We may hope that this exhibition will break down the last remaining prejudice that has operated to prevent the establishment of workshops for soldiers, which have been found of so much advantage in India."

YOUTHS' CLUBS.

An eminent English writer, speaking of growing youths between the ages of fourteen and nineteen, thinks it would be well if they could all be placed under extinguishers until they became young men. As this sentiment has not met with any great amount of opposition, we are bound to consider that it meets the views of a large and respectable class. Few people have any real sympathy with the hobbledehoy. If he is intelligent he asks troublesome questions, and is crammed to overflowing with a great deal of knowledge that most of us have learnt and have forgotten all about. He is painfully precise upon rules of grammar, names and dates of history, and problems of arithmetic, and he soon becomes a bore. If he is stupid he is generally troublesome in other ways, and is often gluttonous, clumsy, and obstinate. Whether intelligent or stupid, however, he thinks himself fit company for men who would rather be without him. He soon finds that something is wrong, although he hardly knows what. He becomes ashamed of his youth, because he sees that others have little sympathy with it. Failing to find companions of his own age and tastes, he stretches his neck and stands upon tiptoe. His cap is changed for a premature hat, his jacket for a premature coat, and his toffy for a bad cigar. He turns his back upon cricket, rounder, peg-in-the-ring, and a dozen other healthy out-door games, and looks towards hot billiard-rooms and frowsy casinos. He may, and most probably does, grow into a sharp, active, average man; but for want of some social resort and recognition after school hours his youth is cut short, and he becomes, in every sense, a forced plant.

This is the social condition of thousands of middle-class boys, who, naturally enough, like "working-men," are not tempted by the icy attractions of "Mechanics' Institutes," or who are not fortunate enough to find a cheap cheerful coffee-house, in some corner of which they may read, drink tea, look at chess-playing, and be tolerated. Thousands of other boys belonging to a lower class, who live up courts and back streets at nights, and who work hard in shops, offices, or in carrying parcels all day, have nothing to look forward to after labour in the shape of steady settled recreation. Their means, appearance, and habits do not lead them to "Mechanics' Institutes," or coffee-shops, and they are not often attracted by the bare slates, desks, and copy-books of an ordinary evening school. It is for this class that "Youths' Clubs" have been started, with a feeling on the part of the promoters that something more was required by tired boys than a few hours of hard instruction. Amusement and friendly intercourse one with another, freedom of action within certain bounds, with book education where it is demanded, are therefore provided for a small weekly payment.

The first of these youths' clubs was started at Dover, by the Rev. Henry White, now chaplain of the Chapel Royal, in the Savoy, Strand. It has been in existence more than five years, and numbers, we believe, between one and two hundred boy members. Silverton, in the Woolwich marshes, started next, with a mixed club for boys and men; but as it has broken through the main idea of the parent institution it has hardly any claim to appear in this list. Sevenoaks followed in 1860, with a club of thirty youths, a fair number for a small inland town, or village without a railway; and Islington came next, in the spring of the same year, with a promising institution of a hundred boy members. The next on the list is Bayswater, which started in the latter part of the same year with eighty members, and which has sent out a fairly trained band of juvenile instrumental musicians. The Dover and Islington institutions are the most encouraging on the list, because they are more nearly self-supporting than the others. The Central Institution in London, which is under the management of the Rev. H. White, the founder of these clubs, will shortly be re-opened, either in Endell Street or Swallow Street, and an endeavour will then be made to found a "Union" for more distant clubs, on the principle so successfully carried out by the Rev. Henry Solly.

The London Central Club, which numbers about two hundred members, was opened in January, 1860, at the Lowther Arcade Exhibition Rooms, and remained there until it was lately driven out by the Italian ice-vendors. It is now seeking rooms in one of the streets we have mentioned above. The idea of the founders and promoters has been to fill up that gap in the life of working boys which comes between their leaving school and their attaining manhood. The plan has been to fit up two large rooms, one for reading and amusement, the other for classes and lectures. The reading or club room will be made as light and attractive as possible, with plenty of gas, pictures, and a neat wall-paper. Many friends of the working-classes, when they start an institution, forget that the eye requires food as much as the mind, and think they have done all that is necessary when they have provided a building like a cab-stable or a wash-house. This hardly does in these days of Exhibitions and Crystal Palaces, and the managers of "Youths' Clubs" are too alive to the necessity of making things pleasant to fall into this error. The club-room will be well supplied with books, magazines, newspapers, chess, draughts, tactics, and other games, and the library will be honestly filled with sound fiction and readable volumes. The rooms (as before) will be open every evening from seven until ten, and the classes held will deal with history, geography, writing, chess, arithmetic, drawing, French, singing, and English grammar.

The subscription for each member, if fixed upon the old scale, will be sixpence weekly, with a shilling entrance-fee, which will buy admission to all the privileges of the club, and to the classes, concerts, and lectures. The lectures will be given gratuitously, like the tuition, by friends of the institution, and will always be on "popular" subjects. Sometimes the members, who are chiefly youths employed in shops, printing and stationery establishments, or as messengers in offices about the neighbourhood at wages vary-varying from six to ten shillings a week, have united to give mixed musical and elocutionary entertainments, and they will doubtless do so again. On the more serious side of the institute prizes will be distributed to those pupils who may distinguish themselves by their diligence and good conduct in the several classes.

When this Central Club was in operation on this system at the Lowther Rooms, the average weekly attendance of the lads was about one hundred and twenty, and they paid up their weekly subscriptions with cheerful punctuality. Looking at the boys as they sat in their club-room, it was impossible not to see that they felt amongst their fellows. The youngsters played at chess or draughts with each other, and on whichever side the victory turned there was none of that uneasy feeling that occurs when a boy overcomes an elderly opponent. The babble of youth was not checked by any angry glances cast from under spectacles. Some of the members read their newspapers, other magazines, and none of them felt that they were standing in the way of people old enough to be their grandfathers.

Looking at the educational plan of these institutes, it may be easily supposed that the "club" is only a school under another name, and that the members, although they pay a fair subscription, are over-managed and coerced into improving their minds. The Rev. Henry White assures us this is not the case. "In carrying out our plans," he says, "the greatest possible liberty is granted to the members in their choice of studies and amusements. No unnecessary check is given to their freest and pleasantest intercourse one with another. The good result of this dealing is seen in the constant and unwearying attendance of a large majority of the members, and in their close and affectionate attachment to their teachers, and to one another. This treatment has only *utterly* failed in a few instances. Those failures have led to the abandoning the hope with which the institute first set out of *reforming* the unruly and evil-disposed. It has been proved that a system strict enough to reform the wayward and wicked must work harshly and with discouragement upon those who are willing to use liberty without abusing it. This experience has led to the belief that the institute must not pretend to be *reformatory*, though it is most truly *preventive*."

There is a little too patronizing a tone in these remarks, and a slight forgetfulness of the fact that each boy pays an annual subscription of £1 6s. a-year, besides his small entrance fee. This is as much as is paid by many members at full-blown institutions, and more than is demanded at many "literary institutes." It is not the fault of the existing boy members if their numbers and subscriptions are not sufficient to defray the expenditure adopted; they have no representative voice in controlling this expenditure or in framing the rules of an institution which ought to attract enough members to free it from a dependence on charity.

The difficulty with this central boys' club has hitherto been the payment of rent, and the Rev. Henry White thinks that his institute cannot be entirely self-supporting. Subscriptions and donations, to the extent of more than £200, were therefore obtained for the club at the Lowther Rooms, including a voluntary rate of £50 from the parish of St. Martin's. Mr. W. H. Smith, the treasurer, and an earnest friend of this club, also gave it the most substantial assistance, so that the published accounts show a proportion of only one-fifth self-help to about four-fifths charity. The central London working boys, unless we are much mistaken, can certainly do much better than this if they are only properly approached and treated.

These clubs are yet in their infancy, little advertised, and consequently little known, and struggling with all the pecuniary embarrassments of young institutions. The cause of the Lowther Room deficiency may be easily traced to a very heavy rental, and a large expenditure upon repairs and fittings. Those who have faith in the permanent value of these clubs should not fritter away their strength in injudicious rentals, but should at once take steps to purchase cheap long leasehold premises on the principle of annual payments adopted by the building societies. They should enlarge the basis of their club, in London particularly, by admitting boys from ten years of age to nineteen, instead of shutting out all who are not fourteen years of age. Town boys of the class these clubs are provided for leave school to go to work at a much earlier age than fourteen, and are often little men when country youths are boys. The friends of these institutions should also never forget that they are trustees for the boys and not their masters; and that a clear balance-sheet, where the members' subscriptions equal the payments—as they easily may—will nourish more self-reliance amongst the lads than all the precepts on the slates, or all the books in the libraries.

PASSING THE BOTTLE.

HALF the intemperance in England is due not so much to a love of drink, as to a listless, unthinking, mechanical compliance with forms and usages. In private society, the absurd custom of health-drinking and head-bobbing has been judiciously got rid of, after an existence extending over half a century. Excessive indulgence in wine is no longer encouraged and stimulated by the "good manners" of the dinner-table, and those who enter the drawing-room, after the banquet is over, with flushed faces and filmy eyes, must proclaim themselves drunkards, pure and simple. At public dinners, the enduring monotonous system of "toasts" is still an incentive to intemperance. No matter what fiery poison is put before you under the names of "port" and "sherry," you must empty your glass to the Queen, the Prince Consort, Albert Prince of Wales, and the rest of the royal family; to the army and navy, the chief object of the meeting (whatever that may be), and the chairman and vice-chairman. If you happen to sit amongst a temperate knot of men, amongst the reporters, for example, who have work to do, you may go through these "toasts" with comparatively little drinking; but if your seat happens to be in a prominent part of the room, and some would-be loyal maniac thinks proper to shout out "bumpers," you may have to consume a pint or two of trash in obedience to custom.

Twenty years ago, Mr. Dunlop published a book upon the artificial and compulsory drinking usages in Great Britain and Ireland; and though many of the empty and injurious customs he censures have been driven out since 1840, by the slightly improved habits of all classes, too many yet remain as supporters of intemperance. He was able to enumerate at least three hundred of these drinking usages, spread over about ninety-eight trades and occupations; and we shall only be giving publicity to the contents of a very useful though half-forgotten book, if we describe a few of these convivial laws of society.

We pass over Scotland and Ireland, and turn to England, properly so called.

Amongst shipwrights, the apprentice is drunk into his trade and drunk out of it. He has to find two pounds for his "footing," to be expended in drink, and from one to five pounds for the same purpose on his "loosing," or termination of his apprenticeship. Launching is always a great drinking festival for the men, and every tradesman interested in the rise and progress of the vessel—block-maker, painter, plumber, glazier, joiner, and others—has to pay drink fees to the "shop" at one period or another. There is "caulking-footing" and "keel money" given by the owners and employers; "chip-money," about three shillings, extracted from every pair of sawyers in the yard; besides other drink-tributes exacted when the lower deck beams are got in. A workman pays ten shillings on his marriage, and is fined one shilling for drink if he comes to his "yard" on a Monday morning unshaved, or with dirty shoes or a dirty shirt. The non-payment of most of these penalties is met by various punishments. Sometimes the jacket of the offender is nailed to the board with large nails, or the hat is mopped with tar.

In foundries the practice is very similar. "Footings" and "loosings" cost just as much, and the money collected is spent in the same manner. Shifting vice or lathe, moving to a better situation in the work, birthdays, national saints' days, and orders given to brass, iron, coal, timber, and tin merchants, are all marked with a certain amount of compulsory drinking. When a workman goes abroad he has to pay twenty shillings, and ten shillings when he returns. An operative being made a foreman incurs a fine of ten shillings for drink money.

One great evil of this system is, that when these fines are not paid, either from poverty or upon principle, many acts of tyranny and injustice are committed. Tools are hidden or destroyed; personal injury is inflicted on the offending workman, or his work is damaged so as to be valueless. Masters and merchants suffer from this system as much as the operatives; and it has been no uncommon thing to burst steam-boilers by over-pressure, in order to revenge the want of due treating!

Amongst whitesmiths, the apprentice "footing" ranges from ten shillings to a guinea, according to the circumstances of the parent. If not paid, the boy is "knocked here, shoved there, and kicked about." Amongst blacksmiths, a journeyman (sledge-hammerman) pays for "footing" two shillings and sixpence, and a smith, five shillings. Chain cable manufacturers, curriers, joiners and carpenters, and sail-makers, are all burdened with similar drink usages. Every stage in each trade is marked with a particular fine, and the custom of "backing," or adding to the amount of these fines by a compulsory subscription amongst the men, only makes matters worse. Tribunals are formed for the purpose of trying all questions relating to drink fines, and a man is said, under these circumstances, to be tried under the strong beer act. Coopers, sawyers, rope-makers, turpentine distillers, stone-masons, tailors, blockmakers, coachmakers, coach-spring makers, skinners, and watchmakers, are all victims to the same senseless customs. Amongst sawyers there are drink fines for men falling into the pit, for a log of wood falling into the pit, for changing pit, and for dirty shoes on Monday. The smallest fine often causes a general subscription for the purpose of "starting a drink." Wetting a new saw, or opening the first log of mahogany, have each their particular fines; and not only in this, but in most other mechanical trades, the work is so surrounded by such drink rules and regulations, that scarcely a day passes without a "spree."

To go through a list of the trades where these drink usages prevail would fill a volume. The system is the same in nearly all cases—drink fines upon entering or leaving a workshop, the same at every stage or mishap in the trade, or on every occasion that can be strained into an excuse for extortion. Riggers, painters, carvers and gilders, saddlers, gunmakers, brass-founders, plane-makers, weavers, shoemakers, hatters, bricklayers, upholsterers, printers, cotton-spinners, millwrights, glassmakers, paper-stainers, and a hundred other bodies of intelligent workmen, are content to labour under and support such a baneful and tyrannical drinking system. Festivity and good fellowship amongst workmen are pleasant, proper, and profitable things in their way, but they are not to be cultivated by such a forcing process. There is no real enjoyment in being forced into compliance with an absurd and pernicious custom; in forcing others; in drinking at all hours and all seasons; in taking liquors which are absolutely nauseous, until an artificial taste is acquired for them; in listening to dull comic songs, and applauding them mechanically; in responding to "toasts," without feeling any sympathy for them; and in pretending to enjoy long rambling speeches that have neither beginning, middle, nor end. All these things are merely excuses for drinking and killing time, and nothing more. There is a senseless hypocrisy about them, which ought to be repulsive to thinking, straightforward men. It would be less odious, where no desire for rational, voluntary, and harmless recreation exists, if the time-killer would sit down openly with a piece of salt and a pitcher of drink, that he might prick up his thirst with one hand, and pacify it with the other. The nuisance would also be less if the sot would get drunk in bed, because a vast deal of trouble, expense, and mischief would be saved by such a proceeding!

THE GREAT HOUSE MYSTERY.

It must strike any man of average intelligence, even if he has not been brought up in a shop, a warehouse, or a counting-house, that the quickest and surest way to dispose of an article is to mark it with the lowest selling price. In the eager race for trading profit, those shops and bazaars must surely run the quickest where everything is marked with plain figures. The opposite, and, perhaps, the more aristocratic system of abjuring labels, may sometimes produce an exceptional profit through a transaction with an ignorant buyer; but if the hundreds and thousands of timid people are taken into account, who never even inquire the prices of various articles, for fear of exposing their ignorance, that profit will be largely overbalanced by a considerable loss. I may take myself as a fair specimen of these individuals. I have money in my pocket, and I love to look at the shop windows. If I had been trained as a professional bidder at general auction sales, I should probably have known the value of all things, from a muslin to a grindstone, without the aid of a ticket. As, however, I have not had the advantage of this training, my money remains in my pocket, the unmarked diamonds, sables, workboxes, silks, and watches remain in the shop windows, and I remain a free sight-seer, paying nothing for my show.

When I take up my newspaper every morning at

breakfast, and look through that portion which is always interesting—the advertisement part—I am pleased to find that no such mystery with regard to price is affected by any sellers, except one numerous and important class. All kinds of property appeal to the great public to be bought, and, with this one exception, very properly state the exact money that will buy them. Wine properly wraps itself in no cloak of selling secresy; book property is scrupulously minute in its particulars of sale ; tea property, clothes property, glass property, and even physic property, come boldly forth to say what they think they are worth ; and it is only house property that stalks behind them.

House rent is the great mystery of London. Ricardo's theory of rent was difficult to get at, but the practice seems more difficult still. Take any newspaper sheet containing the usual house-letting columns, and see how rigidly all the advertisements avoid stating the terms per annum. One or two babbling proprietors may do it, by way, perhaps, of appearing singular, but no one who valued his order ever ventured beyond hinting at a "moderate rental." Most people would suppose that houses were the identical property declared by M. Proudhon, the French philosopher, to be a theft, and that the owners were consequently fearful of declaring their value. Particulars are freely given about "healthy situations," "gravelly soil," "proximity to a railway station," "picturesque locality," "decorative repair," with the number of rooms—often without measurement—and remarks about their suitability to a large or small family; but the all-important fact of the rent—the thing that, in most cases, determines the "eligibility" of the premises—is carefully concealed from the expectant reader. By going across London, or writing to a certain agent's address, this fact may be learned, and when learned, after much delay and trouble, may prove that earlier knowledge would have saved you much labour. The same secresy is observed at the premises which are to let; and you can get no information as to price either from the window-bills or the housekeepers. You wander through the empty rooms, and end with the carpetless front parlour, where a policeman is mending boots in his overtime, or an aged female is trying to warm herself over a half-a-pint of fire. If you ask the policeman about the rent, he will refer you vacantly to the agent's address in the window; while, if you speak to the old woman on the same subject, she may probably tell you, in her ignorance of the higher combinations of the currency, that the landlord only asks eight hundred a year (for a ten-roomed house), if he can be sure of a respectable tenant!

Of course, I know that house agents are at the bottom of this mystery, and that their constant reference to themselves is done to secure their commission, and perhaps increase their clients. I have no objection to the owners of house property intrusting its letting to these middlemen, nor to these middlemen issuing "cards to view" an empty barn, as if it were Chatsworth or Dulwich College. If this is done, however, in a business way, the contract between principal and agent ought to be so precise, that the latter should never be left in any doubt as to his remuneration. Let the house-owner honestly pay the commission after he has instructed his agent, under whatever circumstances the property may be disposed of; let the house agent always advertise the fullest particulars as to terms; and let no wretched house-seeker be further badgered by having to seek a dozen agents as well as a dwelling.

PANTOMIMES.

Those who are inclined to sneer at the present age for being too eminently practical, who believe that poetry is dead, that the ancient faiths are dried up, that imagination is over-ridden by hard facts and a cold-blooded realism, should read the announcements of the Christmas pantomimes. Every dead wall, every newspaper, every shop that will take in a play-bill, in town or country, is filled with tidings of other and strange worlds. The good old nursery stories are kept alive, the wildest legends are accepted with childlike faith, and the dreams of fairy-land are more than realized. The rough costermonger in the street, the gentle child sitting at its mother's feet, the knowing boy returning from school, the busy shopkeeper, the household drudge, the old and young, the rich and poor, have, for once, got something in common. They look forward to that night when the green curtains rise on a thousand magic groves, when blue-nosed demons emerge from caves, when bright-eyed fairies float on gossamer clouds, and when painted philosophers, with little veneration for appearances, expose the hollowness of the every-day world. The lessons that may be gathered from pantomimes are not to be despised. With all our vast educational organization, there are still large classes who are reached by no school except the theatre or the music-hall, and the glimpse of something beyond a daily round of beef, tobacco, and beer, conveyed even through such a tinselled medium as a theatrical bower of bliss, is better than nothing to those whom no churches have been able to attract.

The philosophy of pantomimes is a subject on which volumes might be written, filled probably with as much rubbish as half the commentaries upon Shakespeare. A broad design for a philosophical pantomime was once sketched out by Samuel Taylor Coleridge, in which Charles Lamb and Cottle ought to have played the clown and pantaloon. We have unphilosophical pantomimes in private life every day, and men who are nothing if not half-developed clowns. A vast amount of misdirected animal spirits, of physical energy, of contempt for conventionalities, is hourly let loose in the world, which only wants the patched cheeks, the checked stockings, and the bag-breeches—the outward and visible signs of clownhood—to complete its identity. There was once a notorious Marquis of Waterford, who was essentially an inferior clown; and there is now a notorious Mr. Windham, who is strongly moved by the spirit of pantomime. We need not maintain our assertion with a melancholy catalogue of names. The clown has always a warrant for all that he says or does in some corner or other of humanity.

The character now presented to an admiring public as the central figure of the harlequinade—or "comic business" of the pantomime—is not the growth of a single age, or of one country. The bustling drama in which he takes the leading part, under the old English name of Clown, is probably the oldest existing stage-play in the world; and he is not the invention of one author, but of many men and many minds. To some extent he is a born thrall of tradition. He staggers about with the weight of many centuries on his back. He is probably more ancient than the horse-rider in the circus, the posturer with the bent back, the juggler with the four brass balls. His movements, whims, and fancies were laid down when the earth was very young; and they will be transmitted from generation to generation until it becomes withered and old. In days when the freedom of thought and speech was doled out by grasping officials—when Rabelais and kindred authors took to clowning in literature to convey their hatred and contempt for fine old crusted authority, the clown doubtless grew apace in reckless humour. As a tolerated jester he did the work of smothered reformers, and yet escaped the gallows or the stake. The same licence extended to schoolboys during the holidays was doubtless then extended to the clown. He made faces before his ushers, and burnt his masters in effigy without reproof. Now, in London, in 1864, he has probably no more freedom of action than he had in the dark ages. His movements—his utterances—his quips and cranks—are jealously watched over by a court lacquey. The metropolitan stage ought to be very pure when the master of its ceremonies is a Lord Chamberlain.

Many innovations have been introduced into the pantomime from time to time, some of which have only maintained their popularity for a brief season. The ghastly Pierrot, or clown of the French stage, was transplanted as a companion for the English clown; but he never struck root. The dandy was another shadow which had its day—flitting between the four chief pantomimists in the comic action—and now his place is often filled with tumbling sprites. The introduction, or fairy opening, has been made more splendid by different managers every year, and mines of wealth have been lavished upon elaborate transformation scenes which required half an hour to unfold their beauties. Natural accessories have been introduced in aid of the artificial resources of the scene-painter and machinist; Madame Vestris and Mr. Beverley being the first to outstrip all competitors in the ingenuity and beauty of their combinations. Living nymphs were planted in graceful positions in the scenery, and solid structures took the place of painted views. Some of the effects produced were of unsurpassed beauty, and each combination strove to outdo the last. Much, however, as the old Lyceum management did to advance transformation scenes, and exhaust all the variations which could be played upon this source of attraction, they still left something untried for another gleaner in the same field. Mr. Callcott's lake of looking-glass, reflecting a forest of opening ferns containing half-hidden nymphs, exhibited at the Lyceum during Madame Celeste's management, a few seasons ago, surpassed all former transformation scenes in rich, calm, poetic beauty.

There can be no doubt that the undue development of this taste for scenic splendour has rather overshadowed the "comic business" of pantomime, and checked the supply of good clowns. We have now been many years watching for the advent of a new Grimaldi, but he has not yet appeared. In Grimaldi's days the comic business was the pantomime; the opening was strictly introductory, and, though giving scope for good pantomimic acting, was never allowed to overbalance the harlequinade. This was an inducement for a man like Grimaldi—the son of a ballet-master—to devote himself to his art. What he did, if done well, met with instant recognition and approval. His smallest comic efforts were as much noticed by the press as the more ambitious performances of the leading tragedians. Criticism spurred him on, and rewarded him for his exertions. His successors may be less clever, and they are certainly less fortunate. Newspaper theatrical criticism has now fallen to a very low ebb, and ranks very little above mere reporting. Criticism applied to pantomime has scarcely any existence. Twenty theatres now stand in London, where formerly there were only half a dozen, and all these establishments produce their pantomimes on the same night. If any daily journal has a William Hazlitt on its staff, it can only send him to one theatre, and the rest of the houses, with their entertainments, have to be noticed by the rank-and-file of the working staff. Parliamentary, law, police, and general reporters, suddenly bud into critics for one night only, and struggle through their work according to their lights. If the names of all the costumiers, composers, mask-makers, scene-painters, and stage-managers, pressing forward for publicity, are got safely into print, with the names of the pieces, a hazy account of their plots, and a play-bill description of their leading scenes, this is as much as we can expect. A sound dramatic critic is hardly made under a quarter of a century's training; and, therefore, we have no right to blame the reporters. Unsound critics, with their unsound, or negative criticism, make unsound actors, and this is one great cause of the decline of pantomimists.

How deeply the clown, with all his sayings and doings, his domestic life and his theatrical life, has engaged our thoughts and affections, may be gathered from our literature. We have a thousand stories in which he figures as the hero, and where as much sentiment and effect have been drawn from the contrast between his public and private life as the French have drawn from *Paillasse*—the mountebank. The wonder, admiration, and affection which children have for clowns are wide-spread and genuine. An actor of our acquaintance was once in company with a little child who knew that he was connected with the stage, and seemed to regard him with envious interest. The actor drew the child towards him, and tried to engage it in conversation. The child had evidently something on its mind to which it wished to give utterance, and, encouraged by the actor's manner, it at last said, "How near have you ever been to a clown?"

The biography of our greatest clown has been put together by our greatest writer of fiction; and as a record of a real man who worked without talking, who was not always soul-musing, making his life a poem, and taking huge springs for leaps which were never executed, it may be read with advantage by the side of Carlyle's "Life of Sterling."

ACTORS.

THE plain, homely family funeral of Frederick Robson, which took place lately at Norwood Cemetery, however consonant it may have been with English taste and feeling, was far from complimentary to dramatic art. When a man who was unquestionably the most original English actor seen by the present generation, is carried to his last resting-place with no more organized ceremony than generally accompanies the burial of a popular publican, we cannot help thinking that graveyard demonstrations are rewards for social rather than artistic distinction. It is true that Frederick Robson committed the unpardonable offence of dying out of the season, and was buried at a time when no person of importance could venture to be seen in town; it is true that he was somewhat recluse in his habits, especially during the last two unhappy years of his life—that he was only a nominal member of one or two leading clubs, and the pet of none; it is true that his share in the management of the Olympic brought him nothing but a little solid profit; but this is hardly enough to account for his unimpressive funeral. Are we to assume that the lingering belief that actors off the stage are still "vagabonds," and the practical but ungrateful feeling that no more amusement can be extracted from the dead comedian, had something to do with this seeming neglect?

The first impulse, on witnessing a funeral of this kind, is to say that "they manage these things better in France;" but a little reflection and inquiry will largely deprive us of this consolation. An actor like Frederick Robson could hardly have been buried in Paris at any season without being honoured with a procession formed of many distinguished men in literature and art, and with several orations over his grave, in which acting would have been glorified. So far the outward and visible tribute of respect would have been without a flaw, but the social position of the actor would still have remained unaltered. How unsatisfactory that position is still in France may be judged from the manner in which a recent honour has been conferred upon M. Samson. That fine and famous comedian—the father, so to speak, of the Théâtre Français company; the oldest, most respected, and most celebrated member of a national theatre which has much of a college in its constitution; Professor at the Conservatoire, and formerly the teacher of Madlle. Rachel—has lately retired from the stage, and the other day he was decorated with the "Legion of Honour." In the decree announcing this gift it was expressly stated that he was decorated as Professor—his career and fame as an actor were not even alluded to. The French press could hardly pass by such a slight to a great profession without comment, and it strikes them as remarkable that after all the national struggles to obtain "equality," the old prejudice against actors which existed in Molière's time, and which Napoleon I. found so dominant that he confessed he *dared not* give the "Legion of Honour" to Talma, for whom he had the warmest regard, is still as strong as ever. Exceptions excepted, as in all professions, there is nothing in the lives of the leading French actors to justify this prejudice. In private they are the most quiet and respectable of men, the most affectionate fathers of families, and the steadiest citizens. They are not only as good as their neighbours, but very often better.

Dramas are not the only things connected with the stage which we translate from the French. Much of this prejudice still exists in England, and with as little justification. It is in vain that actors constantly show themselves to be the most provident members of society; that they seldom appear as insolvents or bankrupts; that divorce and police courts are seldom troubled with their doings; that they pay taxes, educate their children, and behave with almost studied propriety. As a class, they have never enjoyed the social position to which they are fairly entitled. Though they are no longer designated "vagabonds," they are often treated as such, or are patronized with a show of condescension which is equally offensive. Shakespeare, to all appearance, is idolized; but the followers of his art—the art which he wrote only to sustain—are either vulgarly slapped on the back, or frozen with two-fingered politeness. Thousands of well-meaning but mistaken people will laugh at or sympathize with an actor on the stage, who would regard him as a half-tamed gorilla if they met him "in society."

It is very difficult to indicate the causes of popular prejudice, but one, I fancy, may be found in the licensing system. A theatre is one of those shops, the supply of which the Legislature, in its wisdom, has thought proper to check, and the conduct of which it has thought proper to superintend. The paltry party political objects which led to the establishment of the stage censorship in Fielding's time are now forgotten; but the Lord Chamberlain's power still remains. A business which is under the constant supervision of a fastidious Court functionary may easily be regarded as a very immoral business, and the persons who carry it on as somewhat dangerous traders. The stage, which is always as moral, neither more nor less, as the age in which it lives, is, of course, not purified in any degree by this Court censorship; but the fact that a censorship of any kind exists is sufficient to nourish doubts about the respectability of actors.

Another cause of the low estimation in which actors are too generally and unjustly held may be found in the conduct of certain female members of the profession. No fortress is stronger, so we are taught, than its weakest point; and managers who love and respect their art and its followers may profitably turn their attention to this point in their encampment. The time, let us hope, has long passed when shameless celebrities can be advertised upon the stage, but interlopers of less notoriety still get first appearances at certain theatres, for which their admirers, doubtless, give solid consideration. Critics, so-called, are whipped up to notice these strutters in pink satin; and the sugar-and-water criticism of the day generally lets the well-known scandal down gently. There are other capering *lorettes* more permanently connected with the drama than these poor butterflies of an hour, who might be profitably weeded out, as all the talent they possess would hardly set up an ordinary singing-chambermaid. I am not blind to the many and exceptional temptations which beset theatrical young ladies—temptations which deter so many managers from allowing their daughters to follow the profession; but knowing how many estimable women have been great actresses and good wives and mothers, I see no reason why the stage should ever be made an excuse for profligacy.

THEATRICAL SLANG.

The "Slang Dictionary," just published by Mr. Hotten, is the best and most complete work of its kind we have seen, but it hardly does justice to theatrical slang. It gives a few specimens of those corruptions or ornaments of language which the stage and its professors have called into existence, but it makes no pretence of having exhausted the subject. The subject, perhaps, is inexhaustible, if technicalities are to be included as slang, and these technicalities soon pass current beyond professional circles. Many respectable members of society are amateur actors; while few are amateur shoemakers or engineers, and stage terms are thus picked up by young ladies and gentlemen, who are rather proud of their knowledge.

It is impossible to say what reporter first called actors "disciples of the sock and buskin," but the phrase is now stereotyped as slang of the first quality. The stage being so much indebted to the French, the French language is pillaged to enrich the vocabulary of theatrical slang, and a part is never a part but a *rôle;* a female dancer is always a *danseuse;* a female horse-rider is always an *equestrienne,* and an actress is always an *artiste.* A dashing style of performance is called *abandon,* and people who patronize a particular theatre are called *habitués.* Sometimes the technical class descriptions of French actors and actresses are imported, and we hear a young man called a *jeune premier* (when he often ought to be called a *jaune premier*), a leading actor called a *premier* or a *grand premier*, a comedian called *premier comique de genre*, an inferior comedian called *deuxième comique*, an actor of old men called a *père noble*, an actor of general parts called *grande utilité*, an actress of common parts called a *soubrette*, and an actress of young girls called *ingénue coquette*. The English adaptations of these terms sound even more absurd to the unprofessional ear—especially when printed in the brief, direct form of a theatrical advertisement. When a manager tells us that he wants a "singing chambermaid," "a first and second old man," "a walking gentleman," "a gentleman to take the heavy lead," another gentleman for the "second bus" or "general utility," that he is "open to stars," that "a few good niggers may write," and that "silence is a negative"—it is not easy at first to decipher such a riddle. Professional advertisements are generally more or less technical in style, but none, we believe, are half as technical as theatrical advertisements. They have also a marvellous power of self-assertion. We are always reading about some "glorious hit," some "unprecedented success," some "startling novelty," some "unparalleled," "unequivocal," "acknowledged," or "world-renowned wonder." Here is an advertisement which is a good specimen of this style :—

"SECOND TO NONE!

"Meritorious and Mirificent Career of the Mercurial

"LYDIA LATIMER, the Most Legitimate Mirth-provoking Serio-Comic Vocalist and *Comedienne* of the present day. Second Year in the Provinces. Now Engaged, with increasing favouritism, at the People's Concerts, Manchester. Fourth Call Nightly. Disengaged March 20th, 1865."

The comic songs which are considered so mirth-provoking are often advertised in the same strain :—

"The Best Comic Song is the one Just Published,

"THE WEEPIN WILLER, written and composed by Harry Clifton, and Sung by him with immense success.

"'She sat by the side of the bubblin water,
"Under the weepin willer tree.'

"Sent Free for Eighteen Stamps.

"Hopwood and Crew, 42, New Bond Street."

It is not easy to see the fun of this, but perhaps it lies in the bad spelling; and sometimes an advertisement, like the following, shows a just appreciation of such humour :—

"GEORGE LEYBOURNE, the Great Comic Vocalist, on his Moke, 'Will, Oh!' at the London Music Hall, Manchester, Tenth Week of uninterrupted success. N.B.—G. L. will back his Donkey against any Comic Singer in the World."

That music-hall singers and performers are all classified like actors and actresses, is shown in this somewhat hysterical announcement :—

"Lingard, Lingard, Lingard (the Greatest Comic of the day), Miss Julia Lamartine (the Fascinating Sentimental Balladist), J. D. Kelly (the Ethiopian King), Miss Julia Weston (the Successful Characteristic Vocalist), Professor Thomas (the Champion Swordsman), Albert Steele (the Delighting Comic), Miss Annie Abbot, Brothers Clarke (Burlesque Duettists), Miss Emma Mowbray, *Les Freres* Fritz (the Lively Eels), Madame Losebini and Miss Constance (the unrivalled Duettists), Sam Collins (the only True Delineator of Real Irish Character)."

Sometimes the most tempting offers are made to what is called "talent,"—talent being a slang term for persons of marketable ability :—

"WANTED, TWO YOUNG LADIES, as Waitresses in a Free-and-Easy; one that could vamp on the piano or sing a song occasionally preferred. A lengthened or permanent situation given to a young person in the above line.

"Address, J. M., 15, Curzon-street, Burnley."

It is curious to note how catching this free-and-easy style becomes, and how great authors, like Mr. Charles Reade, have mastered it in a few lessons:—

"READE *v.* CONQUEST.—The Plaintiff in this case warns Dramatic pirates that his Stories, 'Clouds and Sunshine,' 'Peg Woffington,' 'Christie Johnstone,' 'White Lies,' 'Art,' etc., etc., are all founded on Registered Plays, and the indirect appropriation of a *single character, or scene, or vital situation* in them, will instantly be followed by an Injunction and an action at law. The exceptions are 'Love Me Little,' etc., and 'The Cloister and the Hearth.' These excepted, it will be perilous to Dramatize this Author's works without his consent Nor is it the least necessary. He is as open to fair and loyal Dramatic business as to any other."

We have only one critical remark to make with regard to this little production by the author of "Very Hard Cash"—it wants "Silence a negative" tacked on to the end to make it complete.

Theatrical slang, technicalities, and swagger, however, are not confined to professionals and professional journals; they creep into theatrical notices. Reports of performances, hurriedly written late at night, are not generally pure models of English composition. The first word is chosen rather than the best word, and whole phrases are imported from the green-room. A successful performance is described as "a hit likely to create a *furore*," or the piece is said to be "a go," or to have "went well," or to be a "sensation"—though sensation is an old slang term for a glass of gin. A comedian who made grimaces is accused of "mugging;" a lady who forgot her part is said to have "stuck," or to be a *débutante* if she made her first appearance; if the applause is so great that the actors walk before the curtain, they are said to have been "honoured with calls;" if the piece is considered good, it is said to be "likely to draw," or to be "a draw;" if the elocution of any actor is somewhat pompous, he is said to "have mouthed it;" if the piece is short and funny, it is called a "screaming farce;" and if it is short and stately, it is called a "*comedietta*" or "*petite comedy.*" When mongrel language like this is used by journalists, we can hardly wonder that managers are encouraged to use it. The warmed-up French dishes presented at most of our theatres are seldom disguised in the cooking. Our drama is not only French in origin and construction, but its characters generally retain their French titles. These titles are often terrible stumbling-blocks to the actors. We have heard fourteen different pronunciations of the word "*Monsieur*" in one piece, in one night, at one theatre. This peculiarity is as distinguishable at the Theatre Royal Lyceum, under the management of M. Fechter, as it is at any minor house in the suburbs. The cheapness of bad translations may partly account for this slovenly transplanting of dramas, but the same determination, to use Anglo-French-Argot-Slang, is shown in every corner of our playbills. If three or four female dancers come on to caper for a few minutes, this is called a "*divertissement;*" if a hornpipe, a comic song, and a solo on the trombone, are thrown in as a make-weight between the piece, they are called collectively a "*mélange,*" and sometimes, by way of variety, an "*inter-mezzio.*" A gentleman is never addressed as sir, he is always "*Mesoo,*" or "*Mossoo,*" according to the fancy of the speaker; and a lady is always "*Murdarm,*"

"*Mad'moselle,*" or "*Mam'selle*"—the latter being an abbreviation almost as vulgar as "*mum*" or "*mim.*" *Geneviève* (pronounced "*John Veve*") is the Sarah Jane of such half-translated dramas, and *Henri* was never known to be written Henry, or pronounced otherwise than "*Hongri.*" A bagpipe cannot be introduced on the stage without being called a "*corna musa,*" and a penny whistle in the same slang becomes a "*pastoral tibia.*" A thimble-rigger is a "*prestidigitator;*" a conjuring confederate is a "*medium,*" or an "*omniscient spiritualist;*" a successful entertainment is never visited by crowds, it is always "patronised by the *élite* of society;" a singing head, as vulgar and obvious as the old Bartholomew fair doll-trick, is called an "*Anthropoglossos;*" a youthful actor is sometimes an "*infant prodigy,*" sometimes a "*Juvenile Roscius;*" a tawny actor from the West Indies, or from the Southern States of America, is called an "*African Roscius;*" a man who plays upon the banjo, and dances flash dances, is called a "*negro delineator;*" and a woman like "Miss" Menken, the female Mazeppa, who trades upon her impudence, is called a "*gifted creature.*" This language is common both with managers and journalists. A manager is either "a popular caterer," or "a daring *entrepreneur;*" and an old actor is sometimes called "*a veteran.*" It is fashionable to talk of the *métier*, or "*platform,*" of particular actors and actresses, instead of their ability and position;—to say that Shakespeare's plays "keep the stage," and that the *Colleen Bawn* had "*a long run.*" If a piece is not very brisk, it is said to "*drag;*" if it is long, it is said to want "*cutting.*" Actors will think nothing of calling Hamlet's great soliloquies "*bits of fat,*" or of speaking of King Lear as "*a heavy father.*" Street-tumbling is expressively called "*mouldy-grubbing,*" and any action on the stage is known as "*business*," sometimes shortened to "*bus.*" Painting the face for any particular character is called "*making-up*," and the paint is generally called "*war-paint.*" If the theatre, or "*house*," as it is more technically termed, is badly attended, this is called "a frost;" or if it is filled with orders, or "bits of paper," as they are termed, it is said to be "well-papered." Some more daring geniuses take a higher flight than this, and we remember an advertisement of "*Tom Sayers's Champion Circus*," in which it was said "the fabric is daily and nightly warmed by not less than four thousand delighted spectators, consisting of rank, wealth, and beauty." Warming a fabric with rank, wealth, and beauty was not all that was promised by the gifted and courageous Sayers and his managers. He appeared in connection with Heenan, and "the admirers of science and skill," we were told, "will find in the entertainment of these brave men a pleasurable excitement heretofore unknown. They will appear precisely as they appeared on the 17th of April before five thousand persons at Three Guineas a head, excepting that in this case their apparel will be unobjectionable, even to the most fastidious of either sex."

Theatres are all known by slang abbreviations, and we have the "Vic," the "Lane," the "Lymps," the "Bird," the "Garden," the "Sour Balloon," etc., for the Victoria, Drury Lane, Olympic, Grecian, Covent Garden, and the Bower Saloon.

The technicalities proper to the stage—the terms used in speaking of the various parts of a theatre, can hardly be classed as slang, until they are used unprofessionally. It is very necessary that theatrical workmen should have fixed names for the materials they are called upon "to work." When they speak of "sky-borders," "flats," "wings," "floats," "counter-weights," "flies," "vampyre-traps," "heavy-sets," etc., they are only using the recognised language of their craft. The call-boy who says "overture's on, gentlemen," and the stage-manager who tells the prompter to "ring up" are not creators of slang—that task is left for the audience to perform. The audience is generally very willing to perform it. When the upper scenery interferes with the view of the gallery visitors, there is always some sharp youth to shout out "lower the blue;" and the technicalities about the "prompt," and the "O.P." side of the theatre are supposed to be familiar to everybody. A chance reporter, writing an account of a theatrical accident, once described a witness as "a gentleman who sold fried fish on the prompt side of the house."

MUSIC HALLS.

THE Music Halls have been somewhat roughly treated of late by writers who have little sympathy with the amusements of the people. Their entertainments have been roundly declared to be coarse and vulgar, their associations demoralizing, their frequenters debauched and ignorant. A few of those pithy sentences which practised writers know so well how to put together have described them as combining the attractions of the gin-palace with the immorality of the old theatrical saloons. Their singers have been pictured with cracked voices, their comedians as thick-headed dolts, and their proprietors as red-nosed publicans. Embezzling clerks, weak-headed shop girls, pilfering warehousemen, prize fighters, betting men, skittle sharps, and degraded women, have been catalogued as their most constant visitors and supporters. We have been told that the minimum of bad flashy music is doled out at these pernicious places with the maximum of bad gin, bad brandy, and worse cigars. Each visitor is represented as only dallying with his drink and ballads, his pipe and nigger dancing, while the great sacrifice of the evening is being prepared for his amusement. A spangled acrobat is said to be kept like an ancient gladiator on the premises, to risk his life every night on the flying trapèze for the final gratification of these brutal tavern patrons.

These depressing descriptions of places that are growing daily in popularity are not the production of M. Assolant and his Anglophobist friends, and they are, therefore, tacitly accepted as truthful and reliable. What would have been howled at as a gross caricature if it had appeared in a French journal, is received with meekness when printed in a few English newspapers. A nation which has been caricaturing the French people for eighty years is the first to cry out when caricatured by French writers in return. When caricatured, however, in its own language, by its own superfine instructors and friends, it is quite ready to believe that it is as black as it is painted.

If music halls and their frequenters were quite as low, vulgar, and degraded in the main as these social satirists make out, we should be the last to shed a drop of ink in their defence; but a pretty long and intimate acquaintance with most London places of amusement has taught us to question the correctness of these depreciatory sketches. We are not about to defend everything that is said and done in music halls, nor to assert that their entertainments are always regulated by the very highest standard of taste; but, knowing how superior all of them are to the low sing-songs they have replaced, we think they merit a little fairer treatment than they have lately received. One of their proprietors, at least, started with an honest desire to make his money by giving a really elevating entertainment at the lowest possible price; and as long as the Canterbury Hall remains under its present management, and gives what it does for sixpence, it will form a triumphant answer to any ignorant libel on first-class music halls. It is not Mr. Morton's fault that his public want amusement instead of instruction, that they like a song better than a lecture, after a hard day's work—that they are natural enough not to affect a love for oratorios when they have it not, and to prefer an operatic selection with a few good tunes in it. It is not his fault that a love for physical displays exists amongst them—as it does, we hope, in all healthy, full-blooded working men—and that they like a good gymnastic display on the flying trapèze, without wishing the slightest harm to the performer.

The puking nonsense that has been lately written upon this new variation of ground and lofty tumbling is only fit reading for a consumption hospital, or for bread-and-butter misses at a boarding-school. A few flying bars that are never sixteen feet from the ground, and are generally swinging harmlessly at an elevation of eight or ten feet, a line of mattresses far more comfortably padded than a military bed, a well-trained gymnast, perfect in wind and muscle, who swings from one bar to the other, occasionally throwing a few summersaults, constitute the whole machinery of this terrible trapèze. In no case, by any possible accident, short of one of those flukes through which the best man is sent to his account by a bit of orange peel or a split pea, can the acrobat be killed, and it would only be by great clumsiness and ill-luck that he could break a limb. Thousands of men would run the same risk for one-hundredth part of the same price; nay, do daily run worse risks for much smaller payments. In days when grave professors, chiefly for muscular excitement, hang themselves over precipices by bits of twig, or grasp icicles almost as brittle as barley sugar to save themselves from certain death, it is useless to write snivelling articles about M. Leotard and his followers. Many a poor sailor runs greater risks nearly every day of his life; and many a poor soldier sells himself to a more dangerous profession for a shilling a day. Many a street tumbler thinks himself well rewarded by a few pence for feats that often place him in as much peril as those for which M. Leotard gets a Lord Chancellor's wages.

So much for the danger of the flying trapèze, and its character as a brutal and brutalizing exhibition. If it were all that the effeminate imagination of its opponents picture it, the music-hall keeper could hardly be blamed for supplying it. He has to please his customers like any other tradesman, and he is not bound to be too superior for his business. If trapèze is demanded—trapèze must and will be supplied, and the fogyism which demands the intervention of the Lord Chamberlain is simply ridiculous.

The high musical performances at the best music halls are not so inferior as they have been represented, and they are sufficiently perfect for an average audience. Of course the band, chorus, and solo singer are better at one place than at another; but everywhere an honest desire is shown to do justice to the music. The Canterbury and Oxford Halls deservedly take the first rank; and after these come Weston's and the Islington Philharmonic. Outside places, like the Raglan, Wilton's at the East-end, and Knightsbridge Halls, and others, are of a lower stamp, and rely more upon miscellaneous attractions.

The comic portion of the entertainment is the least satisfactory part, judged by a very lofty standard of wit and humour. The songs certainly are not more forced and unnatural, hard and senseless, than hundreds of productions which are favourites in "society;" but still they are not so good as the sentimental ballads. Good comic songs—full of true humour and character—are very rare; the taste to appreciate them is rarer still; and, therefore, the music halls can hardly be expected to shine in their humorous selections. Some few of the comic performers, like Mr. Mackney, have the true artistic spirit and a considerable share of natural fun, but the majority of them are barely passable. Occasionally they try to make vulgarity take the place of humour, but not more so than many petted low comedians at legitimate theatres.

Much as music halls have increased since the Canterbury Hall was built in 1851, none of them exceed this place of amusement in architectural, musical, and fine art attractions. The noble gallery of pictures attached to the concert-room is an addition which no other music hall possesses, except the night concert-room known as Evans's, in Covent-garden Market. Those who wish to compare the past with the present, may first visit the Mogul in Drury-lane, and then pass on to the Canterbury Hall. The improvement in this class of popular amusement during the last five-and-twenty years will thus be brought strikingly before them. Let us hope that another quarter of a century will bring an improvement for our successors equally striking. Little is gained by cavilling in a narrow, illiberal spirit at what is, and what always will be. There are many worse places of so-called amusement in London than its half-dozen leading music halls. Frowsy *pose plastique* entertainments; coarse, idiotic "Judge and Jury" rooms; and cellars where "spicy" songs may be enjoyed while greasy chops are being devoured, may be attacked with far more justice by public moralists. These are mostly "swell" resorts. Concert-rooms, like the "Canterbury" and others, where two-thirds of the audience consist of tradesmen and working men, with their wives, cannot be very degraded. A mixed assembly, in which a few respectable women have a place, is sure to preserve a certain decency of behaviour, while a gathering of men is not always to be trusted.

Evans's Concert-room, it is true, has purged and lives cleanly, although it harbours none but town and country gentlemen; but its entertainment is not one degree above that of the ordinary music halls. The same singers troll there after they have done in earlier quarters; the same acrobats —those that can be accommodated in the more limited space—fling their limbs about there at 1 A.M. as they have before done in Lambeth or Islington at 9 P.M.; and there is nothing in the performance to justify the exceptional praise which has been lately bestowed upon this "Cave of Harmony."

OLD "MOTHER MEDIUM."

A FEW years ago, before "spiritualism" came into fashion, we had a low class of publications called fortune-telling books, and a low class of sybils called fortune-tellers. The publications were issued by such distinguished publishers as Ryle and Co., of Seven Dials, and they bore such titles as "Napoleon's Book of Fate," "Mother Shipton's Dream Book," "Mother Shipton's Prophecies," "Norwood Gipsy's Popular Dream Book," "Mother Shipton's Prophecies by Cards," "The Gipsy's Oracle," and "The Universal Dreamer." These books, which were sold for a penny or twopence each, found their way into most kitchens, and were often consulted by cooks, housemaids, and footmen. Like all oracles, they were often somewhat obscure in their promises of health, wealth, marriage, and large families, and those who read them with the eye of faith were naturally anxious to have their mysteries explained by competent judges. This encouraged the visits of old women whose power of reading the secrets of the other world was not accompanied by a respect for property. While these women foretold the future to gaping listeners they stole pieces of family plate, or made their dupes help them to silk dresses and other sundries. Such irregular proceedings in the kitchen and servants' hall soon aroused the indignation of the dining and drawing-rooms, and a police raid was made upon all fortune-tellers. The books were raked out of dresser drawers and bandboxes, and burnt, while the old women were prosecuted as thieves and impostors. The kitchen was severely lectured for its "ignorant superstition," and the dining and drawing-rooms thanked God for the benefits of education.

Old Mother Palmcard, turned out of the kitchen, and condemned to six months' luxurious idleness in a prison, had ample leisure for reflection. Far from being reformed by her gentle punishment, she was only convinced that she had made a mistake, and that more money was to be obtained above stairs than below stairs. Too old to alter her own course of action, she merely had her daughter instructed, and that lady, strong in all the showy accomplishments of the hour, instead of being prosecuted as a fortune-teller in the kitchen, was admired as a "medium" in the parlour. Educated delusion was found to be a more pleasant and productive thing to work upon than ignorant superstition, and old "Mother Medium" was fairly started in business. "Mother Medium's" success encouraged the growth of many imitators or competitors, and the power of communicating with the other world soon became one of the recognized professions. Brass plates were put on street doors, cards were printed, advertisements were inserted in certain journals, special "organs" of the profession appeared weekly or monthly, and very business-like circulars were issued. To show that we are not drawing upon imagination for these statements, we print a circular of this kind which was put into our hands a few days ago, and which is circulated without any fear of police interference:—

THE GREATEST DISCOVERY EVER MADE IS THE MEDIATION WRITING DIRECT TO, AND FROM, THE SPIRIT WORLD, IN ONE MINUTE! WITHOUT ANY MECHANISM, EXCEPT PEN, INK, AND PAPER.

MRS. DUKE SAUNDERS, Sibyle Medium, has the extraordinary gift of holding communions and conversation for any length of time and anywhere with the departed in the spirit world, who are not dead, but living, to give the most delightful intelligence of the spirit world they have passed into since they have left the earth; who hail with joy being able to write to their loved ones on the earth, to identify themselves to their bereaved friends. Now if this be true, surely it is the greatest phenomenon ever heard of, and opens the widest field for inquiry and consolation ever known; for what can be more charming than to write to our beloved ones just gone from us, and in a few minutes to receive an answer telling us they are actually more alive now than when on the earth, because they have left the dead material body, and, as St. Paul declares, are a "spiritual body," and are elevated to that sphere they have earned on the earth. What can be more reasonable to the scientific mind than to believe the higher spheres, or planets, are inhabited, as well as our planet the earth? And as we know man has got the power of sending his message from one city to another, is it not reasonable to believe that God has given his progressive spirits, who are in his keeping, in the spirit-world, the power to communicate from one sphere to another sphere, as easy as man can from city to city? If this be denied, it gives more power to man than God! Man's power is mechanical electricity—God's power is spiritual electricity—which as far surpasses the electric telegraph as heaven surpasses the earth! and is a law of nature not yet understood, but is revealed to me through this marvellous writing, which swallows up death in victory! through which many prophecies are written to me! I here declare I have no desire to keep so great a privilege to myself, because I have the power given me to teach others—either believers or sceptics!—to enable them to write to their loved ones, quite independent of me, after I have taught them; who can investigate the truth of this statement for themselves—for what we can do ourselves we know to be true—teaching others will be the best means of making this great gift known. I can commune with the Spirit nearly as soon as it has left the body; Time is no barrier; for no spirit can resist my call!

I have the communions of Adam, God's first man, who has given an account of the universal law, which God gave him; also Father Abraham, Noah, Moses, Aaron, Solomon, Lorenza, St. Paul, St. Peter, John the Baptist, John the Evangelist, Josephus, the Jewish historian; Pilate, Herod, Amphion, King of Thebes; Daniel, and the other prophets, Stephen, Timothy; the Sibyls of the Delphi Temple, and others; Queen Elizabeth, Mary Queen of Scots, Pope, Milton, Lord Bacon, Lord Hastings, the great Sir Isaac Newton, who gives a philosophical explanation of this mediation writing; Swedenborg, who contradicts much he has written; John Bunyan, Titian, the great painter, communicates a full account of his method of painting; and Van Eyck, the inventor of oil painting, gives me his secret of oil painting, so the secret of oil painting by the old masters need never be lost again. Shakespeare, Byron, Burns, and Thackeray write poetry to me. Shakespeare has written his own life from the spirit-world, because I have written him all that has taken place at Stratford relative to himself. Napoleon Bonaparte, Howard, Hall, Sir Matthew Hale, Sir Robert Peel, Sir Francis Burdett, Bloomfield, the Duke of Buckingham, the Duke of Bedford, Sir Benjamin Brodie, Dr. Whately, Lord Lyndhurst, Lord Clyde, Robert Owen, Miss Catharine Sinclair, the Duke of Wellington, Sir John Franklin, Lord Auckland, Hon. Miss Eden, Lady Craven, George IV., King of England, and many others; three communications from the Duchess of Kent, to write to her daughter the Queen Victoria; a great number from our lamented Prince Consort, who has come spontaneously ever since he left the earth, requesting me to write to his beloved Queen, which I did on the 16th November, 1862. And it is by his request I now make it public for the consolation of the world. A book will be published with the communications of all the illustrious characters, as soon as the subscription list is filled up. Subscription, 7*s.* or 10*s.*, according to the binding. The title is given from the spirit world—"The Spirit World; or, the Spirit of the Spirit World." Which will be the most wonderful book ever published—all written by inspiration. Communions and séances held in London, Croydon, and family residences.

FEE.—Teaching to write, £5 (no fee accepted until taught); private communion for one only, £1 1*s.*; communion for three, £1 10*s.*; evening séance, not to exceed seven, £1 1*s.*; communions sent by post, by sending right name or names, and where died, to secure identity (postage stamps enclosed), 10s. Engagements from home, with carriage expenses, in addition to the above fee. Three days' notice will be required to meet engagements. All letters for reply to be addressed to Mrs. Duke Saunders, Keeley Road, Croydon, Surrey. To learn to write independent of me requires from one to three days only, an hour a day.

N.B. Take care of this circular for a friend, as no other will be issued. This circular is printed on the two inside pages, that it may be framed if desired.

Much comment upon a document of this character is not required—the circular speaks for itself. Old "Mother Medium"—like all her tribe—has, doubtless, a good knowledge of the extent of educated delusion to which she addresses herself. There are hundreds, possibly, who believe that she enjoys the confidence of Shakespeare, Swedenborg, Titian, Van Eyck, the late Prince Albert, and the friendship of Thackeray, Byron, Burns, and other departed celebrities. When the volume appears, if it ever appears, in which the communications of these spirits are to be printed, there will be thousands as blind to its absurdities of style as they are now blind to the defects of the wretched literature, science, and art which the "spirit-world" has, at present, given us.

NEST-BUILDING APES.

A LITTLE holiday group, lately standing before M. Du Chaillu's nest-building apes, in the British Museum, bitterly lamented the fact that these animals were not alive. A similar feeling of disappointment was recently experienced at Liverpool, when Mr. Walker arrived from the Gaboon, or Baboon River, bringing to land only a few stuffed skins instead of a tribe of living Gorillas. The public mind has been so prepared by wonderful stories about this missing link of humanity, that thousands were ready to welcome it with all the honours accorded to the Japanese Ambassadors. Lord Monboddo was taken down once more from the dusty library shelf; the theory of progression was looked at with kindly tolerance; and the pot-bellied African stranger was met half way with the acknowledgment that he was all but "a man and a brother."

This sympathetic yearning towards the nest-building ape is probably caused by one of those mysterious affinities which run through the whole animal world. It would be so easy to show that certain gorillas are nest-building men, or that certain men are nest-building apes, that we can hardly wonder at the interest taken in our newly-discovered cousins. If anything would prove that M. Du Chaillu has not been guilty of giving to hairy nothings "a local habitation and a name," it would be the large and easily recognised family of nest-building apes, who have long been taking very active parts in the drama of life. Few of us can lay our paws upon our hearts and say honestly that we are unworthy of this classification. We are constantly gathering the big and little twigs—constantly edging ourselves in from all disasters—constantly making ourselves snug. There is small need to go to a distant howling wilderness for a few dry skins to prove that the nest-building faculty is cultivated by a large and industrious class.

Since the days of Lord Bacon (not to go too far back into the mists of antiquity) it is probable that nest building has been cultivated with great success. We find traces of the art in chapels, churches, and palaces, in town halls, picture galleries and industrial museums. It may be seen in full development at such places as South Kensington; but shops, warehouses, public offices, and a hundred other places are equally governed by it. It reigns almost as absolutely in Tottenham Court Road as it does in Downing Street; in Belgravia and May Fair as in Lombard Street or Chancery Lane. It may be called by various names—such as prudence, industry, success, or, property qualification; because language, like figures, is given to us to conceal the truth.

A very good sample of the nest-building ape—shrewd, active, and watchful—may be seen at the Museum of Universal Taste. He is the main prop of that comfortable institution, and is prepared to raise any number of such nests at the shortest notice, and on the most unreasonable terms. The nest of this knowing ape was first built of the humblest twigs—a structure hideous, but cheap, and therefore not calculated to alarm the British tax-payer. Thick and squat as it appeared, it was the thin edge of the wedge. By slow and silent degrees the nest spread into something between a show and a school, and while it professed to improve the lower orders of the east, its home was at the extreme west of London. Minor nests were built for a number of minor apes; grants of money were got from ear-wigged parliamentary committees; and at last the thick end of the wedge—the full-blown nest—was allowed to emerge from behind the official curtain.

Another thriving specimen of the nest-building ape may be seen any day in the person of the Rev. Mr. Tabernacle. He has covered himself in with a very eligible and valuable freehold by shouting out the Gospel according to St. Lucre. Nothing less than an absolute command of a well-built nest would satisfy the acquisitiveness of this calculating apostle. The hat went round very pushingly for twigs in the name of the Christian faith, and the backward in giving were reminded with sternness that the labourer was worthy of his hire. The nest, like many other similar nests, will always command a good market price, as the title to it is made clear by a good store of worldly precaution.

The official and clerical nest-building apes have worthy companions in the persons of their commercial brethren. The trading ape, wedged up in snug quarters by his cash-books, and ledgers, is generally distinguished for his power of nest-building. He has surrounded himself with banks, insurance offices, and a thousand varieties of nests, each one furnishing homes for other apes, more or less enterprising. In the language of commerce, a nest is often called a "basis of operations," a pretty and expressive name, and one that is not at all offensive. The trading ape generally manages to build his nest, whether he is honest and successful, or dishonest and unsuccessful. In the first case he buys a few small palaces, and takes rank as a merchant prince; in the second he arrives at a smaller degree of comfort and elegance, through a marriage settlement. The nest in the last instance is built with creditors' twigs and put out of the reach of hungry assignees by a legal family conveyance.

The legal profession, who so often build or destroy other people's nests, furnish a very good number of these particular apes. Starring barristers who neglect every case that does not lead to notoriety; who address juries from half-built nests only to collect more twigs, or to be lifted bodily into a warm woolsacky retreat, are certainly no unworthy members of this species. The web-spinning lawyer, who partly feeds the barrister—who looks out from a bower of bills of costs—is about as fine a specimen of the "nest-building ape" as any fancier of the tribe would like to examine. They all have one little fault—selfishness—a little too strongly developed; they all believe devoutly in the same worldly-wise maxim—each one for himself and God for us all. And yet are they not all "men and brethren?"

PAUPER TESTIMONIALS.

We are not going to say anything harsh or unkind about he poor—to jump upon those who are already down—lthough we are compelled to quarrel with a few paupers. n theory, we believe, a pauper is one who has nothing in he world, who resides in a workhouse, and is maintained t the public expense. In practice, however, it occasionally appears that paupers have the command of money nd property, the power of granting rewards, and of preenting testimonials. The matron of a metropolitan workouse lately received a gift in the shape of a handsome ing, the purchase-money of which was subscribed mostly n halfpence or farthings.

This gift was described as a remarkable testimonial, nd we quite agree with the description. Testimonials re either investments of capital, made for a purpose, and iven with a "lively sense of future favours," or they are uxuries which certain good-natured people have a fancy or indulging in. These gifts have become so common f late, and so notoriously a part of our great advertising ystem, that they have lost all the value they ever had as igns of merit on one side, and appreciation on the other. Sometimes the manager of a theatre insists upon having he presentation of a testimonial to a popular actor proided for in the engagement; and sometimes the actor stipulates for the right of making the same ostentatious gift to the manager. Sometimes a body of workmen combine to present a testimonial to a foreman or an employer, forgetting that certificates of character are not given by servants to masters. If a servant stays with one employer for twenty years, he is a living proof of that employer's fairness, liberality, and amiable qualities, and electro-plated teapots or platters would not add to the weight of this testimony, although they might interfere with the healthy working of trade. There is no saying how much bad and uncertain labour many an employer has tolerated, after receiving the fatal goblet, or how much tyranny a workman may have endured from a master, rather than fly in the face of a former testimonial.

If the lowest kind of labourer, however, thinks fit to subscribe to a testimonial, he is spending money that he has fairly earned, whatever may be thought of its application. This is not the case with the pauper. He is not a labourer; he lives only to receive, not to give; he has no capital to invest, either prudently or imprudently; he has no right to indulge in luxuries. While he "sits enchanted in workhouses" where there is no work, he is a parish pensioner; and even when he is employed in any humble task, his wages are not his own, unless they show a balance after paying for his lodging, board, and clothing. It is always pleasing to know that good feeling exists between workhouse inmates and workhouse managers; but such "remarkable testimonials" hardly prove this, procured, as they must be, with the ratepayers' money.

MUTUAL TESTIMONIALS.

It is not often that we step out of our character as literary journalists to advocate the claims of a particular club, association, or trading company; and we are only induced to do so in the present instance from a conviction that a mutual testimonial society is destined to supply a great and constantly increasing public want.

Who has not hungered, at some period or another, for a testimonial and its accompanying presentation? Indeed, testimonial presentations are coveted more than the testimonials themselves. It is so delightful to find yourself the centre of attraction; to hear yourself addressed in those unqualified terms of admiration which are peculiar to testimonials and after-dinner speeches; to see the box which contains the plate brought forward, carefully closed, or the tea-service standing up in the middle of the table, under an impenetrable cover, as if you were not at all aware of the form and value of the approaching gift: finally, to rise up, beaming over the top of your glittering acquisitions, and tell the company how utterly unworthy you know you are of them. This is indeed the proudest moment of your life—no matter what the testimonial, or who the presenters. Of course, it is better to have a diamond ring than a silver snuff-box; a duke to present it from a company of lords, than a publican from a number of admiring cricketers;

but the peculiarity of testimonials is that they set aside all questions of value, and leap over all barriers of rank. The master of a workhouse has been gratified by receiving a substantial token of his paupers' regard, purchased with their united, determined, and desperate savings out of —— we are really not in a position to say exactly what. The leading member of a pantomimic company has received an appropriate acknowledgment (a wooden leg, perhaps) from the assembled carpenters and machinists of the theatre, for his urbanity and skill in the most trying positions of trap-sinking, leap-catching, and suspension. A principal tragedian has become the centre-piece of a spectacular ceremony, in which a massive goblet has been put into his hands (according to agreement) by the lessee of the establishment, the one attired as Macbeth, the other as Macduff, and the whole of the witches and soldiers of the tragedy being present to applaud the crowning of merit. The superintendent of a cotton-mill has been astonished by receiving his full-length portrait, painted in oil, and paid for by a penny subscription of the workpeople, as a reward for he does not know exactly what. In like manner, the Fossil Association, for the promotion of looking back, have elected the Earl of Cryptgrub an honorary member, as a testimonial for his liberality in throwing open for public inspection the ancient pump of St. Aloes the Martyr. The captain of the "Wheezy Neptune" penny steamboat has been presented by the youth of London with a mounted meerschaum-pipe, for his boldness in destroying that oppressive regulation which forbade all smoking abaft the funnel.

Hundreds of such cases of rewarded merit must have come within the observation of every discerning man, and shall thousands of instances of painful neglect be passed over unnoticed? It is not given to us all to be masters of workhouses, an affable clown, an overwhelming tragedian, a superintendent of grateful factory hands, the proprietors of historical relics, or the popular captain of a popular steam-boat. Most of us are compelled to walk in a way of life upon which the shadow of a testimonial and its presentation has never fallen. Some of us have been tantalized with waking dreams, excited with feeble promises, and sickened with deferred hopes.

It is, therefore, to supersede the delicate and troublesome labour of organizing testimonial-presentations, and to assure to every man—no matter who or what he may be, as long as he is a subscriber—a public and satisfactory acknowledgment of merit, that the Mutual Testimonial Association has been established.

The plan of the association is very simple. What has been found to work with advantage in the case of Christmas goose-clubs, or coal-clubs, is applied with but few alterations to the ordinary testimonial. A payment of a certain sum (which has yet to be determined upon) shall secure to each member, according to a rotation to be decided by lottery, the gratification of receiving a graceful and showy work of art, with all the honours of a public presentation. The association, in its corporate capacity, shall take the lead in thus exalting its individual member; who will, for the time during which the ceremony lasts, become detached from the general body. As each subscriber who has been a receiver will be compelled under a stringent rule to join the amiable ranks of the givers, the system will ensure the desirable result that everybody shall, in succession, present something to everybody. That nothing may be wanted to secure the perfection of the presentations, the Mutual Testimonial Association have arranged with several social orators of undoubted talent, who will undertake that the speeches, while warmed with the proper degree of personal friendship, shall be worthy of the most classic efforts of the ancient Greeks and Romans.

In one important respect the Mutual Testimonial Association will differ from the goose-clubs and coal-clubs, before alluded to. In those societies the prizes or drawings are not only consumed, but nearly all the members require to receive them at the same time. With the Lord Mayor's festival comes the necessity for fire; and with Christmas or Michaelmas comes the demand for poultry. A certain weight of coals and a certain number of birds have thus to be provided for each subscriber. This will not be the case with the articles presented by the Mutual Testimonial Association. Each member, according to the chance of the lottery, will wait his turn; and, as the evidence furnished to the society's promoters and projectors has proved that every material testimonial finds its way to the auction mart within a certain number of months, the rate of subscription will be proportionately low, for, with a little care and management, one specimen of metallic art may be made to do the whole presentation work of the Mutual Testimonial Association.

THE TWO CLERKS.

A GREAT noise has lately been made about competitive examination for the Civil Service, and it is looked upon by many people as a great root and branch reform. It is one of the prettiest inventions of a compact governing class that has been seen for some time. It is not contrived in the interests of financial economy, nor to honestly sift the corn from the chaff, but to test the ability of an army of applicants by a highly ornamental standard of education. There is nothing like it in the whole trading and commercial world. A knowledge of the classics, of ancient and modern history, of mathematics, of Shakespeare, taste, and the musical glasses, is not demanded of every clerk who applies at the door of a merchant's counting-house. He is asked if he knows the difference between debtor and creditor, between his right hand and his left, if he can cast up a column of figures, or balance an intricate account. If he can write legibly, his testimonials are looked into, and, if they are satisfactory, he is engaged at once; but only on trial. His whole life of servitude is nothing but a constant trial. The moment he fails in his work he is discharged. He is not made to feel the moment he is engaged that, behave well or ill, so long as he shuffles through his work, no matter how slovenly, he is safe for life. The only hold which he has upon his employer and his position is the punctual fulfilment of his duties. The only hold which his employer has upon him is the payment of his market value at the appointed time. There is no sentiment or patronage on either side. The clerk knows if his master were to die to-morrow he would very speedily get the same salary elsewhere; the master knows if his clerk were to leave him that day he could get another at the same price in the course of the afternoon. On both sides there is perfect freedom and perfect independence. Fidelity of trust is not secured by paying the clerk three times his value. There are responsible offices whose business it is to guarantee honesty for a small annual premium. There are doubtless many faithful servants and scrupulously honest men in the world, but policies of insurance have neither human feelings nor human frailties, and they cannot err. All this may sound very harsh and unfeeling, but upon no other basis could the affairs of this world be carried on. The affairs of Government must belong to another world, for they are managed in a very different manner.

The Government clerk braces up his nerves and his intellect, and hastily crams his memory for a Civil Service Examination. He is questioned on things he will never have occasion to know in the discharge of his official duties, including possibly the names of Homer's ships, and a list of Actæon's hounds; and he displays a knowledge which he had not yesterday, and which he will probably lose to-morrow. He passes, and in a few days he finds himself in the receipt of a salary which he is very glad to get, but which he was never asked if he would accept. Its amount is not based upon any estimate of his market value, but is a proportionate step downwards from the Lord Chancellor's or the Prime Minister's stipend. The clerk is perfectly satisfied, for his duties are light, his prospects are good, and he receives at starting about three times his value. When financial reformers complain of this in the House of Commons, they are answered that the situations of Government are all so highly responsible as to require high salaries to be given to secure fidelity in those who fill them. Guarantee Societies, and their operation, are not so well known in Downing Street as in 'Mincing Lane or Cheapside. How should they be, when the money so lavishly expended is given by the nation, and is never likely to fail? Merchants go into the Gazette when their expenditure has been unwise and excessive; nations only borrow or repudiate. When the Government clerk retires in full health, after a not very lengthy period of service, he receives every year as a pension always one-half and sometimes two-thirds of his salary. If his office is proved useless, or even mischievous, and is at last abolished, after a severe parliamentary struggle, he applies for ample compensation, if it is not voluntarily thrust upon him, and immediately obtains it. That his position is more than acceptable to him is proved by his tenacious retention of it. Rare, indeed, is it to see a resignation of a Government official, and when a discharge of officers really takes place, from the natural death of a department (a very rare occurrence), it is lamentable to see the helpless condition of the outcast wanderers. They are like men who have been shut up in a dark cell for half a century, and who are suddenly sent forth into the full glare of daylight. They find their level, but it is generally a very low one,—the level of their market value; and there are no magic doors open where, by a competitive examination,—the parrot-like trick of uttering a few common-places and answering a few questions,—they can attain a degree, of permanent remuneration allotted with little reference to the labour exacted in return.

One-half of the civil expenditure of Government might be swept away, and the Civil Service be improved by the operation. The whole system of patronage should be rooted out, our ministers being fully paid as it is, without having this other inducement to fight for office. There should be no more favour shown in filling up an under-secretaryship than in appointing an under-butler. Vacancies should be advertised in the newspapers, and those got who are qualified to fill them, and who will do the work at the market price. The hours of labour should be lengthened, the recesses shortened, pensions, compensations and life appointments abolished, guarantees for honesty exacted, and superintendents of departments appointed, who should be paid by a percentage upon the savings of their offices, and not by a premium upon the waste.

A NEW MONUMENT.

There are not wanting many distinguished authorities in this country who declare the national debt to be a national benefit. We are told what a stimulus it gives to native industry; and with what awe it strikes neighbouring and belligerent states. We are favoured with a picture of all Europe trembling before a nation that can bear on its shoulders eight hundred millions of liability, and whistle as it goes for want of thought. It is a fine sight to see a people paying eight-and-twenty millions of interest every year; and a fine specimen of logic to prove that because they appear contented, this payment must really do them a deal of good. It is not, perhaps, made quite so clear as it ought to be how the working man is benefited when the tax-gatherer takes half-a-crown out of every pound he earns, and hands it over to another person called a fundholder. It is admitted that every working man is taxed up to thirty per cent. of his income, and as the interest of the national debt is three-sevenths of the present national expenditure, it follows that this proportion of industrial taxation must go in this direction. The working man may sometimes think, in his hours of reflection, that he could do much better with those numberless half-crowns, by spending them on himself, than anybody—especially the tax-gatherer—appears to be able to do for him. His wife may possibly share the same feeling when she looks at her faded dress; and she may share it much more deeply still when she looks perhaps, at some of her faded children. To add to the bitterness of the deprivation, they are left in utter darkness as to what they are paying for. The sum is surely, though occultly, demanded, and yet no bill of particulars is delivered. They may be told how grandly they are keeping faith with the national creditor; but this information is far too vague to dispel their ignorance. They may hear, in a general way, if they are painstaking and bent on knowledge, that the ministers of the last hundred years have lost a costly American war, and gained a costly victory over France, and another over Russia. When they press still further to be told how these things concern them, they will either be pushed on one side, or ordered to call at a more convenient season. When a financial reformer enlightens them at last, they are often prompted to shake off their burdens by an immediate and ill-considered emigration.

The actions, however, of common people of this class are entitled to no more respect than their ignorant opinions. When the voice of learning, influence, and authority proclaims loudly that national debts are a blessing to the country, though, in defiance of all known arithmetic, it is only the weakest of intellects that would not believe it. If the voice of authority is right—as, of course, it is—it should not be left to bawl itself hoarse, when so many plans might be carried out that would aid its useful teaching. We will only take one that particularly strikes us, by way of example. Why is the national debt—our own national debt—never honoured by the erection of a substantial monument? The men who helped to create the debt are raised in stone to the clouds, but the debt itself can boast of no columns, except the columns of the Exchequer ledgers.

If the debt works only half the good that is claimed for it by its supporters, it is worthy of any distinction that a grateful people can bestow upon it. As an educational instrument, a pillar, such as commemorates the fire of London, would be of infinite value. Let its surface be inscribed with a short history of how the eight hundred millions was spent; of the cost of the American war, in which we were not able to do ourselves an injury by retaining an expensive and unwilling colony; of the cost of the French war, in which we fought against an idea that still exists in full vigour upon the French throne; and of the cost of the late Russian war, in which we succeeded in freeing Turkey from Russian domination for about the space of half an hour. Let this be done, and the seven hundred and fifty millions sterling that went in these three chimerical enterprises, will tell their instructive story to every man who reads as he runs. Such a monument will rival in importance the far-famed column on Fish Street Hill, because it will represent a far greater amount of destruction and waste; while, in appearance, it will resemble that well-known Bastille pillar that spires upwards in Paris, recording the names of those men who perished in besieging the hateful prison, and thought that, by sweeping away its stone and mortar, they had triumphed for ever over injustice and wrong.

MY M.P.

We have all got our peculiar fancies for Members of Parliament, and I have got mine. Some people like a giggling member, some a flowery member, and some a jaunty member. Some like to be represented by a lord, some by an author, and some by a retired prize-fighter. Some never object to a member who sits *on* them rather than *for* them; and others like to see their town or borough always in print, dragged about at the heels of their representative, like a tea-kettle at a dog's tail.

None of these members, I must say, exactly hit my taste—perhaps because my taste is somewhat eccentric. My Member of Parliament is not a popular member; he is not on the right road to become a minister; and he can hardly be called a popular man. He is not an Irishman, nor yet a Scotchman, nor yet an Englishman in the narrow and provincial sense. He cannot see the advantage which his country derives from Quixotic wars, nor the particularly English character of money at ten per cent., bread at a shilling the four-pound loaf, hundreds of thousands of the population declaring on the parishes, and a full "Times" column of mercantile bankruptcies in every Wednesday's and Saturday's "Gazette." He does not throw up his hat when intelligence arrives of the seizure and destruction of so many thousand quarters of the enemy's corn, because he knows that the inevitable result must be a considerable rise in that article of produce on the next market-day in Mark Lane. He is not surprised when he hears of European complications at a time when the diplomatic horizon looks peaceable and calm, because he knows how such a state of things may occur at any moment, while four millions of armed men, to say nothing of volunteers and ambitious officers, are prowling about the civilized countries of the world, and following fighting as a trade.

My Member of Parliament is considered, in certain quarters, to be a common, vulgar man—a man of no breeding, a man of no blood. He is admitted to be clever—decidedly clever—clever in his way, such a way as it is; but very crotchety and unreliable. Whippers-in of party-clotted Governments have never been able to make anything of him, and they have, at last, resigned the task in despair. He is said to be sulky in temper, unsociable in habits, a vegetarian and a teetotaller, because he never accepts a ministerial invitation to dine. He is accounted impracticable; he is said to be rash; he is stigmatized as factious and destructive; and he is known to be troublesome. He is so dreadfully sceptical that he believes in nothing—not even in the perfection of Government departments, although they are headed by the leading men in the State. He cannot participate in his country's joy that the Right Hon. James Baggs has been invested by the Ministry of the hour with the First Lordship of the Rotten Fleet Department, because he knows how the same rapture will be exhibited when the same able administrator is transferred, in due course, or under a political convulsion, to the Home Office, the Exchequer Chancellorship, or the Board of Trade. My Member of Parliament cannot bring himself to think that any man can have properly qualified himself for each and all of those varied departments, before he had any idea that the mantle of Burke was about to descend upon him, in the shape of a small and manageable borough, in the gift of a patron too aged to represent it himself, or holding an hereditary seat in the Upper House. My Member of Parliament has never been taken under the sheltering wing of such a venerable or noble patron; has never benefited by circulars issued from large wholesale City houses to every small tradesman who happens to possess the political birthright of a vote, and who happens to stand on the debit side of their ledgers. He has never reaped any advantage from publicans being suddenly gladdened with an increase in the billeting allowance for soldiers of more than two hundred per cent.; nor from the magisterial appointments of a county being suddenly multiplied more than ten-fold.

He has never gathered a rate, an adherent, nor a committee man, because the royal fountain of honour has been made to play for the pleasure and profit of those in office, and has obediently scattered the spray of its decorations over every dirty political outcast pushed forward to be scented and washed. The whole civil, military, naval, and miscellaneous expenditure of forty millions every year, though fruitful of support to those who conduct it, is barren to him, and it only exists as a force against which he has long contended, and will always have to contend to the end of his factious impracticable days.

My Member of Parliament has not moulded himself upon Pitt and Fox, because he does not believe in the wisdom of the first, nor in the common honesty of the second. As he does not shake the senate all the night, and shake the dice-box all the morning, or shake the treasury money-bags into his own pockets when the chance occurs, there is very little hope of his taking Mr. Fox as his model, or being taken as a model by those who have been taught to worship Mr. Fox.

His estimate of Mr. Pitt, and that heaven-born minister's policy—especially in finance—is so peculiarly unfavourable, that my member of Parliament must either be an "atheist," or what would have been considered one in those stormy political days. How many of the mean, scurvy scoundrels, the dangerous rebels, the un-English supporters of the "Corsican tyrant," and the traitorous villains who reviled Mr. Pitt, are now honoured and sacred in the memory of unblemished children and admirers, it would take a long, long chapter to tell. As my Member of Parliament, if he had sat under the heaven-born minister, would have been equally shunned and reviled by the virtuous, disinterested supporters of that great and infallible man, it is fair to assume that another fifty years of the future will improve his reputation, as fifty years of the past have improved the reputation of the "atheists" and low radical wretches who went before him.

My Member of Parliament has the misfortune to be afflicted with a knowledge of figures—a dangerous gift—which has done more to render him unpopular in the "House" than even his "factious," "impracticable," and independent votes. He cannot learn the advantage of national debts, though he has often heard them called "flea-bites" in the course of debate; but his voice has little authority when he exposes the fallacy of such arguments, and the pressure of such burdens, because it *only* appeals to facts and principles, and not to a practical experience of the Chancellor of the Exchequer's chair. To have actually received a deputation of capitalists, who come to propose for a loan, or to have actually touched a Treasury warrant, or directed the payment of Exchequer bills, is the sole teaching supposed to furnish that necessary amount of wisdom to the oracle, which gives it a claim to the attention of the House. My Member of Parliament has a disagreeable knack—disagreeable to those in office—of kicking the financial sores of the administration, for which he is accused of obstructing the business of the day. He gives a deal of trouble to under-secretaries and political fags, for which his name is held in abhorrence, and used as a bogie to frighten junior clerks. He is not easily put off with an incomplete answer; and when he has shown an eleven years' deficit of five millions sterling in the whole Rotten Fleet Department, he is not satisfied to be shown an annual saving, on the other side, of sixty-one pounds, the result of reducing the hundred-a-year pensions of a storekeeper's foreman and an inspector of shipwrights in one of the dockyards—about thirty pounds each. When he hears of a Post Office Government contract to pay three thousand pounds a fortnight for carrying ten pounds' worth of letters to America, by way of Galway, and bringing another ten pounds' worth of letters home, he does not scruple to tell the only possible and gifted Government that they are purchasing their political support at the dearest market-rate.

My Member of Parliament has often been asked who he is, and the reply, in the early part of his career, was not considered satisfactory. He is not a contractor looking for a job; he is not a barrister looking for a place; he is not a weak-minded man of property, ruled by a wife, who is looking for a title; he is not the nominee of a landed patriarch; but simply the representative of a large, wild, untameable constituency, and nothing more. This is not the sort of member to be received without a struggle; and he is consequently closely watched, that he may be found tripping in history and the letter H. His principles, of course, are of little importance in an assembly which is governed, not by measures, but by men; and his doctrines are received with the same contempt as the preaching of the Apostle was some eighteen centuries and a half ago, when it was not looked upon as the Gospel according to St. John, but the raving of a fanatical fisherman who was hopelessly mad. What makes the matter worse, his speeches are coherent, close, and finished; he is perfectly acquainted with the subject upon which he speaks; his historical allusions are without a flaw; and his aspiration and use of the talismanic letter H are worthy of a curate, or a pedantic schoolmaster. Those who are eager witnesses of his perfection in this latter trick, or accomplishment, are silently compelled to admit, that he satisfies their highest notions of all statesman-like skill, and of the whole duty of man.

SUCKING BRITANNIA.

ONCE every year—on or about the day known as All Fools' Day—the country has to listen to its financial statement. This statement, or Budget, is made by the Chancellor of the Exchequer—an officer who comes in and goes out with ministries. This Chancellor may, or may not, be an able man; his notions of taxation may be brilliant or commonplace; he may be industrious, he may be indolent; he may be full of ingenuity, bold in expedients, and sound in principles, or he may be nothing more than the mere mouthpiece of a Treasury clerk; but, for the time being, with the sanction of Parliament, he governs the national balance-sheet. Having collected estimates of the probable national expenditure, or Rule Britannia side of the account, for the twelvemonth under consideration, he goes to the other, or Suck Britannia side—amongst the sugar, gin, malt, bill-stamps, and tradesmen, to see where the money is to come from. On the Rule Britannia side of his department—in his palatial drawing-rooms—he dispenses his millions with an open hand; while, as Britannia's factor, he collects some of his pence by taxing lollipops, and seizing poor men's bedsteads.

Since the days when Chancellors of the Exchequer were invented, the country has had some eccentric and jocular financiers. • The more eccentric and jocular the financier, of course the more comic were the taxes imposed. One inventive genius in the art of Sucking Britannia thought it would be a good thing to tax bachelors, and an equally good, though somewhat contradictory thing, to tax widowers. This was in 1695. When the bachelor or widower tried to escape from this tax by getting married, the clever financier had him on the hip with another impost. Marriages were taxed as well as celibacy, and even births and burials were made to contribute to the Treasury. Later financiers revived most of these imposts, adding to these taxes on deaths and christenings. The tax upon the birth of children was revived at a time when the good citizen was exhorted to increase his family, when the expenditure was very heavy, the National Debt growing apace, and financiers began to see an excuse for a large outlay in a large and increasing population.

A great advance has been made during the last quarter of a century in the art of sucking Britannia. The amount drawn from the resources of the country is still large—some think, with good show of reason, unnecessarily large—but it is drawn with less determination to favour the few at the expense of the many. The general apathy and ignorance existing with regard to the details of national finance, is an encouragement to Exchequer Chancellors not to do their duty. Our budgets, in all probability, would be wiser and more just if general education included something about taxes and taxation. At present, with the exception of the small doses of political economy administered at the universities, it includes nothing. Knowledge about the National Debt, the Consolidated Fund, and direct and indirect taxation, may be picked up by inquiring youths, as savages pick up the knack of wearing dress-coats and riding in cabs; but this can only be done by "self-help" and studying, not reading the newspapers. Few public teachers step forward to teach such lessons, the task not being showy and popular, but occasionally a speaker or lecturer is found who cares more for utility than popularity. Such a lecturer has appeared lately in the person of Mr. Thomas Hankey, the well-known banker and member of Parliament, who judiciously employed what little leisure he had during the parliamentary recess in delivering a descriptive lecture on taxes and expenditure.* Mr. Hankey is not an avowed financial reformer, and seems inclined to support the existing state of things, but the value of his lecture will be found in its clear statement of details. How little, the lecturer considered, was known of those details, even in banking circles in the City, may be gathered from the fact that the lecture was delivered at the Bank of England Library and Literary Institute. At this dead season of Parliament we may profitably employ a few of our pages in giving the substance of this lecture, with a few remarks which may seem to us good in passing.

In former times there used to be a great state officer called a Lord High Treasurer, who often had no treasure to guard, and who often had to deal with payments in kind, which might be wool or any other material. This treasurer, however, has been superseded by a set of commissioners appointed by the Crown, whenever there is a change of ministers, the chief of whom is called the First Lord of the Treasury, and is generally, though not necessarily, the prime minister. The financial duties of the ministry, however, are always performed by another of the commissioners, called the Chancellor of the Exchequer, whose special duty it is to see that the proceeds of Sucking Bri-

Published by Effingham Wilson.

tannia are equal to the cost of Ruling Britannia. He calls for estimates, some of which, such as the amount required to be spent on the army and navy, are supposed to be considered by the cabinet, that is, by the ministers in a body, and when these estimates have been approved, their total is ascertained, and then begins the task of selecting the taxes. If the Chancellor of the Exchequer has to propose a larger expenditure than his last year's or expected forthcoming income will meet, he has then to ask Parliament to sanction an increase in some old tax, or the imposition of a new tax; but if he can make out an excess of probable income on paper, he asks it either to reduce or abolish one or more existing imposts. When his scheme has been sanctioned by Parliament, his duties may be considered theoretically at an end. The heads of each department, such as the army or navy, ask Parliament to sanction their own estimates, and when there is no special representative of the department in the House of Commons—the House in which all money bills originate—the duty then devolves upon the Secretary of the Treasury, but not upon the Chancellor of the Exchequer. The Secretary of the Treasury is the generally recognized authority respecting the expenditure of the country, excepting for the army and navy.

The estimates, having been already laid before Parliament for some weeks previous to their being taken into consideration, are then put to the vote in the House of Commons, and when voted, the first step, but only the first step, has been gained. No money can really be got at until an Act of Parliament has been formally passed for a transfer of money from the Exchequer Account at the Bank of England or Ireland. This Act is very properly called a Consolidated Fund or Ways and Means Act, and it directs the Comptroller of the Exchequer to obey a royal warrant granted by the Crown to the Lords of the Treasury, and to order a transfer of money from the Exchequer Account to such other accounts as require money for those services in ruling Britannia which have been specified in the votes of the House of Commons. It is the duty of the Speaker to take care that no larger sum is granted for the use of the Treasury in this way, than the total amount of the votes which have actually been passed from time to time in Committees of Supply. Formerly, a much larger proportion of the expenditure than at present was sanctioned by previous Acts of Parliament, consequently, a much smaller sum came annually under the control of Parliament. All the money received on account of the government is considered to belong to the Consolidated Fund. It is paid in as received to the Bank of England or Ireland, placed to the Exchequer Account, and cannot be touched without the sanction of an Act of Parliament, either passed at the time, or which has already been passed, and is then in full force. Towards the close of every session the financial legislation is completed by the passing of an Appropriation Bill, which appropriates every separate vote that has passed the House of Commons during the session, and completes the "ways and means" necessary to meet these votes.

This is the extent of parliamentary control over the cost of ruling Britannia, and it is now necessary to describe the general heads of our annual national expenditure.

First and foremost in the account is the charge for interest and management of the National Debt, and this amounts, in round numbers, to about twenty-six millions sterling. Those who are inclined to make the best of a bad bargain—and amongst them we must include Mr. Thomson Hankey—see in this debt of eight hundred millions a gratifying proof of the soundness of our credit, and not of the fatal facility which governments have of borrowing. Nothing is more easy than to pledge the earnings of posterity. This debt is eminently a fighting debt. It began with a sum of more than half a million at the Revolution of 1688, and increased to nearly thirteen millions during the reign of William the Third, under the title of the "King's Debt." At the accession of Queen Anne it was called the "National Debt," and it increased during her reign to thirty-six millions. George the First received it at this amount, and passed it on to George the Second as more than fifty-two millions; George the Second passed it on to George the Third as one hundred and two millions; and George the Third, owing to the American War of Independence and the French revolutionary war, with subsidies and aids to European powers, found it one hundred and two and left it eight hundred and thirty-five millions. George the Fourth—"the finest gentleman of Europe"—passed it on to William the Fourth as seven hundred and eighty-five millions—decreased fifty millions—and William the Fourth passed it on to Queen Victoria as nearly seven hundred and eighty-eight millions. In Queen Victoria's reign, up to the close of March, 1863, the debt has been increased by a little more than twelve millions. The interest which has been paid on this debt from 1691 to 1863 (inclusive) has amounted to more than two thousand two hundred and thirty-six millions sterling. The debt is chiefly a funded or book debt, and is managed by the Bank of England—the earliest creditors of the country—at an annual charge of about two hundred and one thousand pounds.

The next item in the account is for various charges on the Consolidated Fund, of a permanent nature, amounting to one million and eight hundred and eighty-four thousand pounds. More than four hundred and five thousand pounds of this sum is apportioned for the Civil List and pensions granted by the Crown. This is a national grant, in place of all the former hereditary income of the Crown, which is divided into six classes, and any surplus from one class cannot be taken to supply a deficiency in the other. For this reason, a prudent monarch is compelled to be economical, and not to pay fancy prices for Windsor Castle Theatricals, or works of promising young artists. If we add to this sum about forty-three thousand pounds for the repairs and maintenance of the royal palaces, and one hundred and two thousand pounds which is paid to the other members of the royal family, we shall find that it requires about five hundred and fifty thousand pounds every year to support the dignity of the Crown and of the royal family.

The next item to the Civil List is one of about two hundred and seventy-four thousand pounds for annuities and pensions. This list includes kings, heroes, and ex-ministers of a certain standing, and one reverend gentleman who, as ex-Hanaper-keeper, and ex-patentee (not inventor) of bankrupts, receives eleven thousand three hundred and eighty pounds, or nearly three times as much as the son of the Duke of Wellington.

Next come salaries and allowances, more than one hundred and fifty-six thousand pounds; then diplomatic salaries and pensions, more than one hundred and seventy-one thousand pounds; and then a charge of more than six hundred and ninety thousand pounds for courts of justice. This is made up of salaries to judges and compensations, owing to reforms in the administration of justice, and the large round sum we have given, excludes a few odd pounds and a mysterious sixpence.

A group of "miscellaneous charges" follow, which includes Russian-Dutch Loan and Greek Loan (both war charges), Annuity to Greenwich Hospital, and sums devoted to the improvement of harbours in the Isle of Man (one-ninth of the revenue received from customs in that island), ten thousand pounds devoted to "secret service," which is only part of the sum annually placed at the disposal of the Crown to be used in this way, and between sixteen and seventeen thousand pounds paid to his Royal Highness the Prince of Wales, as Duke of Cornwall, to compensate him for loss of duties on tin.

These sums, with the interest on the National Debt, together amount to something over twenty-eight millions, and are commonly called the charges on the Consolidated Fund. They have been created by general Acts of Parliament, and are not, therefore, necessarily brought under the annual consideration of the House of Commons.

The remainder of the annual charges for ruling Britannia amounts to something over forty-one millions, and this sum is subject to the annual control of Parliament in the votes given in what is called Committee of Supply. The first two of these charges—about sixteen millions and a quarter, and nearly eleven millions and a half—are for the army and navy, the total being nearly twenty-eight millions. Ten years ago our fighting expenditure was only sixteen millions, but the Russian war raised it to a level from which it shows no symptoms of sinking. We get for this outlay about one hundred and fifty thousand effective men of all ranks in our army, and about seventy-six thousand men in our navy, with one hundred and fifty vessels of war in commission.

The next item in the account of expenditure is for Miscellaneous Civil Service, and this amounts to about eight millions. These charges are divided in the votes of the House of Commons into seven general divisions, such as public works (a bricklayers', plasterers', and gardeners' division); salaries, out of which are paid all the public officers of the thirty-six public offices, except those provided for in the Consolidated Fund, and the clerks in the War-offices and Admiralty; law and justice, which absorb about three millions and a half; education, which absorbs nearly a million and a half; colonial charges, superannuations and retiring allowance, and miscellaneous charges. We then come to the cost of collecting the public revenue. This was formerly deducted from the income received by the revenue departments, and consequently no annual estimate was ever submitted to Parliament to show at what cost the public revenue was collected. A change, however, and a very important one, was made chiefly in 1854, since which the whole of the expenditure has been brought before Parliament, and annually voted in Committee of Supply. The total cost of the three departments—customs, inland revenue (excise), and post offices—and land revenues and superannuations—is about five millions and a half. The number of clerks and others employed by the customs is about five thousand three hundred, with an average salary of about one hundred and forty pounds; in the inland revenue, about five thousand, with an average salary of about one hundred and sixty pounds; and in the Post-office, about twenty-five thousand, with an average salary of about eighty pounds.

These sums, with a special vote of a million for fortifications, amount altogether to nearly seventy millions and a half, the cost of ruling Britannia for a twelvemonth; and we now have to examine the other side of the account, the income side—the side on which Britannia is sucked always as much as she will bear sucking.

The first great source of revenue is found in the customs duties—customs, many sound financiers think, that would be more honoured in the breach than in the observance. These duties produce about twenty-four millions—the chief sums being about six millions and a half drawn from sugar and its varieties; nearly six millions drawn from tobacco and snuff; five millions and a half drawn from tea, and nearly three millions drawn from spirits. The other heads of customs revenue are wine, corn, coffee, fruits, wood, and timber (a protective duty), pepper, and a few other articles. Our tariff about twenty years ago contained about one thousand articles which were forbidden to sail in untaxed, but now the tariff contains only fifty-one articles so taxed. Even with this great reform, however, it is far from being perfect, and those who believe that we enjoy free trade in corn will be surprised to hear that an annual million sterling is still drawn from this staple article of food.

Next come the duties collected by the inland revenue department. These are divided into excise, stamps, land and general taxes, and income and property tax. The excise duties are levied principally on two articles, spirits and malt, the first producing nearly nine millions and a half, and the second nearly five millions and a half. The other divisions are licences, railways, stage-carriages, game certificates, hackney-carriages, and sundries. The taxes on railways and carriages are all bad, being checks upon the free circulation of goods and men.

The Stamp Duties are collected from legacies and successions (a tax upon capital and not upon income), from fire and marine insurances (a tax upon prudence), from probates of wills, deeds, bills of exchange, penny stamps on cheques, etc., producing altogether about nine millions.

The first item under the head of taxes—officially so called—is the Land-Tax, the oldest impost in England, which produces about one million. It is based on a valuation made in 1695, which no one supposes can represent the value at the present time, but any attempt to rearrange this tax so as to produce more money would be nothing less than confiscation. The Assessed Taxes are raised on inhabited houses, male servants, carriages, horses, mules, and dogs, hair-powder, and armorial bearings. They produce about two millions every year.

Next comes the Income and Property Tax—a very direct tax—first invented or applied in England by Mr. Pitt, and successively repealed and reimposed by many Chancellors of the Exchequer. Of all the various modes of Sucking Britannia, this is the one which is the least popular, both with financiers and the public. If all the income sucked from Britannia were to be sucked in this way, Britannia would have to be ruled, as she was thirty years ago, at half the present cost. This prospect appears so awful, that the tax is not popular with tax-makers. The public dislike the impost because it is a direct stand-and-deliver tax, and prefer to be quietly bled to death by the indirect operations of Customs and Excise. The Income Tax now produces about ten millions and a half.

Next is the income derived from the Post-office. The gross produce of this department for letter-carrying and banking is about three millions and eight hundred thousand pounds; and the total expenditure in carriage of mails, buildings, postage-stamps, salaries, etc. (about three millions), being deducted from this, leaves a profit of about eight hundred thousand pounds. This is a nice sum for a Chancellor of the Exchequer to receive for the use of the country; but it can only be looked upon as a tax upon the free circulation of thought. Such a tax, no matter how collected, is bad in principle, and can hardly be good for the country. The average number of letters now passing annually through the Post-office—irrespective of newspapers and parcels by book-post (seventy-one millions, and nearly twelve millions, respectively)—is quite twenty for each person throughout the kingdom; and the sooner the Post-office profits are spent in improving the Post-office service, or in reducing the postal charges, the better for these active correspondents.

The next item is three hundred thousand pounds derived from Crown Lands—a class of property which is not very productive. The gross income from these lands is only about four hundred and thirty thousand pounds, and many quiet observers, including Mr. Hankey, are puzzled by this remarkable barrenness. There is a tradition, meandering through old law-books, which is painful to all taxpayers, that these Crown lands were once sufficient to pay all the expenses of the State, before a large number of royal prodigals took to running through the national property. William the Conqueror's income from this source, according to a reliable estimate, was equal, in our present money, to something like six or seven millions per annum, without taking into consideration the increased value of property. Now the forests—the anything but merry green woods, and part of this property—cost more than they produce, showing an annual loss of seven thousand pounds. If this was the case in Robin Hood's time, no wonder his Chancellor of the Exchequer set the practice of thieving.

The last items on our list are the miscellaneous receipts, a group that amounts to about two millions and three-quarters. Here we have small branches of the hereditary revenue (an insignificant sum): about one hundred and thirty thousand pounds paid by the Bank of England for the privilege of issuing bank-notes, or creating capital to the extent of fourteen millions; fees of public offices, a large proportion of which consists of charges on private bills (railway and public company bills), sufficient to pay all the working expenses of Parliament; a sum returned by the King of the Belgians out of his pension, seemingly to promote as much book-keeping as possible; and a receipt of seven hundred thousand pounds from the sale of old stores, which represents a loss of a million and a half, and an annual sop thrown to auction-room jobbers. These are followed by what are called extra receipts—a large part of which is the profit on coinage—more than sufficient to pay the whole cost of the Mint. The profit is made on the silver and copper coinage, and chiefly on the latter. Gold, being the standard coin, is manufactured free of charge, to keep it steady in value. Next, in these miscellaneous receipts, comes the profit made from those useful but not very lively government publications, the Gazettes of London, Edinburgh, and Dublin; then follow the repayments from India for military charges; the colonial contribution towards the cost of our Post-office services (which we have before taken into account); the unclaimed wages and effects of deceased merchant seamen, which are paid into the Exchequer after six years; a saving on the issue of parliamentary grants, paid back in cash; ten thousand pounds received from the public as "conscience money"—partly from people who think they have defrauded the revenue, and partly from enthusiasts who wish to pay off the National Debt; a surplus remaining unappropriated from former votes of supply; and sums derived from the Malta and Alexandria telegraph contractors, the Emperor of China, in the shape of an indemnity; and from the capture of slavers, and other sources. These sums end the miscellaneous receipts, and when the whole account is added up, we find that the result of Sucking Britannia—the total income from revenue of all kinds—is a little more than seventy millions and a half. The total amount received from taxation, exclusive of the Post-office, is about sixty-seven millions, and the cost of collection, excluding the Post-office, but including superannuations, is about two millions and a half, or three and three-quarters per cent. as they say in the City.

This simple account of Ruling and Sucking Britannia only gives the pure income and expenditure of the national balance-sheet, leaving out certain items which always appear in the official statement. These items, on both sides, generally reach another eighteen millions, and represent certain financial operations of the government. There are the balances standing to the credit of the government at the commencement of the financial year—the 1st of April, or All Fools' Day—the money borrowed from the Bank of England by the government, under parliamentary restrictions, and partly repaid during the year; the temporary advances so borrowed and wholly repaid every quarter; and the creation or redemption of additional debt. The last item may be interesting to those who wish to watch the progress of the National Debt. The repayments of advances that are not temporary, includes an operation by which the silver and copper coin finds its way into circulation. The Mint buys copper and silver, and coins both, as before stated, at a profit, but the coin is only issued to the Bank of England, or to other parties willing to give the full nominal value for it, because they require the small coinage of silver and copper for the wants of their customers. Only those persons who require the coin for such purposes would give twenty shillings' worth of gold to receive only eighteen shillings intrinsic value in silver, or probably not above seven or eight shillings intrinsic value in copper.

One of the cleverest inventions to conceal the real pressure of taxation was the so-much-a-head theory. When financial reformers complain that the active expenditure of the country has increased sixfold during the last seventy years, they are referred to the population returns, and told that seventy millions a year, drawn from thirty millions of people, is only about two pounds five shillings a head. If taxes were paid to Chancellors by sucking babes, idiots, paupers, and a number of other similar persons, there would be some fairness in this poll-tax calculation, but the chief heads in the country who pay these seventy millions a year are heads of families. If Britannia really believes in this head theory, with how much disgust must she regard those constantly occurring cases of death from starvation which are a disgrace to the country? It would surely be better to give up a little of our great and glorious expenditure, than to support it by squeezing five and forty shillings a year from those who are dying of hunger.

SOCIAL REFORM.

The cry of Social Reform has been raised a little too often of late. People hear this cry issuing from Tory lips, and they hail it as an augury of the happy death of ancient prejudice, forgetting that social reform is always one of the most dangerous, because one of the most stupifying doctrines of what is called enlightened despotism. Social Reform is a thing admirable in itself, and a pure and noble object in men who devote themselves to it purely for the sake of the classes most likely to benefit by it; but it is not so good, and far from so praiseworthy, when it merely represents a feint of political tactics, performed for the purpose of distracting attention from subjects and principles of far more vital importance to the just and equal government of the country. Political science, or the science of political justice with its even distribution of rights and duties, is not the science of guiding the sewage of a country in the way it should go; it is not the science of ramming a distastoful alphabet and the promise of a better world down the starving throats of agricultural scarecrows; it is not the science of improving the architectural aspect of a city until it takes a foremost rank in the note-book of the *dilettante* tourist; it is not the science of white-washing the dwellings of the poorer orders; for all these things can be done, and are done, much better under Governments where political science is despised, and the last spark of liberty is trampled out. Political science in a free country, possessing the machinery of a representative Government, means more—far more—than is contained in the surface allurements thrown out, in most cases, to satisfy the conscience of the benevolent, to dazzle the ignorant and unthinking, and beget a state of paralytic contentment in the mass. In a country where the mere cost of the Government oscillates between the round sums of seventy and eighty millions sterling, drawn under a mixed system of direct and indirect taxation, from the highest capitalist down to the humblest peasant in the land, it is difficult to know upon what logical principle any contributor to this ministerial mine of wealth is denied his voice through his representative, first in the amount and manner of its collection, secondly, in the amount and manner of its distribution. Putting the claim to equal political rights upon no higher ground than this finance section—no unimportant section—of our administrative machine, upon what principle or pretext can any man who is called upon to contribute directly or indirectly to the funds of Government (and who is not?) be excluded from the power of exercising the elective franchise? He pays his just share towards the expenses of protection to person and property, and yet he has no voice in determining the mode, extent, and cost of that protection. It is no answer to such a man to say, "Entrust us with your money without a murmur, for see how beneficially we expend a portion of it." It is no gift to him that you return him, in the shape of social reforms, perhaps one-tenth of what you take from him in the shape of taxes. As the case stands at present, you rob him of all that you take from him, merely palliating the injustice by expending a portion in what you may consider a manner conducive to his welfare, although his opinion may differ very widely from yours upon the beneficial character of your expenditure. It is no justice to such a man, if he is the meanest tax-payer in the land, to bring in a so-called Reform Bill, when the patience of the most patient people in the world is tired out, which shall just pass him over by a hair's breadth, because, perhaps, it may go no farther in the path of electoral extension than a good, substantial lodger suffrage. Such a man may be clean, may be healthy, may be well housed, well fed, and well clothed, but so probably was the born thrall of Cedric the Saxon, and while the political condition of the labouring man remains as it is, he cannot pride himself upon having attained much advance upon his ancient prototype.

Abundance of capital, causing the dissemination of comparative wealth with its attendant comforts amongst the general body of the people, has always done more than any despotic ordinances to stifle a cry for fair and equal political rights. Social Reform, as it tends to increase the material happiness of the people in a given direction, may, if dishonestly advocated, be easily converted into a political sop to appease the hunger, for a time, of those who are craving for more serious and substantial aliment. The just and rational cry for political justice is not to be silenced by the schoolmaster's pen, the builder's trowel, the painter's brush, or the scavenger's shovel.

TABLE TALK.

HYLAS. Sit down, good master mine, and draw thy chair near this sea-coal fire. The air bites shrewdly on the Northern road.

PHILONOUS. True, most hospitable host; and the wind is none of the most gentle. "Marry child," said the fisherman's wife, as she closed her lattice-window, "but there will be fearful work at sea to-night." You know the quotation—Cornish melo-drama, about smugglers, Act 1st, Scene——

HYLAS. Right well; with the tea-board thunder, and the snowstorm formed of shreds of rejected and confiscated plays. But draw round; here shall no uncouth blast cause those masterpieces of dental skill to rattle, or tip that classic nose with blue.

PHIL. True, most high priest of comfort. I am not ignorant of the manifold allurements of thy snuggery. In some such room sat Cowper when he wrote that cosy epic "The Task."

HYLAS. Thy taste is not for the "cup that cheers but not inebriates," hypocrite as thou art. Fill thy beaker full of the warm south, and take the bottle off that detestable crochet mat, which Betty always pushes under my nose to remind me of my weakness.

PHIL. Is it a *gage d'amour* that thus offends the too sensitive nerves of my friend?

HYLAS. No; alas!

PHIL. Then give me an account of the acquisition of this masterpiece of needle art.

HYLAS. 'Twas at a fancy fair at Chiswick. Lounger and idler as I am, in an evil moment I lounged into this hot-bed of charitable extortion. My eye caught that of a lovely being, who with beautiful humility condescended to officiate at a counter. Some fascination bound me to the spot. I received unconsciously that worsted platter in one hand; I tendered with the other a five-pound note—the only money I had about me. I looked in vain for change. I only received a peculiarly gracious smile, and an overpowering curtsey. I began to understand my position. I, a stern disciple of Ricardo, had been swindled into doing a benevolent action—into subscribing indirectly to the "Fund for promoting Vaccination in Central Africa!"

PHIL. And the name of the fair swindler was ——?

HYLAS. The young Countess of Fitzwheedle.

PHIL. I cannot sympathize with you. You received full value in gazing at the beloved one. Besides, you should carry small coin with you. I have two pen-wipers at home that cost a sovereign. One represents a donation of ten shillings to the "Ragged Schools of St. Tothill-in-the-Fields," applied, I suppose, to mending the breeches of the young alumni, which the Countess of Fitzwheedle could not do, of course, with a crotchet needle, except through the medium of a "Fancy Fair." The other represents an equal amount applied to the removal of the Church of St. Consols in the Money Market from the immediate contact of Mammon—(a contact so close, flanked as it was on both sides by banking houses, that the filthy lucre must have oozed through the party walls)—to the more congenial neighbourhood of Ultra Belgravia. Should I have ever entered into either of these vast enterprizes but for a little Fitzwheedledom? Never. It is the cheapest and most efficacious way of collecting the lounging benevolence about town. It——

HYLAS. Say no more—special pleader. Your light temperament and strangely constituted mind can, of course, see no more impropriety in removing a church through the agency of a fair, than in relieving a decayed clergyman by a benefit at Cremorne Gardens.

PHIL. An aspersion on my organ of veneration. Now, for the influence of authority in matters of opinion. You will admit that Drew—the self-constituted oracle of our club—is not a man that any one would accuse of want of respect to religion in whatever form it presents itself?

HYLAS. Granted.

PHIL. Yet has Drew often regretted to me that he missed the chance of winning the celebrated Boydell Bible at a raffle! A Bible won at a raffle!

HYLAS. A curious amalgam of incongruous ideas, certainly.

PHIL. Yes; but I have not done with you yet. You know old Corderoy the Baptist; elder and main prop of Parrellelogram Chapel?

HYLAS. Well.

PHIL. He sees Ichabod written on the walls of a theatre. He would not allow his family to go to a concert if it were not an Oratorio—nor admit a pack of cards to defile his door-step. Yet this serious, and no doubt sincerely religious man, allows his children to play at a kind of Scriptural Whist, with square pieces of cardboard, each containing passages from the Old and New Testament. These are dealt out to each partner, and without ever thoroughly comprehending the game, which is intended to blend wholesome recreation with religious instruction, I have found myself leading off with Isaiah as trumps, and have become the winner of two chapters of the Psalms, and a chapter and a half of Revelations!

HYLAS. Incredible!

PHIL. Not at all. It is your "serious" people that fall into these absurdities, from an incapacity of perceiving an incongruity in the relations of certain ideas, and a total want of the sense of the ludicrous. The Rev. Sydney Smith would never have introduced scriptural cards to his family, or rattled the dice-box at a Bible raffle: but speak of such a man to Messrs. Drew and Corderoy, and they shrink from him as a scoffer and a latitudinarian.

HYLAS. A most able defence, and the judge is bound to acquit you without any imputation upon your character. Pass the bottle. A cheerful object is a well-made, well-filled bottle. I can understand all that has been said and sung in its praise. It is the chief instrument in the art of internal and external domestic fortification. Calm and benevolent as it looks upon the table, full of joy and power, ready to give up promptly and ungrudgingly all that it possesses for the gratification of others, yet may you see it sharp-toothed, keen, savage, and grinning like a crocodile, when, broken in pieces, and arranged in that firm mortar along the outer wall, it presents a formidable barrier to the midnight invaders of the peaceful villa. Nor is it less repulsive to the young gentlemen at the adjoining academy who are longing to invade your fruitful orchard: for your wine bottle, although a jolly dog, has a true sense of the impropriety of unlawful pleasures, and opposes them accordingly. I like to watch its demure appearance as it serves out the single glass of ginger wine at the children's dinner. It has an affinity and an understanding with the old domestic, and exerts an equal degree of respectful authority over the party. How different is its air now with us two old boon companions and men of the world, eh? Look at its cork stuck jauntily on one side like the Artful Dodger's hat!

PHIL. A very pretty prose Anacreontic; and one that would have entitled its composer to a perpetual chairmanship of the "Jolly Nose Club," if he had lived at the commencement of this century. But how long has Bacchus marked you for his own?

HYLAS. Ever since I became conscious of possessing some degree of intellectual strength, for I hold that it is only your man of parts who is fit to be trusted with the free use of the bottle. The great mind becomes greater under its influence, the little mind staggers under it and falls. It is like Milton's scheme of education; it requires a race of intellectual giants. But find your giants, and then!——

PHIL. Modest, truly! You are not unlike the worthy magistrate who has a stern admonition for the drunken costermonger swept from the gin-shop door, and a smile for the fuddled swell who has been dining at his club. Claret against Hodges any day.

HYLAS. And very proper magisterial conduct too. He knows that in the first case drink is the master of the man; in the second, man is the master of the drink. The lower orders of society are not yet in a fit state to be entrusted with drink any more than with universal suffrage. You must first raise them morally, intellectually, and physically in the social scale. I am not a mere theorist in these matters; I act upon my principles.

PHIL. In what way?

HYLAS. By enforcing temperance, not inculcating it.

Look at the dustmen! What regulates their every movement? Beer. What is the one idea that pervades their mind—except a confused notion that everything is dust, and to dust it must return—not excepting overcoats, walking sticks, and umbrellas—I say again, beer. Their very blood must be beer, fermenting as they walk, but I do not help to supply it! A cool tankard of toast and water is always by my orders kept soaking for them in the kitchen to slake their burning thirst.

PHIL. Thou art indeed a practical philanthropist!

HYLAS. On boxing-day I have ready a collection of tracts which I distribute as appropriately as I can. To the turncock I give "Aqua Vivarius on the Defilement of the Thames;" to the scavengers "Cloaca Maximus on the Drainage of London;" to the "waits" a little work called the "Principles of Harmony;" and to the postman, who has, I understand, a large family, I apportion "Philo Progenites on Over Population."

PHIL. And are overwhelmed with gratitude in return?

HYLAS. On the contrary, I am looked upon as a madman—the fate of all reformers who are in advance of their age. No matter; here comes Betty with the supper.

PHIL. Strange that with all our command of the past, an impenetrable veil should be drawn between us and that unknown benefactor who first had the boldness to test the value of the oyster as human food. It is not a tempting morsel to look at, this mixture of shell and slime which I hold in my hand; but education and experience teach me that it is savoury to the palate—very savoury. Simple and easy is the act of transferring to the mouth each plump and juicy native, but what a world of prejudice and nausea must that great unknown have overcome before he could determine upon that now simple act? We have all had our ears dinned until they are deaf with the names of Columbus, Vasco de Gama, Cortes, Raleigh, Cook, Ross, Harvey, Jenner, Watt, Franklin, Brewster, Davy, Wheatstone, etc., etc., but the great gastronomic unknown is not amongst them. Rather than find the lost books of Livy, or the author of Junius, would I hear the name of that universally respected, admired, and beloved shadow.

HYLAS. How fleeting is the gratitude of a gourmand—evaporating with the morning's indigestion!

PHIL. A base insinuation; but it touches me not. Whole nights have passed with me in waking dreams of island rocks, and long sad mournful beaches, on which in solitude the Sea Pie stalked.

HYLAS. The what stalked?

PHIL. The Sea Pie is not a very poetical name, I admit, for a bird!

HYLAS. Oh, the Oyster Eater: Hœmatopus Ostralegus.

PHIL. Exactly; homely and suggestive as the name is, how welcome must the bird have been to some poor shipwrecked outcast, as stalking before him on that hopeless barren beach, it showed him with its chisel bill the way to treasures far more precious than a jewel mine. This is the first glimpse that humanity got of the invaluable art of oyster eating.

HYLAS. Your natural history is sound; your inference is fanciful, and, in all probability, just. It would make a worthy addition to the Pseudodoxia Epidemica of Sir Thomas Browne, or a pretty chapter in a new work to be entitled "Vestiges of the Natural Dishes of Creation."

PHIL. The best of all dishes. Look at this oyster, with its Doric simplicity, and its Doric strength, and compare it with that highly artificial production on the table—that composite frippery—that stratified crudity—a pork pie.

HYLAS. The cherished luxury of Leicestershire thus vilified! Provocative of indigestion as that pie may seem to you, it was put together by a lovely cousin at Melton Mowbray, whose fair hands are equally skilful in rendering a sonata of Beethoven, or in compounding the gastronomic mysteries of the kitchen.

PHIL. Trusting innocent: it is a painful duty to have to undeceive such confiding simplicity, but it must be done. Melton Mowbray is evidently unknown to you.

HYLAS. It is.

PHIL. Know then, that rural as its name may sound, it is a manufacturing town, and its staple product is the pie of which we have a specimen on the table. It possesses several factories, with a regular staff of operatives. Its population in 1850 was——

HYLAS. Fudge!

PHIL. I have seen the mills at work in this little alimentary Manchester. I have heard the dinner-bell sound at twelve, and have seen the well-conducted, orderly workpeople turn out to their humble mid-day repast, after working all the morning upon the raw material of pies. "May good digestion wait on appetite," I ejaculated, as they wound away in the distance. That pie is not a hand-made production of your fair cousin; it is a dyspeptic abortion, turned out by machinery!

HYLAS. Well, let it pass, man of delicate appetite:—

"I cannot eat but little meat,
  My stomach is not good,
But sure I am that I can drink
  With him who wears a hood!
Both back and side go bare, go bare,
  Both foot and hand go cold;
But belly, God give thee good ale enough,
  Whether it be new or old!"

I think old Bishop Still must have had you in his eye when he chaunted that episcopal lay some centuries ago.

PHIL. I admit, without shame, a love for the fine old English drink. Give me a pot of good beer and the "Religio Medici," and the world may wag as it will.

HYLAS. Porson Redivivus!

PHIL. It is a relief to escape for a time from the din, rattle, and weak refinement of the present, into the monastic calm and vigorous coarseness of the past—to take up an old thoughtful book that has not been vulgarized by *enterprising* publishers, and hawked about the town in penny numbers!

HYLAS. Rabelais, Montaigne, and others have themselves placed a most effectual barrier against any such levelling proceeding, by a freedom of style that the "weak refinement" of the day can hardly tolerate.

PHIL. Allah be praised! they have. Are we to have nothing *caviare* to the multitude? Is everything to be turned inside out, and exposed in the market-place?

HYLAS. We must not turn up our Conservative noses at "progress."

PHIL. "Progress" is a dream! Look at the so-called "Free Libraries." What is their condition? Dying for want of support. A subscription so small as a penny a month cannot be extracted from the pockets of the enlightened multitude. No, my friend, the principle of "progress," interpreted in the popular sense, does not exist; and if it did, push it to its logical conclusion, and what would be the result? Two nightmen debating "Berkeley's Theory of Matter," while their offensive vehicle blocked up the thoroughfare! Let me chant you a stave on that subject called "The Refined Drover."

He sits with his flocks, and pipes all day
  With an oaten reed and pastoral song;
He's quite relinquish'd the pipe of clay,—
  For smoking, he thinks, is decidedly wrong.
He's quite left off the drinking of beer,
  And taken to coffee and tea instead;
And spirits he never takes, for fear
  They should, as he says, "get into his head."

And then he has grown so very humane,
  He never now pulls a lamb by the tail;
He's quite left off—as it caused them pain—
  Stirring them up with a ten-penny nail!
His gentle ways are pleasant to see:—
  You never hear him companions abuse;
And "lauk-a-daisy," or "deary-me,"
  Is about the strongest oath that he'll use.

In coffee-houses he sips his tea,
  And lingers over the Quarterly's page;
Or looks at the "latest news," to see
  What is going on in this wonderful age.
And if he getteth a leisure day,
  He'll to the Royal Academy go;
At skittles he never cares to play,
  He thinks the game is decidedly low.

And then he dresses so very neat—
  He looks very much like a banker's clerk;
As he drives his flock along the street,
  He's often the theme of general remark:
If you saw him on a rainy day,
  You'd think him a most fastidious fellow,
As through the mud he picketh his way,
  Under a beautiful silk umbrella!

HYLAS. Well sung; but a *reductio ad absurdum*, more satirical than just. You do not deny the existence of material progress?

Phil. A general advance in the standard of living? Certainly not; and for that very reason would I sweep away all visionary schemes for forcing knowledge upon "the masses." If material progress be a fact, let it work out its intellectual effects unaided, unmolested. Depend upon it that everything the most sanguine optimist may desire will follow in its train. To attempt to do more, is to adopt a hot-house expedient for raising unnatural flowers upon an uncongenial soil—showy to the eye, but wanting in root.

Hylas. We pass from grave to gay, from lively to severe; and at a time when, if our magnums of 1836 vintage had done the duty usually ascribed to them, we ought to be wallowing under the table, we find ourselves proving my theory respecting drink, by discussing one of the great social problems of the age!

Phil. A hint to conclude. The bottle is empty, and the fire has died out. Give me my life-preserver and my hat; and, until our next meeting, fare thee well!

COMMON-PLACE.

HYLAS. The more I examine our current literature, art, and criticism, the more grieved am I to find how largely they are eaten up by the dry-rot of insincerity and common-place. I wander into the exhibition of the paintings of that debateable painter, Turner, who, with delightful modesty, has left a thousand pounds to defray the cost of his own statue. I see an "effect" upon canvas that I think I could fairly imitate by throwing a dozen eggs against that virgin, unsoiled wainscoting opposite. Not so, thinks the able critic of the public journals; it is with him "Wonderful! worthy of Dubbin in his best days!" I go to the theatre on a great tragedy night. I hear a voice issuing from a figure draped in classic folds, declaiming with insincere elocution the words of the Poet. In the morning the able critic informs me that it was "Wonderful! worthy of Dubbin in his best days!" I go to a theatre celebrated for its farces. I see the chief actor of the place in a new part, made to fit him like a coat or a boot. I find coarseness and buffoonery where I expected humour and a true embodiment of character. Not so, thinks the able critic; it is with him, "Wonderful! worthy of Dubbin in his best days!" I go to a concert, where there is to be a pianoforte solo by a renowned performer. I hear, for one fleeting moment, the echo of an old familiar air, and see a clear case of assault and battery. In the morning I read that it was "Wonderful! worthy of Dubbin in his best days!" I take up, at the reading-room, the last new novel. I find in it neither plot, character, nor style; but the able critic declares it to be "Wonderful! worthy of Dubbin in his best days!"

Philonous. Verily, my friend, thou art hard upon the modern Longinus. Thou surely wouldst not have painter, actor, musician, and novelist above the comprehension of their appointed judge, or the universal critic above the comprehension of his audience? The author or performer in this case is worthy of his critic, the critic worthy of his patrons.

Hylas. Too true; but that does not modify the pernicious tendency of such trash. The common-place in criticism begets common-place in literature and art; and common-place in literature and art begets common-place in criticism. I would root up all such worthless weeds in the garden of literature, and afford room and nourishment for the growth of more sturdy and useful plants.

Phil. Hast thou fairly gauged, O great Reformer, the Augean stable thou art about to cleanse?

Hylas. I have; and that mouldy metaphor of the Augean stable brings before my mind a long list of common-places, that must be eradicated once and for ever. When the noble lord who is at the head of her Majesty's Government has given what the Opposition choose to consider a lame explanation of certain foreign treaties, I know that the next morning I shall be asked triumphantly by the Opposition organ, "Is this a man fit to be intrusted with the guidance of the vessel of the State through the shoals and quicksands of continental diplomacy?" If the noble lord has not shown what the Opposition choose to consider due respect to the Liberty of the Subject, the Privileges of the House, or the Royal Prerogative, I know that the able Editor will tow the Ark of the Constitution out of dock the next morning, and I shall be asked if the noble lord is the person to be intrusted with the care of that venerable craft.

PHIL. True, my friend; and these faded flowers of metaphor are not confined to any particular soil, they are spread over the whole area of journalism. The remarks of the Leader of the Opposition in the Government organ of the same morning are summed up as being, at one and the same time, the Avatar of Protection, and the Hydra head of Faction.

HYLAS. Yes; and if it were a mere party trick, one might let such things pass, upon the principle that the end justifies the means. But the virus has sunk deeper—into the very heart of our general style. A crowded, ill-ventilated law court—no great rarity, we all know, in this metropolis—is *forcibly* described by the *powerful* writer as the Black Hole of Calcutta. The ticket-of-leave man, when he is treated in the philanthropic vein, is feelingly alluded to as the Pariah of Society.

PHIL. All these points are the time-honoured ornaments of the literary mosaic style, a style that is like a set of dominoes, often broken up—shuffled, and formed into fresh combinations—nothing new ever being added, nothing taken away. The fault, if any, does not lie with the man-of-all-work called by courtesy a writer; it is not his duty to originate, he has merely to select. If a statement has to be contradicted he falls naturally into, "we have yet to learn;" if anything has occurred requiring a graphic description, it is simply and promptly disposed of with, "This may more easily be imagined than described." If any public character has distinguished himself in a remarkable manner, it is stated that "the mantle of Dubbin has fallen upon him;" and if "a great parochial question is shaking London to its foundations," we are told "that if St. Spankus is only true to herself, she cannot—she will not fail!"

HYLAS. Exactly; and if all this were put forward with less arrogance, one might feel disposed occasionally to let it pass, for it is possible to have a surfeit, even of the sublime and beautiful; but when I hear such patchwork called Thunder, the Lever of Archimedes, etc., and when I see the smirking, self-satisfied writer, shadowed through the empty transparency of his production, devolving his rounded periods, and evidently considering himself equal to Gibbon *plus* Johnson, it makes my blood boil!

PHIL. A good wholesome fit of indignation does no man any harm; but a great reformer, like yourself, must be above all little infirmities of temper. It seems to me that if you have sworn to run amuck against common-place, you must attack the system from all points—in fact surround it, and, trust me, you will find the task no light one.

HYLAS. I know it; but I am not daunted. If we take common-place while she is in her caustic mood, we shall find that to admit any merit in a man who happens to be of aristocratic origin, and not an inspired pot-boy, is to be accused of Flunkeyism. To be an advocate of order and method in the conduct of public business is to be stigmatized as a Red Tapist. To represent anything of City origin and City interest is to be classed at once with Dinners, Turtle Soup, and Bloated Aldermen. And when common-place is in her playful mood, she affects to regard "Bradshaw's Guide" as a maddening complexity—a differential calculus; looks upon the policeman officially as an unknown quantity, humanly as a body magnetized by a leg of mutton; and finally, with admirable taste and humour, divides the cubic contents of the house-dog into a given bulk and number of sausages.

Phil. Yes, and it does not end here, for every fool one meets in an omnibus or at a public dinner, repeats with evident relish those painful witticisms.

Hylas. It is the number of persons who take up, repeat, and are influenced by common-places, that discourages the reformer. For example:—a respectable wholesale cheesemonger in the City of London, finding his business too extensive for his premises, resolves to pull down his warehouse, and rebuild it in the style and on the scale that are now prevalent. The contract is settled: a scaffolding is raised—a perpetual cloud of dust annoys the passer-by for two days, and at the end of that time not a brick of the old building remains standing. Now it happened that in the year of our Lord one-thousand-six-hundred-and-ninety-two there lived in London an architect (who shall be nameless), whose mission or speciality it was to design and build an immense number of Metropolitan churches, and as the City then was much more like London proper than it is now, the largest proportion of these structures, of course, fell to its share. In due season the architect died, and after the lapse of a few years, when time had begun to throw a poetical haze around the works of the man, the cognoscenti, who rule the public taste, arrived at the conclusion that England never had seen, and probably never would see, his equal! All his works from that moment—bad, good, excellent, and super-excellent—became objects of solicitude and veneration! Now, oddly enough, one of these churches—the worst by many degrees of the whole set—had been erected in a nook at the back of the cheesemonger's warehouse, as the custom was in those days; and when that vulgar receptacle of merchandise was razed to the ground, the half-buried antiquity stood full, with all its beauties exposed to the public gaze. It certainly was not an ecclesiastical building, as we understand that style of architecture in the present day, and as it was understood in the Middle Ages. It looked like a pile of porticoes taken from one of our modern squares, and mounted one upon the other, gradually decreasing in size as they reached the top. However, it was a production of *the man*, and as such it caught the eye of able editors, at a time, too, when during the parliamentary recess social subjects were at a premium, and political subjects at a discount. Leaders appeared in certain journals, in which the old general rules were followed for such a subject. A comparison was drawn between Paris and London, highly flattering to the former, highly damaging to the latter, and winding up with this triumphant question—"Shall the only glimpse that London has obtained for centuries of one of the *lightest* and most *fanciful* productions of one of her greatest sons, be immediately shut out from her sight by the Goths and Vandals of trade? Never!" And half London echoed "Never!" The men who wrote the articles neither cared for nor believed in their subject; if they had I could have forgiven them, for earnestness and sincerity always command respect. The multitude, who took up the cry—it was a good common-place cry enough for them—knew, felt, and cared as much about the subject as their blind guides; but as it was not too profound, and easily understood, it furnished fair average conversational material for a few weeks, during which time none dared to advance a contrary opinion. At the end of this period some equally interesting topic, similarly treated, took its place—the Vandal cheesemonger had re-built his premises, and the pyramid of porticoes was again under total eclipse for some centuries to come.

PHIL. A very interesting story, from which, I suppose, you infer that a common-place subject, treated in a common-place manner, and addressed to common-place people, is the one thing needful to command success?

HYLAS. I do. If I were an artist I would draw eternally dead animals of all kinds, mix them up with Royalty of all ages, fix the *locus in quo* at Windsor Castle, turning it for the time into the semblance of a poulterer's shop in Leadenhall Market, and—I should succeed.

PHIL. My dear friend, you must not judge a painter by his works "done to order."—Lambseer is a man who has communed much with nature, and she has been kind to him.—The familiar is not always the unpoetical.

HYLAS. There spoke your mysticism. However, I will not dwell upon Art. Let me go into society; what do I find there? Common-place ruling paramount. Have I been to Paris? Yes. Have I been to Baden-Baden? Yes.—There are no other known places in the world. Two young ladies sit down to the pianoforte to sing a duet, "Two mermaids are we," with a tira-la chorus of inordinate length. A stout florid nymph sings in a cheerful tone, "Oh! let me never hear his name!" A nervous man timidly renders a bluff song about "the fruits of the soil;" and a thin melancholy-looking youth turns his hair back, and intones through his nose a comic ditty (save the mark!) about "Lord Lovel."—A low common-place standard of taste creates a demand for such things, and the demand produces the supply.

PHIL. I am afraid I cannot question your facts; and you are, therefore, at liberty to make your own deductions.

HYLAS. If I wish to depict foreign or provincial character, and to be generally understood, I must adhere to the strict rules of national characteristics. I must make the Frenchman light and superficial; the German heavy and profound; the Italian moody and revengeful; the Scotch cautious and penurious? the Yorkshireman keen and unscrupulous? and the Irishman warm-hearted and impulsive.

PHIL. This is nature according to the rules of art.—If we are not always satisfied with the accuracy of the portrait as compared with its original in the world of reality, we cannot say that it does not harmonize with its prototype in the world of fiction. As in some of the old comedies you only required to hear a man's name to know what his course of action would be; so in modern fiction your author gives you a shrewd idea of his plot, when in the first page he informs you that "Rinaldo Rinaldino was the last scion of a noble Florentine family," etc.

HYLAS. True; and more than this; a well-known phrase will give you the key-note to a man's character.—I will give you a few illustrations in a dictionary form.

"*A well-informed man.*"—This is a person who knows something of the peerage, a little geography, has read Macaulay's History of England, and can give a few original anecdotes of George IV.

"*A retired tradesman.*"—He carried on business many years as a woolstapler, and retired to Camberwell, at the age of fifty-eight, with a competency realized in trade. He tried reading at the "Institute," and gardening upon his land for six months; but finding that a rural and inactive life did not suit him, he entered the service of his successor in business at a nominal salary, and died in harness, as a porter in the same establishment that had long owned him as a master.

"*The Architect of his own fortune.*"—Lord Brickdust—the most able and learned Chancellor that ever graced the woolsack—was the son of a cat's-meat man at Bethnal-green. Often has he reverted, with tears in his eyes, to the time when his mother used to send him to fetch his father from the skittle-ground, where he often found him in a state of intoxication.

"*A man of powerful intellect.*"—At the time Dr. Forginn edited the "Quidnunc" morning paper, he used to dine at the Grampus Tavern, in the Strand. I have seen him leave the room at a quarter to one in the morning—not a line of editorial matter then written—as drunk as four bottles of port can make a man; go over to his office, dip his head for several minutes in a bucket of water, sit down refreshed, and in half an hour dash off a couple of those startling leaders that only he could write, shaking the effete administration of the day to its centre; and after that light his short pipe, and walk quietly home to Uxbridge in company with his constant companion, a Newfoundland dog.

"*No one's enemy but his own.*"—He was gay without being vicious. His faults were of the head rather than the heart. He was guilty of many a foolish action, but never of a meanness. He might have married an heiress if he had become the Elder of a Chapel. As it was, although the beggar never solicited his charity in vain, he died leaving a few debts unsatisfied, and not sufficient property to defray the cost of his funeral.

PHIL. A very fair catalogue of character, truly; enough to start a popular author in business. Before we conclude, I think I can add another to the list, a kind of supplement to the last, in the shape of one "whose heart was in the right place." He was young, impulsive, generous to a fault; as capable of committing a daring and desperate act, as he was of performing a benevolent action. I watched his short erratic career with almost a fatherly interest. He saved four people from a watery grave; but failing in rescuing the fifth, he provided for the widow and children. What might not have been augured from such a brilliant opening as this? Alas! in a moment of youthful impetuosity he attacked and rifled the York coach with some reckless companions, and was hanged at Tyburn for the crime. Kind, generous, impulsive, but rash and misguided young man! thy heart was in the right place, although thy hands were in the wrong pocket.

MR. DICKENS AND HIS CRITICS.

HYLAS. There is nothing more unfair in criticism than to judge an author by the standard he has created for himself. The minor plays of Shakespeare are not only abused, but in some instances their authorship is discredited because their strength is measured against the gigantic proportions of a "Macbeth" or a "Hamlet."

PHILONOUS. One need not go to the Elizabethan writers for proofs of this injustice, when we have a case before us in the person of Mr. Charles Dickens.

HYLAS. You allude to the reception of "Little Dorrit." Let us suppose that the author of this work had appeared for the first time, and laid this production at the feet of the critical public. How it would have stood out from everything around it. Everyone would have felt that here was a new power developed or developing. The humour, the pathos, the poetic command of language, the photographic fidelity of description, the enlarged sympathies, and the knowledge of the workings of the human heart—all these qualities would at once have been admitted, and all existing fiction literature would have been searched in vain for a parallel. While, however, the divine harmony of the "Old Curiosity Shop" still lingers in the ear, while the incomparable pictures of that most perfect fiction are present to the eye, it is easy to declare any new effort of the old master weak and artificial in comparison; but how largely is such a declaration seasoned with ingratitude, and a forgetfulness of the fount from which the criticism is drawn?

PHIL. True. I quite agree in your estimate of the literary value of the "Old Curiosity Shop." To me there is a charm even in the evidences of indecision of design in the opening chapters of the work. I enter into the innermost confidence of the author. I see the vague idea grow by degrees under the inspired touch, till it is moulded at last into the perfect creation.

HYLAS. The undecided tone at the opening of this exquisite prose poem may have arisen from the writer being unconscious at the time of the power of pathos within him. Wonderful as "Pickwick" was—profusely luxuriant in characters all individually marked, and indicating in their speech their peculiar characteristics, a sufficient answer to those who deny the objective force of Mr. Dickens's creations—still we had yet no sign of that rich mine of poetry and feeling, that command over the emotions of his readers, provoking tears and laughter at the same moment—a power that only falls to the lot of the pure humourist. It may have been that when the pen was again taken in hand, the writer contemplated a varied continuation of his first successful fiction, and this hypothesis is favoured by Mr. Pickwick and several other characters being retained in the introduction. But from the moment that we enter upon the story of little Nell the writer feels the new strength within him, and the result is, in my opinion, one of the most beautiful fictions that the world has ever seen. From the time when the door of the old house closes upon little Nell and her grandfather, when they start upon that long pilgrimage hand-in-hand—a pilgrimage that ends, as millions know, in the death of the child at the old village, what a long and varied panorama passes before us, each picture perfect in itself, each character in harmonious keeping with the plaintive story.

PHIL. It may be urged that Quilp is introduced as a forced contrast to the child in a way that does not conceal the art, and that the drawing of that domestic Caliban is tinctured with exaggeration.

HYLAS. The contrast is not more forced than that between Ariel and Caliban; and with regard to the portrait of Quilp, I may quote the words of a distinguished critic, referring to Shakspeare's kindred creation: "It is not pretended that such beings are, but if they are, they will be as he has pictured them." Against this let us set the artistic skill with which everything that concerns Quilp is drawn, the perfect keeping of his life, his environments, and his death. With regard to the structure of the story, find me, amongst the boasted productions that preserve the unities, any one that can excite that breathless interest which we all feel in the long, painful journey of the old man and his child; and with regard to the pathos, find me an equal amongst any one of the writers of "sentiment" whom England has delighted to honour.

PHIL. If I cannot do that, I fear that I can find you many writers now, of no mean authority, who are trying to prove that the god of our idolatry is nothing but a brazen image.

HYLAS. They attempt to pull down the idol more for political than for literary reasons. Mr. Dickens, in common with all men of quick sympathies and high imagination, is totally opposed to what he considers the hard, dry, unfeeling dogmas of political economy. He looks round upon society, and he sees much injustice, much misery, much poverty, and much crime. Not believing in the great economical doctrine of "let alone," he cries out for more government; and knowing the present government to be bad, he cries out for better government, echoing the old cry of "red tape," and adding two new cries in the shape of "Barnacles" and "Circumlocution Office." Now, if there is one principle thoroughly established, it is this, that everything which a Government undertakes can be better and more economically performed by individuals acting under the stimulus of private gain; and for this reason, that with individuals there is the penalty of ruin if they fail; with a Government there is no such penalty. In the first case it is the Bankruptcy Court, in the second a fresh grant.

PHIL. Yes; and I do not see that any care exercised, by examination or otherwise, in the selection of public servants, will obviate this; for if you grant the power to discharge an official in any case of gross mismanagement—and examination is useless without this—you must entrust it to the care of some higher official, who will have no interest in executing so disagreeable a task; and when an occasion arises the natural indolence of man will find a hundred excuses for remitting the sentence.

HYLAS. Exactly; and this brings us to the logical conclusion, that as all Government administration is necessarily bad, the true object of reformers is to endeavour to reduce rather than improve it. "Red tape" is an old grievance, not worth the power that has been expended against it. In many cases it is synonymous with order and method; and those people who consider much government to be good, surely ought not to cut out these two qualities from the system.

PHIL. Mr. Dickens flies in the face of political economy, forgetting that its great masters are working to the same end as himself—the good government of society. When these writers, after a careful logical analysis of the social system, come to the conclusion that self-interest is the one guiding principle that regulates the intercourse and transactions of men, when they check the open hand of charity by proving that it is ineffectual to cure the misery it endeavours to relieve; when they strike at the root of any sympathy between employer and employed, by laying down that commerce cannot be conducted unless the greatest amount of work be exacted for the smallest amount of pay; when they work out the theory of population, and demonstrate that the only real cure for the social evils around us is self-restraint as regards marriage, and a check upon the production of men; it is not the presumptuous insect on the leaf preaching to his fellow worm, it is not even the one-sided theorist, who says, "These principles are good, these principles are bad;" it is the calm philosopher dissecting the little world beneath him, and without prejudice, without passion, without poetry, without delusions—oftentimes, it may be, with a heavy heart, laying bare the innermost workings of the system.

HYLAS. The duties of poetry are well defined. They are the refining of the human mind, the education of the emotive sympathies, and the spiritual alleviation of the sufferings of humanity. When poetry leaves this useful sphere of action, and attempts the reorganization of society, what is the result? An impracticable socialism. When poetry, not content with ruling over the wide domain of fiction, pushes its territory into the regions of fact and history, am I to be stigmatized as a fiction-crusher if I endeavour to beat it back? Who can measure the fanaticism, the practical misery, the heart-burnings, the disputes that have arisen, the lives that have been sacrificed, because the barriers between true and false have been broken down? For God's sake, let the purple hues of poetry be kept from the hard outline of fact; let the poet, the historian, and the statesman be kept apart.

PHIL. You cannot suppose—nor can the bitterest opponents of Mr. Dickens imagine—that, with all his force and originality of intellect, he is above the comprehension, if he thought proper to apply himself, of those abstract principles which are of vital importance to the welfare and good government of the country?

HYLAS. The question is, not what he is capable of, but what he is. I, for my own part, think it no easy task that a mind of Mr. Dickens's unequalled imaginative power should work in direct opposition to the dictates of that imagination, and throw off the accumulated sentiment of a life.

PHIL. His opponents do not add to the force of their remarks upon his political principles, when they endeavour to detract from his wonderful literary merit, by treating him as one of the herd of mere comic writers, the Jan Steen of literature, whose mission it is to make men grin and silly women cry—perhaps the most eminent buffoon of his day.

HYLAS. When the turmoil of the present century, with all the virulence of its political debate, and all the petty jealousies of its literature, shall have passed away; when those who penned the stinging epigram or the caustic satire shall be weak, or dead, or dying—dying, and anxious to give worlds to cancel many a brilliant injustice which their hasty pens have put upon record, then, and not till then, shall we arrive at a calm estimate of the value of the writings of Charles Dickens. Even now I love to picture him far from the din of the critical Babel, surrounded by those delicate and beautiful creations of his fancy, that ideal family, the children of his pen. There, in the twilight of his study, I see him sitting with his arm round Nell, the favourite child. Her face seems worn and sad, but when she looks up in his eyes, it becomes suffused with heavenly light. At his feet rest little Dombey and his sister, hand-in-hand, and nestling to the father who has called them into birth. Poor Joe is there, the fungus of the streets, crouching like a dog beside the fire, grateful for food, and warmth, and shelter. I hear the clumping of a little crutch upon the stairs, and in hops Tiny Tim, the crippled child. Above them hover the shadowy forms of other children, children who on earth were poor and suffering drudges, workhouse outcasts that the world had turned adrift, but which are now on high, a blessed band of angels. And yet this man, great critics, is only a mere buffoon, and nothing more? Truly, a fit companion for that low player of the olden time, who wrote "King Lear," and acted at the Globe.

MR. DICKENS AS A READER.

The highest order of imaginative literature, in which the creative faculty predominates, is limited in the form and amount of appreciation which it receives by the sympathetic and imaginative capacity of its readers. No matter how sharply and carefully its outlines of character may be drawn, how deeply its impressions may be engraved upon the page, how broad and effective may be the colours that complete its filling in; it appeals to the intellect or fancy, and not to the senses, of its audience, and every reader becomes the possessor of a reflected image which he has himself assisted to a great extent in creating.

With the dramatist, before his productions are moulded into a shape to live in the eyes and memories of his audience, and stamped as current coin, every form and colour of dress, every detail of scenery, every delicacy of bye-play, every situation, every tone and gesture, has to be drawn with a minute and unwavering hand, and firmly impressed upon the mind of the actor by the author. This once done, the stage-carpenter, the scenic artist, the costumier, and the performer join together to raise a solid concrete structure upon an abstract foundation, that produces a uniform impression in its coarse, broad, palpable features, without regard to the inequalities of critical and mental power on the part of the audience. Of course the more subtle touches of nature, the half-hidden delicacies of light and shade, are only revealed to the select few, who have an affinity with the creative artist; but still enough remains for the rough and untrained mass, and every labourer who can command a sixpence may come direct from the brick-field or the coal-pit to listen to the singing Ariel floating in the sky, or to see the haggard witches dancing on the barren heath.

Not so is it with unrepresented, unillustrated literature. Immense and incalculable as is its circulation, it is circumscribed in its influence and effects. The measure of its publication is no index of its power. Thousands take it and read it mechanically; hundreds cultivate an acquaintance with it because it is the fashion; tens of thousands read it with the scales of prejudice before their blinded eyes; while millions stand in hopeless ignorance, and let it pass untouched. The greater the value of a book as a literary production, the more will the circle of its influence usually be narrowed. The very shape, aspect, and garments of the ideal creatures who move through its pages, even when drawn by the pen of the first master of fiction in the land, will be faint and confused to the blunted perception of the general reader, unless aided by the attendant pencil of the illustrative artist. For the sharp, clear images of Mr. Pickwick, with the spectacles, gaiters, and low-crowned hat—of Sam Weller, with the striped waistcoat and the artful leer—of Mr. Winkle, with the sporting costume and the foolish expression—more persons are indebted to the caricaturist, than to the faultless descriptive passages of the great creative mind that called the amusing puppets into existence. Mr. Leech, Mr. Cruikshank, and Mr. Browne are all pictorial expositors of Mr. Dickens to the senses of those who are incapable of seeing vividly with the mind's eye the form and aspect of pure, unaided literary creations. So well do publishers know the advantage of illustrations, even when they address a highly-educated class of readers, that, rather than have no pictorial accessories after the fact, they were willing to let Mr. Thackeray etch for his own works, although he knew and felt himself to be the worst artist that ever appealed to a cultivated public.

This pictorial illustration answers to the dressing and scenic appliances of the stage, appealing only to one sense, the sense of sight; but there is another mode of illustration, appealing to the ear, enjoyed by the drama, but denied to literature—elocutionary illustration. In the dramatic work, every shade of expression, every step in the gradual development of character, every happy point of language, finds a universally understood mouthpiece in the person of the author-prompted and intelligent actor. While thousands are simultaneously made acquainted with literary beauties in the acted drama, which they would never have discovered without the assistance of a trained or inspired guide, the unacted drama—the great literature of our country—is lying worm-eaten upon dusty shelves, is passed imperfectly in conversation from mouth to mouth and ear to ear, or is haltingly read by men whose intellect, imagination, and sympathy are sick, and lame, and blind. The circle of really appreciative, unaided readers, who are blessed with calm judgment, clear perception, and pure literary enthusiasm, free from personal jealousy and sectarian prejudice, is smaller, much smaller, than those men care to admit who wish well to literature, and who follow it with a conscience and an inspiration.

Some feeling of this may have prompted Mr. Dickens to become the elocutionary illustrator of his own works;

and if not, it may be well that he should adopt it, until what was, and is still perhaps, a mere experiment, shall assume the settled form and character of a determined and required mission. The popularity of Mr. Dickens, immense, world-wide, and well-earned as it is, is little guide to the literary appreciation of his worshippers. They are nothing when they become critical. Pickwick—a reflected picture of the cockney-sportsman literature of thirty years ago—touched as it is by the hand of genius, and full to overflowing with the rough, unshapen riches of a young, great, and original literary creator, is still clung to as an enduring monument of Mr. Dickens's power; while those two unequalled twin fictions upon one stem, "The Old Curiosity Shop" and "Barnaby Rudge," are passed by in silence, if not forgotten. While such generally imperfect estimates exist of the relative value of Mr. Dickens's creations, it is fair to assume that half the delicacies of composition, the touches of nature, the tone and importance of minor characters, and all those innumerable graces of the highest literary art which are half hidden from the vulgar and uninquiring gaze (because they do not lie in hard, coarse lumps upon the surface), must be, to the untrained masses, as a secret mine of wealth, until thrown open by the labours of a discerning eye and a discriminating judgment. Many men there may be who are capable of doing this, but none so well qualified as the author himself, especially when, as in the case of Mr. Dickens, he is endowed with the physical capabilities and the dramatic talent to give a vitality to his own mental conceptions.

Mr. Dickens's readings, or illustrations, as we prefer to call them, are running, critical commentaries upon his own works. With all the self-possession, the flexibility of voice, and the facial expression of a trained actor, it is not surprising that Mr. Dickens should be able to cause his own creations to live and move before our eyes. Possessing all the bodily requirements, the conception of character alone is wanted; and there is abundant evidence of the existence of this in the creative fertility of his books. No original dramatic author, no writer of dramatic fiction in the form of novels, whose characters impress their forms upon the page in their own language out of their own mouths, can fail to be in heart, mind, and soul a natural mimic, or actor. Every character in Mr. Dickens's novels, drawn in the first instance from observation, must have been dramatically embodied—acted over, so to speak, a hundred times in the process of development and transference to the written page; and the qualities of voice, nerve, and presence being granted, Mr. Dickens merely passes over that ground, in the face of a large and attentive audience, which he has often passed over before in the undisturbed privacy of his study. Where the pure actor's art is shown, as distinguished from the dramatic quality inherent in all character-creators, is in certain small alterations of the text of his printed book, so minute as to escape the eye of any but a critical observer, but purposely made to produce effective points. It will be sufficient to name one instance in the "Christmas Carol," where the text seems to be improved in a literary sense by the elision of several words coming after, and destroying, to some extent, the effect of a well-known passage. In the glorious account of the Fezziwig ball, in the printed book Mr. Dickens winds up the description of Mr. Fezziwig's dancing by saying he "cut—cut so deftly, that he appeared to wink with his legs, and came upon his feet again without a stagger." In Mr. Dickens's vocal embodiment, he leaves out all the words that come after "legs," saying, with a spasmodic shake of the head and a twist of the paper knife, "He cut—cut so deftly, that he appeared to—wink with his legs."

It is not only in small verbal alterations that the critical effect of Mr. Dickens's elocution is shown. Half-neglected corners of his works, rich in humour and character, are lighted up with all an author's enthusiasm, speaking through an actor's talent; and groups of perfect, well-defined beings are revealed, like insects in a microscope, to the wondering gaze of hundreds, who before this were probably scarcely aware of their existence. The "Christmas Carol" is rich in having two such groups. There are the merchants upon 'Change, who discourse upon Scrooge's death, all of whom stand forth clearly under Mr. Dickens's dramatic treatment, and especially the great fat man with a monstrous chin, whose individuality is as strongly, as humorously, and as forcibly marked in half a dozen lines, as that of Scrooge himself throughout the volume. Then comes the perfectly Shaksperian scene in the rascally rag shop, with old Joe, a very Verges of infamy, the charwoman, the undertaker's man, and the laundress, Mrs. Dilber—all higgling over the wretched rags of the dead Scrooge. Repulsive as the picture is, there is hardly a word that can be spared; and the old huckster, with the two women, stand boldly in the eyes of the audience, until their master chooses to dismiss them. As an example of the objective force of the writing, and the power of embodiment on the part of the reader, this scene ranks second to none in the book—not even the well-known sketch of the Cratchit dinner, in which Mr. Dickens conveys the geniality of the situation in a degree it would be impossible to attain without an appeal to the senses. Admirable and glowing as every word of the description is, it reads almost tame after witnessing the new life which Mr. Dickens is enabled to breathe into it. Language is a wonderful and a powerful instrument in the hands of a master; but it always leaves something unconveyed of the brightest conceptions of the highest inventive genius, and this something Mr. Dickens is enabled to add through the medium of his talent as an elocutionary illustrator.

The "Christmas Carol" presents little opportunity for a sustained impersonation. When Mr. Dickens throws himself into Bob Cratchit, leaning over the elbow-rest upon the reading-table, with a meek, subdued voice, and a mild timid expression of countenance, he gives an instantaneous impression of the poor, feeble, struggling clerk, which lights up the whole history of his past life. But this is merely an indication of dramatic power not allowed to develope, for Bob Cratchit is swept away by the progress of the story, and the stream of level narrative and eloquent description rolls solemnly on. The glimpses of Scrooge's early life—the fine imaginative picture of the first of the three Spirits—the account of Marley's ghost, with that exquisite touch of humour where the two back buttons of his coat are said to have been seen through his transparent body (both sketches equal to anything in the "Arabian Nights")—the flirtations of Topper and the niece—are all read, described, or embodied in a highly impressive, finished, and humorous manner.

The contrast between the Scrooge of the earlier part of the book and the Scrooge of the latter part is drawn with a fine discriminating eye for change of character in the same individual; and every word in the conversation with the boy out of the window respecting the purchase of the goose, is watched for and listened to by the audiences like celebrated passages from a great standard play.

In "The Chimes," the group, consisting of Alderman Cute, Filer, and the red-faced man, is as suggestive as anything in the Carol, although of a purely satirical character. Mr. Dickens's personification of these three men is perfect in the rapid gradations of voice, and is quietly enjoyed, as all satirical embodiments generally are, instead of being coarsely applauded. Mr. Dickens is hard upon the political economists whenever he gets a chance; but his keen shafts of ridicule only hit the hollow pretenders to the science, leaving its great axioms untouched. It is the old quarrel between the imaginative and the logical faculty. There are more great social mistakes made by the heart than by the head; and Mr. Dickens will one day shake hands with Mr. Malthus, and find to his astonishment they have been both working for the same end.

The wheezy porter of Sir Joseph Bowley is a platform creation of the highest dramatic order, built up out of a few lines in the book, which an ordinary reader would pass by. The chandler's-shop woman with the wonderful name, the off-hand medical attendant, Richard drunk and Richard sober, Lady Bowley, the clerk, and the solemn humbug, Sir Joseph Bowley, are all brought prominently forward; and the lines that divide them, when they appear in groups, are marked with an ease and precision that Mr. Dickens will not improve if he reads or illustrates for twenty years. The two girls—Lilian and Trotty Veck's daughter—are very beautifully and delicately conveyed to the audience; but the two greatest impersonations are Will Fern and the old ticket-porter himself. The contrast is very strong between these two characters; but this only serves to show alike the genius of the creator, and the talent of the illustrator.

The tall, gaunt, fierce, hungry, magistrate-hunted labourer, Will Fern, stands in the flesh before the audience, and is one of the most powerfully-drawn and impressive portraits in the whole range of Mr. Dickens's present readings. The country voice is a country voice, not too highly coloured, but forcible and natural; and the whole embodiment can hardly fail to impress upon a reflecting audience a painful social lesson, which they will not easily forget.

Trotty Veck is made manifest through a voice modified from Bob Cratchit's; and, as in the case of the meek, over-worked, ill-paid clerk, the idea of physical and mental weakness is very clearly conveyed. The trot home with Will Fern's half-starved child-niece, Lilian, and the plaintive chant of "Here we are and here we go," produce more tears and laughter combined than anything within the whole range of the acted drama.

The story of Little Dombey, selected from the novel, is poetical, humorous, and pathetic, affording scope for two sustained impersonations, Toots and the Child. Little Dombey's voice, and his gradual fading away, are very beautifully rendered, and are fair examples of the more refined and delicate imagination of their writer. Toots is a thorough dramatic creation upon the platform, both in voice, face, and gesture. Utter vacuity is required, and it is admirably conveyed by facial expression, while the deep voice coming from the half-open mouth is one of the most original and amusing effects produced by Mr. Dickens. Dr. Blimber, Mr. Feeder, Miss Blimber, Miss Chick, the Doctors, Mr. Dombey, and Mrs. Pipchin, are all clearly and carefully portrayed; while the last belongs to a class of women whose peculiarities Mr. Dickens is especially happy in depicting. The miscellaneous reading presents many features not possessed by the complete stories: the chief being that two characters—Boots at the Holly Tree Inn, and Mrs. Gamp—rest for a longer time in the eye of the audience, testing Mr. Dickens's power as an actor of sustained parts: while the selections from "Martin Chuzzlewit" crowd so many performers in a small space, that the polyphonic ability of the reader is severely tried. Mr. Dickens comes out of the trial with much honour and perfect success. The soldier's story opens the reading, and it is an example of a level natural tale, well told, without any straining after effect. It serves as a contrast to the story which immediately follows it, told by Boots at the Holly Tree Inn.

This story is not a story in the strict sense of the term, but a very beautiful idea, delightfully worked out through the medium of one of the most humorous and natural pieces of low, groom-like, stable-like characterization that ever came from Mr. Dickens's pen. It was published in one of the Christmas numbers of "Household Words"—a journal in which lie many fugitive pieces which show no falling off of power in the author of the "Old Curiosity Shop." Boots at the Holly Tree Inn, as an example of low comedy drawn from nature, is worth a hundred fancy eccentric portraits like Sam Weller, whose character is largely marked by the vices of a bygone literature, which happily is now utterly buried and forgotten. Mr. Dickens's embodiment of Boots is remarkable for ease, finish, and a thorough relish for the character. The swaying to and fro of the body, the half-closing of the eye, and the action of the head, when any point in the narrative is supposed to require particular emphasis to make it clear, and the voice sounding as if affected by the chewing of a straw—all assist to make a perfect example of pure comedy acting. It was a very happy notion to place such a pretty story in the mouth of such a man; and the audience, while they watch with interest the progress of the fanciful episode in the life of the little runaway children, are amused by the broad humour and strong individuality of the simulated narrator. The boy-child, when he gets an opportunity of speaking in his own character, is very clearly conveyed to the audience by Mr. Dickens.

The selections from "Martin Chuzzlewit," in which the immortal Mrs. Gamp is a central but not an all-important figure, present a very wide range of personation for Mr. Dickens. There is the pompous Pecksniff, who does not come out very clearly; Mr. Mould, very oily, full of small talk and common-places, with a keen eye to business, who is most admirably portrayed; the old half-phantom clerk, a fine representation; and Jonas Chuzzlewit, with the agonized, restless face, gnawing his finger nails, a perfect example of elevated acting. Betsy Prig, with the masculine voice, is not pleasing. She may convey the author's idea of her; but she is comparatively ineffective as a platform portrait. The minor characters come out well as they revolve at different distances round Mrs. Sarah Gamp, who is a dramatic creation of the highest order. There is no fault to find with Mr. Dickens's embodiment of the immortal nurse, for no amount of study could improve it; and if it fails to produce an impression upon the audience commensurate with its artistic merits, it is because the character, coarse in itself, is so broadly and deeply impressed upon the printed page, that nearly every reader is able to build up for himself a clear idea of this great friend and confidant of doctors and undertakers.

Mr. Dickens, as a writer, may put in a just and indisputable claim for having directed the main course of the literature which now flows around us. From the smallest writer in the smallest magazine to the lofty Baron Macaulay himself, there are traces of the great fiction-creator of the day. Everything that is now drawn or described must be drawn or described from the life, and not produced from the fevered imaginings of an unfed brain. Some carry the lessons of their master too far, and become mere reporters and takers of brokers' inventories. This style is not a true reflex of Mr. Dickens's, for the great gift and charm of humorous analogy is wanting.

If we look at the so-called comic publications of the day, we see Mr. Dickens's forms of satire and types of character nourishing pages that seem to have no power of creating food for themselves. Entertainments are sustained by that which he originated; the stage is beginning to surrender; and the very organs which set themselves up as his opponents are full to overflowing with illustrations drawn from his works.

Mr. Dickens scarcely knows the force of the engine which he holds in his hands—has scarcely mastered the scope and destination of his great design. He is now delighting elegant wearers of opera-cloaks and carriers of bouquets, dangling loungers who come to satisfy an idle curiosity, and stout well-to-do middle-class citizens, who have been blessed with the taught ability to read and write. Descend a little lower in the social scale, and we come upon a land containing thousands—nay, millions—who are only to be reached through their eyes and ears; to whom a printed book is a black, blurred, mysterious mass, notwithstanding many Acts of Parliament, educational commissions, and school-houses remarkable for their imposing style of architecture. Yet these people are men and women with hearts and souls—people willing to be taught, if they can be taught easily (for at forty, in the intervals of heavy labour, it is a sore task even to learn to read)—people ready to pay for being taught—people who know little, and never will know much, of moral principles, and who can only be reached and improved through their emotional sympathies.

Here is a wide and a fruitful field for Mr. Dickens to cultivate, and in such a cause they gain a dignity who descend.

CONVERTING THE HEATHEN.

Of late years, amongst the varied, visionary, disastrous, unproductive, and even dishonest applications of capital, there has sprung up, or further developed, a new trade—that of converting the heathen. Organizations small in their beginning—mistaken in their principles—selfish, wasteful, and ineffective in their practice, have been swelled into most mischievous importance, by the arts and devices of the theological platform, until the public are led to believe, by secretarial reports, and leading articles of religious newspapers, that the whole duty of man consists in taking Bibles into the midst of sandy deserts, and begging, borrowing, or stealing, a miserable native to act as a converted decoy, attracting fresh subscriptions, by stimulating the dying enthusiasm of flagging supporters. Men whose religious creeds should have taught them to respect the domestic affections, or to cultivate those affections in the untutored savage, where they found them either deficient or totally wanting, have bought children from parents for buttons, bits of glass, old nails, or a dirty blacking-bottle, and, taking advantage of those imperfect natures they were sent out to correct, have not hesitated to burk the children of the heathen in the name of Christianity, in order to find favour in the eyes of the magnates of a Missionary Society, and create a sensation at a religious tea-meeting.

The missionary lion of the day is Dr. Livingstone. His

book is *the* book of the season: and as a contribution to geographical science, I am glad to welcome it for what it is worth. My purpose is not to deal with that book, but with Dr. Livingstone, and his speeches in the large commercial towns. Dr. Livingstone is a man of great physical and mental energy—a man who cannot fail to arrive at sound conclusions as to the prospects of missionary enterprise in the interior of Africa. Does he not feel that these missions ever have been failures, are failures, and always will be failures, unless backed by the strong tyrannical arm of colonial government? Why does he hound on the commerce of the country to take mercantile possession of another India? Why does he tickle the ears of commercial Christianity and Christian commerce with accounts of rich tracts of country, because he finds the rank luxuriance of the jungle where he expected nothing but oceans of sand? Because he is only acting in conformity with a system which works with a slow, silent, never ceasing force, and tends to what?—the formation of a bloody arena, like India has lately been, and will doubtless be again, where the ground-down people of a country contend against a ruthless usurper, with all the fierce energy and brutality of political hate, and all the fanaticism of an insulted religion. Dr. Livingstone knows well—or ought to know if he reads history with filmless eyes—the different steps by which we arrive at the formation and anarchy of a Possession or a Colony. First, there is the meek, quiet missionary, in many cases, when not spoiled by a society, a hard-working, conscientious, God-fearing man, who visits a new country, and, gaining the confidence of the natives, is welcomed to their homes, and shown by simple-hearted confiding people the beauties of their birth-place. Expecting to find a race of rude cannibals with eccentric tastes and powerful digestions, he is agreeably surprised, and his report overflows with wild honey. The next step is a settlement of peaceful traders on the coast, who, somehow or another, persuade their government that annexation is the one thing needful for the benefit of all parties. Annexation and military occupation take place; and the people are governed with an iron rod, that one party may trade with them, and the other party convert them. Missionary schemes and military government increase in intensity, until at last the miserable natives rise in rebellion. We have had the same thing before in our own country and in classic regions, and it has been lauded under the name of patriotism. The conclusion, I need not say, is Fire, Famine, and Slaughter.

Dr. Livingstone wishes to direct the greedy eyes of civilization to a tract of country ten times the size of India; remarkable for its vegetation and scenic advantages. Dividends are not usually got out of scenery and jungles; and I thank God that commerce is so sick and weak at present with overgorging, that he might as well try to galvanize a corpse as to extract a stiver for his purposes from the wasted capital of the country! I thank God that it is so, because I feel that, rather than have another India on our hands, it would have been better that the great missionary's bones were bleaching in the desert, or that he had been brained as he sat at the hospitable board of the unsuspecting African.

If he will boldly preach the doctrine of the extinction of the untutored savage I will admit his logical consistency, while I question his humanity and justice.

Some missions there are that, with the widest and most ambitious objects, have exhibited such a lamentable want of practical skill and business tact, so much dishonest and false principle with such feebleness of execution, that their history ought to be a warning and an example to every chapel, platform, society, and religious organ in the kingdom. At the head of this unfortunate list—pre-eminent in failure, where failure is the inevitable rule and not the accidental exception—stands the Patagonian mission, a society which seemingly has attempted a gigantic task with a very liliputian capital.

Its commencement in the year 1850 was most inauspicious—the founder, Captain Allen Gardiner, R.N., with his six companions, who formed the crew of the "Ocean Queen," that sailed from Liverpool in the autumn of that year for Picton Island, Tierra del Fuego, being all starved to death.

The next step taken by the Patagonian mission was the building and fitting out of a vessel called the Allen Gardiner, eighty tons register, which was ready for sea in the latter part of 1854. This brought them in communication with a sea-faring-man of a serious turn, one Captain W. Parker Snow, who offered to conduct the expedition as an unpaid officer; this offer was accepted, but a small nominal salary was awarded him under an agreement, and he was allowed at his own request to take his wife with him. His troubles in connection with the mission now commenced. He was instructed to man his ship with no other crew than men who combined what he might consider practical seamanlike qualities with what the society might consider a sound adherence to certain theological doctrines. Such men were not easy to find in the neighbourhood of Wapping and Ratcliff Highway, nor in the over-hanging streets of Portsmouth, nor on the canal quays of Bristol, where the vessel was to start from. After much labour and difficulty, he succeeded in procuring two pious officers, and the promise of two men. He paid their expenses to Bristol, and they joined the ship along with an indifferent seaman partly blind, a young man, a landsman, a Hindoo cook, an unmanageable cabin boy, a surgeon, a catechist or teacher to the mission and natives, a joiner, a house carpenter, and a mason. The outlay of preparing the vessel for sea fell upon Captain Snow, who worked for masters who were liberal in instruction but chary of money. The mission had nothing yet to show in the way of results, and probably subscriptions flagged, the interest taken in the enterprise being based upon a shadowy recollection of three interesting natives of Tierra del Fuego, who were brought into this country in 1830, and who were taken out of it again to their native soil in 1833, plus a smattering of English language, useful arts, the European costume, and perhaps with some of the vices of the civilized character implanted upon the rude energy of the savage nature. Their names were Jemmy Button and York Minster, boys, and Fuegia Basket, a girl.

Captain Snow himself is a man who acts upon the old Puritan maxim of fearing the Lord and keeping your powder dry. He is no scoffer, but a devout believer in the efficacy of prayer; a fit companion for old Howell, the Admiralty secretary in the time of Charles the Second, who prayed when washing his hands and after putting on a clean shirt. "The Allen Gardiner," notwithstanding the efforts and personal labour of her commander, left Bristol, in October, 1854, leaky, lumbered fore and aft, her decks covered with timber, but fortified with prayer. A clergyman who was to have gone out, and acted as third mate on board, was not ready in time; and he was to follow in some vessel bound for the Falkland Islands.

When the unfortunate vessel got out to sea, the captain discovered, too late, that, for all purposes of practical seamanship, and even for the general harmony and subordination of the crew, it would have been better—far better—if he had disobeyed the rigid instructions of the society, and had manned his vessel with the usual dirty, tobacco-chewing, rum-drinking, swearing, average Ratcliffe Highway seamen, instead of the saintly crew that he had collected with so much trouble and expense. Several of his companions, with two of the seamen and the boy—the inspired boy—took upon themselves to denounce him to perdition whenever they were ordered to do anything they did not like. If told to go up aloft in a case of emergency, they took to chaunting hymns and comforting each other with passages of Scripture. The sailors' cabin must have been quite a little heaven below. The catechist taught that religious duties made a man independent of all secular authority in a vessel. Truly a very troublesome crew to manage by any means short of a rope's-end.

The devoted captain was still left without funds to cheer him in his troubles. He was annoyed by attempts to undermine him (though for what earthly reason I cannot imagine, as he was doing everything for nothing); he was perplexed with very indefinite, numerous, and contradictory instructions from the Society, and he was strongly exhorted to do something, and send over some graphic and well-written account of a visit to the natives, to raise the funds of the mission from the very low ebb to which they had fallen.

He resolved to carry out a clause in his instructions which told him to try and discover Jemmy Button, the eldest of the three native Fuegians, who had returned from England primed and loaded with civilization for the work of converting the miserable natives.

Captain Snow found the natives addicted to yelling, and he established friendly relations with them by out-shouting them through a speaking-trumpet. He thumped their backs and they thumped his back, and he submitted to be hugged by them, although they were very stinking and full of vermin—much like many poor creatures in our own country. He found Jemmy Button as dirty as his neighbours, if anything even below their level. Nevertheless they were all happy, and refused to leave their beloved shores on any account. Jemmy liked England, but he loved Fuegia: and he would neither quit, nor allow any child of his to quit, his native land. All the savages were firm in refusing to allow their children to be taken away: the bits of glass, the old nails, the buttons, and the blacking-bottle for once had lost their charms; and as Captain Snow was not a man to use force and deceit where fair offers were of no avail, the cherished idea of the Society was nipped in the bud—that of conveying the young native Fuegians and Patagonians into the Falkland Islands, to tend in practical slavery the Society's cattle—to build houses, to fish, to seal, to take sea-birds, and to be prevented from running away—and all for the benefit of the mission.

The devoted captain had a spy set upon his actions; he had to pay wages and charges out of his own pocket. He was instructed to buy an island, but no money was sent to him to complete the purchase. He had to discharge, pay, and send home his crew at the expiration of their term of service (except the two mates, who had quarrelled with him some time before, because, there being no clergyman on board, he had performed once instead of twice a daily service of public prayer; and they had been discharged by their own wish to go on shore and convert the wretched sailors and bigoted papists): finally, he was supplanted by a missionary and party sent out from the Society, and left, after two years' hard service, without money, to sell his books and instruments, and buy a passage home for himself and wife.

There are many labourers employed in the missionary vineyard who go forth from a country of religious toleration with principles that savour of the old days of Smithfield and the stake. There are also many men who, in whatever sphere they moved, would always meet with admiration and respect. These are the men who form the bulwarks of religion; whose energy and example are all required, and more than required, to counteract the injury done to their faith by the vicious dogmatism, tyranny, and intolerance of their uncongenial brethren. These are not the men to hound us on to take material possession of China—exclusive China—where the plan of Ningpo and Shanghai is as thickly studded with our mission-houses as a nursery-garden is full of hot-beds. These are not the men to map out India into doctrinal districts, and teach, like the despised Mahomet, the pure faith at the point of the sword. These are not the men to draw alluring pictures of the interior of Africa, that a legacy of blood and rapine and murder may be left to their successors, and that millions of poor, despised creatures yet unborn may learn to curse their names and the religion that they taught. And it is to these men, and their higher wisdom, that I address myself when I ask them to consider whether, while they are expending their time, labour, and treasure in arriving at the result of exhibiting a converted negro upon a religious platform, they have not lost more valuable ground in causing those men, whose adhesion is worth having, to turn their backs upon the faith that they represent, and to close their ears to all creeds, until something more of humanity is mixed with the designs of religion.

IGNORANT EDUCATION.

I AM a working man. I go to my factory every morning at six, and I leave it every night at the same hour. I require, on the average, eight hours' sleep, which leaves four hours for recreation and improvement. I have lived at many places in the outskirts, according as my work has shifted, but generally I find myself at Mile End. I always live near the factory where I work, and so do all my mates, no matter how small, dirty, and dear the houses may be; and sometimes it strikes me that three shillings a week is rather a high rent to pay for a little, dirty, badly-ventilated room, in a back street at Stepney. However, the landlords won't take less, because they have always got customers at that price, and, looking at it in that light, I don't see why they should. One or two of my mates have tried the plan of living a few miles out, and walking to business in the morning, like the clerks do in the city. It don't do—I suppose because they have not been used to it from boys; perhaps, because walking exercise at five in the morning don't suit men who are hard at work with their bodies all day. As to railways and omnibuses, they cost money, and we don't understand them, except on holidays, when we have got our best clothes on.

Now, what I am going to talk to you about, Sir, is the attempts that you gentlemen at the west-end are so fond of making, every now and then, to improve our mental condition. I dare say you all mean well enough, but, unfortunately you don't know anything about us. Talk of the ignorance of the lower orders, why, it's nothing to the ignorance of the upper classes. A working man, like any one of my mates, is employed, we'll say, in making boilers. Before he's allowed to work independently, he passes, at least, a seven years' apprenticeship in learning his craft and the nature of the material with which he has to deal. But a gentleman has only to reach twenty-one years of age, and come from college into possession of a large fortune, and he may set up at once as a benefactor of his species, without knowing anything whatever of the business. Some of these gentlemen, well-intentioned enough, no doubt, are very fond of starting Working-men's Colleges, for the improvement of our minds. It might be thought rude, but it would be very proper, as it is very necessary, for working men who want to be improved, to start a college to teach those members of the upper classes how to improve us. Don't let me be misunderstood, Sir, in what I am saying. Of course I can see the great superiority which our ignorant educators possess over those other members of their own order—those lounging Don Giovannis of Pall Mall, who do nothing, as our preacher says, but eat, drink, and make merry, because to-morrow they will die. I only speak as I do, because I am anxious that what work is done shall be done in a workmanlike manner. I need not take up your time, Sir, with any account of those first failures of the educators—the Mechanics' Institutes. You know as well as I do, that those which have survived have come to be mere places of recreation, and not of instruction for our class—a mixture of the concert-room and the dancing academy. The places that have been raised in their stead—what few there are—are called Working-Men's Institutes, Reading Rooms, and such like. They are generally started by a clergyman, who gets some philanthropic lord to put his name down as president, and a baronet to put his name down as vice-president. Neither of these gentlemen ever come near the place. Then a council, or something of the kind, is formed amongst the well-to-do tradesmen of the district, with, perhaps, a lawyer, a doctor, and one or two other clergymen. Then they take a room and fit it up; and I think, Sir, badly as I may describe it, you will recognize the kind of refuge provided.

It is a long, dark room, generally an old work-shop, with bare brick walls, which they cover half way down with a coating of white-wash. They half fill it with low, narrow, hard, bare, wooden forms, extremely uncomfortable to sit upon, and they block up the fire-place, and plant near the centre of the room, a round, black gas-stove. Then comes the decoration of the walls with one or two rude maps—a coloured geological chart—and a bill of some assurance company, in which one or more of the council is interested. The place is then lighted with a few butchers' flame gas lamps, and I must say, that the general aspect is not cheerful. There is also a small inner room, fitted up with a few more maps, bills, forms, and shelves, on the latter of which the library of the institution is kept.

The books are not numerous—that cannot be helped; and they are not well selected—that, in some measure, can be helped. A library is always, to my thinking, a tolerably correct index and reflection of a man's mind, and that is why the collection of a set of books for an institution of this kind should not be left in the hands of one, or two, or four, or even of all the managing committee. They select such works as *they* know something about, and not such as the intended reader wishes to read. Gifts of books are sent, very often, in the same spirit—a spirit of literary, theological, and philosophical proselytism. Then a course of lectures is arranged, about three times a year, comprising many very good subjects; treated cleverly enough by men who do not understand the working-classes, and who take no pains to adapt themselves to their feelings, their comprehension, and their peculiar mode of thinking. The same spirit—one of self—governs the lectures as well as tho books. The attendance, after a little while, falls off, and the institution becomes merely a very inferior and limited lending library—useful as far as it goes. The clerical founder, and one or two of the committee, who expected great things, become proportionately disheartened, and they cease to attend, wondering at the supposed apathy of the class they were trying to benefit, instead of trying to find a cause in the way they administered their plan.

It seems to me, Sir, looking at it from my point of view as a working man, that all such schemes fail—because they do not aim, first of all, at making the people *comfortable.* We are made up of senses as well as mind, and we require to be warm and snug—to have society—to have colours on the wall to please the eye and pictures to satisfy and cultivate the taste—matting, if not carpeting, to walk upon, and a chair, and not a form without a back, to sit upon. We crave these things first, before we venture upon the cold, abstract ground of improving the mind; and if you, gentlemen, cannot help us to these things at present, wait, and gather strength until you can. One prominent success is worth a hundred failures. In the meantime, a few of our class will go to the glittering gin-palace, but more to the warm coffee-house, where, for a few pence, they can get their books, their papers, their chess or draughts, and their coffee.

Another project, Sir, of an educational nature, that has been before the public at different times, is the throwing open the library of the British Museum at night, for the benefit of the labouring classes. Let them do it if they think proper, but do not let them expect much from it. As a rule, Sir, I believe that the same readers would be found there at night as in the day; and, for my own part, if I went, I am sure I could not settle down to read. I willingly admit that the place is very harmonious and beautiful—perhaps too beautiful—but I could no more settle down to study there, than in the Colosseum or the Crystal Palace. The very light, beauty, and colour of the place all help to distract the attention. My opinion is that nothing can do any real service to a working man *inclined* for study, but a good *lending* library. As you cannot raise men of learning and genius like cucumbers, so you cannot keep determined men down. I have read that a carpenter's workman, named Lee, became, by his own efforts, one of the greatest professors at Cambridge. Good. Let any man who feels that he has got the same will and power within him go and do likewise. He will find plenty of means to help him at hand. It was only yesterday that I passed a large book-stall, where, in an egg-chest outside, divided into twopenny, threepenny, and fourpenny compartments, were bundled heaps of good sterling books, that the real, earnest workman would find of some service. When he cannot get a Cicero or a good grammar for the price of a pint of beer, then let him, or rather his patrons, grumble that he is neglected.

AN AGREEABLE RATTLE.

I WAS walking along Lombard Street, one Friday afternoon, a few weeks ago, in no very cheerful mood, for the Bank had just raised the rate of discount one per cent., and I had several promising joint-stock schemes which I wished to place upon the market. What can be done at seven per cent. is simply impossible at eight, and I felt much like a man who is kept out of his property.

While in this unpleasant frame of mind, I came suddenly across a friend who was hit as hard as myself, but who was of a far more elastic disposition.

"Eight, Sam," I said, "I hardly expected it."

"We shall have it higher," was the annoying reply, "if these joint-stock schemes increase and multiply."

"Don't talk like a money-article," I rejoined; "you may just as well try to mop back the Atlantic."

"Or swallow California," he retorted.

"In ten years' time," I said, somewhat pompously, "no business requiring more than fifty thousand pounds' capital will be found in any other form than that of a limited liability company."

"Don't prophesy, but tell us what to do during the next eight days."

"I have no idea."

"I have; we'll go to the Low Countries. A week's

tour will do us both good, and give the 'precious metals' time to flow in, and ease the market. There's something soothing in our present condition, to go where little is thought of but money-making, and where the greatest banker bears the pleasant name of Hope."

I agreed almost mechanically to this plan. We dined in the neighbourhood of Cornhill, and, to be strictly truthful, I may mention that we got outside a twopenny omnibus at the corner of Bishopsgate Street.

"To start the journey cheerfully," said Sam, "I'll give you a conundrum. Why need our conductor have little fear of the cholera?"

Of course I gave it up.

"Because (as you heard him tell the driver) he's got ten insides."

When we reached the "Flowerpot" we were asked to get down, and form two more "insides" to oblige a costermonger.

"I've often been asked to get outside to oblige a lady," said Sam, "but this is quite a new sensation."

A few minutes before seven o'clock in the evening we arrived at the Shoreditch Station. There seemed to be something very strange, if not radically wrong, in starting for "the Continent" from this quarter of London; but there was little time for reflection. In less than two hours we found ourselves at Harwich—that is, at a platform and a pier with a few beacon lights, and we tottered at once on board a floating hotel, the steamer "Avalon," belonging to the Great Eastern Railway. For those who like a little sea, there are no channel steamers fitted up with more regard to the passengers' comfort than these Rotterdam and Harwich vessels. We took a light supper, went to bed, got up in the morning, and really washed and dressed ourselves—an operation that is not often performed on board a short-passage steamer, for want of conveniences. At seven o'clock we were pleasantly taking our breakfast coffee on deck, as we floated up the Maas to Rotterdam, and criticising scenery which is more remarkable for the industry that made it than for any picturesque quality. Land reclaimed from the sea has the same characteristics nearly all the world over; but rural Holland has contrived to give herself a distinctive character by the introduction of many windmills.

We took the Dutch custom-house officers on board from a boat in the river, so that our luggage was examined before we arrived at Rotterdam. When we got to the pier at eight o'clock, we had, therefore, nothing to do but to walk quietly on shore, and to enter an omnibus like ordinary citizens.

"Halloo!" shouted Sam, "there's some imposition here. Where's our old friend, Rip Van Winkle, with the conical hat and balloon breeches? Where's the immortal hero of the 'Cork Leg.'"

Sam's observation was only too well founded. The men were dressed in that sad imitation of evening costume which is peculiar to Thames pilots, and it was only the poorer women who wore caps, or metal head-dresses, like helmets.

Every Dutchman smoked in the omnibus without asking leave, and a boy about six years old sucked a cigar instead of a sugar-stick. We arrived at an hotel, and were received by the master, who was smoking, and by two waiters, who had evidently just put down their cigars. We dined at a very good *table-d'hôte*, where a pint bottle of Medoc was given to each of us, as part of the dinner, and where cigars and pipes were introduced almost before the dessert. We walked over the bridges, along the quays, and under the pleasant shade of the trees in this Dutch Venice, admired the flowers in the windows, and laughed at the mirrors so placed amongst them that the inmates of each house could see the whole traffic of the street. While so engaged, we became suddenly conscious of an unpleasant, overpowering smell.

"What can it be?" exclaimed Sam, who was accounted a wit. "It can't be decayed tradesmen, the town's too thriving."

"Decayed vegetables," I answered.

Decayed vegetables it was, for on some of the canals was floating a thick scum of cabbage leaves, lettuce leaves, corks, stalks, bits of wood, and potato-parings. Men in black mud barges were dredging some of the streams, and some of the canals looked like the old pictures of the Fleet ditch, at the period when it was an open sewer, and not a shining river. The bargemen are not assisted by horses, but have to pole their craft along by digging into the bed of the river with their noses over the savory flood. The canals not only run through the streets, but under them; and looking down a grating in the middle of a roadway, we saw a Dutch Charon and his companions smoking in the cool shade of a tunnel. The roads are not very smooth, and the bridges are constantly being raised for the passage of large craft, so that riding in hack carriages is not common. These vehicles are three shillings and sixpence an hour—a price far above the Continental average. In other respects—hotel living, for example—there is no difference between Dutch or French, and Belgian prices.

"The people are wonderfully like the English in appearance," remarked Sam, "and wonderfully like them in their love for money making."

"The worst preparation for a journey," I returned, attempting to be philosophical, "is to start with a belief that human nature is not the same in all countries. Conditions of living may differ——"

"Exactly," interrupted Sam, showing a decided determination to cut me short; "if you want a barber here, you go to a shop where a brass dish is fluttering before the door, like a gold fish at the end of an angler's rod; if you go to a place where the usual barber's pole is sticking out across the street, you either find yourself at the Burgomaster's, or at the office of some foreign consulate. Places where they work—their workshops, in fact—they call workhouses. Now in England a workhouse is the last house where you would look for industrial activity."

From Rotterdam we went to Amsterdam by the railway which runs to the Hague, Leyden, and Haarlem, and found that such travelling in Holland was slow, but punctual. Sam thought that Hague had been politely altered from Ague, out of compliment to royalty, which had fixed its residence there, and certainly the country looked remarkably swampy. The fields, intersected by dykes instead of hedges, looked like a vast billiard-table, but rich and luxuriant.

"Ah!" exclaimed Sam, suddenly bursting into poetry,

"'How weary, flat, fresh, and profitable,
Seem to me all the uses of this world.'"

"What must be a Dutchman's feelings," I remarked, in a true spirit of cockney pride, "when he first sees our Greenwich or Primrose Hill?"

"Or what he is even more likely to see," returned Sam, "the *Montagne de la Cour*, at Brussels."

In Amsterdam we, of course, found another Dutch

Venice, with canals even more putrid than those of Rotterdam. "Her home is in the sea, and the rotten cabbage-leaf clings to the marble of her palaces."

The old Spanish houses here give the city a very picturesque effect, though as fast as they are undermined by the ever-encroaching water, and fall or are pulled down, they are replaced with Parisian-looking houses. The French have a wonderful power of propagating their ideas. French shops are on the Dutch quays and boulevards, and the French language is largely spoken by the natives. The general aspect of many of the canal streets reminded us very forcibly of Lower Thames Street, but the houses had a grand and noble look, although chiefly devoted to business. In Amsterdam, and some part of Rotterdam, the Englishman may see what life the old citizens of London led before it was the fashion to live out of the City. The cellars are devoted to goods, part of the ground floor to offices, and the drawing-room floor—large and lofty, in most cases, like the hall of some old City company—is the dwelling-house of the family. Above these are bed-rooms, divided by a storehouse for mere goods, from which drops a crane-chain, when required, in front of the drawing-room windows. In this store-room — amongst the bales and tubs—the female domestic servants are fond of sitting on a Sunday evening, reading a book, or doing a little needle-work, and flirting with their sweethearts in the distance.

Everywhere we came across the everlasting pipe and cigar, the churches even smelling of tobacco during service time like a taproom. The actors at the theatres did not exactly smoke during the performance, but they spat upon the stage, which is almost as bad. We went to an open-air concert, where we heard the best band in Amsterdam; but though the selection of music was ambitious—embracing all schools, from Wagner to Auber—the execution wanted fire and precision. Leaving this concert we passed through the Jews' Street, a street that rivals Petticoat Lane, or the Jews' Street in Frankfort. The Jews in Amsterdam reach sixty or seventy thousand. The maniac noises and gesticulations made to sell a few pennyworths of pickled cucumber, showed us unchecked competition in its wildest moments. The only calm man in the jumping, shrieking, bawling crowd, was an old, bent, sallow-faced hermit, with blinking sore eyes, dressed in greasy rags, who watched over a few old Hebrew books displayed in a dirty basket. Perhaps there was something in him of the spirit of Erasmus, but why was he so dirty?

Before we left Holland we had some idea of going to Germany, but the trains to that country were so slow—something like twenty miles an hour being an express pace—that, as our time was very short, we gave up the notion.

"Do you understand much German?" I asked Sam, who was somewhat daring as a linguist.

"About a sausage and a half," he answered, as if that was quite sufficient.

"Then, I think," I returned, "we'd better go to Belgium."

To get to Belgium we had to go back to Rotterdam, and we made another railway circuit, this time by the way of Utrecht. The country was still as flat as a billiard-table, and as fresh as much water could make it. At Rotterdam we went on board a steamer, much like the Rhine boats, and sailed up the Rhine to Dordrecht, and from there to Moerdyk. On board this steamer we met the only two very fat Dutchmen we had seen, well fed and well dressed; "clothed," as Sam put it, "in turtle and fine linen." They gulped Dutch bitters before we started to give them an appetite, and as soon as the vessel began to move, they plunged down into the cabin and took their places at a very good *table-d'hôte* dinner. Here they ate bits of every dish, drank several French and German wines, and then went on deck and ordered coffee. As soon as the coffee was consumed, they sipped brandy and sugar, and by the time that was consumed we had arrived at Moerdyk. Here the Dutch-Belgian Railway awaited us, and we took our places for Antwerp. The travelling was just as slow as on the Dutch-Rhenish line, broken by an examination of luggage at the Belgian frontier. The passport nuisance is now happily got rid of in most parts of the Continent, thanks to the liberality of the French Emperor.

Antwerp may be shortly described as a fortified monastic town, with a fringe of docks—a combination of Canterbury and Wapping. The great election struggle between the clerical and liberal party was at its height, and the people in one of the low quarters were erecting an image to a favourite saint. The most poetical thing about the churches is their clear, ringing, musical chimes, and next to that their grey, worn exteriors. Many of them, however, are in such a state that they are obliged to be restored, a process which largely destroys their picturesque character. The interiors are mostly overloaded with decoration—bright wooden carvings, wonderful in their way, marble altar-pieces and pictures, all piled up together, or over each other, until the effect produced is that of a bazaar, like the Pantheon in Oxford Street. The grand simplicity of the Rouen churches is wholly wanting. Much, of course, is made of Rubens; but Rubens—colour excepted—was of the earth, earthy, and sadly deficient in true religious sentiment. Here, as in Holland, French house architecture is gradually replacing the fine old Spanish style, and the Hôtel de Ville is being restored in a way which makes it look like the Carlton Club.

From Antwerp we, of course, went to Brussels—that little Paris, which every man should see who wishes to thoroughly enjoy the greater city. Everywhere we appeared to be meeting our compatriots, the travelling English. At our hotel in the *Place Royale* we were treated like true Britons, and were supposed to be pining for beefsteaks at every hour in the day. To make this supposition more unjust, we, in common with the rest of the English, simply breakfasted upon eggs and bread-and-butter, while the only French party in the house were devouring beefsteaks and potatoes. The "Cock-a-Doodle-Doo" coach called for us every morning to go to Waterloo, and the guard of the "Cock-a-Doodle-Doo" aroused us every morning with the "British Grenadiers," badly played on a cornopean. Instead of going, however, to the field of battle, we mused upon the emptiness of human glory. The blood that was spilt on that great day has merely manured the fields until they show an exceptional fertility, and has sustained an English four-horse coach for many seasons.

While resting at Brussels we felt a growing desire to use the travellers' privilege of grumbling at the dinner-table. Sam began it. They brought us a leg of mutton and "trimmings," and when abroad, we like to leave the cookery of our native land behind us. The joint, as is too often the case when foreign meat is cooked in the English fashion, was decidedly, hopelessly tough.

"Do lambs ever have wooden legs, like Greenwich pensioners?" asked Sam.

"Why?" I inquired.

"Because if they do, we've got one of them by mistake."

The French wine was bad and dear, but still we ventured upon a little champagne.

"What brand is that?" asked Sam, showing me the cork.

"*Perière Jouct*," I answered.

"Ah!" said Sam, "*Perière Jouet, e i o u*, and sometimes *w* and *y*."

When some very suspicious-looking beef was brought on by way of an *entrée*, Sam was compelled to address himself to the waiter, and he said:—

"I don't mind dining *à la carte*, but I object very much to dine *à la carle* and horse."

"*Oui M'sieu*," replied the waiter, who hardly understood a word he said, and who immediately brought him a *hors-d'œuvre* of boiled salmon.

In the evening we attended a very good open-air concert, where the music was much better, although the admission fee was only half a franc, than it was at our two-franc concert in Amsterdam.

We also went to a popular half-franc theatre, called the *Théâtre-Lyrique*, where three or four thousand people, chiefly of the middle class, were assembled to witness a six-act drama entitled *Le Jésuite*. The plot of the play was of the *Hypocrite* class, designed to show the baneful influence which Jesuits may obtain over the female members of families. Every time the Jesuit came on, every time he moved across the stage, or made a "point," the whole audience howled at him like good-humoured wild beasts. The actor, a Frenchman, was popular, as was shown by great applause at the end of the piece; but the demonstration was made against the Jesuits. After witnessing this piece and its reception, we were not astonished at the electoral excitement which we met with everywhere.

Having seen that the Hôtel de Ville, the fine old houses near it, the old palace, and the mannikin were still standing, in spite of the French architectural invasion, we started for Ghent, where the electoral fever was still more strikingly manifested. The grand old market-places, vast, half-deserted areas as large as Russell Square, with the grass growing at their sides, were filled with nearly the whole population of the city. The voting was by ballot, the ballot-boxes were kept open until late at night, and yet no evil resulted, either from the mode or time of voting.

"It seems a pity," I said, "that a people who show so much political life, should allow their country to be the hot-bed of protection."

"It seems a pity," said Sam, "that a people who show so much political life, should wear one of the clumsiest sabots ever tolerated. The economy of wooden shoes I can understand; but there must be much bad conservatism lingering in a country where the people shuffle about in a sabot like a barge, which has to be kept on the foot with hay stuffed behind the heels."

From Ghent we went to Bruges, another fine, old, half-deserted city, where the grass was growing in some of the streets, and bare-footed friars were to be met with in the clerical quarters. The size of the grand square struck us here, as at Ghent, and we easily imagined how much more important these cities must have been than the City of London, before the latter threw down its walls, and spread over the adjacent country.

From Ghent we went to Ostend, and after carefully inspecting it, admitted that it was one of the most sensible watering-places which we had seen for a long time. Nearly everything in the shape of amusement is ranged along the sea-shore. There is an admirably paved and raised promenade, more than a mile in length, and on the land side of this is built the Kursaal, the bath-rooms, and a number of restaurants and cafés. The visitors live here by the sea-side, and not, as in English watering-places, at frowsy lodgings. They get all their meals exactly when they want them, at the restaurants and sea-side hotels, and have no quarrels with lodging-house servants about fragments of cold mutton. Here, I am happy to say, I saw some of my countrywomen, whom I gallantly consider to be the loveliest ladies in the world, and whose complexions appeared brighter by contrast with the sallow cheeks of the Belgian damsels.

"There's the kind of girl," I said to Sam, pointing out one of the most charming creatures on the promenade, "who's calculated to make sunshine in a shady place."

"The most disagreeable quality in a woman," he replied. "A girl that makes sunshine in a shady place would light a fire in the dog-days, and we all know what that would lead to."

The time had now arrived for us to turn our steps homewards. Our week had expired; the Bank rate, as we had expected, had gone down one per cent.; and I, therefore, proposed that we should return from Antwerp by the long sea-passage.

"Do you know Dr. Johnson's definition of a sea-voyage?" asked Sam.

"I do," I returned. "Imprisonment, with the chance of being drowned."

"My sentiments exactly," returned Sam, "and I think in days when we hear of Cork pilots and Deal boatmen being lost at sea, we ought not to play the fool as amateur sailors."

"These are nice sentiments for a descendant of the hardy Norsemen."

"I'll give you my sentiments about the hardy Norsemen," said Sam; and he immediately burst into the following song, which was original if not conclusive:—

"The hardy Norseman came over the sea—
Luff, boys, luff, on the starboard bow—
The 'shortest sea-passage' and rail chose he—
Pipe all hands to the starboard bow.

"Then the saltest old salt rose up and spake,
'Haul up coals to the top-gallant mast—
Show the hardy Norseman we're wide awake,
Pipe all hands to the top-gallant mast.'

"'You come from the land of the Vikings, boy
(Pipe all hands to the starboard bow),
All Ratcliffe Highway wishes you joy
(Now, then, luff on the starboard bow).

"'The sea is rolling now mountains high,
(Let out reef on the larboard stem)
We'll sail with the wind and the cloudy sky,
(Let out reef on the larboard stem).'

"Said the hardy Norseman, 'I hate the sea,
So haul away, let me get on shore,
For pitch-and-toss don't agree with me,
So haul away, let me get on shore.'

"'What do I hear?' roared the rough old tar,
('Knock that fly off the mizen mast).
Is the hardy Norseman a land-lubbing cur?
(Knock that fly off the mizen mast).

"'It cannot be that a Viking's child,—
(What 'r'ye doing to the jib-boom sail?)
These men are enough to drive me wild
(Take in reef in the jib-boom sail!)

"'It cannot be that a Viking's son,
(Who's carved my name on the quarter-deck?)
Can despise the fame which his fathers won,
(Who's carved my name on the quarter-deck?)'

"Said the hardy Norseman, 'the stormy sea—
Haul away, let me get on shore—
Had no more charms for my fathers than me,
So haul away—let me get on shore.

"'We're hardy Norsemen, and not Jack tars—
Why can't you hold the vessel still?—
Only used to horses or driving cars—
Why can't you hold the vessel still?

"'We're hardy folks at a steeple chase—
Oh, haul away, let me get on shore!'
Then the captain howled, with a purple face,
'Hold on, let the lubber creep on shore!'"

Of course, after this, we returned by the way of Calais and Dover, and found the money-market like ourselves, in a most healthy condition.

NIGHTMARES.

The yellow curtains are closely drawn, but there is still a sickly glare about the room. Shadowy forms glide in and out. There is a hum of voices, and a distant roar of wheels. The orange lies untouched; the fumes of vinegar are in the air; the watch clicks hurriedly beside my bed.

* * * * *

I find myself one of a large crowd assembled in an open space before a town-hall, listening to an orator on a platform. I cannot say much for the character of my companions. Thieves and costermongers form the majority, and the man who is pouring forth a flood of eloquence is one of the same class. It is an election meeting under the principle of Universal Suffrage, and the Bohemians are about to return one of themselves. Never, perhaps, before was a meeting so unanimous, and if society loses in one respect it gains in another, for certainly never before did so many pickpockets join in the show of hands.

I reach a building remarkable for the external beauty of its architecture. It is built in a style called the semi-crystal—half glass, half ornamental brickwork. The approaches to it are laid out as an Italian garden—union of the choicest flowers and the most artistic statuary. Here are the great criminals in the world's history. On one side stands a marble representation of the gentle Greenacre in the habit as he lived. Near to him is placed the penetrating Sheppard and the bold and impulsive Turpin. Right and left, along the several avenues, are the minor heroes of the "Newgate Calendar." Scene of enchantment, in which crime is made so attractive, what is it that I stand before? I am answered: the great philanthropic Model Prison. It is full to overflowing of those fortunate individuals who have given up the struggle of life for perpetual ease in an earthly paradise. Thousands have been turned away from the doors, and crime is practically annihilated. By instituting a system of rewards instead of punishments, the stimulus to crime is apparently increased; but when the power of reward is known to be limited, the motive for exertion is diminished in the exact ratio that the hope of gaining the prize is decreased. Thus the great social evil, which has withstood for centuries all attempts at uprooting, is quietly nipped in the bud by over-nourishment.

I am again in the broad thoroughfares of the world. Hurrying on, with head bent forward and knitted brow, is a man earnestly bent upon business that seemingly brooks no delay. From the opposite direction lounges up to him a time-wasting, prosy bore, who checks the progress of the earnest man by the familiar process of button-holding. Scarcely has his finger touched the accustomed right hand breast button—scarcely has the drawling, rounded sentence issued from his parting lips—when, with a shock, like that of a galvanic battery, the button explodes—the bore is on his back in the gutter, and the man of action pushes on.

What neighbourhood is this, where trade, having outgrown its narrow receptacles, overflows upon the footpath? Are we to be edged into the gutter by encroaching butchers? Here am I walking along an interminable avenue of meat—legs of mutton hanging above my head, like the rich clusters of grapes in a Chatsworth greenhouse; sheep hooked up by their legs with their heads downwards, and their bloody noses dripping at my feet. As I move along I am supposed to be there, not from necessity, but from choice, and I am addressed with rude familiarity by greasy men with fearful knives and cleavers, and asked to buy the carrion that obstructs my path! I emerge at last from the unwelcome shade into the broad glare of the July sun. An overdriven bull sweeps past me, seeking a place of safety. He hesitates—turns and returns, and at last seeks the friendly shelter of an assurance office. Mysterious influence! Can it be with the view of insuring the short remainder of his wretched existence? Alas! no living actuary has calculated upon such an application, and they do not entertain such risky lives. There is nothing for thee but to resign thyself to the sacrificial axe, and to help to fatten the child whose mother thou hast just gored to death!

A crowd of people pass me with short balance-poles in their hands, which they poise like rope-dancers. Propriety is in their footsteps, but intoxication is in their eyes. Thanks to the invention which they hold in their grasp they neither require a cab, nor come under the observation of the policeman. Their course is straight as an arrow from the bow. What is man without the appliances of science? Take but these regulating instruments away, and each helpless bacchanal collapses upon the pavement.

I did not hail an omnibus—no matter; he opens the door. Four drunken Greenwich pensioners block up the entrance, their wooden legs crossed like hurdle bars. He pushes me in, and slams the door. I struggle forward, and the legs snap under me, like pieces of tobacco-pipe, but the victims sleep on. I reach the corner unmolested. Next to me sits a man with something in his arms, which he nurses like a child. Is it a child, done up in a newspaper? No; it is an enormous turkey in a putrid state; and ever as its nurse sways to and fro with the motion of the vehicle the abomination threatens to scratch my face with a protruding claw. Shall my nose be at one and the same time offended with a stench, and endangered by a talon? Never; but how to release myself? Sleep hangs heavily on the eyelids of all. All save one, a sharp old man, with a large stick, near the door. I catch his eye. He understands me. One blow, and the conductor's arm drops lifeless by his side. I am free once more.

I enter the coffee-room of a tavern. Standing before the fireplace, with his coat-tail over his arms, is an over-dressed young gentleman, who looks with cool impertinence at every person in the room. His principal occupation is to ring the bell every five minutes, summoning a waiter each time upon the most frivolous pretexts. Little does this troublesome coxcomb know that, by a mechanical arrangement, the coffee-room bell acts in connection with a kitchen boiler, and that every time it is pulled it pumps up a gallon of water from a well under the premises. I see a sardonic smile upon the face of the sallow waiter, who is called and recalled a dozen times in the course of a simple luncheon. He is amply, although silently, revenged; his elegant tormentor—lounger in the Mall, and chosen one of Belgravia—has unconsciously filled a kitchen boiler.

What melancholy place is this? I thought to find a railway-office, and I enter a charnel-house. A sombre union of the booking clerk and the undertaker hands me a ticket. I see it all. I am at the funeral station of the Negropolis Railway. I take my seat in a jet-black carriage. Two sombre porters place a corpse, like a portmanteau, in the luggage-van, having first labelled it with a black-bordered ticket, inscribed "Choking Cemetery." A sedate driver passes to take charge of the engine. Is he sedate? His raiment is solemn; but the man is not always indicated by the covering. Another sedate-looking man, with a red nose, and crape garnishings, takes his place as guard of the funeral train. A muffled bell tolls, and we move on. At first, the pace is decorous, as befits the occasion, but gradually it increases, until at last we attain a speed of several hundred miles an hour. I can hear the bones of the corpse rattling against the sides of its prison house. Alarm is useless, and communication with the driver impossible. Why am I here at all; the corpse is none of my race? I am the victim of circumstances. We come to a turn in the line—a fearful jerk sends my head forward against the walls of the carriage: a crash follows. The corpse has burst its bonds, and is standing up, blood-stained, amidst the ruins. Powers of mercy, what can it mean? Has the end of all things arrived? Do I hear the dread angel's voice booming through the awful trumpet like a waiter: "I'll take the Globe after the last man!"

THE END.

CPSIA information can be obtained
at www.ICGtesting.com
Printed in the USA
LVHW040027180422
716440LV00005B/391

9 783752 590784